For Kate
with best wishes
Richard Greene

The
Day
After
Midnight

The
Day
After
Midnight

RICHARD A. GREENE, M.D.

G

GADD & COMPANY PUBLISHERS, INC.

The characters and events in this book are fictitious. Any similarity to real persons, living or dead, is coincidental and not intended by the author.

pp. 145-146: *A Tribute to Dalton, Massachusetts, The Home of United States Currency*: S. Donaldson

Gadd & Company Publishers, Inc.
An Independent Division of The North River Press Publishing Corporation
292 Main Street
Great Barrington, MA 01230
(413) 528-8895
Visit our website at www.gaddbooks.com

Printed in the United States of America
ISBN: 978-0-9774053-8-1

To Sally and Nat
of blessed memory

Acknowledgments

The staff at Gadd and Company Publishers: Larry Gadd, Cia Elkin, Rachel Kaufman, Bryn Davis, for their enthusiasm, support, creative advice and for shepherding me though all the revisions.

The ladies I am privileged to work with: Jan Clark, Bev Doyle, Kathie Gennari, Debra Lussier, Elda Spring, Adele Vogel, for their interest and encouragement and for advice on Patty's wardrobe.

Rabbi Dennis Ross

Massachusetts State Police Lieutenant (ret.) Peter Risatti

Raymond Conway, M.D., Harold F. Sherman, M.D., Raymond Sabatelli, M.D.

My wife, Lindsay, and my son, Mark, for letting Charlie and Patty live with us for all these years.

The
Day
After
Midnight

Chapter One

"What do you mean there's two guys from the FBI in the waiting room who want to talk to me?" I asked, repeating Helen's statement, my voice getting higher and faster toward the end of the sentence. I had been minding my own business trying to earn a living and being helpful to people when Helen, the emergency department secretary, left her desk to come back and tell me this. I was with a patient and I'm sure she got a thrill and would have a story to tell her friends when she got home. It might start with, "Well I was in the ER with a very badly sprained ankle and three FBI agents came to talk with the doctor there." Who knew how the story would evolve, how big the fish would grow, with each telling of the story. I wished Helen hadn't told me this in front of the patient, but it was done.

What would the FBI want to talk to me for?

Helen said, "Well? Will you talk to them?"

"Like I have a choice? Sure I'll talk to them." I wouldn't think you could just brush them off and say, "No thanks, I gave at the office". Or, "No, I'm busy, could you come back later?" I doubted if they were here collecting for the FBI intramural softball team.

But I had a patient in front of me. Nothing is more

important than the patient in front of me. *Focus, Charlie, focus.* This forty-eight-year old white female turned her ankle going down the stairs at work. She didn't hear a pop but it hurt immediately and began to swell *and what could they possibly want with me?* She could scarcely bear weight on it, it was quite swollen and black and blue and I hope this doesn't have to do with some dark days I had some years ago. She had point tenderness under the lateral malleolus, which is that outer bump of your ankle, *and I always pay my taxes and seldom speed more than a little.* The posterior tibial artery and dorsalis pedis pulses were good, the toes were warm and when pressed the capillary refill was brisk *and I always thought I was a fairly good person and I go to synagogue once in a while and sometimes I even pay attention. Focus, Charlie, focus!* Be objective, render the patient the best effort and concentration you can, forget any of your own issues until you are on your own time.

We got several radiographic views of the ankle. To my eye they looked okay. I didn't see any tiny bony chips where the deltoid ligament might have torn from the bone. The mortise of the ankle, where the calcaneus is held in a square recess by the tibia and fibula, all looked symmetric and okay. I saw no obvious fracture and there was no bony displacement. There could've been a hairline fracture that I didn't see, but the radiologist in this little hospital was already gone for the day.

I wanted to hurry this up and get done with this lady so I could embrace my fate with these FBI guys, but I've learned the hard way that whenever I rush and cut corners it inevitably comes back to bite me in the butt.

So I told the lady, who was very nice by the way, that she certainly had some tendinous and ligamental tearing, but that the worst she might have was an invisible hairline break and that was how I'd treat her. I told her I wanted to make a plaster splint.

My hands were shaking as I unrolled several rolls of four-inch plaster tape. I've been driving since I was seventeen and in all those years only two or three times did I see a police car right behind me in the rear view mirror. No flashing lights, no siren. I hadn't done anything illegal but my face would turn sweaty and red like it is now. The cop would follow me mile after mile; I must've done something wrong that I wasn't even aware of. I got the plaster tape wet, squeezed it between my shaking fingers and then snaked it through a soft cotton tube called stockinette. The whole thing was about three feet long. I bent it into a U, fit the bottom of the U under her heel, the tops on the inside and outside of her leg just beneath her knee and then molded it to conform to her ankle bone. Then I wrapped a four-inch Ace bandage around the whole thing and remembered getting called to go to the principal's office when I was a little kid. It could only be bad. I didn't know what I'd done bad enough to get called to the principal's office. It was down a long hall. It was my death march. But it was okay. I'd forgotten my lunch and my mother dropped it off and they called me to come get it.

This kind of U-shaped plaster splint is called an ice tong splint because of its shape. It supports the joint reasonably well but allows for swelling to occur. It would keep the ankle stable till tomorrow when she could see the orthopedist. I told her to keep off it; keep it elevated; put an ice pack on it, and I gave her a prescription for Motrin. I explained everything to her and wished her well. She said to me, "Thanks for everything, Dr. Davids, I hope things go well for you with those FBI men because you look guilty already."

"Well, they probably just want to talk to me about

3

some patient I've seen who they must have an interest in." First rational thought I'd had in fifteen minutes.

The nurse finished her up, fitted her with crutches and gave her the instruction sheet and told her to call the orthopedist today so she could be seen tomorrow. I went to wash the plaster off my hands and arms. I didn't get any on my tie. I had taken my watch off but I never take off my wedding ring and there was plaster stuck on it and on my fingernails. I didn't have the patience to keep scrubbing. Hell with it.

I was trying hard to ignore my biggest fear. Three years ago, in 1984, my arm got twisted to do some stuff I really didn't want to do. Got twisted hard. I had to give medical care to some bad guys. Secretly. It went on for a year and then it was over. I hoped it was over. I've hoped ever since that it wouldn't come back to haunt me. I can keep a secret and I hadn't let out one word.

Margaret came over and handed a towel to me, "Wash your face, Charlie," she said harshly. She said everything harshly since they took out half her larynx. I never asked her which half. Sometimes patients came to the ER and heard her voice and said, "You should try some Echinacea for your throat" Margaret would say: "Oh, really, does it work for cancer?" Meddling busybodies.

I did what I was told and spread the towel out on the counter in the cast room to dry, ran my fingers through my hair and headed up front. Margaret was right behind me. Practically touching. I came up behind Helen at the front desk and asked her if the only two people in the waiting room, the two men wearing suits, were the FBI guys. Margaret raspily said under her breath, "No, Charlie, those two guys are evangelists and they're here to convert you." I rolled my eyes and shot a sideways glance at her. I walked through the waist-high swinging door at the front desk into the waiting room. The outside doors were open and I could smell the sweet, warm, summer air coming through them. I walked over to the men. They put down their magazines and started to get up.

"Hello gentlemen, I'm Charlie Davids. Did you want to talk to me?"

The guy on the left was wearing a grayish-blue suit. He was my height but stockier, had short brown hair, a round face with blue eyes and slightly tanned skin. He had a short thick neck. His facial skin had an orange-peel texture like you get from bad acne as a teenager. He handed me a business card and said, "Hello Dr. Davids, I'm Special Agent Morse with the FBI and this is Special Agent Fremont." Fremont was taller, thinner, had thinning gray hair, a ruddy complexion and a big Adam's apple. He would be the easier one to intubate. He also handed me his card. Margaret was still right beside me and she took the cards from my hand before I had a chance to look at them. "Is there a place where we can talk?" Moore asked.

"Of course. We can go back to my office."

"Why don't you all come sit down in the coffee room?" Margaret suggested, and she went ahead of us to banish anyone who might be there.

Morse, Fremont and I were in the coffee room. I asked them if they'd like coffee or a cold drink and they said no. Margaret was back beside me and hoarsely croaked, "Don't you guys have badges?"

"Yes, of course we do," and both men reached into their suitcoat pockets in unison and came out with their worn black leather badge wallets, which Margaret inspected closely.

"Excuse me, Ma'am," said Morse, "who are you?"

5

"Mrs. Palumbo is a close personal friend." I said.

"Are you a nurse here?"

Margaret was standing there with a dumbfounded look on her face. She was wearing white shoes, white tights, a white dress, a navy blue cardigan with a brass pin that said, Margaret Palumbo, RN, Nursing Supervisor. She put her hand on her hip and looked from Morse to Fremont and back again and croaked, "You guys are from the FBI and you really have to ask me that question?" Margaret had brass balls. The two men looked at each other and then at Margaret.

"Would you mind if we spoke with Dr. Davids privately?" Morse asked.

"That's up to Charlie." When Margaret spoke it always sounded like there was static in the background.

I turned to her. "Its okay, Margaret, thank you."

"Okay. Holler if you need anything," and she left the room. Then I realized what she'd done. This room had no door and it had an intercom. My office had a door and no intercom.

We sat down on the modern wood and vinyl padded chairs.

"Dr. Davids, we'd like to show you some photographs of some men and ask if you recognize any of them."

"I'd be happy to look at them. What is this about?"

"Let us ask the questions, okay?" said Fremont. I gave him a hard look. Morse handed me a large manila envelope. The return address said "FBI—Springfield". This was the kind of manila envelope that had the flap closed by a red string wound around two red paper washers. I opened it up and inside were a bunch of big glossy photographs. There were about ten of them. I moved to a seat that had better light. They were not very good photographs. Perhaps they were taken with a telephoto lens. Some were taken at a steep angle and were enlarged so much that they were grainy. Maybe they were surveillance photos.

I looked at each photo quickly at first and saw no one who was easy to identify. Then I went through them more slowly. I tilted the photos this way and that to get the glare off the glossy surface. I looked at the faces, the body habitus, the way the hair was combed, the eyeglasses, the background. I spent five minutes looking at them, which is a long time. I wanted them to see I was making a concerted effort. They were ten different men, from young men maybe in their twenties to older men in their sixties. All were clean-cut, respectable looking white guys. No one that I recognized.

"No one that I recognize," I said at last. They had been silent while I'd been studying the photos. "Who are these guys?"

"We're not authorized to tell you that," barked Fremont.

"What is this about?" I asked again.

Fremont slowly turned his head from his partner to me and sighed, as if I'd annoyed him by asking a question. "If you don't recognize any of these men then there is no point in discussing this any further," Fremont said.

I shrugged and put the photos back in the envelope and handed them back to Fremont.

"You're sure you never saw these people before?"

"I don't recognize them. There's lots of people I meet I don't remember. I've met thousands of people and their relatives here in the ER. I can't remember all of them. People say hello to me in the supermarket and I nod back politely with no clue who they are and I just presume I saw them at work. You know what I mean."

"Okay. We're done here. Thanks for your time."

The FBI guys left. While I was busy with them a few patients came in; nothing serious. Margaret said, "What was that all about?"

"Damned if I know," I replied. "Thanks for the moral support."

"There's that. And, I was curious."

The rest of the day in the ER puttered along uneventfully. Business was steady but not hectic and by the time my shift was over at eight that evening I'd almost forgotten about the FBI visit.

It took four minutes to drive home to our little bungalow on Gilmore Avenue. Patty was living there when we met, renting with an option to buy. It was convenient to both the pharmacy where Patty works and the hospital, so soon after we were married we bought it.

It was an adorable little bungalow. It was on a quiet, residential, tree-lined street, one of two similar bungalows amongst larger houses. The house was built in the early nineteen-hundreds, sometime later an extension was added on the back to enlarge the kitchen.

I parked my Subaru wagon in front of the house and bounded up the porch steps, my footfalls loud on the wooden porch. As I entered the living room Patty was coming up from the back of the house with a big smile. A hug and kiss later we were in the kitchen, talking. I was looking through the mail. Although I'd had supper at the hospital cafeteria with Margaret I had the munchies and I explored the refrigerator and emerged with a Genesee Cream Ale and some tuna salad. We told each other about our days.

"And then there were these two FBI agents who came to see me," I said, and I told Patty the whole story.

"What were they like?"

"The first guy, Morse, was thick-bodied, my height, in his forties. The other guy was thinner, older, taller.

Both of them were gruff. Neither of them were very engaging. They weren't trying to get me to like them. I was polite, I offered them a cold drink; they refused." Patty laughed when I told her how Margaret asked to see their badges and how they asked if she was a nurse.

"So you didn't recognize anyone in the photographs?"

"Nope."

"No one at all even slightly resembling the people you were mixed up with a few years ago? Not the people, not the patients?"

"Nope. None that I could recognize."

"Not Sal?"

"Definitely not. Time wouldn't weaken my memory of his face."

"Hmmmm," Patty said, "they were big photographs?"

"Yeah. Eight by ten or so. Almost the size of a piece of typing paper."

"Were they smooth-textured and glossy?"

"Yeah."

"Did they hand them to you one at a time?"

"No, they handed them to me in a big manila envelope."

"Did you see them handle the pictures at all?"

"No, I didn't."

"Hmmm. I wonder if they were trying to get your fingerprints," she said. Her brows were furrowed and she was staring at the business cards they had given me.

Chapter 2

The following week Morse and Fremont visited me again at work. I didn't know how they knew my work schedule. I didn't know why they kept bothering me at work when I could be very busy with important things having to do with other people's health. Sometimes real important things. Maybe they prefer to work nine to five. I am a physician in an emergency department in this cute little rural seventy-bed hospital in this cute little town of Great Barrington in the southern part of Berkshire County, that is as far from Boston as you can get and still be in Massachusetts.

After medical school I moved to Pittsfield, which is the biggest city in Berkshire County. Actually I lived in Dalton, the next town over, but I worked in Pittsfield at Berkshire Medical Center. That's where I did a three-year residency in internal medicine. It was an excellent training program. Residency is the anvil on which we young doctors are forged. We work eighty-plus hour weeks, admitting sick people to the hospital, working them up, drawing bloods, getting lab tests, X-rays, all guided by the attending physicians. Get a lot of experience, see a lot of sadness, learn a lot, cry a little, get some confidence, meet lots of people from many different walks of life. See a lot of people get better, give a lot of people bad news, see a lot of people die. We all found it hard, but most kept better separation between the medical pathos they saw every day and their own psyche. I took it home with me; couldn't help it. But I dealt with it.

When those three years were over I took the two-day board exams in internal medicine and I passed them. Barely. That was a coup for me because I was a good enough student but not a great one. And not such a good test taker, and these exams are difficult and there is a not insignificant failure rate. There are those who, even though they may be excellent doctors and clinicians, do not pass the boards. Not everyone takes them.

After a grueling dozen years, of pre-med in college, med school, internship and residency I was ready to coast for a while. I took a job working three or four shifts a week in the ER of Fairview Hospital in Great Barrington.

Emergency work has its pros and cons. You are working for someone else; it could be boring; it could be tragic; but when you are on you are on and when you are off you are off, and I didn't need a pager and there were not ongoing problems to deal with or rounds to make every morning. I thought I would do it for a couple of years until the right conventional practice opportunity came along.

The Berkshires are a great place to live. They have scenic beauty with mountains, forests, rivers and lakes. People have been coming here for 150 years for

11

restful bucolic vacations. The wealthy have enjoyed the Berkshires as a place to build their summer mansions, which with false modesty they called "cottages." Edith Wharton had a home here and Herman Melville wrote Moby Dick here. It has Tanglewood, the open-air summer home of the Boston Symphony Orchestra, and the Berkshire Theatre Festival presents a summer stock theatre of a very high level. We've got the wonderful Clark Art Institute in Williamstown, where I proposed to Patty, right next door to Williams College. There is Berkshire Community College that also hosts much theater and music and in Great Barrington there's a small liberal arts college called Simon's Rock of Bard College.

There is a small but vibrant Jewish community with five synagogues, Patty and I were married in one of them, and an active cultural calendar. There are five alpine ski areas, and lots of places to go cross-country skiing. The Appalachian Trail runs through the whole county and there are dozens of other hiking trails besides that one. There are endless miles of charming country roads with stone walls, old barns, venerable sugar maples, period colonial homes, pastoral views, the occasional deer and turkey and raccoon, and the number of black bear is on the rise. I'd have to be nuts to leave this place. Patty thinks so too. So here we remain. I've been at Fairview over five years now.

I've been on interviews in the northeast for regular jobs as an internist. They interest me less and less. And as the politics and economics of the practice of medicine evolve, as there are more and more regulations and we are controlled more and more by the increasing power of the insurance companies, as we are pressured by the malpractice insurance companies, as the pharmaceutical lobby and insurance lobby and trial lawyer's association lobby all exert their influence on the legislators I am more and more inclined to stay at Fairview and work for someone else. When I'm off I'm off and Patty and I can enjoy each other and all the county has to offer.

I digress. Morse and Fremont visited me again. Since I'm the junior guy on the roster I work more nights than days, yet these guys find me at work again. I finished up with the patient I was seeing, it wasn't busy and I took them back to my office. We sat down. They still didn't want a cup of coffee or a cold soda. I still could not warm up to them.

"Dr. Davids, did you ever practice in Springfield?"

"No."

"What about West Springfield, or Holyoke or Chicopee?"

"No. Why?" These were a group of big cities clustered together about an hour east of here.

"You know computers are a wonderful thing. They are a real work-saver. What they can do in a minute would take a dozen detectives a week to do the old-fashioned way."

And you are telling me this because...

"We got access to the computer system that ties in together all the branches of the pharmacies in those cities, you know, CVS, Brooks, RiteAid, and asked for a list of all prescriptions you wrote within a certain time frame."

And? So? I thought but did not say.

"What we've learned was that in a one-year time period you wrote a flurry of prescriptions for a number of interesting medications for a list of unsavory people."

Uh oh. Do I see an infringement of patient confidentiality?

"We want to know what you can tell us about this"

Without hesitation I spoke. "I don't know what I can tell you. I only practice here. We see lots of people from out of town. Tourists in summer, deer hunters in the fall, skiers in the winter. I don't know where patients take their prescriptions to get them filled. Maybe they'd rather spend an hour in the car and come here than go to some city hospital and wait forever. I suspect if you did the same computer search for a radius of fifty miles in every direction for each doctor here you would find the same kind of statistics." I did not glance from Morse to Fremont as if searching for agreement and support. That would look weak.

"How do you explain the large number of high strength antibiotics, pain medicine, narcotic antagonists that you prescribed in just that one year?"

"I can't. Are you sure that these were prescriptions I actually wrote? It would not be too hard to swipe a prescription pad from here."

"We're here to ask you the questions, doctor."

I could've asked why they were prying into doctor-patient relationships but that would make me seem defensive. Nor would they say, whoops, you're right, we apologize, and then leave.

"So how do you explain those prescriptions, Doctor?" Moore asked again.

I answered immediately, my eyes directly on his. "I have no explanation. I work here. I see patients. I write prescriptions. That's the only explanation I have." We held our gaze. I wouldn't back down or glance away first.

"Okay. That's all for now." They stood up. "If you remember something you can give us a call." And he handed me another business card.

That night, after a late supper together, Patty and I were sitting on the living room couch. I was staring across the room at a lovely framed print of Monet's *Water Lilies*. I bought this for Patty years ago when we were dating. I bought it at the Clark Art Institute, in fact. We were telling each other about our days and were drinking a martini. One martini. We were sharing it. Three years ago on our honeymoon we went to Israel. While we were in Jerusalem, which really is the city where heaven meets earth, we stayed at the LaRomme Hotel. The first night, with jet lag and all, we couldn't sleep, so we went to the hotel cocktail lounge. On each table they had a brochure listing the seventeen kinds of martinis they served. We tried numbers one and two and kept the brochure for future reference. That was the night we ceremoniously frisbeed Patty's diaphragm into the trash and tried to conceive a baby in Jerusalem.

Anyway we had learned that one martini was enough for the two of us and Patty was sitting crosswise on my lap, facing to my right and we were sipping from the traditional conical-stemmed glass. Patty had found a set of them at a yard sale. Like a good analytical chemist she was leading us through a study of different types of martinis, and different gins. So many permutations. With an olive or lemon peel.

I told Patty about my visit with Morse and Fremont and how they were asking me about certain prescriptions filled in the Springfield area.

"You know, whenever I go to a CVS pharmacists' training seminar, they stress again and again, over and over, patient confidentiality. Those guys must've had a court order to get that information. It also sounds to me like you're becoming a very adept liar."

"I know, it's been bothering me a lot. A whole lot. I didn't really lie. I was not able to answer their specific questions specifically. I wasn't being charged or arrested, they didn't read me my Miranda rights, I was

15

not subpoenaed before a court. I didn't promise to tell the whole truth. And if I opened my mouth and told them everything I knew, it might not be relevant to their questions and it could open a Pandora's box for us. And Sal."`

"Well you do have the right to keep private things private. I'm sorry, I didn't mean to challenge your ethics. You're one of the most ethically conscious people I know. You just were not forthcoming. That is your right. To lie is to say something false. The commandment 'Thou shalt not lie' is poorly translated, it is 'Thou shalt not bear false witness against thy neighbor,' which means you can't frame someone in court. You can tell white lies. If someone asks you a question the answer to which would be damning, you aren't obliged to answer it. Like, do you still beat your wife? Do you pick your nose in private? Were you ever in jail? No one needs to divulge anything personal if he doesn't want to. My brother was a Boy Scout. He didn't want anyone to know because it wasn't cool. He kept it a secret. That's not wrong. That's privacy."

"How do you know all this?" I asked.

"At UMass I was one course short of a minor in Judaic studies. You know this. We did a section on the Ten Commandments. Of course there are really six hundred thirteen commandments. Three hundred sixty-five don't's and the rest are do's."

"Unplumbed depths." I said. So smart. So much fun to live with.

We were washed up, teeth brushed and flossed, and in bed. Before turning off the light I rolled towards her, my head on my hand, my elbow on the pillow. Sweet cool summer evening air made the curtains gently move. I looked at her and I swept the hair out of her eyes. "I hope this crap from Springfield doesn't start up all over again."

Without an instant's hesitation, Patty said, "I hate to tell you this, Charlie, this crap from Springfield is starting up again."

I groaned and turned off the lights and kissed her good night.

Many minutes later, when I was almost asleep, Patty whispered, "Charlie, are you still awake?"

"No, I'm not," I answered groggily.

"Yes, you are. I can tell." She rolled closer and kissed me.

"Charlie, would you plumb my depths? Please?"

I slept very soundly until Patty woke me up in the middle of the night. She snapped on the lamp. She was standing at the side of the bed, in her bathrobe, holding a small glass of orange juice.

"Charlie, wake up."

"What's the matter? What's the matter?" I asked, still half asleep. She rubbed her knuckles on my sternum and it hurt.

"Here, drink this, it'll help wake you up."

"What is it? What's the matter?"

"We need to talk. You need to promise me something."

"What? Anything, what?"

"I've been tossing and turning and pacing all night while you've been dead asleep. You need to promise me something."

"Okay, what?"

"If there's going to be trouble for you like there was before, I have to be part of it. Trouble for you is trouble for me. I'll not let you keep me in the dark. You have to let me know what's gong on. You can't try to keep me safe by keeping me out of it. You tried that once. I lost you once and I'm not going to lose you again. Do you promise?"

I thought for a second.

"I promise," I said.

"You promise to tell me everything that happens, recognize that we are in this together and you won't deceive me in the misguided notion that it's safer for me."

"Yes. I promise. I swear. With all my heart."

"Good. Go back to sleep. She took off her bathrobe, got into bed, turned off the light and kissed me. She was asleep almost instantly. I tossed and turned the rest of the night.

Chapter 3

I'd been watching the red illuminated digits on the bedroom clock all night. I wasn't getting any good sleep anyway so at six o'clock I rolled out of bed and traipsed down to the kitchen. I put on the coffee pot and then got the newspaper off the porch. I put some English muffins in the toaster, set the kitchen table for the two of us. I turned on the radio to listen to the news on WAMC, the local public radio station. I had the day off but I had to go in at eight that night. By the time the second set of muffins launched out of the toaster Patty appeared in the kitchen doorway, tall and thin and barefoot in her nightgown, long brown hair, rubbing her eyes and yawning.

I poured her a mug of coffee and put a bit of milk in it and handed it to her. She smiled and took her cup and kissed me and waddled over to the window and looked at the yard and the sky. "I say, Eeyore, I wonder what's going to happen exciting today." She was quoting Winnie the Pooh. She said this most mornings.

"Let's have breakfast and lounge around with the paper. Then I'll go to synagogue and when I get back how about we go for a run?" I had to work that night and some exercise would help me get a better nap before going in.

My father died about six months before and it is a

tradition to go to synagogue each morning to say Kaddish, the prayer for the dead, for a year. I went most mornings, when I could. A very old tradition. I wasn't dogmatic about it. Conveniently there was a little synagogue a five-minute walk from our house. Ahavath Shalom. It was built over a hundred years ago. It had been a secular country schoolhouse that was bought by the local Jewish immigrants and became their house of worship. Through the decades they often didn't have an ordained rabbi but managed to get along with talented lay members.

I was the youngest person by far to show up at these daily early morning minyan services for mourners. A minyan is ten people, the minimum number you need to attract God's attention. Maybe the reason for this is so you wouldn't be mourning by yourself, you could have company and support. There are usually a lot of reasons for each practice in Judaism, they don't always agree and you can make up your own. They were happy to have me there; at least I was another body. Some of the old men there were beyond their period of mourning but they came anyway, out of habit. They got used to coming; it became part of their routine; it got them out of bed and out of the house; they could socialize and support each other; maybe have coffee and play pinochle afterwards. That's probably part of the grand plan, establish traditions that require a bunch of people to get together every day to pray and then talk and kibitz and socialize and interact and strengthen the community bonds. Very clever.

Some of these old men were just delightful and chanted their Hebrew beautifully. There was a retired high school principal, a couple of retired business people. They always said hello to me, would pat me on the back, and ask why my wife doesn't come more often, but they never ever asked me for medical advice or told me about their aches or pains. I appreciated that. So often when people, especially older people, learn I'm a physician I then have to listen to their organ recital as they tell me all their woes about their joints and their sinuses and sciatica and indigestion and how long it's been since they had a bowel movement they could be proud of.

When I returned from synagogue Patty was in her running clothes pushing the vacuum cleaner. She saw me and switched it off. "Oh, hi Charlie, how was shul?"

"Good."

"The dust bunnies had another litter under the dining room table and I couldn't stand it anymore. Go get changed." She resumed cleaning and I went upstairs to change for our run.

We had about a dozen different routes we could take to run according to our mood, the weather, our energy level. Today we decided to run out to Butternut Ski Basin, which was maybe a five-mile round trip. I never used to bother with stretching before running but Patty insists on it. She is a tall, lean, lithe lady. She is five-foot-seven and I'm not sure how much she weighs but I bet she's less than 125 pounds. She has long legs that finally come together about four feet off the ground. She won't wear the sleek silky stylish athletic clothes they have out these days. She wears regular old-fashioned cotton gym shorts and a T-shirt, which I think adds to her charm. She wears her hair in a thick braid down her back. I run in gym shorts long enough to cover the big ugly scar on my left thigh.

After we finished stretching our hamstrings on the porch steps we started north on our street toward State Road, turned right, and in a quarter mile passed Belcher Square. I used to think it was named after Governor Belcher, who was the British administrator of the Massachusetts Bay Colony. But it wasn't named after him. It was named after a Belcher who was a local counterfeiter who they caught and hanged in Albany, New York in the early 1800's. I don't know how he rated a landmark. We continued on Route 23 East toward the ski area. It was bright. It was going to get hot.

Once in a while someone would drive by who would recognize us, wave and gaze at Patty.

I've been running for a long time. I need it; it's a stress reducer. Also it enables me to eat anything I want without gaining weight. Patty is innately more athletic than me, though she denies it; this also adds to her charm. In high school and college she played intramural soccer, and is a better sprinter than I. But she can't sprint for long and I can outdistance her. We both try to keep up a good cruising speed and not just plod along. I always have Patty run in front of me so I can admire her grace and watch her braid swing back and forth.

The summer smells were in the air; the day was bright and was warming up; the fields still had goldenrod and Queen Anne's Lace and purple asters; the distant hills were beautiful. The traffic was light. When we got to Butternut we circled around the parking lot and headed home. Running back on the north side of the road we passed a big marshy area with cattails, bulrushes and a muskrat lodge. From Belcher Square to Gilmore we usually torqued it up and ran faster and harder to finish, exhausting ourselves until we got to our corner. Then we stopped and walked the rest of the way home, recuperating from our sprint, aching, and waddling.

Once I could walk and talk at the same time I said, "I've been meaning to ask, have you heard anything about your teaching jobs?"

"No, I haven't. I've been meaning to make some follow up calls. But I don't want to be pushy."

"Maybe you should expand your range. What about applying to Westfield Community College. It's probably no farther away than some other places you applied, like North Adams State College. It would open up another option for you.

When we got married Patty was working full time as a pharmacist. After four or five months she dropped down to working part time and that suited us much better. With my erratic schedule of working many nights and weekends, we saw a lot more of each other this way. And we were richer for it than if we had her full-time salary. Of course we thought there would be babies by now. Most of the time she worked in the CVS pharmacy on North Main Street. That was where I first met her. Sometimes she would help out in a pinch in a few of the other local pharmacies, but she was getting bored with it. For some time we'd been talking about other things she might do. Like get a master's in public health or public administration. What appealed to her the most would be to teach college chemistry. She applied to Simon's Rock College, Berkshire Community College and North Adams State College.

"You'd be such a good teacher. You could put every day practical science into your basically boring freshman chemistry."

"It would be a lot of fun. I would really enjoy working with kids and trying to make it come alive for them."

We got to the house and clambered up porch steps and plopped in the Adirondack chairs. In a minute I hoisted myself out of the deeply seated chair to go in the house and I came back out with a tall glass of orange juice for each of us. It was a beautiful day and it was not yet eleven o'clock.

A young woman from the neighborhood walked down the other side of the street pushing a baby stroller. She also had a dog on a leash. We waved to each other. We've waved many times though we didn't know who she is.

"We should get some of those," I said.

"The baby or the dog?"

"Both," I said.

"Yeah, we should." We were holding hands and she squeezed mine. I looked at her and she smiled. We watched the young mother until she was out of sight.

"C'mon," Patty said, "let's finish cleaning the house." Another wonderful thing about our little bungalow is that it took the two of us only forty-five minutes to clean it thoroughly from top to bottom.

When we finished cleaning I took a shower. Patty came in and joined me. We got wet and soaped up and rinsed off and then Patty reached up for her shampoo. She lathered up her hair and massaged it through. I stood in the back of the tub watching her. "Patty, I want to ask you something."

"What?"

"Remember last night when you woke me in the middle of the night to promise to include you in everything that might happen with those FBI guys from Springfield?"

"Of course I remember."

"What would you do if I didn't keep that promise? Of course I'm going to keep it, but make believe I didn't. What if I broke the promise, or didn't really mean to keep it and I did hide things from you if trouble started up again. What would you do? Would you be mad? Would you leave me?"

She was rinsing her hair. "Yes I would be mad. You would be violating my trust. No I wouldn't leave you."

We were facing each other. Her back was to the showerhead. She took a big breath, reached up, tilted her head back into the spray, her hands to her hair.

As she did this I could see the angle of her chin from below, the V of the muscles in the front of her neck. As she lifted her arms her breasts rose, as she inhaled her ribs became more apparent. As she arched her back the groove on her abdomen from sternum to navel deepened; her navel stretched to a narrow oval; vertical dimples appeared on each side of her stomach muscles. The contour line of the outer part of her breasts became continuous with the muscle in front of her underarm and continued along her upraised arms to her elbows. If I were a sculptor I know what I would focus on.

"No," she said again, "I would never leave you. I lost you once, that'll never happen again. I wouldn't leave you, but I would beat the shit out of you."

As she said this she was wringing the water out of her hair. Her hair made a thick rope any tugboat would be proud to have on board. At least now I know where I stand.

I went into the bedroom to take a nap before my shift. The room was upstairs in the front of the house. There were gable windows on the front and both sides and a sloping wall from ceiling to kneewall. It had light beige wallpaper with a pattern of little flowers. The floor was spruce boards, partially covered by a braided rug. We had a full-size bed. We tried to get a queen-size bed but we couldn't get it up the stairs. We had a maple spool headboard and footboard that Patty got at an estate sale and had refinished. There was a colorful patchwork quilt on the bed. We each had a bedside table though they didn't match. Nor did the lamps. The three windows had ruffled curtains from the Country Curtain Shop in Stockbridge. We didn't have an air-conditioner because no matter how warm it got in the daytime it always cooled off in the evening. Maybe three or four nights in the summer, the

25

hottest nights, we'd put on the attic fan to pull a draft through the windows.

It was a nice room; simple; old fashioned. It was from another time, one that we imagined was slower, quieter, more wholesome and more gentle. It was calming to me. It reminded me of rooms I'd rented in tourist houses long ago when traveling the rural parts of New England. I opened the window and lowered the shades to reduce the early afternoon sunlight. I got into bed. From the drawer in my nightstand I took out two foam rubber earplugs and rolled them between my fingers to squeeze them down so I could screw them into my ears. I closed my eyes and sighed and listened happily to little crackling noises the foam made as it re-expanded, and the sounds of the house and the street got smaller and smaller and I got sleepy. I began a pre-sleep daydream. I was sitting on the porch just like I was before. Down the street the woman walked toward me pushing a baby carriage. She had a dog on a leash. She smiled at me. It was Patty. With our baby and our dog.

I slept well and deeply. When I awoke, the sun sneaking in around the shades was at a different angle than before. My ears were itchy and I pulled out the plugs. It was almost five o'clock. I luxuriated in bed for a few more minutes and stretched. There were little noises downstairs and I wondered what Patty was up to. I threw back the covers and rolled out of bed. I waddled down the stairs. I was stiff and my knees were spongy after our run.

Before I got to the kitchen I could smell silver polish so I knew what Patty was doing. She'd gotten into the habit of checking out tag sales and garage sales, especially when I would work weekends. We had a very nice assortment of crystal wine glasses and old china plates. And she could tell sterling silver from silver

26

plate, which I could not. We ate off china and silver every night, not just on special occasions. Of course none of it matched; we decided that made the table look more interesting. I didn't ask her the chemistry of how silver polish worked because she'd tell me.

I plopped down opposite her at the kitchen table.

"Did you have a good nap?"

"I did. I was out. Whatcha working on?"

"I got a few pieces several weeks ago and I didn't get to shine them up yet." She held up the spoon she was working on. "Isn't it pretty?" Her fingers were gray from the polish.

"Yup." I couldn't get real excited about flatware.

"I don't think people know what they're giving away. It sure doesn't look like much when they're tarnished. I bet they wouldn't sell them for so little if they were shiny and they could see how nice they look," she said as she continued polishing.

I drank some orange juice. I watched Patty. I went upstairs, washed up, dressed for work and came down to help cook supper.

We chatted while we worked in the kitchen. I was making a salad. Patty was boiling water for cheese tortellini and was grinding basil leaves from our garden to make pesto sauce. While I was sleeping she'd gone to Gorham and Norton grocery and gotten some fixings, including a loaf of focaccia bread with thinly sliced tomatoes and black olives baked onto the crust.

"I think the new guy started today," I said.

"Oh, right. What's his name again?"

"Howard Barker. I think today was his first shift."

"He's an internist?"

"I think his training is in family practice. He moved into one of those big fancy old houses just down the hill from the hospital. He's starting up a practice there; from scratch. I'm sure it'll take a while for him to get busy. It's good for him and it's good for us that he can take some ER time. I hope he has an okay first day."

"Where's he from?"

"I don't know. Midwest, I think."

"What's he like?"

"I haven't met him yet. I'll meet him for the first time in a few hours."

Our dinner was delicious. Fresh basil is a wonderful thing. So is balsamic vinegar. The things I never knew. I ate lightly since I learned how unpleasant it is to go to work the nightshift groggy with a full stomach. Patty had half a glass of white wine. I had water. I sneaked a sip of her wine knowing she would catch me. When we were done and cleaned up it was still too early for me to go to work so we went out for a walk around the neighborhood. I love summer evenings.

We got back to the house. I got my medical knapsack and went over to Patty and gave her a long hug. I hated to leave her at night. Why can't people have their emergencies in the daytime? She never said she got lonely, but she was a good sport. Tomorrow she'll work and I'll be off all day sleeping off the shift. Once in a while she'll stop by the ER and hang out with me or whoever is in the coffee room. In particular she likes to come when I'm changing shifts with Will Connor because he's such a funny guy. He's very opinionated and he and Patty like to have sparring matches. She's one of the few who can keep up with him.

We kissed again and I left for work. "I hope you have an easy night," she said.

Chapter 4

From the instant I walked through the door into the ER I could feel the tension in the air. No one greeted me happily. Everyone was walking around fast; preoccupied. A quick "Hi, Charlie" and then out of the side of the mouth "Boy am I glad you're here!" Sotto voce. I was ten minutes early, as usual. As I walked back to the doctors' room with my knapsack I passed a cubicle with a lady on a backboard and a Philadelphia neck immobilizer. In the next cubicle was a man on a backboard and another neck collar. In the third one was a man I didn't know sewing up a modest laceration on a lady's knee. I stopped and looked at him. He was paunchy, a little older than me, with longish brown hair, big glasses and a polyester tie. I looked at the nurse who was with him and above the top of her surgical mask her eyes locked onto mine and then rolled.

"Hi. I'm Charlie Davids."

"Oh, hi, Charlie, I'm Dr. Barker. I've been looking forward to seeing you."

"Same here. How did your day go?"

"Oh, not bad at all." As he was sewing his tie kept touching the sterile drape. He didn't have a mask on and he was talking into the wound.

"So. Do you have anything to sign out to me?" I asked, wondering about the two people I just saw on backboards.

"There's these three people who were in a motor vehicle accident. I haven't gotten to the other two."

"Oh. You haven't evaluated the other two yet?"

"No."

"Are they injured? Are they stable?"

"I don't know. I haven't evaluated them."

Why the hell not? Did you ever hear the word triage? Did you think maybe you ought to make sure they're stable and maybe get some X-rays and labs cooking before you plop down and start sewing some piddly laceration that could wait until you've checked everybody out and gotten them off those miserable backboards? Maybe he's just killing time doing something easy knowing that he's off shift soon and he can dump on the next guy.

"Okay. Nice meeting you," I said without really meaning it.

So I got into high gear and checked out the people on backboards and did a physical exam, neurological and orthopedic. Both had neck pain, which was hopefully whiplash, and I sent them for C-spine films plus a few others. Fortunately they'd had their seat belts on. An hour later they were both in X-ray and I was feverishly writing up their charts at the nurses station. Howard Barker was long gone. Margaret came up behind me.

"Boy, Charlie, that guy is terrible," she said, raspily. I wondered if the lining of her larynx looked like sandpaper.

"Let me clear this place out, Margaret. Then you can tell me."

I fully re-examined the lady Barker had sutured. She told me how the accident happened, how her right knee had bumped into the dashboard and got cut on some edge of the molding. She hadn't lost consciousness. I listened to her heart and lungs, palpated her abdomen. She had no rib pain, particularly none over her kidney or spleen. She was oriented to person, place and time and had a normal neurological exam. There were no red blood cells in her urine. I discharged her and wrote it all up.

The tech came back with the C-spine films. "See you later Charlie," she said. They know how I work. Neck films are scary. I always read them the same way. Big hospitals always have a radiologist on call. Not at Fairview. We read our own films at night. There are a lot of bones and bony features to look at and it's very easy to miss things in a neck series. It could be very bad for the patient's future if I miss something important. It could be very bad, also, for my future, if I miss something important. It could be very good for the patient's lawyer if I miss something. I always go to the radiology office so I am away from distraction. I read each film twice. Sitting, not standing. I bend open a paper clip and use it like a pointer to trace around each bone to make sure the contours are smooth, that the front of the vertebrae make a smooth continuous arc on the side view, that the soft tissue shadow in front of them is thin and uniform, that no corners are compressed down. All the facet joints have to be uniform.

I read the films twice. First the woman, then the man, then each of them again. You can't be too careful with necks. They looked okay to me.

I got EKGs on these people and got cardiac enzymes to make sure they had no evidence of a cardiac contusion from the blunt force trauma when they hit the dashboard.

I finished up with these two patients, told them everything I hadn't found, sent them home with a head sheet, neck sheet, soft foam neck collars, analgesics and muscle relaxants.

It was almost eleven when I got to the coffee room and plopped down next to Margaret.

"Okay," I said and sipped my coffee, "tell me."

"Well," she rasped, "I don't want to rush to judgment. Maybe the guy is nervous. But it was only a mildly busy day. There was only one cardiac and the only significant trauma was the one you walked in on. He was disorganized. With some cases he was real fast, with some he was real slow. He didn't seem comfortable with the cardiac case. He was real uncomfortable with the three people from the MVA. He went to the simplest patient like an ostrich burying its head in the sand and he left the others on backboards. We kept dropping hints that he ought to evaluate them before he started that laceration but he blew us off."

"Oh," I said. I swallowed hard. "Maybe he's just nervous. The director said he was well-trained. He said he'd been in practice for more than a few years. Maybe he just wasn't used to this place and the way we do things here. Kind of like trying to cook in someone else's kitchen. Everything seems awkward."

"Well, he sure doesn't work like you and Will and the other guys. But that's very generous of you Charlie. That's what I expected from you."

"How did he interact with the staff?" I asked.

"Well, he wasn't exactly snotty but he wasn't as nice as he could've been. I don't really think he made any friends here today. This is all just between you and me, right?"

"Of course," I said. "I can keep a secret. What do you think this guy's future is in this department?"

"Not too good; first impression."

"Too bad. I was hoping it would work out. It would give us a little slack in the schedule."

"I could be wrong," Margaret said.

"Right. When have you been wrong when it comes to understanding human nature?"

She did not respond for a minute. Then she said, "I was really right when I told you Patty was the girl for you."

"Yeah, well," I exclaimed, "that was really obvious. That was a bad case of love at first sight. You know there's a nice old man who I see at shul most mornings, Mr. Franklin, and a few weeks ago he told me a wonderful story, of Basheret."

"Tell me the story."

"Basheret was the name of a beautiful and spiritual young Jewish woman. She was very kind and good. Her wealthy father was afraid she would marry the wrong guy, so to protect her he isolated her on an uninhabited island in the sea. Lo and behold a shipwrecked man washed up on the island, and although penniless, he was a scholar of scripture and a thoroughly good and sincere and honest and loving man. They fell in love, the father approved, they married, all was good. So her name, Basheret, came to mean 'that which is fated.' I don't believe in fate but I like the story."

"Sounds like you, Charlie," she rasped.

"What does?"

"A scholar; a sincere and good and loving man."

"Oh , please. I wish," I interjected.

"So things are good?"

"With Patty?" I asked.

33

"Of course."

"Things with Patty are wonderful. Better than wonderful."

"So how come there aren't any little Charlies running around? We've all been wondering."

"It isn't from lack of wanting," I said, "or trying. Let me ask you something. This also is strictly between you and me. How many times have you heard of an infertile couple who finally adopt and once they have a baby in the house they finally conceive?"

"Several times," Margaret said, thinking. "More than several times."

"Just suppose that one of those couples didn't adopt but they got a puppy in the house. And it woke them up at night and it made noise and they had to take care of it, and their friends and family came over to congratulate them and they had to deal with its feedings and pee and poop and all that"

"And do I think it could have the same emotional-psychological-hormonal influence that an adopted baby would create, and enable them to conceive? Sure, why not? Why not? You ought to try it. You ought to get going at it. Time is running out. How old are you two anyway?"

"I'm thirty-four, Patty is almost thirty-three."

"Well that's not the eleventh hour yet, but you better get into gear before too much longer. I like that puppy idea. Are you going to get one?

"I've been thinking about it for a little while. I haven't mentioned it to Patty yet. I wouldn't want her to know my ulterior motive."

"No, better keep that one to yourself." Her pager went off. She looked at it and made a call. "I have to go upstairs. I'll see you later."

I finished my coffee and got up and stretched. It was eleven. The night was still young. I grinned. Margaret is such a neat person. I wandered around the department and chatted with the receptionist, Helen. Her husband was MacPherson who was a sergeant on the evening shift of the Great Barrington Police Department. He's a good guy. Big guy. No one remembers what his first name is because everybody just calls him Mac. Or MacPherson. Or Sergeant. He'd been a Marine. He'd been in Vietnam. He loves taking care of people. He loves being a small town cop. Just like I love being a small town doc. He thinks he's a Scot because his parents or grandparents came from Nova Scotia. I heard that Nova Scotians are more Scottish than people from Scotland. Mac is fiercely proud of being Scottish. He was born and raised in East Boston and has a speech impediment he tries to pass off as an accent. He calls me "Chollie." Whenever he can he lapses into a phony Scottish brogue and makes everybody groan. In the winter he wears a Tartan plaid Tam O'Shanter cap when he's off duty. He'd probably wear a kilt too, if he could get away with it.

Sometimes when Patty and I are out running we pass him. He is very serious about physical training. He'll nod his head at us but never stop to talk. Sometimes he'll run in his army boots: "Got to keep my feet used to them." He'll run with a five pound dumbbell in each hand: "That's about how much my M-14 weighs." Other times he'll say: "Gotta keep my Claymore sharp." "What the hell is a Claymore?" I asked once. "A big-two handed Scottish battle sword," he answered. I learned later that a Claymore was also an antipersonnel mine used in Vietnam.

I chatted with Helen. I did not ask her what she thought of the new doctor. I asked if I could look at all the charts from 8:00 AM to 8:00 PM. She got them for me. Helen said, "If I don't see you again tonight I hope you have an easy night. Shift change is coming up soon."

I thanked her for the charts. "Thanks, Helen. Have a good night. Regards to Mac."

I went and sat down with the charts in the doctors' room. Barker's handwriting was legible though not neat. His notes were sparse but they were adequate.

Margaret poked her head in the door and started to bark. I laughed. "I'm going home now Charlie. What are you doing?"

"Well, between you and me, I'm looking over Dr. Barker's charts for the day." My feet were up on the corner of the desk, the charts were in my lap.

Margaret looked serious. "I'm glad you are doing that. I wasn't going to ask you to."

"Well, so far, so good. It's all up to the director, you know."

"Good night. Have an easy one," she said

"And I want you to go straight home. No cavorting in downtown Great Barrington for you."

She waved me off and left.

Joan was on with me tonight. Another nice woman. I enjoyed working with her. She was busy restocking the supply cabinets. Some night nurses did it right away in case things got busy and they couldn't get to it later. Other nurses waited until the middle of the night to do it, so if they were nodding off they'd have something to occupy themselves with and not fall asleep.

I reread all of Dr. Barker's X-rays for the day. Looked good to me. I reread his EKGs. Also okay. I brought the charts back up front. I chatted with Joan.

I thought about Patty sleeping in our bedroom at this hour. By herself. I wondered what she was dreaming about. I wondered what position she was in. I wondered which nightgown she was wearing. I wondered what book was on her nightstand. I wondered if she was happy.

I got a couple of hours of sleep on the sleeper sofa

until Joan called me to tell me an ambulance was enroute with a little old lady from a nursing home who fell out of bed on the way to the bathroom and they thought she broke her hip. So did I. Her left leg was about two inches shorter than the right and the left foot was externally rotated. We drew all the bloods she'd need as a pre-op, including a type and cross match for two units of blood, since she would likely have surgery in the morning. We called the X-ray tech to come in and do pelvic, hip and chest films. I started an IV and gave her a pre-op exam. I called the orthopedist and told him about her, that she was fairly comfortable, I'd given her a little Demerol, the films showed a typical intertrochanteric fracture, she was all wrapped up and worked up and ready for him for the OR in the morning. He said thanks and went back to bed. We rolled the lady up to the surgical floor.

Just as I was heading back toward the sofa bed one of the nurses from the third floor came to the department. She had been giving a patient an intramuscular injection in the buttock; an elderly disoriented patient. The nurse, Harriet, had grasped a fold of buttock with her left hand and with her right darted in the needle. The patient was uncooperative and his arm came swinging around to sweep her away and when the needle finally came to rest it was in her palm. Ouch. These things happen. That's a painful place to get a puncture. It is not much of a traumatic problem; it could be more of an infectious one.

So I did the standard needle stick protocol. I examined her and listened to her heart to see if there were any murmurs in case she might get one later. I palpated her lymph nodes, felt for her liver and spleen size, all as a basis for future comparison. I drew blood for the hepatitis panel, cytomegalovirus and all the other tests as specified in the protocol. The patient himself would have the same blood tests drawn in the morning when the phlebotomist made her rounds. Hopefully the patient wouldn't give the phlebotomist a hard time. Probably wouldn't. During the daytime these patients are usually more tractable. Especially if the Demerol hadn't worn off. They call it the Sundowner Syndrome. When elderly patients are in an unfamiliar environment they become disoriented when the sun goes down.

Harriet was a nice lady who'd been a nurse for decades and this was not her first needle stick. When it happened she went to the sink and washed for a good long time with hot water and surgical soap and massaged it, milking some blood out of it. She knew the safety issues and the need to go through this testing. She said he's a nice old man, she wasn't angry with him. These things happen. It's part of the job. She went back upstairs to work and I sat down in the nurses' station to write up her ER chart, the employee incident report and the OSHA needle stick report.

I made it back to my sofa bed and had an hour-long unfulfilling catnap that was shallow and full of work dreams. Not restful. A little while later I heard the hospital come back to life as the seven to three shift was coming in and the night shift preparing to go home. I got up and brushed my teeth in the little sink in the corner of the room, put on my shoes and wandered drowsily into the coffee room.

Will Connor was there already, almost an hour early, holding court. He liked to come in early, to get caffeinated, hoping to find someone he could provoke.

"Hey, Charlie, you should be glad you didn't go to that risk management seminar at the Holiday Inn last weekend."

"Oh, yeah, how was it?" I asked, settling in on the couch cuddling my coffee cup in both hands, smiling, looking forward to whatever outrageous commentary would soon come forth. To get relicensed in this state we need ten credit hours of risk management every two years, amongst all the other requirements. Risk management. How not to get sued. Now and then they'll have a Saturday conference at some hotel. They're awful. They have weak coffee, powdered creamer and small soggy Danish that leave your fingers sticky.

We get harangued by lawyers who once were doctors, or lawyers who think they're doctors. Or lawyers who defend doctors. These people are not in the trenches of real life medical care. Yet they tell us how we should be practicing. How we should discuss each differential diagnosis with each patient and involve them in clinical decision making. That we must tell patients every possible, unlikely and rare side effect of every drug we prescribe. And we should record everything we do or say for the record to be defensible in court. These things might sound reasonable on paper but in real life, so little of it even floats.

This is while the government says there are too many specialists and not enough generalists. Yet they want the generalists to work slower and spend more time with each patient. Where would this extra time come from? As it is, people complain about waiting too long for an appointment and too long in the waiting room.

This is while insurance companies decide to pay less for office visits since the whole reimbursement schedule is too high anyway. More time per patient equals fewer patients per day followed by lower payment per patient, and physicians are supposed to be okay with this? Tell me another industry where this could happen. Maybe that's why I'm not in private practice like I thought I would be by now, and work here by the hour instead.

This is while the malpractice insurance industry in this state imploded because it is so highly litigious that it was not profitable. So they left. All of them. There was a vacuum. The state legislature had a crisis and they invented their own quasi-state government-owned-managed insurance company called "Mass Pro Mutual." And they sent their "experts" out to talk to us about how we should take care of patients with both hands tied behind our backs. They send them out to talk to us about all the things we're doing wrong.

"Everytime you have a patient encounter it is an opportunity to get sued," they say. We know this.

"Every time you prescribe a medication for a patient it is an opportunity to get sued." We know this.

"So," Will said, "there was this speaker who used to be a pharmacist and now is a lawyer. He told us we should never ever under any circumstances prescribe a generic drug."

"Right," I said. "Why is that?"

"He presented the case of a general internist who got sued and lost and there was an enormous cash award. Here's the story. It is so stupid. Not what the doctor did, but how the jury looked at it. It makes me so frustrated just to think about it. This internist had a patient who was an older man who'd had a few mild heart attacks and some mild congestive heart failure. He had this guy on digoxin and Lasix and potassium supplements. How many patients have you seen like that?"

"About a thousand," I said.

"Maybe a million," one of the nurses said.

"So this old guy collapses and he gets CPR and they get him to an ER somewhere and they give advanced cardiac life support and do an EKG and labs and guess what, he has an arrhythmia. And then he dies. And guess what? When his blood tests come back, his potassium is a little low. Ever see this before?"

"Of course."

"So the guy dies and the family is mad and their

lawyer finds the guy's potassium is a little low, like whose isn't if they are on Lasix, and he finds the pharmacist filled the patient's potassium replacement with a generic equivalent of the name brand. And the lawyer scraped up some evidence that the generic formulations of potassium chloride don't always have the same bioavailability as the name brands. So since the internist didn't insist on a brand name and the pharmacist gave a generic and the guy's potassium was low, and we don't even have proof he was taking it or taking it properly or that this was a less potent generic, and he had an arrhythmia, despite still smoking and his fragile past cardiac history, his death was the doctor's fault because he permitted a generic interchange."

"That's bullshit," the nurse said.

"Do you prescribe brand name potassium?" Will asked me.

"I've seen people on generic and brand name potassium and they are all hard to keep controlled. I've never noticed any advantage. I've never prescribed brand name only potassium," I added.

"Are you going to now?" Will asked.

"At five or ten times the cost? Just because some sleaze was able to convince a dumb jury that it really makes a difference? I don't think so. Everyone on a diuretic loses potassium, no matter which one they are on. It's always hard to keep their potassium up. It's no easier using brand name stuff."

"And this sphincter of a lawyer focused on the generic potassium chloride as the crux of the whole situation and blew it up way out of context and was able to convince an ignorant nonmedical jury.

"And he sees himself as a knight in shining armor for his client. A hired gun, win a case for them, win money for them with any tactic or distorted fact he can blow out of context."

41

"And pocket a third of it for himself," The nurse added.

"You know in Canada," Will said, "malpractice works differently. There lawyers only get paid by the hour. They don't get paid on a contingency basis like they do here. There a malpractice case doesn't represent a possible pot of gold for them like it does here. Here so many lawyers just dream of having that one big juicy malpractice case with a multimillion dollar settlement, a third of which would create their fortune and their reputation. In Canada there's less incentive for them to try so hard to win a case with no merit. In Canada the award is decided by the judge, not the jury."

I hate hearing this. It's so depressing. You try so hard to help people, you've studied and trained so long to learn. And it is such a difficult system. Everybody is different. Not everybody responds the same way to the same drug. Not everybody heals the same way. If medicine were simple and straightforward everybody would be doing it. You could learn it in a trade school in two years, like an auto mechanic.

Five percent of skier's boot-top leg fractures result in a bony non-union. Across the board. Happens to everyone if you do enough of them. Then you need surgery. But if you are the patient, it's the doctor's fault because he must not have set the bone right. As if he didn't wrap the plaster around the fracture properly. The way some people think.

"I hate going to those meetings and hearing those horror stories. If they made medical school applicants go to those risk management lectures I bet half of them would change their minds," I said. "I better get going. I want to get home before Patty leaves for work."

I drove down the hill from the hospital. I got caught at the light at Main Street and stared at the wall of Searles Castle in front of me and St. James Episcopal church to my left. The light changed and I turned left on Main Street, passed the church, turned right onto Bridge Street, passed Harland Foster's hardware store and crossed over the Housatonic River, which was low and muddy this time of year. I turned left on East Street, right on Cottage and left on Gilmore. Patty's car was still on the driveway. Good. Home in four minutes.

Patty heard my steps on the porch and greeted me with her big smile. She gave me a kiss, asked me how my night was and then she gave me another one. She was dressed for work. She was wearing a coral-colored Izod shirt, pleated khaki chino slacks and espadrilles. She had on small gold ball earrings. No makeup. She didn't need any with her dark brown eyes and long eyelashes. She had a little pink in her cheeks and a few cinnamon orange freckles on her cheeks and nose. Vermillion lips, an engaging smile.

On her left wrist was a little black plastic digital watch. On her left ring finger was her wedding ring. It was reddish gold. It was her grandmother's, who had come over from Austria at the turn of the century. Patty's grandparents name had been Cohen but somehow in immigration it became Caine and has been ever since.

I wore my father's wedding band which had been his mother's. She'd come over from Russia around 1910. I held Patty's hand and played with her ring as she sat on my lap in the armchair finishing her coffee. My forehead was on her shoulder, my eyes were closed. I was drowsy. My left arm was around her back, my right hand holding her left, her right hand holding her coffee cup.

"Go to bed, sleepyhead. I have to go to work."

She slipped on her white pharmacist's jacket and went out the door. I heard her car drive away and I wondered if she'd be dispensing generic or brand name potassium chloride today. I wondered what her thoughts would be about Will's story.

I read the morning's Beagle (the *Berkshire Eagle*) on the porch but was too tired to really pay attention. I went upstairs to the bedroom, undressed and got into bed. I squeezed down the little earplugs, screwed them in and listened with pleasure as they crackled and expanded and I fell asleep.

Chapter 5

We had big plans. It was the first time we had a day off together in a while. It was August and we needed to get in all the summertime recreation we could. I got up early and went to say Kaddish. When I got home Patty was in our little backyard garden picking chives to mince with onions for an omelet. We had coffee and orange juice with the eggs, and thick pieces of toasted wholegrain sourdough bread from the Berkshire Mountain Bakery in Housatonic. We had butter and locally made blueberry jam. We dined elegantly on our mismatched tableware, eating even breakfast with china, crystal and silver.

After breakfast I cleaned the kitchen. We had a rule. He who cooks shall not clean. Patty put the bikes on the rack on the back of my car. I changed and then we headed out for our morning's activity. We were going to do bike trip number eight from the *Berkshire Bicycling Guidebook*.

As we drove south for ten minutes towards Sheffield I asked if Patty had read yesterday's *Eagle*.

"Yeah."

"Did you see the article about the man and the boy in Ohio who drowned?"

"Yeah, I did. How awful."

There had been a very rainy week in Ohio and when it finally cleared, all the rivers and streams were engorged. A man was walking along the stream with his eight-year-old boy. They were in awe of the raging torrent; it must have been amazing to look at. You can imagine hearing the father say, "Now, Johnny, don't get too close!" The kid falls in and is swept away. The father jumps in after him. A few hours later they fish them both out. Dead.

"That guy was doomed," Patty said.

"How do you mean?"

"He was at the brunt of a no-win situation."

"What do you mean?"

"Well, there were a limited number of outcomes. The kid falls in. If the father did nothing and the kid dies, he'd never forgive himself, nor would anyone else, for the rest of his life. If he jumps in and saves the boy, then he's a hero, but it was a suicidal risk. Or he could jump in, the boy survives but the dad dies and the kid goes through life with the guilt of falling in and his father dies trying to save him. Or the father jumps in and survives but the boy doesn't and the father replays the terror, the shock, the tragedy over and over again for the rest of his life, like biting on a sore tooth every five minutes. Or he jumps in and they both die, which is what happened. I think those are all of the permutations."

"So what are you saying?"

"That only one of the outcomes was acceptable: they both survive, and that sounded most unlikely given the description of the flume. Any other outcome would be horrible."

"You're suggesting it's better the father died so he wouldn't have to live with the memory of the tragedy, of seeing his kid swept away? What about the poor guy's wife?"

"I think it's a tragedy any way you look at it."

"You think he'd prefer to die than live with the tragedy?"

"I don't know what he would prefer. But to be right there, to see it happen, to see it unfold, to see the boy washed away, to see the desperate look on his face as he was helplessly swept away, do you think the father in a hundred years could ever get past that? How could you live with that image, that memory, being right there? It's like a Greek tragedy."

"Lots of people witness tragedy and go on," I said.

"Yeah, but how many really want to? How many of them continue to exist but don't really live? I mean, to witness such a tragedy so up close and personal. It would be a lot different if you hear, hours later, that something like this happened. God forbid if you got some horrible form of cancer and your days were numbered, at least there's some time to prepare mentally. Or if, God forbid, you were killed in a car accident and I found out about it later, at least I was removed from it, not a witness to it, not a part of it like this man and his boy. I'm just talking about different levels of shock value. There are things you can prepare yourself for, and things you don't have a chance to, that hit you so much harder. Do you have any clue what I'm talking about?"

"I never looked at a situation like this so analytically. I was just being emotional because the story of that man and his boy is so sad and tragic."

"And I agree wholeheartedly. And all but one resolution are bad ones. And tragedy can break your heart so badly that living prolongs the tragedy."

We parked on Main Street in Sheffield. It was a beautiful summer morning, the dew was drying and it was partly sunny or partly cloudy, take your pick. Partly cloudy after that morose conversation. We put the water bottles in their baskets on the bikes; folded up the map into my shorts pocket; put on helmets and headed north.

We turned left on Covered Bridge Lane. The Upper Sheffield Covered Bridge was built in 1854. It's a real wooden trestle-style covered bridge spanning the Housatonic River. It's ninety-six feet long and cost fourteen hundred dollars to build. Naturally it is one-lane. We walked our bikes into it. Halfway through the bridge Patty stopped me. We looked out the windows at the river flowing beneath and beyond us.

"Know what else they call wooden bridges in New England?"

"No, what?"

"Kissing bridges," she said. "See?" And she put both arms around my neck and kissed me long and slowly, and it got my heart rate up. We bumped helmets. Finally we disengaged, and as our lips parted they made the sound of a bubble popping.

"Yeah, I'd say this is a good place for kissing." We got our bikes, which were leaning against the sidewall, and continued on our way. Patty rode ahead of me on her red touring bicycle. We turned right on Boardman Street and rode south with expansive fields to our right. To our left was the forested valley wall. We passed the occasional farmhouse and barn, sometimes a smaller, newer ranch house or split-level. We pedaled up slight inclines, then coasted down gentle slopes. We passed hay fields; we passed cornfields.

At the Balsam Hill Farm on Hewins Road we saw a big green and yellow John Deere tractor with huge rear tires and an enclosed cab pulling a red Ford New

Holland manure spreader. It was going around and around in circles as big as a high school quarter-mile track and there was a dark brown cloud spewing out the back. Its odor was palpable. Thankfully we were coasting downhill and didn't need to breath deeply.

We passed the tractor and then a farmhouse and a huge dull red barn. Beyond the barn was a field full of Holstein cows, black and white. There were a few near the side of the road and we stopped to look. They did not seem terribly aggravated by the flies landing on their pretty faces. They had long delicate eyelashes. Their ears flopped back and forth. Each cow had a yellow plastic ear tag with a number on it. You could see the muscles on their foreheads bulge and relax, bulge and relax, as they chewed. They looked like they had a rim of creamed spinach around their mouths and chins. They were clean except from the knees down, which were muddy. Their tails swished. The udders were big and pink.

We communed with the cows a few minutes more and got back on our way. We were in the warm sun on a long uphill stretch for ten minutes then Patty called for a water break. We found a grassy spot on the shady side of the road. We plucked water bottles out of their carriers and gently laid our bikes down on the grass. We gazed off into the distant fields and low hills and faraway mountains and clouds.

"Are you a little blue today?" Patty asked softly.

"Oh, I don't know. Maybe I am."

"You seem a little diminished."

"I've been thinking about my father."

"Good thoughts or sad thoughts?"

"Oh, nice thoughts. I miss him." I took another swallow of water and could feel a little road grit on the nipple of the water bottle. "I wish I had more of his things."

Patty came up close to me and stood right in front of me. She smiled. "You" she said loudly and poked me in the belly with her index finger. "You, You," she said, gently slapping both my cheeks at the same time. "You You You You You!" she said as she slapped me on the chest, hard.

"What are you doing?" I said, laughing, backing away, trying to protect myself.

"You You You You," she said as she danced around me, patting me hard, slapping me on various parts of my anatomy as I tried to avoid her blows.

"What's the matter with you?" I asked in a high voice, laughing as she beat me with her crazy chant. She kept going after me. Suddenly she stopped.

"Cross your arms and hold your shoulders," she commanded. I did.

"You are now holding about the most precious thing your father ever possessed! You're holding his own flesh and blood. His legacy. Flesh and blood. You are the child he created, you're the kid he carried in his arms, whose butt he wiped, whose education he paid for. He's in your head, he's in your heart and soul, what the hell else do you need?

"Sure it's nice to have his ring, his mother's ring, but big friggin' deal. It's a trinket. If you saw his ring among a dozen others in a pawnshop you couldn't tell it apart. It doesn't have magic powers. It doesn't have his electromagnetic imprint from being on his finger for so many years. Sure it's nice to have it but it's just a trinket. It's just stuff. We are not a people who worship relics. You resemble him. You have memories of him. You cherish your love of him. You are of him. You have you! What the hell else do you need?

"When was Abraham around, eighteen hundred BCE? Thirty-eight hundred years ago? How many generations is that? How many times throughout those generations did our ancestors live with nothing, or next to nothing, How many times did they have to flee with just the clothes on their backs? Don't get weighted down with the baggage and burden of stuff.

"Focus on the memories. The love isn't in his stuff; it's in you. You have you, you don't need anything else. You've got his flesh and blood, what more could you want?

"Oh, Charlie," she said and closed the distance between us and we hugged. We were sweaty. "Oh, Charlie, are you bonding with those nice old men at synagogue and wondering when you'll be saying Kaddish for them too?" She said this talking into my shoulder. I didn't really answer.

"Maybe you should think about not going anymore."

I thought about that. We were now sitting on the grass, side by side, crosslegged, looking out across the valley. I was playing with a blade of grass. I had it between my thumbs, up against my mouth, and I was blowing across it like a reed. All I did was get lightheaded and get spit all over my hands.

"You do it like this," Patty said, as she nonchalantly picked a green blade of grass and set it between her thumbs. She took a deep breath and while gazing at the view brought her thumbs to her lips and blew a noise that was so loud and raucous and penetrating that it rivaled the town fire horn at noon.

I tried and tried and she showed me again but I couldn't get it.

"You know over the years in medicine I've met a lot of nice people. People I like. People I would want to get to know. But the reason I meet them is because they're sick. And sometimes they get better and sometimes they don't and I can't always know who will and who won't. And I get sucked in and get personally involved and engaged and they die and I feel like hell and then I do it again. And each time it happens I get this pain in my heart and it festers. And as the years go by, and I do it again and again, I remind myself there's a difference between liking them as a patient and liking someone as a friend. I'd like to like them all as friends but it'll hurt too much. Am I making sense?

"It festers and it putrefies and each time I get over it it becomes encased in a layer of scar tissue in the middle of my chest and I try to protect myself from this sorrow but once in a while little squirts of pus leak out and get into my system and make me sick for a while until the scar toughens again. As I get older I get a little better at it. Maybe I am a little better at resisting it. Maybe I don't let myself get as close anymore. Maybe I'm better at realizing that I can enjoy these people, enjoy the interaction, the humanism in the rapport with them, the touching, but maybe I'm more aware of their fragility, that they are on thin ice, they could fall through and die and I'm more cognizant and I don't get my heart in it as much as my mind.

"Other people—Will, MacPherson, the EMTs, the other docs—I'm sure some of them feel this way sometimes, but not as much or as sharply as I do. It's the job. Do CPR. Run the code. If people die, so be it. Move on. It is never easy for me. I know people have to die and in some cases of extreme disease or age it's a blessing, but for me there's always a loss."

"Then why do you keep doing this? Why don't you change careers?" Patty asked.

"I could never give this up. I love this. I get to do precious things for people. Every day. It's a privilege. But that doesn't mean it ought to be easy. This is just the price I have to pay. It's the price I choose to pay. Did I ever tell you about Father Donovan?"

"Who is Father Donovan?"

"He's a Jesuit priest who was a chaplain at BMC when I was an intern."

"Tell me about him," Patty said.

"Okay, but this is a long story," I warned her. "It was late August. I'd been an intern for two months and was terrified to see how little I knew. All summer we interns were taking care of Edward Mortin, who was dying of leukemia. He was a little older than us, in his mid-thirties. All day and all night we'd get paged to give him his pain meds. He was on Dilaudid and other stuff that was given IV and for policy reasons the nurses couldn't give it and the house staff had to do it. We all got to know him. He was a nice, quiet, kind guy who had no hair and was only flesh and bones after his chemotherapy. He was subdued, resigned. He had a wife. She was pretty. They had two little girls, and even though children weren't allowed to visit on the wards, everyone turned their heads and these girls were there often.

"By late August he had a bad case of the dwindles. I went in on a Sunday morning at eight and I was on call that night. Naturally that was the day Edward was going to die. The SOB had to die on my shift. So all day long I was running all over the hospital as usual, admitting people from the ER, answering pages from nurses, running around doing scutwork, getting arterial blood gases, getting called to see patients on the floors who had headaches or who were throwing up again or were having chest pain. Edward Mortin was one of them and he was really in a tailspin. He had a fever because he had no white blood cells and no platelets either. I was drawing blood cultures and swabbing him everywhere to look for a source of infection; checking urine samples for maybe a kidney infection. And giving him Dilaudid.

"When I realized that he was going to crash and

burn and there wasn't really a damn thing I could do about it I began to choke up. I kept thinking about his wife and kids. I was losing it. But I had to keep running around the hospital working. It was all I could do to keep from crying. Edward's fever went up and he went into a coma. His wife was there. I called his oncologist every few hours. 'Keep him comfortable,' he said. It was so different from what I was accustomed to. For the first two months of internship so far we had always done something. We never stopped. We did CPR, we put people on ventilators, we got CT scans, we started triple IV antibiotics, we put in SwanGanz catheters. We were always pushing, always pro-active, until they were flatlined. This was a new concept for me then, though I'm used to it now.

"I got called to Three East Green for a lady with chest pain. I was barely keeping it together. I examined her and rolled in the EKG machine and as I was hooking it up these two young nurses, who I'd worked with all summer, appeared and were standing side by side at the foot of the bed like the Bobsy twins, looking at me. I was surprised. I looked at them wondering what they were doing. When I asked them, they said, 'We're just here to help you if you need anything.' Two of them. Usually I wouldn't even have one of them. I think they knew I was losing it and were keeping an eye on me."

"So what does this have to do with Father Donovan?" Patty asked.

"I'm getting to that. I told you it was a long story.

"So all afternoon I'm running around being an intern and I keep checking Edward, and of course his wife is there. His pulse is getting threadier and threadier and his respirations are getting shallower and his heart sounds are getting more and more muffled and his blood pressure is getting lower. He's really circling the drain. And around eight o'clock in the evening he dies and the nurses call me to pronounce him. It's all I can do to keep it together. I've got all this I have to take care of, probably sixty people on Three East, another fifty or sixty on Five South and Five West, plus whatever new admissions the ER sends up. There was one other intern on in CCU/ICU and the stepdown unit and one resident supervising us both. So I'm using all my energy to keep up my protective force shield, you know, like on Star Trek, to keep the Klingons out so I can keep it together and do my work.

"So I go up to his room and ascertain that he's dead and I give Mrs. Mortin my sympathies. I'm afraid if I say any more I'll lose it. Then I go to the nurses' station and write it up and document it. Then I close myself in a utility room and pull out my little Kaddish card that I kept in my lab coat pocket. I started to say Kaddish for the poor bastard but I couldn't get through it."

"You didn't want to say it at the bedside?"

"No, I didn't want to say it in front of anybody, in front of her."

"Why?"

"She wasn't Jewish, she wouldn't have understood it. Besides, it wasn't my place to say a prayer in front of her and her dead husband. After a few tries I got through it and I'm leaning over the sink splashing cold water on my face and my goddamn beeper wouldn't leave me alone. But I finally get a grip and get it together and I come out of hiding and get back to work. But every now and then the Klingons break through again and I have to run off and find a place to collect myself.

"So it's about eleven o'clock at night and I'm in the small Three East conference room. One of the nurses comes in and says, 'Charlie, you have to go cry somewhere else, we're going to be giving report here in a few minutes.'"

"She sounds like Nurse Hatchet in the movie *One*

Flew Over the Cuckoo's Nest," Patty said. I shrugged.

"So I left the room. I don't remember where I was headed but in a little while I saw Father Donovan walking down the hall toward me.

"He was tall and slim and had gray hair and was a regular guy and talked sports and everybody adored him. He reminded me of Bing Crosby as Father O'Malley. I don't know if he could sing. He used to help the police out all the time. He'd help them talk people out of suicide threats. Once he put on a bulletproof vest and went to talk to some angry guy who'd taken hostages. He was a local hero.

"So he came up to me and said, 'Dr. Davids, can you spare a few minutes to sit and talk with me about something?' I figured it must have been about Edward. We went off somewhere, I can't recall where, it was probably the on-call room. I was happy to help him, but what with I didn't know yet. We sat down on a couch. He turned to me and put his hand on my shoulder.

"'You're really suffering, aren't you, Charlie?' The dam broke. It all came gushing out. I wouldn't let myself cry but I couldn't hold it back so I sat there quivering. I was trying so hard to compose myself. When I finally could talk he asked me to tell him what happened."

"Did he know that you are Jewish?"

"I told him. He said that he had surmised it. 'Good,' he said. 'It's good to have a religious orientation.' He asked me what happened. So I told him how I'd started my internship eight weeks ago, that every week it got harder. When I drove to work in the morning, as I approached the hospital, I could sense a silent scream growing louder and louder, the collective pain and suffering and angst of all those people inside that building. How much grief those walls had absorbed over the decades; how could they still stand? Each time I saw the housekeeping ladies wiping down and disinfecting a bed I wondered how many lives had ended there, cradled in that very mattress. I told him how we all bonded with Edward over the summer as we pumped the strongest narcotics into his veins. I told him about the Klingons and the force shield.

"He asked me if I knew the difference between sympathy and empathy. He said, 'Sympathy is when you feel sorry for someone. Empathy is when it keeps you up at night. Empathy is being impacted by it. You are an empathetic physician. And you know what? You always will be. But it'll never be this bad again. You won't need to suffer this much again, ever. That does not mean you'll be any less empathetic. You can quote me on that. Do you know what else happens to people as empathetic as you? The rewards are sweeter. Did you ever lance a boil, Charlie?'

"I told him no, but I'd seen it done, and Father Donovan said, 'It's a painful thing to go through. It hurts badly enough to have one and much worse to have it lanced. But once all the pus comes out and the pressure is released, you feel so much better. Charlie, I think you just got your boil lanced, didn't you? It's been developing all summer. You know what else, and you can quote me on this also, you'll be better for it and stronger for it and you'll remember it vividly the rest of your life. Tonight you passed a major spiritual milestone in your life.'

"I said, 'Thank you, Father, you've been very kind.'"

"'Wait I'm not done yet,' he told me. 'You know what else? You're too hard on yourself.'

"'How can I be too hard on myself when there's a whole hospital full of people who are depending on me and I break down like this and can't function? What happens if the other interns look at me and wonder if I'll be able to pull my weight?' I asked him.

"'That's not it, Charlie. The problem is not with the patients or the other interns or even with the Klingons. The problem is the force shield. You don't need it. You can let the Klingons in. They're not so bad. You can deal with them. Just like you are now. The harder you try to compose yourself, the more energy you put into your force shield, the more brittle you become. Just let it out. Lance the boil, get the pus out, get better, get on with it. All summer your boil has been ripening and you just finally got lanced. You had a catharsis.

"'You've been trying to be a super intern. You've been dealing with all this tragedy and at the same time you're striving to fulfill all your duties, as a doctor on call on a weekend, with all these patients who might need you, desperately need you, at a moment's notice. And you're beating yourself up about it because you see your psyche as a doctor being tested because you think you have to be as ready and capable as a swat team and here you are grieving. And you're wondering if you're cut out for this and wondering if you made the wrong choice. You made the right choice but you know what, it's just that it's harder for you in the beginning than for the others. But you'll persevere and you'll get over this and be stronger for it, without any conscious effort on your part at all. Your emotional psyche is going to learn from this. It'll never be this bad for you again.'"

"He sounds wonderful," Patty said.

"He was wonderful," I agreed.

"And I'm sure you took all that empathy with you when you were taking care of all those gangsters in Springfield. Six years after Father Donovan you went toe to toe with the mob and you prevailed."

I stared out at the tops of the hills across the valley, at the sky above them. "I don't know any other way to do it," I replied in a whisper.

We didn't speak for a little while. "You know, Maimonides said the practice of medicine is a religious undertaking."

"You could have been a rabbi, Charlie."

"I'm not smart enough."

"You're smart enough."

"I'm not religious enough. I have doubt."

"You're religious enough."

"I love you, Patty. I never told anyone that story before. About Father Donovan."

"I love you, too. I didn't know it was that hard for you. You're very courageous Charlie, doing what you have to do when it's hard and you're scared. Every sick patient is a vicarious threat, isn't it? It must be a tough way to live. Kind of like shell shock, all those patients. Kind of like vicarious post traumatic stress."

I nodded. I was exhausted. More from telling the story than from the bike ride.

Chapter 6

We finished our bike loop in a couple of hours and by the time we got home it was lunchtime. There was a big car parked in front of our house. I parked in the driveway and as Patty and I were getting out of our car, Morse and Fremont were getting out of theirs. They must've had a pleasant and relaxing morning sitting in their car on a nice shady street in the summer. It was warm and they'd been in the car with their suit coats on. Probably hiding their guns.

We walked over to them. "Good morning, gentlemen. This is my wife, Patty. These are agents Morse and Fremont. Would you like to come in and have a cold drink? Some iced tea?"

When I was a kid I was always excited when a workman came to the house. I was curious. I wanted to help. I offered to hold the flashlight for the plumber or the oil burner man or the guy who came to read the water meter.

They were sitting with Patty in the living room. I came in from the kitchen with a tray with four tumblers of iced tea with mint leaves from the garden and lemon slices even though the men said they didn't want any.

"So, how can I help you guys?"

"You better help us this time. We've been out here two times already and you haven't helped us the least bit." Patty and I looked at each other.

"We want to know how come we found your fingerprints in Springfield."

"Why not? I've been to Springfield many times. I've been to West Springfield, Holyoke, I've been to lots of places. Boston. New York City. Jerusalem."

"That's not much of an explanation, Doc," Morse said.

"How do you know they are Charlie's fingerprints?" Patty asked.

"His prints are on file from when he got his gun license," Morse said. Patty looked at me as if to say, "I didn't know you had a gun license."

"And we confirmed them when you handled those photographs the first time we met." Patty shot me a glance as if to say, "I told you so."

"Speaking of gun licenses, do you have a weapon, Doctor?"

"Not anymore. I had a shotgun once. I sold it a few years ago. At a sporting goods store up in Pittsfield." Patty looked at me as if to say, "I didn't know this."

"Any other weapons?"

"No."

"What about a large capacity Smith and Wesson nine millimeter semi-automatic handgun you bought in Lawrence in nineteen eighty-four?"

"Oh, that. I forgot about that." Patty gave me a puzzled look. They were watching our every movement.

"You forgot about that," he repeated.

"I lost it."

"You lost it."

Why does he keep repeating everything I say? Probably to rattle me. I will not let myself be rattled.

"Yes, I lost it. And I filled out a lost firearms report. As required. As you probably already know. At the Dalton Police Department."

"You know, you really should be more forthcoming and cooperative. You're supposably this good conscientious helpful law-abiding doctor but we're not seeing any of this at all. We could make things difficult for you."

"All right, gentlemen, I've heard enough," Patty said forcefully. "How dare you come in here unexpected, asking probing questions without any explanation at all and then make these thinly veiled threats? It's time for you to leave, please." Patty said this loudly and as she stood up they looked at her legs.

They got up from the couch and Morse extracted a business card from his shirt pocket and extended it toward us.

Patty put her hands behind her back. "We don't need it. We already have one."

As they went to the door Fremont stopped and pointed at the mezuzzah on the molding of the doorframe. We got it at the Hadassah Hospital gift shop in Jerusalem. He looked at Morse and then me and Patty. "I see you have your Jewish good luck charm on your door. That's good. You're going to need some luck."

"That's the second threat you've made," Patty countered, "And let me expand your knowledge base just a little so you don't make the same error again. A mezuzzah is not a good luck charm. It is a conspicuous reminder of our obligations."

"You should be a little more mindful of your obligations to your local law enforcement," Morse shot back.

"I want you men to leave, now," Patty said, and

slammed the door loudly behind them. Morse and Fremont walked off the porch and got in their car. They fidgeted around a little before putting their seatbelts on, probably getting their guns in a less uncomfortable position. They drove off. We stood in the living room looking out the big window and watched them drive off. Patty had a scowl on her face; her hands were on her hips.

"What do you think?" I asked after they disappeared down the road. I picked up one of the tumblers that nobody drank from.

"Those guys, those guys are just a pair of thugs. What's the name of the shorter guy? Morse? He's a moron."

"Why?"

"He's an idiot."

"Why?"

"Did you hear him say 'supposably'? What kind of person actually uses the word 'supposably'?"

We were on the front porch, sitting in the Adirondack chairs. We waved at our anonymous neighbor pushing the baby carriage and walking a dog on a leash.

Patty turned to me. "When the hell did you get a gun license?"

"Back a few years ago. When I got mixed up with Sal. I spoke to Matt in the Midwest and that was one of his useless suggestions."

"And you got a shotgun and a handgun?"

"Well, the shotgun I got when I was in school. I had a classmate who taught me how to shoot skeet. It was fun, but I lost interest."

"So. Do you still have the guns?"

I turned and looked at her, surprised. My stomach twisted. "No. No. I don't have them anymore."

"Oh. I thought when you said you lost it and filed

63

a report, that it was another of your creative deceptions."

"No. I did lose it. You make it seem like I'm a nefarious schemer."

"No. I know you're not. How come I didn't know anything about this stuff with the guns?"

"I don't know. I don't like to talk about it. Or to think about it. It's dark."

"What happened to the handgun?"

What do I tell her? The truth or another fabrication? "The truth is, it got taken away from me. I'd rather not go into it. The fabrication is that I lost it when I was hiking in October Mountain State Forest. It's a felony or something to lose a firearm and not report it. I didn't want to tell the police the real way I lost it or I would've had to tell the whole story with Sal. So I made up a story that I had it in my knapsack and when I packed up after lunch I must've forgotten to put the gun back in. I didn't realize it for a few weeks until I unpacked the knapsack. I went back to find it but I couldn't. That's how I filled out the police report."

"So in order to not break the law by not reporting a gun loss you broke the law by making up a story."

"Patty, please don't give me a hard time. I was having a hard time back then. I was doing the best I could. I didn't know what to do."

"Okay, I'm sorry, I'm teasing you. You're getting pretty good at evading the truth though."

"Thanks a lot. But don't I have to? I can't tell them anything or I'll have to tell them the whole story and our only safety depends on me keeping the secret. You know this. I have a right not to talk myself into trouble. I haven't told any boldfaced lies that incriminate anyone but myself."

"Guns," Patty said. She took a deep breath. A sigh.

"I hate guns," she continued. "I've always hated

guns. I don't mean the stuff we saw on television in the sixties with Bonanza and Gunsmoke and that Hollywood nonsense. I don't mean squirt guns in the summertime. Real guns. When I see a policeman with a gunbelt I want to move to the other side of the street.

"Remember, we grew up in the sixties. My parents were always talking about the escalating war in Vietnam. Every week in the paper there would be pictures and obituaries of local soldiers who got killed. So many young men. Teenagers. Just out of high school. Dead.

"I would lie in bed at night and wouldn't be able to fall asleep because all I could think about was when would my brothers get drafted and what would be their fate and what would be our fate? I never told my parents about my fears. They just saw me as a silly little girl with pigtails. Sometimes at night the Levinsons would come over. They were good friends of my parents. Next-door neighbors; two doors down. Sometimes, after I would go to bed, I'd hear them sitting at the kitchen table having tea and talking about all this stuff. The Domino Theory. What the hell did playing dominoes have to do with Vietnam? What the hell did I know?

"I was in fourth grade in nineteen sixty-three and one Friday in the fall, just after lunch, one of the other teachers came to the door and said something quietly to my teacher who then vanished into the hall for what seemed like forever. When she came back she said that school was closing a little early because President Kennedy had been shot and he was having brain surgery that very minute in Texas. My mother was waiting for me outside of school and we picked up my brothers and we all walked home together and my mother explained that a bad guy had shot the president in the head and they were trying to fix it. I hadn't taken anatomy yet and my conception of a head was that it was

65

very much like a cantaloupe. In the grocery store once I saw a cantaloupe fall on the floor and there was the melon all mushed up with all the seeds oozing all over. Or maybe it was because it was just after Halloween and someone read me the story about Ichabod Crane and the Headless Horseman who carried a pumpkin thinking it was his head. Maybe I morphed it into a cantaloupe. But, that's what I thought Kennedy's head must look like. All because of a gun. A real gun."

We were still sitting on the porch. Patty was to my right. She was speaking slowly, softly, staring across the street, her gaze not wavering as she gave this soliloquy. It flowed out smoothly, without a sense of angst or restraint. It was warm, and sunny, and I stared at her profile as she spoke, not wanting to disturb her train of thought.

"We were glued to the TV all weekend. It was one of those old, oval, black and white screens with a big lens in front that you had to sit pretty squarely in front of to have no distortion. And there were John John and Caroline, who was the same age as me, and all the special military honor guards, the horse with no one sitting in the saddle and boots in the stirrups backwards, it made no sense to me. The Levinsons came over. My brothers would go out and play catch but I stayed. All across the country people were grieving. All this heartache just because of one guy with a gun.

"Then, on the Sunday of that weekend, around lunchtime, there was a flash on the TV that the guy they'd arrested the day before, Lee Harvey Oswald, got shot in the belly and died. And this was when he was surrounded by a bunch of cops and prison guards. Mr. Levinson said something about it sounding like a set up. I thought a set up was like a set shot in basketball.

"And of course as an undercurrent before, during and after all of this was the Cold War. That was another term I didn't get; the Iron Curtain too. *Life Magazine* had photos of smiling suburban families building and stocking their fallout shelters. Seemed like something everyone should have. Kids could use it as a clubhouse. I could use it as a doll house. I wanted to know when we were going to make one. My father said we weren't going to. I couldn't understand why not. He said because if we had a fallout shelter, he would have to have a gun. I asked why. He said it would be to protect us from people who would try to take it over. But I still couldn't understand why; why wouldn't they have one of their own?

"So JFK was in sixty-three and a few years later somebody with a gun killed JFK's baby brother, Bobby, just two months after Martin Luther King, Jr. was shot on that balcony down in Memphis. Each time I envisioned the same squashed melon.

"And a year or two after that, I was a teenager by then, I was in bed, and it must have been ten o'clock at night, and I heard the phone ring, which was pretty unusual that late. I heard my parents' hushed, startled voices. My mother tapped on my door and opened it an inch and asked me if I was still up. She and Dad were going down to the Levinsons; someone was sick; my brothers were in charge; they'd be back as soon as they could.

"The next morning I found out that Mr. Levinson had shot himself in the head in his garage.

"How could he do something like that? Why would he do something like that? Why did he even have a gun? Must have been cantaloupe seeds all over the place. His little daughter Suzie, the one who talked funny, did I mention her? She had a botched tonsillectomy and had a paralyzed vocal cord on one side and sounded like she was talking through a kazoo. She was a few years younger than me; she was nice; I don't know why I didn't hang out with her more. Well, she went off the deep end and was hospitalized. My parents were very worried about me and my brothers, especially since Mr. and Mrs. Levinson were like an aunt and uncle to us. We had barbecued hamburgers on Sundays in the summer for all those years; we spent so much time with them.

"I was stunned, I was dopey, I didn't know how to process all this information. Mr. Levinson? At least the soldiers and JFK and Bobby and Martin Luther King, Jr. were strangers. But Mr. Levinson?

"What was a nice Jewish man like Mr. Levinson doing with a gun, anyway?

"My parents would come and sit with me. I'd be doing homework or reading a silly girls' magazine or watching a TV program and one or the other would just come and sit near me. Not saying anything necessarily, just being near me in case I had something to say or ask.

"I'd lie awake till all hours of the night. If other young men in America could get drafted and die in Vietnam, why couldn't my brothers? If Mr. Levinson could take his own life, why couldn't my father?

"I guess my father got tired of waiting for me to ask. 'All through life people have problems,' he told me. 'Those problems don't go away when you get to be an adult. There are lots of different ways to deal with problems. Poor Mr. Levinson must have labored under some terrible problems. I don't know what they were. But the solution he chose wasn't a good one and he hurt himself and everybody around him terribly.' Again, with a gun.

"I asked my father why Mr. Levinson even had a gun in the first place. It turns out he was a social worker who worked with people who were in and out of jail; a probation officer or a parole officer or something like that. It was a slightly dangerous job. He carried a gun. They all did.

"My father told me not to worry, he didn't have a gun. 'Everyone has problems,' he said, 'and when problems get too big you find someone to talk to about them. You come to us or you go to your best friend or a teacher you like, or the rabbi, or your doctor. Even if they don't have the right answer they can help you search for it.' He said he would never do that to me, what Mr. Levinson did to Suzie.

"Needless to say we were all shaken up for a long time. My parents went to the funeral but we kids didn't. I never saw Mrs. Levinson or Suzie again. They moved away, we weren't told where. I think my parents silently made a point of not talking about the Levinsons anymore. But I didn't stop thinking about them. Ever.

"What is it about guns, do you think, that it makes it so terribly easy? So devastatingly easy? That a twitch of a finger can explode a man's cantaloupe, with about as much thought? If Mr. Levinson didn't have a gun, would he have cut his wrists? Or sucked in car exhaust? I sure don't know. But maybe other methods give you just a little more time to think about it, or to chicken out, or to smarten up, or whichever it is. Guns. Such wickedly destructive, unforgiving little tools.

"That's why I hate them."

We migrated into the kitchen and were making sandwiches for lunch. Patty sent me out to our little garden. I came back with more mint for the iced tea, some Bibb leaf lettuce and our third ripe tomato of the season. This is the Berkshires. You can't put your tomatoes in the ground until Memorial Day and then you're lucky to get a ripe one by mid-August. We planted Early Girls and they were late. But they were good. We toasted bread. I put on a thick layer of Hellman's Lite Mayonnaise so that it could hold a whole lot of immitation bacon bits. Then the lettuce and tomato, for our version of a BLT. Bread and butter pickle slices. I had two sandwiches. Delicious. We ate on the front porch.

This was to be our day together for outdoor activities. So far our bike ride was interrupted by my morbid internship story. Then we came home to be aggravated by Abbott and Costello. In the afternoon we were going to go canoeing. What would befall us next?

While Patty cleaned up the kitchen I took the bicycles off the back of the car and put them away in the garage. I put the life jackets and paddles in the car. Patty came out and helped me put the canoe on top of the car and lash it down. It was a nice old green fiberglass canoe I bought a couple of years ago from some guy in town who had it on saw horses in his front yard with a For Sale sign on it. We'd had fun with it and explored quite a few of the county's lakes and ponds. Today we wanted to paddle up Wood's Pond. It isn't a pond really but a wide marshy part of the Housatonic River in Lenox and Lenoxdale on the west side of October Mountain.

We drove out of Great Barrington, past a few antique stores, the Jenifer House, and the WSBS radio station on the flats north of town. Farther up Route 7 we passed Monument Mountain on the left and then Windy Hill Farm on the right. This is a picturesque farm with cultivated fruit trees and nursery stock going way up the hillside to the horizon. After that the road levels out and it is wooded on both sides. Then comes a huge swamp on the west side, full of brush. It's just about impregnable in the summer but in the winter ice fishermen will hack their way in there. I know only one name for this swamp and it is very disparaging. Another mile or two and the vista opens up to a huge marsh and on the high ground on the far side you can see the row of mansions on Ice Glen Road in Stockbridge. This town is very charming and is steeped in history. It was first settled by Reverend John Sargent. The famous eighteenth-century theologian Jonathan Edwards lived, preached and wrote here also. His grandson was Aaron Burr. The artist Norman Rockwell helped make it famous with his street scenes, most notably with his painting of the huge, rambling Red Lion Inn that has command of Main Street.

We followed Route 102 into Lee, the gateway to the Berkshires, Exit 2 on the Massachusetts Turnpike. It was named after General Charles Lee in 1775. Lee was one of George Washington's most experienced generals. He was said to be loud and large, and liked food, spirits and dogs. He was irascible and he bumped heads with Washington enough that he fell into disfavor with him.

Unlike Stockbridge, Lee is a real town. People can live and work and shop in it. It has two lumberyards, three hardware stores, a drug store, quite a few pizza places, and a couple of no-frills bars. The main street is lined with beautiful nineteenth-century buildings. At the bottom is a small town square, maybe an acre in size, on the north side of which sits a typical Bullfinch architectural-style Congregational church. It has the tallest wooden steeple this side of the Mississippi. The town hall is situated here also. It's called Memorial Hall and was built in 1871 in tribute to the sons of Lee who perished in the Civil War. Inside there is a marble plaque listing the names of those who died. Many of them were in Andersonville, Georgia, and I'm guessing that was the Confederate prison camp that was the basis for the play, *The Andersonville Trial*. Down the hall is the courtroom where the blind judge Hannon gave folksinger Arlo Guthrie a hard time as revealed in the song about Alice's Restaurant.

Across the street is the Morgan House. It has been a traditional restaurant and inn for a century and a half. Next door is McClelland's pharmacy, an 1820 building where you can still go to the soda fountain and get coffee for a quarter and, if he isn't busy, the pharmacist will entertain you with stand-up comedy.

Sitting at the top of Main Street like a crown is Joe's Diner. It's an institution. At any hour of day or night you can go in there, get a good cheap meal and be entertained, and insulted, by the staff.

Taking a right at Joe's onto East Center Street, then turning left onto Greylock Street, you pass some more mills and a few very old colonial homes and their barns. Greylock becomes Mill Street and brings you into the little burg of Lenoxdale, formerly Lenox Furnace. A right onto Crystal Street takes you past the Beloit Jones factory where they build paper-making machinery. The name "Crystal Street" comes from when Lenoxdale had a huge glass furnace. Supposedly the village had the largest single-roofed building in the world in the 1860s. You wouldn't know it now, there isn't a trace of it, and it remains a quaint, working-class village with only a few small businesses.

Finally we turned right at the top of Crystal Street where it intersects with Housatonic Street and drove the last hundred yards to where we parked and could launch the canoe. There is a pedestrian bridge that crosses the river and gives access to a whole maze of dirt roads that extend all the way up October Mountain. Upstream the river widens broadly into the marshy section called Woods Pond and our plan was to paddle up this broad, still section all the way up to New Lenox Road in northern Lenox. Then we'd turn around and retrace our route.

We got the canoe to the water's edge, I grabbed the knapsack and drinks and locked the roof straps in the car. The shore was mucky and once we got out into the water we shook our feet in the water over the side of the canoe to rinse off the muck. "Watch out for snapping turtles," I warned Patty, who replied, "Yeah, right, watch out for PCBs."

The GE plant upstream in Pittsfield let loose a lot of PCBs in past decades. They were used as a nonflammable stable liquid to fill transformer cases; good for transformers but bad for living things, persisting for decades in the river bottom. Despite it getting into the food chain, as warned by signs on the river saying not to eat fish from it, Woods Pond was full of fish, big ugly mean-looking snapping turtles with prehistoric-looking heads, egrets, great blue herons, ducks, and Canada geese. There were several big beaver lodges made of sticks and smaller muskrat lodges made of mud. Patty has told me more than I wanted to know about the chemistry of the polychlorinated biphenyls and from the sound of her information the pond ought to be sterile and our paddles should dissolve away as we use them. But the river looked like it was teeming with life to me. What do I know?

We paddled along. It was a great day, maybe even a little too warm. The sun was strong and made me sleepy. Patty was in the bow. She was wearing a Red Sox ballcap, a loose white T-shirt and faded denim cut-offs with a small, bright red Levi's tag sewn into a back pocket. We paddled past areas of thick blankets of aquatic vegetation, past open areas with ducks and geese and seagulls, past slimy logs with frogs and painted turtles sunning themselves. There were islands covered with purple loosestrife, a foreign plant that is so invasive, but so pretty. We passed a small dilapidated wooden structure in the reeds that might have been a duck blind. It was beautiful and there was so much to look at.

There was a little bump on the water moving along from left to right creating a small v-shaped wake behind it and we hurried up to catch up to see what it was. As we neared it, it disappeared and Patty's best glimpse of it suggested a muskrat.

We chatted about this and that and Patty went on about our unpleasant lunchtime visit with Abbott and Costello.

When we got to New Lenox Road there were a bunch of other people there who were heavy-duty canoe racers out for practice. They had long skinny brown eggshell-thin racing canoes. These guys were intense. They were all thin and sinewy and really into it. They were just setting off for their time trials and we got out of their way. They were gone in a flash. We beached the canoe and got out and stretched. We walked around on the grassy bank, sipped some water, walking funny like people do when they've been cramped up in one position for a while. We walked like flamingoes. Small steps with high knee lifts.

"Do you think you oughta call your friend Matt?"

"How come?" I've mentioned Matt before. I called him for some advice during the tense times a few years ago. I knew him in college. He'd been in the military and had been in Special Forces; had been involved in intriguing stuff he wasn't allowed to talk about. After college he ended up in the New York City police force. Eventually he became a detective lieutenant. He gave up the stress to become an insurance broker in the Midwest. When I was in trouble a few years ago I tracked him down to talk some things over with him, get some advice in his unique area of knowledge. In the long run, it wasn't much help.

"Just to tell him about what's been going on lately with those FBI guys. Instead of us guessing and surmising, he might be able to tell us what they're really doing, if this sounds like a standard operating procedure for some kind of case workup. Maybe he could say they wouldn't be acting this way if you were the object of an investigation but they might if they thought you might have information that could help them investigating someone else."

"I could call him," I said, wondering where I'd call him from. "I could get a roll of quarters and call him from a phone booth outside of town." I hated the idea of this. It brought back memories and made my stomach cramp.

"Why? Do you think our phones are tapped?"

"Who knows? I wouldn't put it past them. I've been tapped before."

"Don't they have to get a court order to tap someone? Isn't it a difficult process?"

"It's supposed to be done that way. But who knows if it always is. If they are trying to convict someone they couldn't use evidence they got with an illegal wiretap. If they are just fishing around looking for clues and leads, that might be indirect evidence that would never come into court. Who knows what they are looking for. It might not even be what we're worrying about."

"It wouldn't do any harm to talk to him. From whatever phone you want." I made a mental note to get some quarters.

It was hot and we were sweaty. Patty's face was shiny with sweat and sunscreen. She had her summer tan despite the sunscreen, the freckles on her cheeks were more brown and less cinnamon and her smile was big and her teeth were white. She took a deep breath while gazing at October Mountain to the east and as she exhaled I could faintly see the pulse in her neck. She finished her water.

"You ready?" I nodded and we got back in the canoe and headed downstream. After a few paddle strokes we were moving right along. I liked this old fiberglass canoe.

"What a nice day," Patty said. "A nice bike ride in the morning for lower body exercise, a nice canoe trip in the afternoon for upper body exercise."

I thought to myself that maybe this evening there could be some middle body exercise.

"I know what you're thinking," Patty said.

"What am I thinking?"

"You're thinking about another kind of exercise."

"I was thinking about how nicely this canoe glides in the water compared to the aluminum ones I used as a kid."

"Yeah, right."

"You know what I was really thinking? How nice a cold beer will taste when we get back."

"And that."

We were halfway back to Woods Pond when the flotilla of canoe racers approached. We got way over to the side and they blew past us. Those guys were tireless. But I don't think they noticed the flora and fauna. Different reasons for doing the same thing.

We got out at the boat access area and tied the canoe on top of the Subaru. We went back to dangle our feet in the water and get the mud off and stretch. We drove down to Tanner's market at the bottom of Crystal Street for some cold drinks. We also got a cold six-pack of Genesee Cream Ale and some chicken breasts and sweet corn for dinner.

The drive home was uneventful; we were relaxed and sleepy from the sun and exercise. The Norman Rockwell Museum was closed for the day so Main Street in Stockbridge wasn't too clogged up. The sun was lower in the sky but it was still hot and the hanging impatiens on the porch were droopy.

Patty helped me off-load the canoe. We carried it

into the garage and set it up into the rafters. She disappeared into the house. I put away the life jackets and paddles and stuff. I could hear the water in the upstairs shower.

I rolled the grill out of the garage over to the back of the house. I filled it with tinder and kindling. It was more fun to use real wood like a campfire rather than charcoal briquettes.

As I was watching it and feeding it more wood Patty emerged from the backdoor. She handed me a cold bottle of Genny Cream. What a woman. Her hair was wet. She was wearing an ivory colored cotton gauzy sundress that was sleeveless, lowcut and ended at her mid-thigh. I could vaguely see the borders of her underwear when the dress was against her skin.

I was thirsty and drank the beer quickly. Once it was clear that the fire was well started I asked Patty to keep an eye on it while I took my turn in the shower. I had a thick coating of sweat and sunscreen on my skin. She was in the garden picking vegetables.

When I got out of the shower I peeked out the window; the fire was doing well. I went to the kitchen and began melting butter for the barbecue sauce. Land O'Lakes. I liked the little Indian girl on the box. While it melted I added some olive oil and I opened another Genny Cream. I measured out a teaspoon of celery salt, garlic powder, onion powder, black pepper and chili powder and paprika. I let the spices simmer a little and went to check the fire. Patty was in the backyard talking to a neighbor across the fence. I poked the fire down and spread the coals more evenly. I brought out the saucepan and four big fat chicken breasts on a tray. Two for dinner, two for leftovers. I painted the chicken with the sauce and put them on the grill. I turned them and repainted the other side. I ran in to set the table and steam the corn. I kept turning the chicken. The fire was cooling down, the chicken cooked slower, the fat dripped out from under the skin, the butter and herbs formed a crust on the outside.

Patty and the neighbor were still gabbing in the yard and I brought each of them a beer.

I had everything on the table ready to serve and went to the back door and whistled. No response. She ignored me. I filled the water glasses on the table and their sides dripped with condensation. I went to the back door again and shouted that dinner was ready. They looked at me, the woman said goodbye and Patty turned and walked toward me, barefoot in the grass.

"Why didn't you let me know you were ready?" she asked. I smiled and shook my head.

Dinner was good. The chicken was hot and moist and spicy. The garden salad with a mustard dressing made with balsamic vinegar was delicious. Sweet corn is always a treat. Patty talked about her dream of leaving the pharmacy. She talked about teaching kitchen chemistry, how baking powder works in a zucchini bread, why hard boiled egg yolks sometimes turn green. How glue works.

We were tired. We'd had a lot of exercise. We'd been in the sun all day, we'd been drinking beer all evening. We went into the living room to watch the news. We were side by side on the couch and Patty was draped over me, half asleep.

They recappped the news of the week. Rudolf Hess, ninety-three, was found dead in his cell at Spandau Prison. He hanged himself. Or someone made it look like he hanged himself. ABC Middle East news chief Charles Glass escaped his Hezbollah kidnappers after sixty-two days of captivity in Beirut. In London, the Order of the Garter was opened to include women. On the local level there was a segment that the Commonwealth of Massachusetts Attorney General's office had scored another success by prosecuting and convicting Mafia Underboss Gennaro Angiulo on many counts, including racketeering; extortion; wire fraud; loan sharking; witness tampering; murder and other related crimes. And in Windsor Locks, Connecticut, not far from Bradley Airport, an unidentified badly decomposed body was found in a manner suggestive of a gangland slaying; dental forensics pending. *Damn. That's only an hour away. Maybe a little more. Only twenty minutes from Springfield.*

We gave up and went upstairs to bed. I opened the window, closed the shades and turned on the attic fan. It was warm. Sweaty. Patty was snoring. Finally she picked her head off the pillow, found me, kissed me and said good night and rolled away to get some cooler air between us.

I smiled and stared at the ceiling in the darkness.

"Addio, dolce svegliare alla mattina." I said.

A moment later Patty groggily asked, "What does that mean?"

"It means, 'Farewell, sweet wakings in the morning.' It's from *La Bohème*. Years ago I took an old girlfriend to Lincoln Center to see it."

Many seconds later I felt her shift her weight and she mumbled, sleepily, "That was me, you moron."

I paused. "It was? Are you sure?" I flinched. "Ouch! No pinching!"

Chapter 7

I woke up five minutes before the alarm was set to go off. It was almost six; it was gray outside. The street was quiet. I could hear Patty breathing beside me. I wasn't sleepy but it felt good to lie in bed. It had cooled off overnight. I kept looking at the digital clock with its big red numbers on the dresser across the room. At one minute to six I got up and clicked off the alarm so Patty could sleep.

I went downstairs and set up the coffee pot. I went out to the front porch and got the newspaper. I peeked at the upper outer corner of page B2 to make sure I didn't recognize anyone in the obituaries.

The coffee was ready and I had my first cup while I scanned through the paper. I poured myself another cup and one for Patty and I carried them upstairs to the bathroom. I set them both on the shelf on top of the sliding shower doors and turned on the water. I stripped and stepped in.

Through the frosted glass of the shower door I saw Patty's indistinct silhouette come in and reach up for her coffee mug. She stood outside the shower long enough to have a few sips and then she put the mug back up. I watched her silhouette as she pulled her nightgown up over her head and slid open the door.

She stepped in and rolled the door closed behind her. Reaching up she put her arms around my neck and we shuffled around in a 180° so she could have the water on her back.

"Shit," she muttered, quietly.

"What's the matter?" I asked.

"My period came."

"Oh." I didn't know what else to say. Every month we were hoping for a blessing. "I'm sorry too," I added and I felt her head move in a nod next to mine.

We stood embracing in the shower, occasionally reaching for our coffee cups. Her back was to the showerhead and we were front to front. My arms were around her back and hers around my waist. My chin was hooked over her shoulder and I was watching the water run down her back. I could feel the vibration of the shower spray on her back. I watched the water run down her back and form a little pool in the groove my forearm made against her. I opened my arms and the pool disappeared. I brought my arms up and cupped her shoulder. I could see a long expanse of her back and undulating chevrons of water converging and diverging, cascading down her back, down her narrow waist, her bottom, and disappear. Buttocks have an unexpected geometry, looking down on them from up here. Looking at them horizontally doesn't prepare you to expect the curvature you see from up here, vertically. It is a curve where the radius lengthens as it rotates, like in a chambered nautilus or a draftsman's French curve.

I crossed my arms over her back again and put my fingers in the grooves between her ribs. I felt the vibrations of the shower spray drumming on her back. I closed my eyes. A few deep breaths later the vibrations coarsened, her back felt like it was trembling but the quality of the shower spray had not changed. I wondered about it. Then she sobbed.

Surprised, I unhooked my chin from behind her shoulder and leaned back so I could look at her face. She was crying.

"What's the matter?" I asked earnestly.

I stepped back and she put her hands to her face and rubbed her eyes and her nose.

"Oh, all I want is to be pregnant. And have a baby."

She was gasping and I could feel her whole frame shuddering with staccato breathing as she cried. Between the gasps she said, "Charlie, we've been trying so hard for so long. Three years. I want to have a baby so much. Our baby." More sobs. "Why is it taking so long?"

I thought it was a rhetorical question, so I didn't answer. Last year I secretly took a semen sample to the hospital to look at under the microscope. I went in early. I didn't want anyone to come in and say, "Whatcha lookin' at, Charlie?" There were lots of the little guys swimming around. They looked happy. They moved actively, chaotically, bumping into each other.
"Patty, we've talked about infertility studies. We've talked about adopting." She began to sob even harder. I'd said the wrong thing. I leaned back to look at her. Her facial muscles were scrunched up like a prune and there was a gob of mucus on her lip. After another minute she settled down a little and though still crying she said, "Charlie, I know you love your medicine and blood tests and hormone levels and ultrasounds and stuff." She coughed and wiped her nose on her wrist. "I'm not ready to think about adopting someone else's

baby and dealing with administrators and social workers and all that red tape. I just want to have our baby. I want you on top of me and inside me and to know that it's going to work. I want to get fat and have morning sickness and backaches and see my nipples turn brown. I want to have labor pains and push and have all that blood and slime and then get a baby. I want to change meconium diapers, I want to feel my breasts swell and ache and feel the baby suck."

She wants to fulfill her destiny as a mammal, I thought. More convulsive crying with some honking and snorting. I didn't know what to say so I didn't say anything. We held each other. She quieted down a little. She leaned back to look at me. Her face was not as pinched. She looked like she was coming out of it, emptied out.

"Oh, I want these things so much. I dream about these things." She looked at me. "Good," she said, "you're crying too," I didn't realize that I was. "We're in this together."

"Of course," I said, "we're in everything together."

We stood embraced in the warm shower, in the dark gray room, the only light coming from the small bathroom window.

"Oh, Charlie, I love you so much. God, we've been in here a long time. Aren't you going to go say Kaddish for your father?"

"Not today. Dad gave me the day off. I want to be with you." I pulled the lever to close the drain in the tub and it began to fill. We were standing there holding each other, twisting a little from side to side. Like rocking a baby.

"Excuse me. I'll be right back." I kissed her on the nose and snuck out of the shower. I wrapped the towel around me and ran downstairs with the coffee cups. I brought them back full, dropped the towel and went back into the tub. It had filled, Patty had turned off the shower and the water was filling the tub through the spout. Patty was sitting there cross-legged with her knees up like a grasshopper. I got in and handed her the mug. I sat down and closed the shower door even though the spray was off. We looked at each other.

"Okay. I'm done. I had my catharsis." She was calm now. Patty faced left, I faced right, neither of us had the spout poking us in the back. The water was deep now and Patty adjusted it to a trickle to keep it hot. Once in a while she'd paddle her hand to push hot water to my end of the tub.

"I have a headache from crying," she said, while rolling her neck in slow circles.

"When we get out I'll give you some Tylenol and a neck massage."

"I'm sorry. It's not like me to complain or carry on or be negative, but it just caught up with me. I had to let it out."

"I'm glad you did. So tell me. When you do get pregnant and you feel fat and have morning sickness and backaches and sore breasts, can I remind you about what you said this morning about welcoming all those symptoms and can I say you asked for it?"

"Of course not. I expect you to be completely sympathetic."

"I need to get out. I'm dissolving in here. I'm becoming broth."

Chapter 8

"Hey, Charlie," Margaret asked with the grinding sound of rusting disc brakes, "are you in the market for a puppy yet?"

"As a matter of fact, I am. I just made that decision this morning. How did you know?"

"Oh, you know, I'm clairvoyant. I know everything. No, really, I just heard that Marjorie on the third floor has some puppies for sale."

As soon as I had a break from patients I ran upstairs looking for Marjorie. She was an LPN on the day shift, seven to three. I went to the third floor nursing station and asked where I could find Marjorie. She was down the hall helping a respiratory therapist give a patient an inhalation treatment. When she was done I tentatively asked, "Marjorie?"

She was a buxom middle-aged woman with fair skin, dark hair and an engaging smile.

"Hi, I'm Charlie Davids from the ER. Margaret tells me you have some puppies?"

"Hi, Dr. Davids, I know who you are. Yes, we have two puppies left."

"Oh good, please tell me about them?"

"Tell me what you're looking for. Are you a dog person?"

"Actually, no, I've never had one, but I want to get a puppy for my wife and me. What are yours like?"

"Well, we've always had Labrador Retrievers. Our mother had a litter of six puppies about ten weeks ago. Four of them we've already sold; we have two left at home. A few people said they were interested but they haven't made any commitment to us yet. It's really time for them to be weaned and get away from their mother."

"Great, when can I come to see them? Would tonight be too soon? I get off at eight."

"No, tonight would be great. Let me tell you where I live."

She gave me directions and I thanked her. "Now, not a word to anyone, okay?"

"Oh, is this a surprise?"

"Yeah. My wife doesn't know about this yet."

"Are you going to tell her beforehand?"

"I thought I'd take it just one step at a time."

"Well, I'm not sure I want to give up a puppy unless I know everyone in the household is into it. But first come tonight and see them and we'll talk.

"Thank you so much, Marjorie. I'm excited; I'll see you later."

I was like a kid waiting for Christmas. The rest of the afternoon dragged. Shortly before my shift ended I called home and told Patty I would be a little late because I had an errand to run. I grabbed my orange medical knapsack and flew out of the department.

Marjorie had a beautiful home. It was a big, old, turn of the century house, elegant with stone on the first floor, cedar clapboard on the top and a slate roof. She led me into the kitchen. In the corner, near a set of French doors, was a big cardboard box. In it was the mother, a big yellow lab named Martha, and with her were her two remaining black puppies.

Marjorie reached in and said, "Excuse me, Martha, let me show off your beautiful little children to Dr. Davids here." She scooped the two puppies out from under Martha, one in each hand, and put them in her lap as she sat down in a nearby chair.

"This one here is a little girl we've called Lucy after Lucille Ball because she's kind of slapstick and loud and rough. This other little guy here we call Mac for no particular reason. You can see he's a little smaller than Lucy."

"He's actually the runt of the litter," said her husband.

"Though that doesn't mean he won't grow to a reasonable size; it doesn't mean he's weak or fragile. He's just petite for now," she said, giving him a little lift by the belly and a kiss on his head.

I was on my knees right in front of her, petting those adorable little puppies. They were cute as hell. I got close to them so I could look at their little puppy faces. Their eyelids looked like they were a little too big and they folded and looked wrinkled when their eyes were open. I got closer and the little Mac licked my cheek and the next thing I knew little Lucy batted off my eyeglasses.

"We told you Lucy was the rambunctious one," Marjorie's husband said as we were still laughing. "Marjorie tells me you haven't had dogs before, is that right?"

"No, I haven't. Patty had one for a little while when she was a kid."

"Do you have children?"

"No. Not yet," I answered.

"Well, if I'm any judge of a dog's personality, I'd say that Mac is the one for you. I think that Lucy will be a handful. Mac is a sweet and gentle little thing. He's very people-oriented."

I was sitting next to Marjorie and I had Mac on my lap. He felt so good. He had a round little belly and my hand just fit between his front and rear legs. He was warm and so soft. His ears were soft as velvet. And he had sharp little teeth, like needles. He seemed complacent in my lap.

"So your wife doesn't know about this yet?"

"No. I wanted to surprise her."

"Do you think she'll be receptive?"

"I think so. I hope so. This little boy is real sweet."

"Yeah, he is," her husband said.

"Do you want to call your wife and have her come over to meet Mac?"

I thought about that. "I could. But that would lessen the surprise value."

"Well, if you want to surprise her, since you don't live far from here, why don't you just drive Mac home and see how it goes. If she's not receptive then bring him right back."

We talked over the details and the price and they put Mac in a little travel crate. They told me how to take care of him, warning me about how bad his first night away from his mother would be. They told me to keep him in his crate with a hot water bottle, lots of towels and leave a radio on softly near him.

I was excited. I thanked them profusely and complimented them on their beautiful home and told them

I hoped to be calling them in twenty minutes to tell them we had a deal. I thought it would work. Once a puppy like this is in your arms or in your home it would be hard to not keep him.

The two of us, Mac and me, drove home. His little crate was in the front seat next to me. When I got to our house I carefully opened the door of the crate and eased him out. I hopped up the steps onto the front porch and as I went through the front door Patty was coming toward me from the kitchen.

"Look what I found!" I shouted happily as I walked toward her and gestured with the puppy in my hand.

What a look of joyous surprise crossed that girl's face! When she saw what I was holding she inhaled, her eyebrows went up, her eyes went wide, her jaw dropped, she bobbed her knees and clapped her hands. She ran over to me and put her hands around Mac as I held him.

"Oh, he's beautiful, he's so cute, he's so sweet!" It worked. "Where'd he come from?"

I told her about Marjorie, and her lab Martha and her litter of puppies.

"Well, you don't look very much like a little runt to me." she said in baby talk. "Is he ours? Did you buy him? Can we keep him?"

"We can if you want to. All I have to do is call them and tell them."

Still holding the puppy to her face, nose to nose, she said, "Of course I want to keep you, you precious little puppy."

"Yes, we can keep him, but only on one condition, this baby talk has got to stop!" I insisted.

Patty turned her back to me and still nose to nose with the puppy she said, "That mean nasty Charlie doesn't want us to talk to each other in baby talk but we will anyway, won't we, because you're just the cutest little puppy baby." As she said this she turned back to me and grinned at me and there were tears in her eyes.

Well, I could see who was going to get all the attention tonight. I called Marjorie and told her that it was an easy sell and she was pleased. She gave me some more instructions and then I went out to bring in the stuff from the car. I set the crate in the kitchen and found a few old towels to line it. I got a plastic canteen for hiking and filled it with warm water. I brought a clock radio into the kitchen and tuned it in to the local classical music station. I put his leash and little collar on the table.

Patty was lying on the living room floor giggling in joy as little Mac was prancing around. It was a Kodak moment. She's going to be a good mother. I sat on the couch and watched the two of them play. After a while I suggested, "You ought to put on his collar and leash and take him out in the backyard so he can do his business."

"I will in a little bit," she said as they continued to play. I shouldn't have said it because a minute later he squatted and tinkled on the floor. "Told you so," I said, as I ran to get stuff to clean it up. I turned the lights on in the yard and Patty took him out to explore. I stood by the back door and watched them. It had gotten cool. Radiational cooling. The air smelled moist and sweet. The stars were all over the sky. Oh, this was good. This was going to be a good thing, to have this puppy in this house.

It was getting late, almost ten o'clock, and we were pooped. Patty couldn't take her hands off Mac. We set out a Pyrex custard dish with water for him and another of puppy chow but he was more interested in exploring the kitchen and playing soccer with an ant trap he found in the corner. We took it away. We'll need to baby-proof the house.

Marjorie made me promise that Mac would sleep in the crate tonight. I put in a towel she gave me that had Martha's scent on it. I also put in the bath towel Patty used that morning. We kissed Mac goodnight and tucked him in. We left the stove light on in the kitchen. The radio was on low and they were playing baroque harpsichord music. We went upstairs and made each other promise that Mac would not end up in bed with us. I picked up a quarter from the top of my dresser. I tossed it and I won so Patty had to get up at three to take him out to the yard for a bathroom break.

We snuggled in bed. Though it had been a nice warm day, most evenings were cooling off in the last week or two. It's a short summer in the Berkshires. Sometimes summer ends in August. The cool nights make the lakes cool off and then you can't go swimming. And then it's not summer anymore.

Patty was enthused. "Oh, Charlie, what a great little puppy! He's so cute! He adds such life to the house. Much better than a house plant."

"Good, I'm glad you like him," I said.

"Like him? I love him."

"You just met him. You can't love him yet. You're infatuated. You're a pushover."

"What do you know? I love him. I'm so excited, I don't think I'm going to be able to fall asleep."

At that we started to hear some whimpering from downstairs. "Why don't you go downstairs and read him a bedtime story?" I suggested.

"I will," she said abruptly, and in a flash she was out of bed and down the stairs. I smiled and put in my little earplugs and was asleep in minutes.

I woke up at about five because something was scratching me and that something smelled bad. I was groggy and disoriented and I turned and was halfway to a sitting position when I remembered our new little family member. In the thin gray light I could see and smell a wet one on the coverlet. Patty was sound asleep. Mac was ready to play. I picked him up with one hand under his belly and he was sticky with something. Yuck. I carried him downstairs and gave him a bath in the kitchen sink. I threw on a sweatshirt and in boxer shorts and bare feet I took Mac out in the backyard for an opportunity to relieve himself properly. He cooperated. That done I put him in his crate, went upstairs with a roll of paper towels and a can of Woolite Spray Cleaner.

I wiped as much as I could off the coverlet, then folded it up and stuffed it in a plastic bag to drop it off at Ried Cleaners on my way to work. I put another cover on the bed so Patty would stay warm.

I made coffee and talked to Mac as I puttered around the kitchen. Nothing noteworthy in the *Eagle*. Mac and I went back out and he helped me do a little weeding in the garden. A cute little puppy. He amused himself batting around some fallen cherry tomatoes and gnawing sticks. He was going to be a lot of fun.

When the two of us turned back to the house Patty was watching at the window. She looked up and smiled. I intended to glare at her, and tried to, but just started laughing instead.

"Alright, so what happened? Marjorie made me promise not to let him sleep with us."

"Oh, come on, lighten up. I kept him company for a while and every time I tried to go upstairs he'd whine. So I'd go back downstairs and after a while I got sleepy and I couldn't stand to think of the little thing so lonely and unhappy so I brought him up."

"So he's training you very well. All he has to do is whine and you'll be right back to entertain him. He'll have you wrapped around his little paw in no time. By the way, he's not housebroken yet."

She shot me a glance. I pointed to the coverlet in the plastic bag in the corner. "I was wondering what happened to it."

"So how long do you think he can stay in his crate at a time?" Patty asked.

"Marjorie said five or six hours."

"Well I'll have no problem coming home at lunchtime to let him out." There was only one stoplight and two minutes between her pharmacy and home. "I could even come home on coffee breaks."

"I'm sure he would appreciate it." We fed him. We finished our granola and oatmeal and the rest of the sourdough bread as toast with jam. We showered and hugged and laughed and got dressed and went to work. Driving in I had a big grin on my face, like I was pulling something over on her. Her nurturing instincts are there, all right.

When I got to work just before eight, there was a message for me to call Marjorie. I did and she asked me how it went last night. I told her it was great and we both love the puppy. Marjorie asked where he slept last night and I told her the dog ended up in bed with us and about my stop at the dry cleaner on my way to work. She laughed and said, "I told you so; you can't make that mistake tonight." I promised her I wouldn't and told her I had a check for her that I would run upstairs for her today.

It ended up being a pretty unremarkable day. Margaret came by and said, "Woof-woof, nooky-nooky." Very funny. An overweight retired lawyer from New York City, with mild congestive heart failure usually well-controlled on Digoxin and Lasix, up in his Berkshire vacation home, must have eaten a little too well and had too much salt on his deli sandwich and tipped

over into a little pulmonary edema. He came in short of breath and with swollen ankles and he tuned up pretty easily with some intravenous diuretics. One of the summer camp nurses brought in two kids who she thought had strep throat and I agreed with her and did throat cultures and wrote prescriptions.

One of the hospital cafeteria cooks came to see me. He had a cold. He was well liked. He was a short roly-poly guy like the Pillsbury Doughboy. He was always friendly at the cafeteria line, quick to laugh with a big smile on his dark sweaty face. He wanted an X-ray because he had a cold. I examined him. His eyes were not watery or bloodshot, his eardrums were normal. His throat was not red. His neck glands were not enlarged. He had no sinus pain and only clear white nasal mucus. His heart sounds were normal. His lung sounds were normal. He had no fever. He had a runny nose, a slightly scratchy throat and a minimal cough not productive of phlegm.

He had a cold. He wanted an X-ray.

I asked him why.

"Erica told me I should get an X-ray." Erica was the kitchen supervisor.

"Why?" I asked.

"She said I should have one."

"You have a normal exam. You are under forty, you never smoked, you have no fever, there are no criteria being met here to justify needing an X-ray. Is there something you're worried about? Do you know someone who had pneumonia or lung cancer and you're nervous and you want to be on the safe side?"

"Erica said to."

"You know, I follow the guidelines for primary care. I don't just make stuff up as I go along. I don't get tests or X-rays just if I feel like it, I have to follow the recipes for taking care of people, just like you follow recipes when you do your job. We follow the guidelines of the American College of Physicians because they know more than I do. And they know more than Erica does about this. But if you have your heart set on an X-ray, I'll order one, although I don't understand why." Could I have handled this better or more appropriately?

He slid down off the stretcher, walked past me and left the department. I looked at the nurse who was with me and shrugged and I felt as if I had done something wrong.

When I went to the cafeteria for lunch with a few of the ER nurses, he was on the serving line. He didn't smile or acknowledge me when I said hello, he just flung food on my plate with unnecessary force. I did not understand this at all.

When I finally got home Patty met me at the door with Mac under her arm. She had a martini in her hand and proposed a toast to our new dog. A fine idea.

"I take it you had a nice day? How were your visits home to see him?"

"Oh, he did great." She hadn't kissed me yet.

"Do I get a kiss?"

"My hands are full."

"Your lips aren't."

She gave me a nice one. She tasted like martini.

"I was thinking," she said as we passed the martini glass back and forth. "Mac should have a Jewish name."

"I didn't know he was Jewish," I responded.

"Of course he's Jewish. Why wouldn't he be Jewish? We adopted him."

"I didn't know dogs came in religions."

"Of course they do, Charlie, don't you know anything about dogs? I was thinking of naming him Maccabee. It's similar to his original name and he seems to respond to it. What do you think?"

95

"I think that's a good name. A strong name. We'll just have to be careful when MacPherson is around, it'll get confusing. Will he have to be circumcised?"

"Of course. Well, castrated, anyway," she replied.

I thought about that one for a minute and had another sip of martini.

I stood straight and stretched to my full height. In a voice lower and louder than usual, I said, "Let me make one thing perfectly clear, my dear: there is a world of difference between circumcision and castration."

Patty put down the puppy and put down the martini glass. She sauntered over to me theatrically, put a hand behind my neck and leaned back. In a deep sultry Mae West voice, she said, "Don't I know it, baby, don't I know it!"

The three of us relaxed and unwound and hung out. The two of them were playing and I was sitting in the armchair, amused, perusing a medical journal. At around ten Patty brought Maccabee outside for a last bathroom break. Then she brought him over for me to kiss goodnight. She put him in the crate and told him to be a good puppy and Daddy would come to let him outside in a few hours.

On her way upstairs she said, "I'm going to bed. Are you going to be reading much longer?"

"No, I'm almost finished."

"Well then, hurry the hell up. I want to make puppies!"

Chapter 9

I was up early as usual. I left Patty sound asleep and I went downstairs. I took Mac out in the backyard. It was still dark and dawn was getting a little later as the summer wound down. It was cool out. I slipped my bare feet into sneakers, slipped a sweatshirt on and the two of us went out into the backyard. He knew not to run away because that would delay his breakfast and he was very motivated by food. And attention. We were quickly back in the house. I gave him his puppy kibbles and put on the coffee pot. It used to be that nothing came before the coffee pot. That was always first. But now I have parental responsibilities. Have to take care of the kid first. Then I went to the front door and got the newspaper. While I was outside I noticed a big sedan idling, parked two houses down on the other side of the street facing my way. I didn't make anything of it.

I went in and had my first cup with the Beagle and the Labrador. Then I brought two cups upstairs, silently walked around our bedroom wafting coffee aroma to try to give her a hint. Then I went into the bathroom and set them on top of the shower doors. I got in and soaped up and marveled at Patty that deeply asleep. I dried off and shaved and, with a towel around me, carried both cups into the bedroom. She was still asleep. I set the cups down and kissed her on the forehead, making a big slurping sound. She opened her eyes and said good morning. She sat up and I fluffed her pillow and put it behind her. I gave her the coffee.

We were sipping coffee and chitchatting and I walked over to the window and peeked out. The sun was up and the big sedan was still out there idling. I put on my underwear and got on the floor and did my usual daily exercises. I did forty crunches. I used to do sit ups but Patty told me they were out of vogue and crunches were better for you. I did some hurdle stretches on the floor. Then I did some pushups and I was done. I used to also do some chin ups or pull ups but I injured my left wrist a few years ago and my grip strength wasn't very good and it was hard to hang onto the bar. Nor was I much help opening a stuck pickle jar and Patty long ago learned to not ask me because it was so frustrating. I also used to play the piano in a coarse kind of way. It was fun and I didn't let lack of skill interfere with having a good time. Since that injury I hadn't played the piano much. My left hand always felt clumsy like I had a mitten on it. I could still play allegro with my right hand but it was more like andante with my left.

As I was getting dressed I chatted with Patty who was still in bed cuddled up in her Lanz of Salzburg flannel nightgown with her cup of coffee.

"Why do you keep looking out the window?" she asked.

"Well, there's been this big car sitting out there idling. "

"How long has it been out there?"

"When I got up this morning and went out to get the paper I noticed it. It was still kind of dark out then. Maybe it was an hour ago?"

She just looked at me across the top of her mug.

"Maybe I'm getting as paranoid as Raskolnikov in *Crime and Punishment*." I picked up the phone and walked back to the window. I called the police.

"Who are you calling?" Patty asked.

I nodded to her as the dispatcher picked up.

"Hello, this is Charlie Davids on Gilmore Avenue. There's been a suspicious car idling across the street for a very long time. Since before dawn. It's a big full-size sedan, with dark paint. It's on the east side of the street facing north in front of number thirty-seven Gilmore."

They said they'd send a cruiser over to check it out. I thanked them.

I was looking out the window as I made the call. No sooner was the receiver in the cradle than I saw the big car sluggishly pull away from the curb and motor on down the street.

I called the police again and told them not to bother.

"So maybe you are getting a little paranoid." Patty said.

"No." I replied. "I think our house is bugged."

I finished getting dressed. I found a flashlight and began going from room to room looking in all the nooks and crannies, behind pictures and furniture. I checked all the phones and unscrewed the earpieces and mouthpieces looking for something that didn't look like it belonged. I looked in the closets. I went down into the basement and followed all the wiring with the beam of light. Patty came down and watched me.

"What are you doing?"

"I'm looking for something that doesn't look like it belongs."

"Like what?"

"I don't know. That's what makes it hard."

"You look like you've done this before."

"I have. And I didn't know what I was doing then either." I eventually got to the corner of the basement where the electrical service came in. I opened the circuit breaker box. I looked at the beige plastic box where the phone line came in. I didn't see anything suspicious. Of course, I don't know what something suspicious looks like.

"I think you're getting a little carried away," Patty said.

Maybe. Maybe not. You don't see too many full-sized four door plain dark sedans these days. It looked like a government car to me. But wouldn't they have more sophisticated equipment so they wouldn't need to have someone sitting out all night waiting in case I said something useful? Who knows? I sure don't.

Mac was out of his cage and we were sitting in the kitchen. I had to go to work soon. Mac was chasing dust motes in the sunshine coming through the window. He was having a good time. He always had a good time. Patty was working half a day today and then had a bunch of errands to do. This included taking Mac to the vet to get his vaccinations and to talk about neutering.

When I got to the hospital Will was holding court in the coffee room. He was on a roll. "Goddamnit Charlie, I feel like I'm working for the R.J. Reynolds tobacco company. All I did all night was take care of people with smoking related stuff. I had a bunch of cardiacs last night, all of them smokers. I had a guy with emphysema who came in really short of breath. He was still a smoker! I nearly needed to intubate him. Another guy came in with a stroke, his hands were purple, his fingers were nicotine stained yellow from his friggin' butts and now half his squash is gone from his smoking. All of this stuff was preventable! I can't friggin' stand it! If I ever go into private practice, God forbid, I'm gonna have a big sign on my office door that says not to come in here if you smoke 'cause I won't be sympathetic when you suffer from problems I can't fix and you could've avoided! Damn! It's so stupid!" He continued ranting and raving as he went down the hall, collected his stuff and left the department.

I'd been up for hours by now, the ER was quiet and we were hanging out in the coffee room. There was an EMT sitting there who worked once a month or so. I think his real job was at the Rising Paper Mill in Housatonic, a small hamlet to the north. He was really gung ho and impressed with himself. Whereas most EMTs wore the usual blue uniform shirt from the South Berkshire Volunteer Ambulance Service, this guy was really decked out. He had the same shirt but it was heavily starched and ironed, had a lot more patches sewn on it. It had epaulets and everything. Instead of regular pants he had on black nylon swat team style military pants with the big bellows pockets on the side of the thighs. They were starched and ironed, too, and they were 'bloused' into shiny black high paratrooper's boots. He wore a wide black leather utility belt; it looked like a policeman's belt and had everything but a gun. It had the usual EMT pouch with a bandage scissor and pen and pad and stuff, but it also had half a dozen other pouches and compartments on it. He was talking about nutrition with the other more normally dressed EMT who was on the shift with him. He was talking louder than he needed to. He was irritating.

I was drinking coffee and looking at the *Eagle* and

sitting next to one of the respiratory therapists I liked a lot. It was hard to concentrate because I was still pissed about the car outside my home this morning. I was frustrated that I couldn't find any electronic evidence of their intrusion into my home and I was annoyed by this bellicose blowhard of a SWAT-EMT who was distracting me from my newspaper. Every once in a while the blowhard would say something annoying and the therapist and I would look at each other and roll our eyes.

The blowhard was still on nutrition and talking about how important it is to take supplements in addition to bean sprouts and curd. And how most people aren't really getting enough of the essential amino acids. I was trying to read about a meeting that President Reagan had with the Israeli Prime Minister but the second paragraph of the article was so full of pronouns like he, him, them that I couldn't keep track of who was doing or saying what and that annoyed me too. I hate it when they can't write clearly enough and you can't keep straight who said what.

"And they don't really teach doctors anything about nutrition," the blowhard said.

I looked at him over the top of the newspaper. I looked at the respiratory therapist and he looked at me and shrugged.

"What did you say?" I asked Rambo the EMT.

"What? We were talking about nutrition."

I carefully folded up the newspaper and put it down beside me. I got up and stood in the middle of the small coffee room. Maybe three feet away from him, facing him. I looked down at him. My hands were in my pockets, real casual.

"Tell me," I said, softly and slowly. "Tell me what my curriculum was for my four years of medical school."

"What do you mean?" Rambo asked.

"I want you to tell me what courses I took in medical school. I want you to tell me what was included in each syllabus."

He looked at me puzzled. "How would I know?" he asked.

"You must know," I responded, drilling my eyes into him. "You just said that they don't teach doctors anything about nutrition. You wouldn't have said it unless you had an accurate knowledge of what they do and don't teach. I'm a doctor. I've been sitting here listening. You must know what my curriculum was in order to say what you did."

"I don't know what you took," he said, a little tense.

"Then why would you go around denigrating people's knowledge? I take my education extremely seriously because I use it every day to take care of sick people. Do you know what 'denigrate' means? It means to paint something black, to insult or to speak damagingly. I happen to think I had an excellent exposure to nutrition. The biochemistry course was beautifully dovetailed with the physiology course especially where the commonality was nutrition."

You could have heard a pin drop. The other EMT and the respiratory therapist were silent and motionless.

Rambo looked left and right trying to think of something to say. "I never hear you guys tell patients about nutrition. I've been reading all these books from the vitamin store, I understand all this."

"You memorized the propaganda put out by companies that sucker you into thinking you need all that crap. Tell me the difference between glucose and sucrose. Tell me what the Kreb cycle is. Tell me what adenosine triphosphate is. Tell me what four molecules come together to form a fat."

He looked around again hoping to find something to say. I was standing about two feet in front of where he was sitting so he didn't really have room to get up.

"But you can't really be healthy unless you take proper supplements. Especially lecithin. I never see you guys recommending lecithin."

"Lecithin taken orally is destroyed in the stomach by gastric acid. Our bodies make our own lecithin."

I spread my hands out, palms up and smiled. "My friend, how can you talk about healthy when you're sitting there with a pack of Marlboros in your pocket and a thirty pound beer gut?"

He was sweating. I sat back down and picked up my paper. I heard Rambo say to his colleague, "Let's go back to the ambulance garage."

"That's a good idea," I said to him, nodding. They left.

"Boy, Charlie," said the respiratory therapist. "That was really something. I never saw you do anything like that before."

"Well the guy was a jerk. I don't mind him being ignorant," I said as I nonchalantly turned the pages. "But I do mind him being arrogant." Actually, it was kind of fun to intimidate him since lately I'm the one getting intimidated.

"You're right. Well, he's a well-known asshole anyway. You know what?"

"What?"

"You'll never have to worry about sharing space in this coffee room with that guy again. He'll keep his distance from you from now on." I nodded and tried to read an editorial but I couldn't concentrate.

It got busy and I was running around like a maniac wondering which complete blood count went with which patient and I was seeing kids with fevers and earaches, adults with forty-eight hours of vomiting and diarrhea, a woman with sudden severe lower abdominal pain who probably had a twisted ovarian cyst, men with various injuries from the woodpile, a fractured ankle from a softball game. If this was all I had to do it was fine, but there was always the worry that there would be something nasty that would come in. I'm always waiting for the ambulance radio to come on; for the other shoe to drop; for the bomb to go off. If it stayed like this it was fine. I didn't get to call Patty at lunchtime like I usually do. I wondered what she was doing.

At six o'clock I had a most unusual experience. It moved me, and I'll never forget it as long as I live. The afternoon rush had quieted down and I was about to go down to the cafeteria with the nurses. A middle aged slender sandy-haired man with bright blue eyes and a ruddy complexion came in. He was vibrating. He told the receptionist and the nurse only that he needed to talk to the doctor. When patients say that it usually means they think they have VD.

I looked at his chart. We were standing in the cubicle next to the stretcher. I looked at the ER encounter form and the vital signs the nurse had written down were normal. His blood pressure was normal, so was his temperature. His pulse and respirations were a little fast but not too much so.

I took the blood pressure cuff out of its little basket on the wall and took his blood pressure again. It was still normal.

"How can I help you?" I asked.

He said softly, "I fear this is going to be a mental health thing, Doc. I never thought I'd hear myself say that." He was almost whispering and he was standing close to me, just within my personal space. "I could be dead right now. Something horrible happened. I mean, something terribly horrible almost happened, and if it did I would have killed myself. The worst nightmare I could possibly imagine almost happened. It didn't. But if it did, and it was so close, so close, Doctor, I'm telling you, that I would have done myself in on the spot. But it didn't happen. I'm so lucky. But for a fraction of an inch it didn't happen. But I can't let go that it might have happened, and I'd be dead now. And I'd be happy to be dead. Do you get what I'm saying?"

I couldn't imagine what he was trying to tell me. "Could you be a little more specific?"

"Sure. Okay. I nearly got my son killed right in front of me. No, he's okay. Maybe he's a little shaken but when I left he looked better than me. No, I didn't try or intend to hurt him if that's what you're thinking.

"I'm forty years old. I'm married. I have a daughter in college. UMass. I have a son at home. He's sixteen. He's my buddy. He's a great kid.

"He's a big strong kid. He plays football. He's a leader in school, not a follower. He wants to enlist in the service after he graduates. He talks about doing something stupid and dangerous and exciting like being in Special Forces or Rangers or a Navy Seal. I hope he'll get some good safe career training like in diesel mechanics. Or that he'll grow out of it and change his mind and go to college.

"He can build things with wood. He understands preload and afterload; vectors of force; stress and strain. He can back up a trailer behind the tractor better than I can. We have a pool table in the basement and I haven't been able to win a game in three years. This kid knows geometry and angles. Every night before bed we have ice cream, leaning against the kitchen counter, talking, rubbing elbows and teasing each other.

"We live in the woods. We have a house I built myself. We mostly heat with wood and I have to cut and split a lot of it, I've been doing it for years. We have a barn and a tractor, and he's good with everything. The kid likes tools. He has a knack with them.

"I'm good with tools too. I'm an assembler. I work in a factory that makes great big machines for papermaking companies. I've worked with tools my whole life. I didn't go to college, I started this right after high school. I went to a tech high school. I'm good with tools and I built our house and I understand angles and cables and I have a rigger's license and I know how to move big heavy stuff with cranes and forklifts and cables and winches and pulleys. So my boy is like me, only better and smarter and I'm proud about it.

"So we were out in the woods, in our woodlot. It feels like I spend half my life there because we need eight or ten cords a year. My son was with me. In the last year or so I've been letting him size up the tree, plan the drop, run the chain saw. I think he's as good at it as I am, he has the knack. I always let him try things, under supervision. I don't mind if he makes mistakes. Once he rolled the riding lawn mower, thank God he was all right, and that's okay because I know he will never make that mistake again. Actually I think he's really more cautious than I am. My wife gave me hell about that though, she says he's just a boy. I'm teaching him to be a man, and I really think he might be one already.

"So we lined up this drop. We expected the tree we cut would fall and would probably hang up against one of several trees and then we'd pull it with a come along, a snatch block pulley and a cable and get it on the ground. It was a big white ash, about eighteen inches across. So of course I'm looking around, checking the other trees in the area, watching him make the cut and he does everything right, just the way I taught him. He undercuts the far side and takes out a wedge, then cuts through above it from the near side. The tree begins to fall, tilts about thirty degrees, gets caught in a big old cherry but not the one I expected. It bounces and then I see this big dead limb about eight inches thick and ten feet long break off the top of the cherry and it's headed right at my son. My heart stopped. I was about fifteen feet away looking up, he couldn't see up well because he had a baseball cap on and he was backing up like I taught him when a tree is going down. But when the first tree hit the second it was kind of springy and it kind of launched that dead limb at him and I screamed and as he turned to look at me he moved a few more inches in my direction and that big damn limb came down and knocked off his Red Sox hat. It hit him right on the brim of his hat, all in a matter of seconds. The limb landed right in front of his boots. Never in a million years could I have seen this happening, never in a million years could I have forgiven myself if he got hurt, or more likely killed. He looked at me. If I hadn't yelled and he hadn't turned he would have been a few more inches away from that bomb."

The guy was white. He was whispering. He was maybe sixteen inches from me and I could smell the fear in his breath. We stood there staring into each other's eyes. His pupils were tiny.

"I didn't want him to know how scared I was. I didn't want this to be a nightmare for him. I ran over and I hugged him so tight that he asked me to loosen up so he could breath. It was all I could do to not cry. And all I could think was that if he was dead I'd take out my knife and cut my throat. Just one big deep slice.

"See this, Doc, I keep this big folding Buck knife on my belt. It has a three-inch blade. I keep it real sharp. It has a nice big handle I can really get a grip on. I use it all the time. When the frost throws around the barn and the doors rack I can shave them down with this. I'm always cutting haystring. When the rototiller binds up with grass stems I can just cut them right off the tines with this thing. Well, I know where the big artery is in my neck. I would've just said to my dead son, "Wait for me, don't get too far ahead, I'm right behind you," and I would've slit my throat and wrapped my arms around him and bled out and it would be horrible but it's the only thing I could've done.

"I didn't have to do it. My son is okay. I'm okay I think. But I just can't stop thinking about that big dead limb coming down and almost smashing that smart and beautiful head of his and I'd have nothing else to live for and I'd be so devastated that I'd want to be dead as soon as possible. My church would say I've sinned and I couldn't care less. I'd have killed him because I didn't foolproof the drop and I didn't see the hazard. I've been doing this for years and I didn't see the hazard. It'd be my fault and I would never ever be able to forgive myself. Nor would my wife who always thought I gave him too much trust. And to my neighbors I would've been the guy who got his kid killed. I'd be much better off dead. For the rest of my life, for every waking hour, I'd be looking up watching that big limb come down to destroy the best thing I ever had in my life."

Wow. I was sitting there, on the edge of my seat, my heart in my mouth listening to this poor man. Talk about being on the cutting edge of life. This was like Shakespeare. I was supposed to know what to say to this guy to make him feel better?

"Come with me." I said. I picked up the ER sheet and we walked to the doctors' room. There wasn't anyone else in the ER I needed to see.

I sat him down on the small couch that was our sofa bed. I pulled the chair from behind the desk and sat in front of him.

"Can I get you a cold drink? A cup of coffee?'

"Would you? A soda would be great. Any kind. My mouth is dry like sawdust."

I came back from the coffee room fridge with a Diet Coke. No caffeine. This guy did not need caffeine.

He popped the flip top lid and raised the can up and took a sip. He had a tremor, he was so distraught. He looked at me. He took a deep breath. He smiled.

"Well, Doc, you ever have a case like mine?"

"No. No. Never. That's quite a story. I'm so glad that this was only an almost tragedy. What do you think is going to happen to you the next few days?"

"I suppose I'll keep shaking and think about it constantly; think about 'woulda, coulda, shoulda.'"

"Does your wife know?"

"No," he said with a snort. "My son and I promised we wouldn't tell her."

"Why?" I asked.

"Because she'd never forgive us. She'd say she told us so."

"How do the two of you get along?"

"Me and my wife?"

"Yeah."

"We get along okay. We love each other. We respect each other. It's changed a lot since we got married."

"How so?"

"Oh, you know. When you're first married, the other person is the biggest thing in your life, like your sun. And then as the years go by you lose your infatuation. It's too bad, really."

This guy was really opening up. Telling me very personal heartfelt things.

"You're really baring your soul. You're really opening up."

"I could be on an autopsy table right now. I could be a lot more opened up."

Good point.

"How do you think your wife would feel if you and your son were found dead in the woodlot? And your daughter?"

"You know, doc, I didn't even think about them. Not at all. This would have been so gigantically horrible for me that I'd have had to do it and I just would have to hope that they'd understand."

"Mr. Jones, what would happen if, say, there was a different scenario. What if you and your wife were home, and God forbid, you got a call that your son was killed somewhere else, a car accident, a drowning, something elsewhere, and you weren't right there? Would that be a different story?"

"Yeah, that would be a totally different story."

"How come?"

"It would be a totally different thing to be right there, seeing my son get killed because of something that I was supposed to have control over, to protect him from, to have it happen on my watch. Does that make any sense to you?"

I paused. "I think so. Both scenarios would be horrible. But the first one is more horrible."

He nodded.

"Do you have any thoughts now of hurting yourself?"

"No. Except maybe by drinking too much."

"I don't think you should do that. How much do you normally drink?"

"I was just kidding, Doc. I don't drink much. I just have a beer or two once in a while."

"I want you to promise me you'll stay away from alcohol in all forms until this storm has blown over. If there's one thing I've learned working in medicine it's that people who are upset and drink make poor choices, bad decisions. Promise me."

"Okay. I promise. Not even one?"

"No, not even one. It's harder to not have the second one than it is to not have the first one."

"I hear you."

"So, tell me. What were you hoping that I could do for you tonight?"

"Oh, I don't know. Nothing happened. I feel better to have told someone about it. I don't know. I feel better."

"Talking is good," I said.

"Talking is good," he replied.

"Would you like to speak to someone from the mental health team? I guess I'm supposed to offer you that. I'm better with broken bones and cut fingers and heart attacks than I am with this stuff."

"No, you're doing fine, doc."

"Mr. Jones?"

"Yeah?"

"Do you have any thought that you might harm yourself in the future because of what almost happened this afternoon?"

"No. Nothing happened. Other than we got real scared. No, I was really just kidding when I said I only might hurt myself by drinking too much. You know, it's like a typical American behavior, in all the movies when something bad happens, the actor pours himself a stiff drink. You know, I am just in a state of shock about what almost happened. Just a matter of a few more inches in the wrong direction would've killed him and me, and horribly changed the life of my wife and daughter and so many people around us. So close to a big tragedy. An inch. Just an inch. Maybe two."

"But it didn't happen," I said, "You won't talk about this with your wife?"

"No, no way. She would freak. She wouldn't handle it well. She'd give me no end of grief and it wouldn't make anything better. For my son or for me."

"Do you and your wife not communicate well?"

He paused. "For this day and age, I think we do okay. We love each other. We've been married for a long time. We're committed to each other. Over the years her interest in me has dwindled. I resent it, but then I guess mine has dwindled a bit too. Sometimes I wonder 'what if', and did I marry the right woman, but on the whole we do okay. You know, so much of it is attitude. It's what you make of it." He stared out the door for a moment, and then turned to me. "Doc, how long have you been married?"

"Three years."

"A newlywed. You're just a beginner. You two probably still have a lot of energy and enthusiasm. You listen to me and don't you lose it."

"Don't you think you could get it back? If you worked at it?"

"Yeah. Maybe. It would take a lot of effort, and it would be hard to sustain it. And it would take two to do it." I nodded.

"So what are you going to do differently?"

"In what way?"

"About your son. About woodcutting. About your wife."

"Oh. I don't know. My daughter is out of the house. I try real hard to get the most out of my time with my son. You know how when you drink tea you squeeze the teabag against the spoon to get the most flavor out of it? I'm always looking for ways to do that with my son."

"That's a great metaphor, squeezing the teabag. I guess it means the same thing as to 'grab the gusto.' Wasn't that a jingle for a beer commercial?"

"Yeah. It was. Miller High Life."

"You know, here in the ER I see a lot of bad things happen, sometimes to people much too young. You never know how much time you're going to have and you need to live it as fully as you can. Squeeze the teabag."

We looked at each other. He gave a little nod.

"How do you think you're going to heat your house this coming winter?"

He shook his head. "I don't know. I've got almost enough wood stacked up."

"Maybe you should stay out of the wood lot until your head clears about this thing that happened today. Do you think of yourself as an expert woodcutter?"

"I did until today."

"Do you have friends who cut as much as you do and have been doing it just as long?"

"A few."

"Do any of them have stories of near misses in the woods?"

"Oh yeah."

"But not ones that imperiled their loved ones?"

"Not that I know of. But I wouldn't think they'd discuss it if they did."

"Why not?" I asked.

"I don't know."

"Too macho?"

"Yeah. That's probably it."

"So. Maybe it's like a near miss in the car when you're on the road and it could've been a bad accident. Have you ever been driving at night and you're tired and you're fighting to keep your eyes open and finally you nod off and you lurch awake to find you're drifting over the shoulder? It's happened to me dozens of times."

"Me too."

"Couldn't they have been similar tragedies?"

"Sort of."

"But you and I don't dwell on those so much because it's so common."

"True."

"But it doesn't make you feel much better right now does it?"

"Not much. No. Nice try. But I do feel better, much better, getting this out with you."

"So, in one sentence, what is bothering you the most right now?"

"That I nearly got my kid killed, then I would've killed myself and that would've messed up the lives of a lot of people around us. And that risk was just an inch away from being a reality."

"But it didn't happen," I said. "Are you religious?"

"We go to church. But I'm not really into it. Why?"

"Some people might say that this was an opportunity. It was a wake up call. It got you to think about those around you. It got you to think about squeezing the teabag a little harder. With your wife. With your daughter. As well as with your son."

"Good point."

"Do you think you're going to be able to sleep tonight?"

"Not likely. I'll probably just be staring at the ceiling all night."

"Would you like a mild tranquilizer? You'd have to promise me to have absolutely no alcohol"

"Heck, doc, now what fun is that? No, just kidding. I can handle it. I can deal with it."

"What was running through your head when you drove up here tonight?"

"We're dead. We nearly died. He nearly got killed. I nearly got him killed. We both could be dead right now."

"Okay. How about squeezing something positive out of this incident. When you're trying to fall asleep tonight and you're staring at the ceiling, instead of saying that over and over again, how about saying, 'I'm

115

going to make my relationships richer with all these people.'"

"I'll try that Doc, it's a good idea."

"Anything else you want to talk about?"

"No. I think I've taken up enough of your time."

"Well I have something to say. I think you're a great guy. I think you're a hero. Because you are doing hard things and you're being thoughtful and purposeful and responsible for your actions and thinking about consequences. And you are a very sincere and sensitive man and you love strongly and deeply. I want to hear from you again. I want you to feel free to talk to me again. I won't tell a soul. You've shared this secret story with me and now I'm in it with you. You can find me here and my name is in the phone book. If you want to talk to a real counselor I can help set it up. Don't forget me. Okay?"

"Okay. Thanks a lot. I gotta go."

We shook hands again and he turned and he walked out of the doctors' room.

I took a deep breath and sat down at the desk and stared down the long empty hallway.

I can learn a lot about life from this job.

Chapter 10

The next day at work I saw an adorable little four-year-old girl whose name was Carole. She was there because her right arm hurt. She hadn't fallen on it; she didn't get in a fight with her other siblings; no one knew what happened. She sat on the stretcher, very quietly, clutching her velour rabbit. There'd been no rough games, no tag, no running and jumping. I spent a few minutes standing there chatting in a friendly manner with her parents. I was trying to get her used to me. I tried to keep it light and not appear heavy or serious. I was trying to say silly things, like, "Oh what a cute little boy you have---Oh, you're a girl? Oh, I'm so sorry. And what a nice little toy bear you have. Oh, is it a rabbit? I'm so sorry, I get so confused. May I see it?" She sat there very quietly, taking it all in but not interacting. Finally I coaxed her into letting me hold her rabbit. I played with the rabbit. I tried to stick a tongue depressor in its mouth but it wasn't a real mouth and it didn't open. I tried to shine a flashlight down its throat but its mouth still wouldn't open. I tried to listen to its heartbeat with my stethoscope but I couldn't hear anything. I told it to take some deep breaths but the rabbit would not cooperate. I sat with the rabbit in my lap.

"You know, Carole, my wife and I just got a puppy last week, about this size. He's black. We named him

Maccabee. He's real cute, but he doesn't sit this still. He is always moving. I was sitting on the other end of the stretcher from her. I got the sense that the parents were impatient and thought I should have gotten an X-ray by now. I took the rabbit by the front paws and walked him vertically across the stretcher. Then I gave him a little swing across the stretcher to the counter. "Wheee" I said as the rabbit swung through the air to the counter. "Do you ever swing like that?" I asked. She still wasn't very responsive. "When I was a little boy I would go for a walk with my parents and each of them would hold one of my hands. And each time we came to a puddle or a curb they would pick me up by my arms and swing me through the air to the other side. And I would giggle all the way through. Do you do that stuff with your parents?"

I heard the mother murmur affirmatively behind me and little Carole nodded her head. I thought so. "You know, when you are little your bones and joints can be a little loose and sometimes it can help to tighten them up." I looked at her, hoping to get a sense that she was following me. "Here, let me give you your little doggy back. What? Not a doggy? Of course, I was thinking of my own little doggy, I'll give you your bunny back." With my left hand I reached the bunny toward her, toward the outside of her right shoulder. She didn't move her right arm, it stayed in her lap as she reached across with her left arm to get the toy.

"Let me show you how I can so easily tighten the bones for you, it doesn't hurt at all, I promise. I held her left hand palm up in my left hand. I held her left elbow in my right hand with my thumb in the crook of her elbow. With the elbow about halfway extended I stretched her arm and rotated her hand inward as I pressed with my right thumb. "See? All better. Wasn't that easy?" She still didn't say anything. "Now let's

118

tighten up the bones in your right elbow. I did the same maneuver on the right side and as I did I could feel a little pop, just a little subtle click, with my left thumb on her elbow. That was the proximal head of the radius of the forearm slipping back into place against the lateral epicondyle of the humerus.

"Well, I think both your elbows are all tightened up now. Do you have any other bones that need tightening? I got a cold pack and sat down next to her. "You want to see something really cool?" She sort of nodded. "Feel this." And I had her hold the cold pack. I reached it toward her right side and she still received it with her left hand. "See how warm it feels?" She nodded. "Watch this!" I said. I took off my glasses and held the pack in my hand. "One, two, three" and on three I made a funny face, took a deep breath, closed my eyes and smacked the cold pack on my head. It made a slapping noise and it broke the little packet inside that released the chemical that starts the endothermic reaction that makes the contents get real cold real fast.

I handed it to the child, to her right side, and she took it with her right hand. I smiled. "See how fast it got cold? Isn't that cool?" She was getting ready to smack it against her own head and I said, "No, no, don't hit yourself in the head with it. Then I'd have to tighten your head bone and I don't know how to do that. I only know how to do it to arms."

She grinned and was passing the cold pack back and forth from hand to hand. "Why don't you hold it against your elbow?" She put it against her left elbow. "Why don't you put it against your right elbow, the one that hurts?" Finally she said something. "It doesn't hurt," she said. Bravo, I thought. So then we started doing Simon Says. She didn't have any reluctance to move her right arm anymore. "Doesn't your arm feel better now?" She nodded vigorously.

I smiled at her and kissed my finger and touched it to her nose. I turned to the parents.

"What was all that about?" they asked.

"It's called the nursemaid's elbow and it's pretty common. It happens to kids this age when they have a hyperextension of their arm and elbow like when you swing them by their arms. You get a little partial dislocation of the smaller forearm bone where it meets the elbow and that little twist I did just pops it back. It's real common and she'll be fine, just don't swing her around by the arms for a couple of years until the bone and cartilage mature.

"Don't you have to take an X-ray or anything to make sure it's not broken?"

"Nah, no point. There's no history of trauma, there's no bruising, no swelling and look how well she's using it now." She was vigorously petting her rabbit with the right arm now.

"Nursemaid's elbow. I never heard of it," said the mother.

"It's pretty common," I said again. "It's one of those things. We see a lot of kids here and this is pretty recognizable."

"I guess," she muttered, and I asked her to contact their pediatrician if there was any more trouble.

I was writing up the chart in the nurses' station and I heard Will's voice down the hall. When I finished I went looking for him since it wasn't his shift and I wondered what he was doing here. No surprise I found him in the coffee room. "What a surprise, what are you doing here, Will?"

"Well, I came in to do some paperwork and I bumped into Boy Marvel, our illustrious hospital president, and he wants you and me to be in his office in ten minutes."

"For what?" I barked. I was resentful. I didn't think much of the guy nor did I like a secondhand message that he expected me to leave my duties in the department to sit in his office and attend to something that could only be about business and not patient care.

"Do you know what this is about?" I asked again.

"Haven't a clue. But if it's anything off the wall, let me do the talking." I nodded.

I choked down a half cup of old, burned, bitter, inky coffee that had been sitting in the pot for way too long and we went downstairs to the administrative area.

The secretary ushered us right in and the president shook our hands and sat us down in front of his desk. He was in his mid-forties and had a thick shock of straight black hair without any gray in it. He had a green three-piece suit. The jacket was on a wooden hanger on a coat rack. The vest had a lot of buttons and bulged over his belly. He sat down and put his feet up on the corner of his desk. They had leather soles.

"So what can we help you with, Mr. President?" Will asked jovially.

"I want to talk to you about keeping the customers satisfied."

I didn't have a clue as to what he was talking about and thought if I kept my mouth shut, I'd eventually find out. But I was being paid to be in the ER, not to be here talking about customer satisfaction.

"Whatever do you mean, Mr. President? Charlie and I are not in business, we don't deal with customers." The president grinned each time Will called him Mr. President. I think it irked him because he knew Will was making fun of him.

"It's the wave of the future, Will. Medicine is a business now. Patients are consumers and we have to cater to them to keep up our market share. It's a new paradigm. This is the way it is."

I took a deep breath. I didn't like this at all. It sounded like he just returned from a high-powered sales meeting and wanted to rev us up to increase profits. "I deal with patients, not consumers." I couldn't keep my mouth shut. "I am not a shopkeeper, I'm a physician." Will shot me a glance that said, "Shut up and let me do the talking."

"You see, Charlie, that's just where you're wrong, that's the old way of thinking. I want you here today so I can begin to teach you the new way of thinking."

"Excuse me but I think they're calling me in the ER," and I was halfway out of my chair when he said, "Sit down, Charlie, I told them to call you here if there's a patient."

Never before did I ever wish that someone would come in hurt so I could get busy in the ER and get out of this office.

"For example, Charlie, you saw a patient who wanted an X-ray. You told him he didn't need one. He came back the next day and Dr. Barker got him an X-ray. Now he's happy. And we picked up an X-ray fee. And he's more likely to come back here for health care the next time. See?"

"Who are you talking about? Are you talking about the cook in our cafeteria? He didn't need an X-ray!" I was incensed. "I did a meticulous exam, he met no criteria for needing an X-ray, one wasn't indicated. I told him that and I also told him that if he really wanted one I'd order it. And he walked away."

"See, that's just what I mean. You're practicing the old way. You didn't make him happy the way Dr. Barker did."

"Dr. Barker ordered an unnecessary expense, gave him an unnecessary dose of radiation. What did it show?"

"It was normal."

"So? What's your point?"

"My point is not whether the X-ray was indicated or not, or positive or negative, but that the patient wasn't happy with you. If you had ordered it, he would have been happy right away and we would have had some more revenue. It's a win-win situation. Don't you get it?" This is the crap that increases healthcare costs in America.

"No, I don't. There is a proper way to practice medicine and part of it is the appropriate use of medical resources. You're turning it into a K-Mart marketing campaign."

Will was uncharacteristically quiet through this. He kept tapping me with his foot, which the president was not able to see with his desk was in the way. I think he was telling me to shut up.

"Charlie, I wanted to introduce these new ideas to you so you could think about them and we'll talk again. Now, Will."

"Yes, Mr. President?"

He paused at this moniker, smiled and exhaled. "Now Will, you had a patient who came in with some upper respiratory symptoms and wanted some antibiotic pills and you denied her." It was preposterous that this flunky of an MBA would have the audacity to tell us how to practice medicine and I was flabbergasted that Will just sat here, smiling so passively. "So two days later the patient came back in and Dr. Barker gave her the antibiotic she asked for, Cefadril."

"But that's not a first line drug for any community acquired infection!" I pleaded.

"Charlie, there you go again."

"How can you say that?" I asked, almost shouting as Will gave me a surreptitious sideways kick right on my shinbone that hurt but I was so mad I ignored it. "Patients don't know what they need! They don't know what's good for them! That's why drugs are by prescription, so they can be intelligently and properly chosen and used! What do you want to do, have a big blackboard in the waiting room so the patients can choose their meds like picking a breakfast in the diner? Should we have specials everyday? Hello, my name is Charlie and I'll be your server today. Our daily special is ceftriaxone, would you like fries with that?" Will kicked me again. Hard.

"Charlie," the president said, soothingly, "I think you need to have yourself a little attitude adjustment and maybe you ought to change your tone."

"Okay." I was steamed. I won't say another word.

"So," Will said, looking at a piece of paper on his knee. I wasn't aware he'd been writing. "Let me get this straight. You want us to be more consumer oriented, to try harder to make the patients, I mean customers, happy. Right?"

The president nodded.

"And we should be very willing to satisfy their requests by ordering X-rays and antibiotics more liberally, right?"

"Right."

"Okay, Mr. President. We'll see what we can do with this. Thank you for having us in for this little chat. May we be excused?"

"Yes, boys, you may. Have a good day."

We left. I was agitated and confused and upset, especially that Will took all this lying down. I was appalled.

As we walked down the hallway I was seething.

"How could you just sit there and take that? How can you put up with that nonsense? I'm going to kill that guy Barker! The president shouldn't have called us there. He should've spoken to our department director, who should then have told us about this. Or he should've punched the president's lights out!"

"Charlie, you got to keep your voice down. Don't get yourself in trouble. Don't you know any strategy at all? Don't you know how to use someone's own force against themselves?"

"What the hell are you talking about?"

"Just wait and see the letter that gets written. I promise, you'll enjoy it and it'll be the end of this abortion of judgment."

"Don't go get yourself in trouble. Don't go get yourself fired."

"Don't you see, Charlie, if anything this'll make our jobs even more secure."

"Will, what the hell are you talking about?"

"You'll see, you'll see, just be patient. You'll like it, I promise."

The rest of the day was pretty routine. An older guy came in with crampy left lower quadrant pain and a low-grade fever. He had a slightly elevated white blood cell count but the flat plate of his abdomen and the left lateral decubitis films were all pretty normal. I talked it over with his attending physician and we decided he probably had diverticulitis. I admitted him, got him started on some antibiotics, got him some mild analgesics and upstairs he went.

There was a guy who was splitting wood in preparation for the winter. He was a big beefy guy and he had a hydraulic log splitters that is run by a small gasoline engine. All morning he was lifting big heavy logs onto the bed of the splitter. As it got later it got hotter and he got tired and his back began to ache. It got worse and worse as the afternoon went on. He would stop to rest and open another can of beer. Finally he lifted the last log (the log that broke the logger's back) and he finished slipping his disc. The poor guy was in agony. He did it like this every year, always did all this work in late summer, did very little vigorous work the rest of the year and he really overdid it. He had all the neurologic signs of a bulging L5-S1 herniated disc. I gave him some Demerol and in five minutes he was much more comfortable and very appreciative. I admitted him for the orthopedist and he went upstairs.

A twenty-two-year-old kid came in with a nosebleed that he couldn't stop. I squirted up some cocaine solution that gave his nose mucosal anesthesia and vasoconstriction. I looked around in his nose with the otoscope, found a tiny little oozing point on the anterior septum and cauterized it with a silver nitrate stick. I put in a little packing and urged him to leave his nose alone and keep his fingers out of it. He protested that he didn't pick his nose. *Yeah, right.*

I went down to supper with Helen and one of the nurses. The cook in the cafeteria still wouldn't look me in the eye. Meatloaf, wax beans and mashed potatoes. Love it. Always did. Ever since grammar school.

There were only twenty minutes left until my shift was over at 8:00 PM and I was doing some paperwork in my office. Helen phoned my extension to tell me there was a gentleman here to see me, not about a medical matter. That could mean anything and was usually someone annoying who wanted a favor. Grudgingly I went up front and there was a man standing right there with Helen at the front desk. He was middle-aged, a little shorter than me, thin, with grayish-brown hair that was beginning to recede. He had a nice earnest friendly smile. He was wearing a nice dark fitted suit. He was wearing it casually with his shirt collar unbuttoned and the yellow paisley tie loosened up a few inches.

"Hi, are you Dr. Davids?" he asked politely. "Thank you for coming out to talk to me," he said almost sheepishly. As we shook hands he backed away from Helen's desk and I instinctively followed him into the empty waiting room.

"My name is Lewis Goldstein. I work for the government. I'm here on behalf of the FBI." He reached into his pocket and extracted his badge wallet. I took it and looked at it. Helen was watching us from across the waiting room. He was Inspector Lewis Goldstein. The other guys had been special agents. He was from the Boston office. If he was a big cheese, he was playing up to me like a modest little mouse.

"Do you have a business card?" I asked. *I'm collecting them.*

"Yes, of course." He fumbled to get one out of his pocket. I looked at it and put it in my shirt pocket.

"What happened to your two other colleagues who've been visiting me lately?" I asked.

"Would that be Morse and Fremont? I don't know, I haven't met them, though their supervisor spoke to me. I presume they've been reassigned."

Out of the corner of my eye I saw Howard Barker come in through the ambulance doors and head down the hall to our doctors' room. He had the next shift. I had nothing to sign out to him, thankfully.

"Is there a time or a place that would be convenient for you and me to sit down and talk for a little while?" Goldstein asked.

"What is it you want to talk about?" I asked.

"Morse and Fremont and I have been working on opposite sides of the same case with the attorney general's office for a while now and we'd like to ask you some questions."

"What could I possibly know that could be of help to you?" I asked.

"I won't know until I ask," he responded quickly. "Where can we go?"

Well, Patty made me promise to keep her in on

127

everything. Why not? I looked at the clock on the wall in the waiting room. "Mr. Goldstein, my shift is over in a few minutes. Why don't you come home with me. We can talk there. Let me finish up and get my things. I'll call my wife and let her know we're having company." He nodded and I went back to the office.

I put my things in my orange medical knapsack, put away the textbooks I had out so they wouldn't be in Barker's way. I said goodbye to the staff and to Barker who was being bellicose in the coffee room. I picked up Goldstein in the waiting room and he agreed to follow me home. In minutes we were at the house. The porch light was on and Patty met us at the door.

"Patty, please meet Inspector Lewis Goldstein. He is with the FBI." She didn't pause or blink at all. She flashed him her Patty smile and shook his hand and welcomed him in. She had her long brown hair brushed back, not gathered in a ponytail. She was wearing a clingy white cotton top with a boat collar, sleeves that ended at mid-forearm. The bottom of her blouse was untucked from her faded jeans and she was wearing sandals.

"Welcome to our little home, Inspector," I said.

"Aah, please call me Lewis," he replied, looking around the living room.

"Okay, Lewis, please make yourself comfortable. It's late for us," Patty said. "Would you like a cup of coffee or tea? A cocktail? I make a good martini?"

"Aah, thanks, I can't have a cocktail on the job. A cup of tea would be nice."

How homey, I thought.

"Good," Patty said cheerfully, "I'll make a pot."

"Gee, Dr. Davids, I hoped we could talk privately" he said to me softly as Patty went into the kitchen.

"Aah," I said offhandedly, "please call me Charlie. And anything you or I have to say we can say in front of Patty."

It was my guess that after Morse and Fremont thoroughly pissed us off and it became clear that we were not going to interact with them in a useful manner they scrounged around and found a Jewish guy, who they had to send out all the way from Boston, maybe thinking that if he was Jewish like us, and was real polite and low key, that we would open up to him.

I thought they usually worked in pairs, so they could corroborate and collaborate and compare notes and everything. Maybe they thought sending a nice, earnest, tired looking Jewish guy by himself would be more disarming. *Am I getting cynical or what?*

Patty was moving back and forth between the kitchen and dining room. I could hear little puppy noises coming from the kitchen.

"Your wife is very lovely," Goldstein said, as an aside. Here it comes.

"Thank you. I think so too."

"Why don't you guys come and sit down in the dining room?" Patty asked.

I led the way into the dining room. It was the room to the right behind the living room, on the way to the kitchen. It was a modest-sized room. We had a nice Hitchcock maple table with understated gold stenciling around the border and four armless Windsor chairs around it. The room was lit by a small brass chandelier over the table. In one corner was a small bookcase. In another was a small side table with a lamp on it, a pair of brass candlesticks, a brass menorah and my father's kiddush cup. There was a colorful photomontage of Chagall's stained glass windows from the Hadassah Hospital in Jerusalem. Patty had set out three linen placemats and set the table and put out a dish of shortbread cookies. She came back with our mismatching china teacups and saucers and shining silverware.

Goldstein took off his coat and draped it on the back

of his chair. He must've left his gun in his car. He sat down and smiled. "It's been a long day for both of us, hasn't it," he said relaxedly as he rolled up his sleeves. Getting comfortable and folksy. Using all the body language to get us to relax with him.

Patty finally came in carrying a delicate china teapot. She poured some for each of us and sat down.

"You have a very lovely home," Goldstein said approvingly. "I hear you're a pharmacist?"

"Yes, I am. And I'm applying to teach freshman chemistry in some of the local colleges."

"That's nice," he said, approvingly. "Did I hear a puppy in the back?"

"Yes, we have a new little black lab puppy."

"Oooh, can I see him? What's his name?"

"Maccabee," Patty said.

"Mac...Maccabee? Like in the Chanukah story? Are you folks Jewish?"

Right. Like you didn't already know. This guy was a little lame.

"Yes, we are," Patty said, "and with a name like Goldstein I presume you are too?"

"Of course," he said. "Well look at that, we're all landsmen."

Give me a friggin' break.

"So, Lewis, have a piece of cake. Tell me, what's a nice Jewish boy like you doing in the FBI and what are you doing here all the way from Boston?" Patty wanted to know.

"Well, actually, I started out as a lawyer. And one of my first jobs out of law school was as an assistant district attorney in one of the cities not far from Boston. You know, it's a pretty structured job, at first it's very exciting, there's a lot of supervision, you get lots of experience. There's a large volume of criminal law out there. After a while I left and went into private practice with an established firm but after a year I was bored to death sitting around in the same office all day doing drudgery stuff like wills and divorces and real estate closings and things. I missed the DA's office. I put my feelers out to try to go back in again and I ended up doing it for the FBI."

"So, what are you working on that you think we could help you with?" I asked.

"Didn't Morse and Fremont sketch it out?"

You know they didn't. "No. They showed me photos. They asked me about prescriptions. Whenever I asked them what this was about, they told me that they'd be the ones to ask the questions," I reported quietly without annoyance in my tone.

Goldstein shook his head. "Tsk, tsk, tsk. You'd think that those guys would have developed better interpersonal skills by now. They sound like a couple of tough street cops."

Now he's siding with us against them to further convince us subliminally that he's a nice guy, on our side, we should like him and trust him and talk to him. It's one of those good cop-bad cop routines.

"Here's the story, Charlie and Patty. There is a lot of organized crime in the northeast. They are in New York City, New Haven, Connecticut, there's a lot in Providence Rhode Island, Boston and all along the big cities on the Route 90 corridor from Boston to Worcester to Springfield. You read the papers. You've heard about Boston politics and the Mafia and the Irish mafia and Whitey Bulger and all that. I work in the organized crime task force. There are a number of people who are in the higher ups of different factions of these organized crime families that we have been collecting information on for a long time. We've been able to indict and convict and put away quite a few of these people. And there are a lot more we're working on putting away." He paused, and looked at me. I thought back to the news report we'd seen on TV recently.

I just looked at him. He set me up to say "So what do you want from me?" but I wouldn't say it. I just looked at him. It was awkward. The seconds ticked by. I wasn't going to give in and ask the question he was begging.

"Mr. Goldstein?" Patty asked quietly.

"Yes?"

"Would you like some milk for your tea? Is it not alright? You haven't touched it."

"No, thank you Patty, it's fine, thank you." He leaned back and took a sip, his eyes locked on mine. He had been leaning forward over the table, his forearms were on the table, his hands were almost at the halfway point on the table between us. He was showing me just how earnest he was.

"So what would you like to know from me?" *Okay, I give in.*

"Did you recognize any of the men in the photographs that Morse and Fremont showed you?"

"No. Not at all. Like I told them," I answered softly.

"What about a series of prescriptions you wrote that got filled in the Springfield area between nineteen eighty-three and four.

"What about them?" I asked. "I write millions of prescriptions."

"Can't tell me anything more about them?"

"No. I can't."

"What about your fingerprints being found in Springfield?"

"What about them?" I asked. How does he know they were mine? Was it one fingerprint or many? How good was the match? I didn't ask.

"You haven't asked me where the fingerprints were found," Goldstein said.

It wasn't a question so I didn't answer.

"Where were they found?" asked Patty. She caved in.

Goldstein turned to her. "Your husband's fingerprints were found in the back of a liquor store. And in a basement apartment." He said this like he was in a courtroom and was producing a damning piece of evidence.

"Well, Dr. Davids? Charlie? How do you explain that?" He wasn't being so folksy anymore.

I don't have to explain it. I don't need to explain it. I'm not in a situation where I need to defend myself.

"I don't know, Mr. Goldstein. I just can't say."

"A few years ago you reported the loss of a rather expensive and sophisticated handgun." He paused for dramatic effect. I said nothing. "It's been found." I said nothing. I just looked at him. I was tempted to escape his stare and take a sip of tea but I just looked at him.

"In all my years at this, of all the lost guns that have been found, you're the first guy I've met who didn't immediately ask where it was found and when can he have it back." How do you explain this?"

"I was just going to ask you where it was found and when I can have it back. You didn't give me a chance to ask."

"So. Charlie. How do you explain this?"

"Like I said, Mr. Goldstein, I just can't say."

He didn't say anything for a few minutes. He paused for dramatic effect. He had a few consecutive sips of his tea. He ate half of a shortbread cookie. Maybe in this long silent period I was supposed to crack and confess. *I did it! I did it! I killed Mr. Green in the library with the candlestick!*

Finally he spoke. "The phrase, 'I can't say' can be taken many ways." He was back to being sweet and soft spoken and folksy. "It can mean, 'I am unable to say'. It can mean 'I don't know.' It can mean 'I won't

133

say.' It can mean 'I could say but I can't because there is something that's stopping me from saying.' It might mean 'I can say this but I can't say that.' It can mean, 'I can't say for sure but maybe I can guess a little.'"

I resisted the urge to cross my arms on my chest, lean back and clench my teeth. I leaned forward and put my arms on the table and looked at him, silently, earnestly. I said nothing. Many seconds ticked by slowly.

"Okay," Goldstein said, "here's what we're guessing. We think that somehow, on some level you either knowingly or unwittingly provided medical care for some of the people we've been investigating. You may or may not have information that could be useful in developing evidence that could be used in their prosecution. There is absolutely no interest in you as an object of prosecution for any involvement you had with them, be it medical or criminal misconduct. You may or may not know anything. You might think that whatever you do know wouldn't be useful to us. But you have to let us be the judge of that. Maybe you were involved with them and you're thinking that if you stay silent you'll stay safe. Maybe you will, maybe you won't. And if you're safe, you won't know for how long. That's a lot of doubt for you two nice young people to live with."

"Are you driving back to Boston tonight?" Patty asked, changing the subject.

"No, actually, I'm staying over. I'm going back in the morning."

"Where are you staying?" I asked, not really interested but just being polite.

"I've got a room at the Red Lion Inn in Stockbridge," he answered.

Pretty swanky accommodations for a guy on a government expense account. We had a few more minutes of polite but useless conversation and then Goldstein got up to leave.

Patty and I stood side by side on the front porch and we watched Goldstein drive off. It was a cool summer evening and the air was fragrant.

In the darkness Patty said, "Have you called your old friend Matt yet?"

"No, I haven't," I replied.

"I think it's time you did."

"I think so, too."

We watched until his taillights were gone.

We ambled back into the house. I wandered around. Patty took Mac out of his crate and brought him into the backyard to do his thing.

I picked up the phone and called the Red Lion Inn. I asked the desk clerk for Mr. Goldstein's room. Patty came in just as I was calling.

"What are you going to tell him?" she whispered? "He's probably not even there yet."

I covered the mouthpiece of the phone with my hand. "I don't really want to talk to him," I whispered back.

"I'm sorry, sir, we don't have a guest by that name."

"Mr. Lewis Goldstein?"

"We have no one by that name sir."

"Could it be that he hasn't checked in yet?"

"We are not holding a reservation for that name."

"Do you have any vacancies tonight? He told me he was going to stay with you tonight."

"No, sir. It's Tanglewood season. We almost never have any vacancies."

I thanked him and hung up. It was hard to know what to believe.

Chapter 11

Our next morning off together we got up early. Neither of us had slept well. We had coffee and a light breakfast and tended to Mac's needs and put him back in his crate. We put on our running clothes and drove to the top of Monument Valley Road. It was still and it was August and it was cool and damp. We both felt the need to run some anxiety out of our systems after our visit the other night from Mr. Goldstein, our friendly Jewish FBI agent. All night I kept thinking of Mr. Jones and his son. We stretched a little at the car because Patty insisted.

"How come you always make nasty faces like you're in pain when you stretch," Patty asked.

"Who me? I didn't know that I did." I stretched some more. "Yeah, I guess I do."

We started at a slow warm-up jog, heading south and slightly down hill on this lovely road. We were in the mood to do some mileage. We passed some old colonial homes, big old barns in varying levels of deterioration. Cultivated fields and fields grown amok. When we were still jogging slowly enough that I could talk, I told Patty about my little meeting with Will and the hospital president. Between huffs and puffs, Patty said, "What a jerk that guy is. He was totally out of line. Not only was that terribly unprofessional, but he went right over your department director's head. I'm more familiar with corporate structure than you are, and that guy committed a pretty audacious faux pas."

We were running through a thickly wooded section and we had a good head of steam worked up and it felt good to be sweating as we slid through the cool damp air. The sun wasn't up over the mountains yet. There were deer tracks in the wet sand on the shoulder of the road.

I told her how people were going to say I wasn't such a nice guy anymore. The cook at the hospital cafeteria throws hate bombs every time he sees me. I told her about my incident with Rambo the EMT. No doubt a blowhard like him would do his best to let people know what he thinks of me.

"On the contrary," Patty said between breaths, "you may be held in greater respect, as if that were possible, because you stood up for yourself and stood up for the seriousness with which you hold your education."

"Thank you, Patty, you've made me feel better already."

"Just wait until later," she quipped, and winked at me mischievously.

Farther on we saw long white fences along the left side of the road leading up to the heart camp. This camp had a really neat concept. It was started long ago by some wealthy person who had heart disease. He had a farm he used as a summer home. He developed it into a special camp for kids who had heart problems. They'd come from all over the northeast to spend a few weeks here in the summer where they'd try to have as normal and active a life as they could given their disabilities, with very vigilant supervision and nursing attention.

We came to a long gradual uphill and we nodded to each other. This was our signal that we were now going to try to kill ourselves. Keeping pace with each other we lengthened our strides, sped up so that it hurt and we chugged up this hill like two little engines that could. Patty: this girl is built for stamina. And commitment. When the hill crested, we slowed to a jog. We reversed our direction and headed back at a more comfortable lope. I was sweating Goldstein out of my system. I don't know where he slept the other night but I hope he slept poorly.

Finally we reached the car. We both were happily tired and felt silly, and we guzzled diet cola once we got the car open, and Patty let loose some loud belches. We were lazy and walked together with our soda cans along the side of the road, stretching, cooling off, taking turns kicking a rock down the road with our toes, amid the moist forest fragrance and Queen Anne's Lace. Maybe soon, when it's cooler, and he's a little older, Maccabee can come running with us.

On the way back we went to the hospital so I could just duck in and pick up my mail and paycheck. I felt self-conscious going into Fairview dressed this way but I got over it. No one saw me or stopped me. I jumped back into the car, where Patty was waiting. She drove. I leafed through the mail as we drove home. There was some medical junk mail and my paycheck and surprisingly, a letter from Will. I tore it open. I read a few lines and smiled. I read it aloud to Patty.

Dear Mr. President,

This memo is to formalize in writing the key points you made in our meeting of August 21, 1987. In this unscheduled urgent meeting in your office you met with me and Dr. Davids, who left his post in the ER to attend at your command. In this meeting you explained the new paradigm of prioritizing patient satisfaction above and beyond standard established medical guidelines of care. We should be willing to obtain patient X-rays if requested, even in the absence of meeting clinical criteria. We should be willing to prescribe antibiotics of the patients' choice regardless of the recommendations of Center for Disease Control infectious disease guidelines.

Both Dr. Davids and I look forward to helping our small hospital see greater revenue and patient acceptance. We look forward to discussing this proudly with the Joint Commission of Accreditation of Hospitals the next time they come to inspect.

Sincerely yours,
    William D. Connor, MD
cc: Dr. Edward Barrow, Director of Emergency Services
Mr. John McElroy, Chair, Board of Directors
Dr. Eric Atkins, Chief of Staff
Dr. Charles Davids, Emergency Physician

When we finally stopped laughing, Patty said, "I can't believe the balls Will has. As much of a jerk as the president is, Will shouldn't so blatantly embarrass him."

"I agree, this really sounds risky. I'm sure the president will really be pissed. But how can he deny it? I was there, too, I was a witness. What he said was unforgivable."

When we got home we could already hear Mac squealing in his crate in the kitchen. Our knees were spongy as we climbed up the porch steps and we moved like we were a hundred years old. Patty let Mac out in the back. He was doing well and hadn't soiled his crate in days. I mixed up some iced tea; we were both still thirsty.

I couldn't resist. I had to call Will. He picked up the phone at home.

"Hey, Will, this is Charlie. That was quite a letter you sent."

"Yeah, well, I told you that you would like it."

"Don't you think that was pretty risky? I hope you don't get yourself fired. He could make a lot of trouble for you."

"Not at all, Charlie, not at all. Do you remember you asked why I just sat there so quietly? You wondered why I didn't argue with him. I kept trying to get you to shut up when you argued with him. We didn't have to argue. Don't you see? We just helped him cook his own goose."

"How?"

"What can he do to us now? Our jobs are probably even more secure now than they were before. He could never fire us, now. All we'd have to say is he's firing us out of retribution because he made a fool out of himself in front of us. We'll never hear a word out of this guy again. It'll be great. McElroy and Atkins and Barrow will go up to him and ask what the hell this is all about, and how could he defend himself? He'll avoid us like the plague! We're golden!"

"Oh, I don't know. I hope you're right, but this is a small place and I wouldn't want to make enemies."

"Charlie, you just don't understand corporate American politics. I've been around longer than you. I was in the Army. It's the same thing. Ask Patty, she's been in CVS for years, she knows how corporate politics works."

"Well, I enjoyed the sarcasm and your courage. I just hope there's no fallout from it."

"Don't worry. Hey, I'll catch you later."

We sat on the front porch in the Adirondack chairs drinking iced tea with fresh peppermint. The day had brightened; the fog had burned off; it was much warmer.

Our next task for the day was to call Matt. We collected our puppy and got in the car. Mac was still leery about riding in the car. We headed north on Route 7 to the K-Mart plaza. On the way we stopped at the bank to deposit my check. I also picked up two rolls of quarters for the pay phone. Each time we got out of the car we laughed as we watched how awkwardly and slowly we moved after our run. We drove over to an outdoor bank of four public telephones. They weren't very private. They weren't private at all. It's hard to find one of those old-fashioned phone booths anymore. I went up to the payphone with the heavy rolls of quarters in my pocket. I picked up the receiver and looked at Patty twenty feet away in the car, with Mac, looking at me. I saw lots of people going in and out of K-Mart. Lots of people were going in and out of the supermarket. This wasn't the kind of place I needed to make the kind of call I needed to make.

We drove up to Pittsfield, another thirty minutes north. There was a little luncheonette on Park Square that used to have one of those nice old-fashioned wooden phone booths. I hoped they still did. It was the kind with a semi-circular seat and when you closed the folding glass door a light and a fan went on.

We got to Pittsfield, we even got a good parking spot. It wasn't too hot to leave the puppy in the car. We left him in the crate in the back seat with all the windows open a few inches. The luncheonette was open, they still had their phone booth and we were famished. We made a beeline for the counter. Patty ordered a seafood salad roll and I had a grilled cheese and tomato sandwich. It was good, too. I wouldn't have to worry about a grease deficiency for a while.

I got into the phone booth and pulled Matt's phone number out of my wallet. I hoped it was still good, I hadn't spoken to him in a couple of years, although we exchanged holiday cards.

"Hello, Aetna Insurance, how may I help you?"

"Hello, may I speak with Matt Adams please?"

"Mr. Adams is in our suburban office today, may I transfer you?"

"Yes, please."

"May I tell him who's calling?"

"Yes, this is Charles Davids."

The phone clicked a few times and then Matt said, "Charlie, how the hell are you?"

"I'm fine Matt, how are you?"

We got the pleasantries out of the way. Finally I said, "Matt, there's something screwy going on."

"Oh, no, don't tell me you're in trouble again."

I told him how nice and quiet our little life had been until Moore and Fremont started showing up, asking questions I either couldn't or wouldn't answer, and about our visit from Goldstein the other night. And that I thought our house was bugged.

"So what did you tell them?"

"Nothing."

"They'd have no trouble telling you were holding back information."

"But I didn't. I didn't recognize any of those photos. I don't know about the prescriptions, though I could guess. I didn't want to know about the gun."

"You said Goldstein told you a little about their investigations. Tell me more."

I told Matt what he said about his organized crime task force and the indictments they'd succeeded in and the ones they were working on but needed more evidence to bolster them up. I didn't think I had specific enough information that would be helpful in court. I didn't know the names of anyone I'd dealt with except Sal. I wasn't going to violate my silence and safety and tell them about Sal.

"Yeah, that's your interpretation of it. And they don't know what you know. They probably hope that whatever pieces of the jigsaw puzzle you have might jive with what they have and would lead them to some useful conclusions."

"So what should I do? Shouldn't I keep quiet?"

"You're always safer keeping quiet. As a private citizen who hasn't been arrested you aren't under any legal obligation to be forthcoming. They're just hoping you'll cooperate being that you're such a good citizen. If they're putting this much effort into developing you, they probably haven't got much of a case built up yet. If I were you, I'd stay quiet, stay polite and don't give them anything at all, don't give them anything that will encourage them. You have the right to remain silent.

"I agree with you that they probably brought in Goldstein from out of town as a ringer hoping he could befriend you and sweet talk you into cooperating. Your instincts are good."

"What do I do about the bug?" I asked.

"That's a good one. It might not be a good idea to ask your friend MacPherson because he'd want an explanation. He probably wouldn't have access to the right equipment anyway. Radio Shack sells some electronic security devices for bugs but they aren't very sophisticated and if it finds nothing it might give you a false sense of security. You said you looked around the house carefully? Just be very careful about what you say inside the house. Check your cars, your coat pockets, and Patty's purse. Anything that you always carry with you. It could be just a little device."

We chatted a little longer and he asked me where I was calling from. He asked why I only called him when I was in trouble and why I never came out to visit him. We hung up and it took a long time to slip the required number of quarters into the phone.

Patty and I left the restaurant. Once in the car I told her about the conversation.

"So he didn't have any sterling insights except to play dumb and keep quiet."

"Yeah."

"I think we both can be pretty good at that."

We decided to go over to my old stomping grounds in Dalton. Our first stop was at Kelly's Package Store. I used to live a few blocks away and was a frequent patron and had struck up a casual acquaintance with Mr. Kelly. Although there were nice package stores in Great Barrington, I liked giving him my business.

We walked in the front door and Mr. Kelly was at his post at the checkout counter in the center of the store. He was a jovial round-faced man with penetrating blue eyes, a gray crew cut and pink cheeks.

"Hi Doc."

"Hi Mr. Kelly. Did you ever meet my wife Patty?" I asked.

"Yes, I have had that privilege," he said while shaking my hand and then he quickly took Patty's hand and she giggled as he slowly brought her hand to his lips and he kissed it. "Yes, I have had the pleasure of meeting your lovely wife. Years ago when you still lived here, where you're still supposed to be living. What can I do for you?"

"How about a case of Genesee Cream Ale?"

"Genny Cream," He repeated. He turned to Patty, "A good budget beer. You know for years I've been trying to sell him up to one of the nice flavorful premium beers or ales. He never let me do it," he said, shrugging his shoulders at Patty.

"I like premium beers just fine. I just don't like paying a dollar a bottle for them when I'm perfectly happy with Genny Cream," I said resolutely. "While you're at it how about a couple of bottles of nice but inexpensive red and white table wines?"

While he was in the back I pulled Patty over to a small framed poem on the wall in the back of the store. "Here, read this."

A TRIBUTE TO DALTON, MASSACHUSETTS, THE HOME OF UNITED STATES CURRENCY

Did you ever live in Dalton in the scenic Berkshire Hills? That's where they fashion paper to make our U.S. bills. If you've lived and loved in Dalton no matter where you roam, when you handle U.S. greenbacks they're a little bit of home. The pioneers whose dream it was built better than they knew. It took much more than paper mills to make that dream come true. For crafts and churches, stores and schools combined to make worthwhile a town with worldwide purpose where loyal workmen smile. Their product—flawless, fine and strong—in paper craft—supreme—is then engraved by Uncle Sam in colors gray and green. I'm glad its coat is verdant like meadows lush and sweet and gray like old Day Mountain a-cooling off his feet. Way down among the green you'll find Waconah Falls' white spray and Weston's Chalet, too, is there, White Rocks and snow in May. The crispness of a brand new bill is Pine Grove tall and straight, its thin dry needles whisp'ring down the path from gate to gate. The coolness comes from Wizard's Glen where ice is found in June from frosty nights and northern lights and skating 'neath the moon The kindly folk who fashion it are friends of your folks, too, They work and play together, they hope and pray that you Will make this good world better, will keep it clean and fair, A symbol true of Dalton, its brotherhood will share. The gracious Dalton people are helping keep the tills Of globe-encircling friendships piled high with U.S. bills Though years may change fair Dalton, ideals can never die, Firm trust in God has brought reward, 'twill keep its purpose high. Oh, you can't lose touch with Dalton no matter where you roam, when you handle US greenbacks they're a little bit of home.

When Mr. Kelly came back with the beer he asked us about the wine and if we liked dry or not, full-bodied or lighter. "While we're at it, Mr. Kelly, Charlie and I have been learning about martinis. Is there an interesting gin you'd like to recommend?"

He looked at her for a few seconds, then shifted to

me and back to her. "You like a nice aromatic gin? I have a real nice one. One with nice botanical flavors that you wouldn't want to obscure with an olive. I recommend the original Bombay gin, not the Bombay Sapphire. Here," he said as he took a bottle off the shelf, "see here, on the label it even lists the different herbs blended in to flavor it. Coriander, lemon peel, angelica and cassia bark, whatever they are, orbis, I don't know what that is either, licorice, juniper berry and almond. You wouldn't want to cover those delicate flavors with a big salty olive. My recommendation? Just a drop of a French dry white vermouth like Noilly-Pratt, the gin, and a small lemon peel. Keep it simple, it's a lovely drink."

"Oh, you make it sound so good, I could have one now," Patty said.

"Are you two becoming heavy drinkers, Doc?"

"Oh, no, not us, we usually make just one small martini and share it. Maybe we have one a week."

"Oh, Doc, that's not enough. You should always have two. Not one, not three. Just two. And you can only have the first of the day just once. But you need two to relax."

"Mr. Kelly, if I have two, I'll fall asleep."

"Well, then, that may be just what you need to do and it helps you."

While we were talking two little kids came into the store. Maybe they were eight or ten. Both had on Red Sox caps and each had an empty soda can. They handed the cans to Mr. Kelly who, without breaking the flow of the conversation with Patty and me, took the cans and tossed them into the bin under the counter. Then he took two pretzel sticks out of a tall glass jar and handed one to each kid. They put them in their mouths, Mr. Kelly waved his lighter under the end of each pretzel stick and they turned without a word and headed out the door. Patty and I watched this interaction and we smiled.

By this time I had the case of beer in my arms and Patty had the wine and gin in hers. We said goodbye and headed out to the car.

"Have you ever seen the Mad Mason's house?" I asked Patty

"Who's the Mad Mason?"

"He's this old codger who retired from Crane's decades ago. He's from Ireland and has a brogue that's as thick as Guinness stout. He lives way up Old Windsor Road past the high school and he's decorated his front yard with all kinds of silly colorful stone constructions. He's got archways, a wishing well, a little stone house that looks like it's for leprechauns. He's got terraced gardens supported by low stone walls and he hooked up the wastewater from his kitchen so it'll water his garden. It's all very colorful; some of the stones and the wooden parts are brightly painted."

"How do you know all this about him?"

"Years ago I went jogging and when I passed his house he stopped me and told me my stride was all wrong and if I really wanted to train properly I'd do this and that and then he told me about his boxing days when he was a young man in Ireland. He was a little nutty but very colorful." We drove past his house slowly and gazed at all the funny stuff we could see from the road. We continued up the road, which was quite heavily wooded, and eventually turned onto Cleveland Street, which took us up to North Street and we soon passed Dalton Tractor with all their big interesting machines out front. A little past there we turned off to take a look at Wahconah Falls.

We put Maccabee on his little leash and gave him a chance to stretch and walk around. He was full of energy and he splashed in the pocket water between the stones at the base of the falls. There hadn't been much rain lately and there wasn't much water coming out of the Reservoir so the falls weren't very dramatic to look at. Sometimes after stormy weather it was deafeningly loud.

We headed back to Dalton and had an early dinner at my favorite pizza place: Benny's. This was a family style restaurant and bar that had great pizza. Great sauce. I didn't know who Benny was but the restaurant was owned by the bartender, Angelo. There was always a serious red-haired lady in the kitchen working hard. We shared a pizza and a pitcher of beer. Genny Cream. It was good. Tired, full and relaxed, we drove back to our home, hoping that nobody was there waiting for us.

Chapter 12

There were no surprises waiting for us when we got home. We fed Maccabee. I put away our purchases. I put a half dozen Genny Cream bottles in the refrigerator. I brought the wine bottles to the basement. When I got back upstairs Patty was making us a martini according to Mr. Kelly's recipe.

We sat on a kitchen chair, Patty sitting crosswise on my lap. The windows were open and the breeze barely moved the curtains. Patty twirled the stem of the martini glass. Mac sat contentedly chewing a rawhide bone.

"Nice gin," I said.

"Uhm hmm," she agreed.

My leg was falling asleep under Patty's weight but I didn't mention it.

We sipped through half of the martini. It took ten minutes. Little sips. Strong stuff. I closed my eyes.

"Listen, don't get too snookered. We have work to do tonight. I'm probably ovulating."

"Hey. Go easy, you know the walls have ears."

"Oh, right, I forgot." She looked around the kitchen for a moment. Then she snaked her right hand under her shirt to her left underarm. Then she pumped her left arm up and down and made an obscene gaseous sound. The things her brothers taught her. "Oh pew, Charlie, what did you have for lunch?"

I looked up at her with mock indignation and rolled my eyes. "Here we are, two sophisticated health care professionals enjoying a cocktail, and I always thought of you as so grown up and mature."

"I don't want to be grown up and mature. I just want to be able to pass myself off that way when I need to. Like at work." Now she was making similar noises with her mouth on the back of her hand. "Charlie, Char-leee, will you please go to the bathroom if you don't mind!"

I grinned. I took the tin watering can she used for the houseplants and went into the half bath off the kitchen. "I've been dying to take a leak all afternoon," I said, "I was so busy I just didn't have a chance." Then I held the can high and began a long slow stream of water into the toilet. Coming from that height it was a loud gurgle and with the large volume of the watering can it went on for minutes.

When the can was finally empty I flushed the toilet, washed my hands and rejoined her in the kitchen. "I feel much better. I had to pee like a racehorse."

"That's what it sounded like. What a bladder you must have!"

If anyone was listening, I hope they were amused.

"Listen, come outside with me, I want to show you something in the garden," I said.

There was just a little martini left and I drained it

151

and put the glass on the counter. I took her hand and the three of us went into the backyard. We sat down on a bench and I spoke quietly in her ear.

"Does it bother you as much as it bothers me that our house might be bugged?"

"Yeah. But what can we do about it?" she whispered back.

"Won't it bother you to have people listening to everything we say and do? And I do mean everything. Even that."

She thought for a few seconds. "Let them eat their hearts out."

"How can we discuss what's going on with each other, about Goldstein and Morse and Fremont, and what happened to me before?" I asked.

"And this is all based on you seeing one four-door sedan once, that happened to drive away when you called the police."

"Yes. But do you really think it was just a coincidence?" I pushed.

"Maybe that was just a one-time deal. The night after Goldstein was here. Maybe he thought he would have stirred up some discussion between us he could use. Maybe the guy in the car had one of those bionic ears, and there's nothing in the house."

"It would be nice if you're right. But we can't be sure."

"Any ideas?" Patty asked.

"Yes."

"What?"

"Disinformation."

"What do you mean?"

I told her my plan.

The next morning at work I called her at home and she picked up on the bedroom phone. I told her, in a soft and nervous voice, that Sal had contacted me and told me to meet him at the Price Chopper supermarket parking lot in Lee at nine that night.

"How come?" Patty asked.

"I don't know. He wouldn't say. He insisted that I show up; that it was important."

"Do you think this is safe?" she asked, following the script perfectly.

"I don't know. It could be unsafe not to show up."

"Oh, no. Now you've got me worried."

"I know. I'm worried too. I'll talk to you later." We hung up. Now, if anyone really was listening, they had all day to plan their surveillance.

At eight o'clock that night, when I finished my shift, I called Patty at home. "Okay, dear, I'm off. Wish me luck."

"Oh, honey, I'm so worried about this. Please be careful. Call me as soon as it's over so I can stop worrying.'

"Okay. I will. I love you." And I hung up.

I dawdled around the ER for a few minutes. I got my stuff together. I went out to my car. I drove slowly out of the parking lot. I didn't notice any cars behind me. I slowly drove to Lee. I parked under a big streetlight in the back of the parking lot near the dumpster. I got out of the car, locked it, and leaned against the back of it. I watched the traffic. I watched people come and go, pushing shopping carts.

It was five past nine and a big, dark blue Mercury LTD sedan drifted up to me. The person inside beckoned me to get in. I got in the back seat. Then Patty drove me, in Margaret's big car, to the back of the parking lot of Lee National Bank, a few blocks away. She parked in a dark corner and turned off the lights. I got into the front seat.

We grinned at each other. We sat there for almost an

hour, listening to the radio, talking and eating a pizza she had picked up at Athena's Restaurant. It had green pepper and onions and it was very good. We each had a bottle of beer.

No police cars came storming in from all directions with flashing lights. No SWAT teams surrounded us. No unmarked sedans cruised through the parking lot. How disappointing.

We concluded that if we really were bugged, they wouldn't have missed an opportunity like that. It made us feel better. A lot better. But it was not absolute proof.

For the next few weeks Patty enjoyed giving me fictitious messages at home. When I'd walk in the house, she would say things like, "Oh, Don Corleone just called. He wants you to call him back." I'd return after a long walk with the dog and she'd say, "J. Edgar Hoover called, he wants to know if you're free for lunch on Wednesday." One time she said, "Jimmy Hoffa wants to know if he can stop by this weekend." She can be such a smartass.

Chapter 13

My next shift at work was a Saturday day. It was the last weekend in August. The next weekend would be Labor Day. Saturday mornings could be kind of nice because it wasn't a weekday and the hospital was much quieter; there wasn't the hustle and bustle of people coming in for physical therapy; the office staff was absent, the lab was on skeleton staff. People were home, not at work or traveling to it, maybe they were sleeping a little later and they wouldn't start getting into trouble for a few hours yet.

I was relieving Howard Barker who was still working a shift or two a week. I hadn't really warmed up to him yet. His private practice was developing slowly. He was overheard telling people, in the ER, "You know, this isn't really an emergency so I can't take care of it here, but if you want to come to my office tomorrow I can help you with this." That's really sleazy. This is a small town. In a rural area. Lots of people don't have regular doctors. Lots of people come to the ER for non-emergency stuff like colds and flus and aches and pains, and we, meaning Will and me and the director, feel that as long as we're helping people we're doing our job.

Barker was still on our bad side because he sucks up to patients and gives them whatever they want even if it's inappropriate and this got us into that fiasco with the president. We've all seen him using his stethoscope on a patient's back through clothing, even a shirt and sweatshirt. You can't hear breath sounds well if the diaphragm of the stethoscope is not on the skin. You can't hear well through a layer of clothing, let alone several. Barker says he can do it because he has very good hearing. I say that's baloney. He's just making it look like he's listening but he's just going through the motions because I think he doesn't really care. Of course, the patients don't know the difference.

So I politely but not warmly went up to Barker to say hello, ask how his night was and if he had anything to sign out to me. He didn't. Good. Then I went to the coffee room. Barker hadn't vacated the doctors' room yet so I didn't move in with my coat and knapsack and stuff. Helen was working, having traded shifts with the usual day secretary. We sat and had coffee. She had a woman's magazine on her lap and I sat down and looked at the pictures with her. We looked at the fashion pictures and passed judgment on what we thought of the models and their clothing and figure and hair and makeup. As we went on page by page we laughed harder and harder and our commentary got more and more acerbic. "She's dressed like a slut. Look at that hair, it must be glued with hairspray. So much makeup, it must be a half-inch thick. Real people don't dress like that, she's got to be real impressed with herself or on the prowl. Look how skinny these girls are, they must be anorexic. They can't be that skinny and have breasts that big, they must be on the pill or had augmentation," Helen said.

After her break was over she went back out to her desk. I set myself up in the doctors' room and started in on the newspaper. In a few minutes she called me and I went out front. The nurse was showing a lady into a cubicle. She was my age. She had long braided blond hair and light skin. She explained that she had a home birth two days ago and the placenta never came out.

Oh.

"Oh. Tell me," I asked, "where is the baby now, and how is it and who is with it?"

"Oh, the baby is a girl, she is home with my mother."

And who delivered this baby?"

"My husband. He's been trained."

"I see. So the placenta never came out?"

"No, the umbilical cord is still protruding."

We were standing in the cubicle. She was wearing a long flowing batik Indian skirt. She began to lift the bottom of it. She had Birkenstock sandals on, legs as hairy as mine and there was the umbilical cord swinging between her knees, brown, dry and stiff with its characteristic curlicues. *Uh oh.*

Her blood pressure was normal, she amazingly had no fever, and she was not short of breath. She sat down on the stretcher pretty comfortably. Her heart sounds were good with no murmurs. Her lungs were clear. Her palms were pink, her eye membranes showed no pallor.

We had her change into a Johnny gown and then I examined the rest of her. Her abdomen was still stretched out and baggy, as it should be. She didn't have any particular tenderness to deep palpation.

157

"Well," I said, a hundred thoughts spinning around in my mind, "there's a bunch of things we need to do." And quickly. This woman was lucky to be alive.

While the nurse started a big bore intravenous line in her left arm, I drew blood for blood cultures and some other blood tests from her right arm. We quickly hung a bag of a gram of cefazolin, a broad spectrum antibiotic, to run in as a piggyback with the IV line. I took a culture swab, and after letting the patient know what I needed to do, I swabbed the most proximal end of the umbilical cord and the introitus. We need to know what germ we're dealing with here.

To have such a big chunk of dead tissue up her uterus with an umbilical wick hanging down into the outside world was an infectious nightmare waiting to happen. She could have been dead by now. She could get real sick real fast. In the old days it would have been called puerperal fever and it was a killer and still could be. God watches out for kids, drunks and crazy people. I asked her if there was anybody with her. She said her husband was in the waiting room.

I paged the obstetrician on call and then I went into the waiting room. There wasn't anyone there. I looked around and then saw a tall, plainly dressed man with thick red-brown hair and beard walking my way with a Styrofoam coffee cup. I asked if he was Mr. Harris, and he was.

The two of us sat down on one of the hardwood benches in the hallway. He was pretty quiet and reluctant to say much. I congratulated him on the birth of his daughter. She seemed to be doing well, he said. I urged him to have the baby checked out by a pediatrician. He gave me a noncommittal nod. I told him his wife told me he'd been trained. "Yeah," he said, "I read a book about it."

I'm all for do-it-yourself projects but I don't think

childbirth should be one of them. If things go well that's great, but things can go wrong real fast and then you could end up with a dead baby, or a dead mother or a baby damaged for life.

I told him that she had a high infection risk and we had started her on antibiotics. "Oh, no," he said, "we want to breastfeed and we don't want any chemicals to get into the milk."

I thought about that for a moment. This guy just doesn't get it. "Sir, although your wife is stable at the moment, she really is in a very precarious situation that could turn very bad very quickly. She's got two pounds of dead placenta sitting in there that by now is probably teaming with germs like staph and strep and a bunch of others, and if they succeed in breaching the membrane between the placenta and the uterus and get into her system she could go into septic shock.

"Septic shock is when your bloodstream is seeded with bacteria which give off toxins that result in circulatory collapse and death. That's why she needs antibiotics, now, and she needs an obstetrician to get that thing out of there." He just looked at me, eyes wide, and nodded. I tapped him on the knee and told him how glad I was that she was here now and suggested he sit with her. I promised to check in with her often and I'd let them know what the obstetrician has to say.

As I was about to go, he said, "We just wanted to have a nice cozy home birth. The natural way. She was great. She went through labor like a trooper. But the placenta wouldn't come out. The book made it seem so easy. But the placenta just wouldn't come out. I pulled on it slow and steady for hours but it never loosened up. I massaged her belly for hours but it wouldn't come out. Why didn't it come out?"

The book made it sound easy. Right. And figure skaters make it look easy. Women used to die all the time

159

in childbirth, hadn't this guy known that? "She might have something called a placenta accreta. It means that the placental cotyledons are too tightly adhered to the uterine wall and won't peel off. I've already called the obstetrician. We'll see what he has to say."

I went back to the doctors' room and pulled an infectious disease textbook off the shelf and began to furiously leaf through it. I ran out to the nursing station and called the pharmacy. I ordered some more intravenous antibiotics. I asked for gentamicin to cover gram negative bacteria, and clindamycin for the anaerobes. This lady needed it all. She was a ticking time bomb.

The obstetrician returned my page. I had met him a few times before and I liked him, though I did not know him well. I told him the story. All he could say was, "I can't believe this, I can't believe this, I wonder why she waited forty-eight hours to come in. Maybe she had trouble finding the place? I'll be right over. You got an IV in?"

"Oh, yeah. A big one. She's getting a lot of normal saline."

"You start any antibiotics yet?"

"Oh, yeah. I got her all cultured up. She is getting cefazolin now and then she'll get gent and clinda. I'm getting all the pre-op stuff done."

"Good going, Charlie. Will you let the OR know?"

"Sure. See you soon." He clicked off.

Wow. This is going to be interesting. I wondered what he was going to do. I didn't know if he could curette out the placenta. Scooping out all that rotten tissue might be too dangerous. It could send a massive volume of germs into her bloodstream. He might have to take out the whole uterus with the placenta undisturbed within it. I wondered if she had any other children. This one would likely be her last.

I got busy with some other patients. One was a regular guy who was working on his woodpile, a common Berkshire pastime for men. He was limbing a tree and a branch fell down and got him on the top of his foot. It was black and blue and swollen and painful. Even if he had safety shoes with steel-capped toes it wouldn't have helped this injury to his instep. The X-ray showed that his second and third metatarsal had undisplaced fractures. I gave him pain meds and had him keep it elevated with ice on it. I spoke to the orthopedist, who would be in to cast it. I would've done it for him.

Another guy came in who was fifty-three years old and was visiting his friends who had a summer home on one of the local lakes. He was from New York City and was having a great weekend. His hosts had a motorboat and took him water skiing. He hadn't done that in decades. He was a pretty sedentary city dweller and was not accustomed to much exertion. Toward the end of his water ski session he began to have pain is his chest, which he thought was muscle strain from hanging onto the tow rope. The guy was complaining of a lot of pressure. We wheeled him into the cardiac room and before he knew it, I had an oxygen mask on him and one nurse got an IV in one arm as another drew bloods from the other and I hooked him up to the EKG. He asked why we were all swarming all over him just because he had such charley horses from water skiing. I didn't look forward to telling him my version of the story. As I was running the EKG they gave him a nitroglycerin tablet under his tongue and within two minutes he was feeling noticeable but incomplete relief. By that time I had the EKG and was reading it and he had ST segment elevations and flipped T waves on the anterior leads confirming he was having heart muscle damage.

His wife was in the waiting room and I went out to ask her to come and join us.

"Mr. Haimes, I have a different reason for your chest pain other than from overexerting yourself when you were water skiing. Rather than harming your chest muscles, you've damaged your heart muscle. You were asking your heart to perform more work than it was able. Your coronary arteries weren't able to supply enough blood and oxygen to the heart muscle to do all that work and some of the heart muscle got choked off a little and is damaged and that's why you are having pain. It's called angina pectoris and the EKG shows me that you are having a heart attack. You're here and you're stable and your pain is much better already and that's all good, but it's always a bit of a fragile situation and there are things we need to do to keep things stable." I paused to let things sink in.

"But how could it be a heart attack? I've never had any trouble with my heart before."

It sounded like a stupid remark but almost everyone says it.

"Well, Mr. Haimes, there's a first time for everything. All day long I see people with things they've never had before. You've never been exerting yourself so heavily at this age before. So, there are some things we do to let your heart rest and not work so hard. We'll keep giving you nitroglycerine, which relaxes your vessels. We'll give you a medicine called a beta-blocker and this stops your heart from beating too fast or too hard. I think of it as like putting a block under the gas pedal of your car so you can't push it down too far; it won't let you go more than twenty miles per hour at twelve hundred rpm and you can't get out of second gear. Another thing we need to do is to give you a continuous intravenous drip of lidocaine. This is a medicine that calms down the electrical wiring system in your heart. Sometimes when you have damaged heart muscle the nerves in the heart that get the muscle to contract in an organized, synchronized manner can get messed up. It's like having static in the system, and when that happens you can't pump blood properly; your pump fails. This medicine makes that less likely to happen."

"I just can't believe this," said Mrs. Haimes, "he's never had any trouble with this before."

"Is there any history of heart disease in the family?"

Mr. Haimes replied, "I don't know. My father died when I was young. I'm an only child."

"Do you know what your father died of?"

"No. They just said he dropped dead."

"It's possible then that he had sudden death from a massive heart attack. There are other possibilities, but that one is near the top of the list. Do you see a doctor regularly at home?"

"No, not really. I only go in once in a great while when I'm really sick or I have a bad cold I can't shake."

"Do you have a regular doctor?" I asked.

"Well, I do but whenever I go I don't usually see him. I might see one of the other doctors at the HMO, or a nurse practitioner."

"When was the last time you had an EKG?"

"Oh, I really can't say."

"Do you know if your cholesterol or triglycerides are high?"

"I don't know."

"Have they been checked?"

"I don't know."

"When was the last time you went in for a thorough overall physical exam with lab tests and health care screening?"

"I can't remember if I ever did."

"How come?"

"Because I only go in when I'm having a problem. They're always so busy there."

"You haven't had your prostate checked? You haven't had tests for blood in your stool? You haven't had your blood pressure checked?"

"They haven't told me I needed anything. I just thought I was a pretty healthy normal middle-aged guy."

I couldn't believe this. He must be one of those guys who only heard what he wanted to hear. No doctor who considered himself a primary care physician would neglect to do these things. Unless I was wrong and they really were that sloppy.

"Your friends whom you're staying with. Do they live here full time? Would they have a local doctor they use who we can call for you?"

"I don't know. Can't I go home?"

Wow. He still doesn't get it.

"Sir, you're having a heart attack. We are doing everything we can to stabilize you in a potentially precarious situation. We need to finish these things and transfer you up to the Coronary Care Unit."

"Wow. It's that bad, is it?"

"Well, everything so far is going well and you're stable. But things can happen; this can be unpredictable. The safest place is to have you here. I'll give a call to the doctor who is on call for the CCU this weekend and he'll be in to carry on with your care."

"You can't take care of me?"

"No, I just work here in the ER."

"Well, if I have to stay, I'll stay."

The X-ray technician came with her portable machine to take a chest X-ray and I got out of her way and let her. When she was done, I finished taking my history and finished examining him. He was a nice enough guy but I couldn't fathom how a guy his age could be so oblivious to his own health care. It seemed that he was in as good shape now as he could be and it was likely he would do well, barring the long list of unpredictable mishaps that could befall him. I got him all tucked in and went over everything with him and his wife, and then once again with their friends.

That done, I went on to see the other patients who had filled up the ER. Nothing serious. A little kid with a bad sore throat and an earache. A sprained ankle. A backyard mechanic whose socket wrench slipped and the back of his hand got cut on a sharp edge of the bracket that positions the alternator against the V-belt. The laceration was dirty and greasy and after I numbed it up, I scrubbed it out pretty hard with a surgical scrub brush.

By the time I got a break for lunch it was almost two o'clock. I went down to the cafeteria just as they were closing. My favorite cook, the one who wanted the X-ray, turned his back to me. I picked up a pre-made sandwich and went back upstairs. I poked my head into the surgical office and the coordinator there told me that the lady was done and gone, the obstetrician had to do a hysterectomy, and that it was really gross, a cup of puss spilled out of the uterus.

I hid out in the doctors' room to have my sandwich and a can of Coke. Margaret found me; she was working three to eleven. She had come in early and we sat and gabbed for a while. The scuttlebutt, she said, was that the other docs and the director weren't too fond of Howard Barker either, keep this under your hat, and his tenure probably won't be long here.

Around five o'clock my buddies Morse and Fremont came to visit me. The department was quiet. Helen was watching with big eyes. Margaret was upstairs somewhere. I wouldn't have thought they'd work on a weekend.

"Hello, gentlemen. What can I do for you?"

"There've been some new developments we'd like

to talk to you about." *Oh. To talk to me. How nice, I might be wrong, but that might imply an actual dialogue.*

Some staff were in the coffee room. I took them into the doctors' room.

"Would you guys like a cold drink?" If I wasn't going to cooperate, at least I could be polite. I wondered what happened to Goldstein.

"No, thanks, Doc. We'd like to show you a picture."

"Okay." Morse opened up a small briefcase and took out a manila envelope, opened it and drew out an eight-by ten-inch photograph. He handled it himself, unlike the first time.

I took the photo. It was in color. It was of a handsome young man. My age maybe, give or take a few years. His hair was on the short side, longer than a crew cut, not long enough to lie flat on his scalp. He had nicely arched eyebrows, like a movie star. His eyes were large and blue. It looked like a studio shot for an actor. He had a nice smile, a medium-sized nose, a very engaging appearance. Like a guy you would want to know. I sat on the chair behind the desk, looking at the photo.

"I'm sorry, I don't know who this guy is," I said.

"This man's body was found last week," Morse divulged, paused, looked at me, waited for me to bite. I didn't.

"There was a kid who got a metal detector for his birthday and he was poking around the edges of a tobacco field in the Connecticut River valley a few miles from Bradley airport. He got a signal, started digging and found this badly decomposed body." He paused, looking at me, waiting for me to respond. Fremont watched me in profile. I wondered what was metallic on the body that the device picked up on. I didn't think they could find anything more than a foot deep. Must have been a shallow grave.

"His name was Anthony Spumoni. Junior. Tony Spumoni, can you believe it? He was a known member of organized crime. He was low level." I wondered how they identified him.

"He'd been missing for a couple of years. He was identified by dental records." Pause. I wondered how he died.

"They did an autopsy on him. Due to the advanced state of decomposition, the information was limited. His bones didn't show any evidence of a bullet or a knife wound. The hyoid bone in the throat wasn't broken so he probably wasn't strangled."

"The coroner is suspicious that he had a blunt force head injury. The most he could find was a possible hairline fracture at the base of the skull.

"Anything to say?" Pause.

"No. Did the poor guy have kids? A wife?"

"As a matter of fact, he had a wife. I doubt if he was much of a husband. Do you know why we're asking?"

I've never understood for sure why these guys have asked me anything. I could think up some guilty reasons of my own, but I didn't know for sure.

"We found his fingerprints in the back of the same liquor store in Springfield where we found yours." Pause. "He was a career hoodlum in the Hartford, Connecticut, area."

I was calm. I wasn't fidgeting. I was calm and relaxed with the knowledge that I was not compelled to give an answer. And they hadn't asked me a direct question. As long as my mouth is closed, I can't get into much trouble. I felt like Thomas Becket. Although eventually Thomas Becket got into big trouble.

Morse and Fremont looked at me, then at each other and then at me again.

"Can you tell us how you think both of your fingerprints ended up in the same place?"

I could guess but I'm not saying.

"No," I said.

"Here's what we think. We think you were brought to this guy because he was injured. Evidently there wasn't anything you could do or maybe he was dead when you got there and then they buried him. We think that your involvement in this was coerced. This guy was a very dirty, involved kind of guy. We've been trying to build a case against some mid- to high-level mobsters. Can you tell us all you know about this guy, who brought you to him, whoever else was there, anything at all that might lead us to building more evidence against these people?"

I sat there and stared at them. "There's nothing I can tell you about it." *Notice the word "can."* I'd open myself up for trouble if I spoke.

We three sat quietly for a moment, looking at each other.

Finally Fremont broke the silence. "Make believe, if you will, Doctor, just make believe that you as a doctor went to see an injured man in the back of a liquor store. You are probably tense and intimidated. You see a man who has what might be a life threatening injury. You aren't in this nice emergency room with the comfort of all your staff and machines around you. You want to help the guy but you have no resources. Do you think you'd be able to recognize and remember other people who were there as bystanders? Maybe one or some of them could have been involved in this man's injury?"

I sat there quietly and calmly thinking this through and trying to anticipate what they were trying to manipulate me to say.

Finally I asked Fremont, my voice barely louder than a whisper, "How many legs does a dog have?"

Puzzled, Fremont said, "Four."

I said, "If his tail is also a leg, how many legs does a dog have?"

Still puzzled, Fremont said, "Five."

"No," I replied, "it would still only have four. Because calling a tail a leg doesn't make it a leg."

"What the hell kind of a riddle is that?" Morse asked.

"I don't know. Abraham Lincoln said it. And I think it applies. Gentlemen, do we have anything more to talk about?" I was hoping I appeared calm and controlled but I could have used some oxygen and nitroglycerin. And maybe a beta-blocker.

"Once again we drove way the hell out here and you continue to stonewall us," said Fremont, and they left.

I stayed in the doctors' room. I held the photograph in my mind's eye. It was true; I did not know who the man was. I hadn't lied. I had seen him before. I had not divulged.

It was three or four years ago, during the dark times. Sal probably called me up and I probably met him after work, at night, in the dark, in the parking lot at the Price Chopper supermarket in Lee. We drove to somewhere in Springfield or Holyoke or West Springfield and cruised through a diminished looking industrial area and parked behind a liquor store. Bob got out of the driver's seat of the van, walked slowly around the front, his coat opened for easy access to his hardware as he scanned the parking lot, the adjacent buildings. He opened the sliding door on the van and I got out with my knapsack. Sal got out too, from the front passenger seat. They closed the van doors and Bob rapped on the steel door of the back of the building.

"That you Bob? Sal?" came a muffled voice from the other side of the door.

"Yeah, it's us, and the doc," Bob replied, and the door opened.

Inside, to the left of the back door was a big area where they dealt with returnable bottles and there were boxes stacked to the ceiling and huge three-foot-wide clear plastic bags full of just Coke cans, or just Budweiser cans. To the right of the back door were shelves and shelves full of cases of liquor, I saw cardboard boxes labeled Fleishman's, Canadian Club, Black Velvet. There was a high desk with clipboards hanging in front of it; lots of magic markers; box cutters. Must've been for inventory and deliveries.

There were carts with wheels to roll around stock; there were handcarts. There were two middle-aged men, two older than that. And then there was the guy on the floor.

I went over to the guy. He was on his back, on the gray concrete floor. Someone had put a few thicknesses of corrugated cardboard under his head, as if it were a pillow. His hair was matted with blood and some blood oozed from his ear.

"What happened?" I asked, of anyone who would answer me.

"What do you think?"

"Sal, I need to know," I volleyed with annoyance.

"He got hit."

"With what? A stick, a fist, a bullet?"

"I don't know. Maybe all three."

"When did this happen?"

"A couple hours ago."

He was a nice looking young man. Nicely but modestly barbered. He had high arched eyebrows like Gregory Peck's. When I examined him and lifted his eyelids, his irises were vivid blue. He was wearing a mock turtleneck sweater, woolen pleated slacks and Europeon loafers.

Even though he was out cold, in a coma, he looked like he was a nice guy. The kind of guy you would want to like you. This was despite my knowing that nice looking people weren't always nice. I'm not quite that naïve anymore. But I was giving this victim the benefit of the doubt.

I was kneeling on the floor looking at him. I looked up at the men and asked, "Has he moved at all since he's been here?"

"No, I don't think so. Did you see him move, Joey, since he got hurt?"

Joey, or whatever his name was, had his back to us. He was at one of the warehouse shelves and was opening up a bottle of Chivas Regal. He helped himself to it. Maybe he owned the place; I never knew. He took a gulp right from the bottle and then wiped his mouth with the back of his hand.

"I didn't see him move. But then I haven't been watching him too close." He took another gulp from the upended bottle and then handed it to one of the other men, who took it eagerly. Charming.

The guy's color looked good, his lips were pink, his fingers were warm and pink, not blue or cold. His breathing was regular. I stood up and got one of the clipboards from the work station and put a fresh sheet of paper on top. I got a pencil from a Seagram's coffee cup. I took the guy's pulse, steady but thready, blood pressure (142 over 78), respirations (18) and temperature (99.1°). I wrote it all down on the clipboard, with the time.

I had to wrestle the guy's shirt off and was reluctant to jostle him too much because if he had a spinal neck injury I could make it worse. I ended up cutting the shirt off using a bandage scissor that I had in my knapsack.

So he was breathing and circulating well enough. I took out a little plastic airway from my knapsack. It is just a cheap little plastic thing shaped like a question mark that you put in a guy's mouth to prop the teeth open and nudge the tongue forward to help keep the airway open.

I put on a pair of latex gloves and began to palpate his skull. I didn't feel any crunchy broken areas. There was a swollen hen's egg on the left back of the skull. He didn't respond at all when I palpated it firmly, trying to see if I could feel a skull fracture beneath it. I couldn't, but what he really needed was to be in a real hospital and get X-rays. He had some blood in his left ear. I used some wet Q-tips to swab out some blood and I looked in his ear with my otoscope. There was blood behind the eardrum, it was dark as a plum. There was a little dusky black and blue area behind the guys left ear and this is called the 'battle sign.' That and the blood behind the ear suggested a basilar skull fracture. Pretty serious.

I listened to his heart and lungs and they were okay. I palpated the abdomen and it was soft and normal. I palpated him all over, from fingertips to toes and everything in between to look for damage. I didn't find any.

His pupils were midsize and they constricted when I shone my penlight in them. Viewing his retina with the opthalmoscope showed normal blood vessels and no bleeding on the retina as might occur with head injury. When I rocked his head from side to side the eyes stayed fixed in his head, like a doll's.

I tapped his reflexes with the rubber hammer and they were all there; brisk. When I shouted in his ear and shook him, he did not respond. When I poked his palm and his feet with a little needle, he reflexively withdrew the limbs.

I sighed and sat back and looked at this man on the floor.

"Well?" asked Sal. I looked at the men, who were still nursing the bottle of Scotch.

"Well what?" I responded, maybe a little insolently.

"How is he?"

"He needs to be in a hospital," I replied.

"No can do, Doc. Isn't it just a concussion?"

Did you learn that on television?

"Not if he's been this deep this long. He at least has a contusion and it could be worse than that."

"What's a contusion?"

"Well a concussion is a brief disturbance of consciousness, lasting minutes, that results from a traumatic impact on the brain without anatomic damage to the brain. This guy has been out for hours, I surmise, since you guys are so soft on giving me details. This suggests at least a contusion, which is an actual bruise of the brain. I can't find any focal deficits to tell me if there is a traumatic laceration of the brain with bleeding. We should take him to the hospital and get a CT scan."

"Forget it, Doc."

"Why?"

"Can't do it. Leave it at that."

"No, I won't leave it at that."

"Doc. Jesus, Doc, he stays here. Anyway he was a bad man. Take it from me, society will be better off if this guy doesn't make it."

"Don't give me that crap again. You say that all the time. This guy is not as neurologically far gone as a couple of the others. You know that. He could still be salvageable. He probably is. Check things out with a head scan, if there is an expanding bleed it wouldn't be a big deal for a neurosurgeon to go in there and suck out the clot and tie off the bleeder. He could live. If he's such a bad man then he could go to jail. It's better than dying here on the floor of a storeroom."

"Doc, just do what you can do."

Damn right. I'm gonna try to do more than you let me.

173

I got my coat and grabbed some of the other guy's coats without asking and put them on the floor. Grudgingly one of the men helped me get the man on the coats. A little padding and off the cold hard floor. On his side. His mouth was going to fill up with saliva and he had no gag reflex and I didn't want him to suck it into his lungs and get aspiration pneumonia.

I sat on my haunches next to him on the floor trying to think of what else I could do for this person. I got up and stretched, and walked around the storeroom. I didn't make eye contact with any of the men. They were standing around, sipping, talking quietly.

I looked at my watch. I'd been there for half an hour. I got the clipboard and took his vital signs again. Everything was about the same. He was still out of it. Neurologically he was stable. Reflexes still brisk. Pupils still reactive. Breathing steady. Still withdraws his limbs to painful stimuli. No more active bleeding from his ear. I rolled him back onto his side.

It was getting late and I was tired and I was disturbed. I found a folding chair and opened it in a shadowy corner and sat down and closed my eyes.

"Hey, Doc, how long are we gonna be here?"

"That's up to you. The sooner we get him to a hospital the sooner we can go home."

"Don't start up that shit again."

"Then I stay here as long as I say I stay here."

A minute later one of them asked, "Why do you need to be here?"

"To take care of him." *You moron.* "To see if there's anything more I can do for him."

I tried to nod off in my chair. But I kept waking up every few minutes to look at my watch so I could recheck him. This man did not need to die.

A few hours went by. At my two o'clock check his exam had changed. The difference between his systolic and diastolic blood pressure increased, his pulse decreased, his reflexes were sluggish and his response to pain was markedly less. *Shit. Shit, shit, shit.* The poor bastard. I kept pulling his eyelids open and measuring the size of the pupils. One was five millimeters, the other four and a half. Not enough of a difference to matter, but the rest of his exam had definitely deteriorated.

"What's the matter Doc?" asked Sal. The guys found a deck of cards and were playing on the inventory counter. They'd opened another bottle and were smoking cigars. They were having a grand old time.

"He's getting worse, that's what's the matter. His coma is deeper. Something bad is going on in his brain. Like he's bleeding into it. We have to take him to the hospital. It's really critical now. He's not going to make it otherwise." I was speaking calmly, quietly, trying to sound reasonable.

"Don't start up with that shit again, Doc."

I was mad. "Come on, Sal, just once, let me take one of these people to the hospital. I'll keep you guys out of it."

"Don't start up, I said. Don't get me pissed off."

"You pissed off? You pissed off? You think I care if you get pissed off? How do you think this poor bastard on the floor would feel? I'll bet he'd be pretty goddamn pissed off, with you guys letting him die right there. I'm a little pissed off myself, did you know that?"

All the men were looking at me. I'd never spoken to Sal this way before. I was mad. I was disgusted.

"Come on. Give me your car keys. I'll take him myself. Just help me carry him to a car. I'll go by myself. It won't be your goddamn problem anymore."

"Doc, calm down and shut up," Sal barked.

"You want me to calm down? This isn't the time for me to calm down. I'm trying to save that poor bastard over there and you want me to calm down?"

"It can't be done."

"Why the hell not? He could be saved. To leave him here, that's murder!" I shouted.

"His blood isn't on our hands," said one of the other men.

"Bullshit! Then you're just as murderous as the bastard who hit him! You guys are pretty fucking blasé about human life, aren't you?"

It got so Sal was looking pretty annoyed. With a sweeping motion of his right arm he swept back his suit jacket, reached under it and his hand came forward with a huge black gun. *Great. Now he's going to scare me. Hey, Sal, you forgot to take the cork out of the end of it. Like he's really going to shoot me, an unarmed guy, a doctor, just because I'm doing my job.*

Sal is a big man. He raised the gun up in his outstretched hand, up just under his eye level, pointed down at me. It was a big black gun that looked like the military handguns in World War II movies. The hole in the end of the barrel was immense. The room was silent. Seconds went by.

His thumb moved and cocked back the hammer. It sounded like vise-grip pliers snapping closed. The click reverberated in the concrete storeroom.

Now I was scared. I started backing up. Sal followed my movement with the muzzle of the gun. He didn't say anything. His expression didn't change.

Now I was very scared. I backed up into the shelves and I heard some bottles jostle. I was sweaty and prickly and I could hear my pulse in my ears. He had my attention. I hadn't said a word since he'd pulled the gun.

"Doc," he said, and then he paused, for what seemed like many seconds. "Doc, I'll shoot you right now and you can die on the floor right next to your buddy there.

Or you can keep your mouth shut and not say another goddamn word and get out of here."

I stood up against the shelves behind me, pouring sweat, my hands holding onto a shelf at waist level behind me, looking at the big dark hole in the end of Sal's gun. I didn't say a word. Sal didn't move. He was holding that big gun pointed right at my face in his big meaty fist. I felt my heart beating, banging around in my chest.

A minute went by; everyone in the room was frozen.

Finally Bob broke the ice. He went over to the guy on the floor, grabbed some coats and brusquely ripped them out from under him. The guy's head made a hollow thud when it bounced on the floor. Bob walked over to me, handed me my coat. "Come on, Doc, let's go."

I took my coat. As I took it Sal lowered that goddamn gun. I didn't say a word and I followed Bob out of the building.

Yeah, I recognized that guy in the picture Morse and Fremont showed me. But I didn't know him. Whatever case Morse and Fremont were working on, they'd have to do it without me.

Until that day I could almost like Sal. I could almost make excuses for him. But what he did that night crossed the line.

Chapter 14

The phone rang in the doctors' room and woke me up. It was the nurse letting me know that a patient was coming in momentarily with belly pain. I grunted acknowledgment and rolled out of bed. I splashed my face, brushed my teeth and emerged in search of a cup of coffee.

I stood in the dark, outside the ambulance entrance, breathing the cool mid-September night air. It was five in the morning and the stars were still out. The air smelled fresh and moist. In another few weeks when the leaves started to fall the air would change and smell musty.

It had been a pretty quiet night. When I came on at eight o'clock the night before there were a bunch of little things to deal with, but nothing critical. Margaret was on until eleven and when things quieted down we sat around in the coffee room chitchatting and playing Hearts. Joan the night nurse came on to relieve Margaret and we hung out for a little while. Doug the friendly night watchman, a retired game warden, wasn't on. At midnight I stretched out on the sofa bed in the doctors' room and took a catnap. At two in the morning I got called to go upstairs to pronounce an elderly patient who had expired.

The lady with belly pain was thirty-three years old and lived in Housatonic. She worked at the Becton Dickinson plant in Canaan, Connecticut, which is about twenty minutes from here. BD makes injection-molded plastic medical supplies like syringes. She was probably going to get needled by some of her own products. They ship their products all over the country, if not the world, and yet they're made right here in the Connecticut Berkshires. Canaan is another very pretty old New England town. The Housatonic River runs right through it, too.

The lady started feeling crummy when she went to bed the night before. She was crampy and achy in the middle of her stomach. She tossed and turned and never really fell asleep. She kept expecting she was going to vomit but never did. Now the pain was more in her right lower quadrant of her abdomen. Her blood pressure was normal. Her pulse was 85, her temperature was 100.5°. Her lungs were clear; her heart sounds were normal. Her belly was slightly distended but when I percussed it the drumming sound was not high pitched. Listening for bowel sounds with the stethoscope revealed only occasional quiet gurgles and tinkles. She was tender all over the lower abdomen, maybe more so on the right side. She did not really display classic "rebound tenderness."

That's when a patient can tolerate slowly pushing your fingers indenting into the belly wall but when you suddenly remove them, the rebound, that's what hurts. It is a clue to peritonitis. She only had mild guarding, which is involuntarily tightening up your stomach muscles when someone is palpating your abdomen, to protect what's in there that hurts.

Appendicitis is easier to diagnose in men than women because women have more stuff in there, like ovaries and fallopian tubes, that can confuse you. The differential diagnosis includes an ovarian cyst, endometriosis, fallopian tube trouble like an ectopic pregnancy, pelvic inflammatory disease and kidney stones.

When I did the pelvic exam her uterus did not hurt when I wiggled her cervix. Sweeping the adnexa on the left side was okay but achy on the right. When I did the rectal exam she clearly had pain when I poked to the right, toward her appendix.

She had a negative pregnancy test, a normal urinalysis. Her complete blood count showed an increase in the number of white blood cells, her sedimentation rate was also up. Her chest X-ray was normal (I didn't expect it to be abnormal but I figured she was going to go to the OR anyway and they'd need it); the flat film and lateral decubitus film of the abdomen looked okay to my eye without big dilated loops of bowel or air fluid levels. I had her typed and crossed for two units of blood, which is a standard pre-operative precaution. We started an IV.

I called the surgeon. He was a fairly new guy in town. Young, about five years older than me. I liked him. He was quiet; funny; a man of few words and they were usually sarcastic. He talked slowly but moved fast; he was very efficient. I presented the case to him in a formal medical fashion. "Yeah, yeah, cut the crap, do you think she has appendicitis or not?" he interrupted me. "Okay, I'll be there in twenty minutes. You wanna let the OR know?"

"I already did."

I took care of the details, discussed it all with the

lady. I spoke with her husband, then she spoke to him. He'd drop the kids at a friend's house and come right back.

It was almost seven, time for the nurses' shift change. The hospital was waking up. The surgeon came, spent five minutes with the patient, made some calls and then sat down with us in the coffee room. Will, who was relieving me, brought donuts. The surgeon wolfed down a Boston Cream and then lit a cigarette. He was lounging catlike stretched out on the vinyl two-seat couch with his leg up on the other seat.

"Charlie," the surgeon asked, "is your shift over at eight?"

"Yes."

"How would you like to scrub in on this case with me?"

"Gee, I'd love to. But I haven't been in an OR since I was in med school. I don't know what kind of assistant I'd be." I'll miss services again this morning. Dad will understand.

"That's okay. I won't need you to do anything that a reasonably bright Cub Scout couldn't do."

"What if you drop dead during the case? Would I have to finish it?"

"I'd prefer it if you'd forget the case and give me CPR. You gonna help me or not?"

"Sure. I'd love to. Let me just call my wife and tell her I won't be home for a while."

When I'm on overnight I usually change into OR greens and a lab coat. They are comfy like pajamas, and good in case I get to sleep. We went into the OR men's locker room and I put on fresh greens, a mask, shoe and hair covers. I went to the scrub sink. I took a scrub sponge and squeezed it, making a popping sound as the plastic wrapper split. Then I stopped to think if there was anywhere I wanted to scratch

181

before scrubbing in. Nope. Good. I started the traditional five-minute hand scrub, box method. Each finger-dorsal, ventral, this side, that side. Scrub sinks have a foot pedal under them and a clock over them. Gotta do it for five minutes. Up to your elbows. Then you use the little red plastic pick that comes with the sponge to clean under your nails. You shake off into the sink, hold your still dripping arms out in front of you with hands held together and with your rear end you push open the swinging door into the OR where the scrub nurse hands you a sterile towel to dry off with. Then they help you into your sterile gown. You put your hands out straight like Frankenstein, push your arms into it and then they scoot around and pull it onto you from behind. If they like you they'll tickle you or give you a little goose at this point, then tie the strings of the gown closed. Then you put on your sterile gloves and there is a proper way to do this so as to not violate sterile technique.

"You wanna prep?" the surgeon asked me. The lady was already on the table with an endotracheal tube coming out of her mouth and a blood pressure cuff on one arm and the IV in the other. There were EKG leads taped on her chest.

I took the long sponge tongs, dipped them in Betadine and began painting her abdomen in ever-widening brown circles.

"Nipples to knees my boy, nipples to knees," he said. He likes a big prep.

"Come on, Leonardo, this isn't fine art. Make believe you're painting a barn. Be fast. Be sloppy. Atta boy."

I splashed the brown Betadine prep soap all over the place like he wanted me to. Three times. That's the tradition. He placed the green sterile cotton surgical drapes around the surgical area.

"Okay. This here is the anterior superior iliac spine,"

182

he said, touching that top part of the hip bone at the lateral right waist. "This here is the belly button." I had my hands planted on the surgical field. Sterile technique dictates that when you are doing nothing you plant your hands somewhere sterile and keep them there so you don't absentmindedly scratch you head or push your glasses back up your nose. "And here is McBirney's point."

"Did you know Dr. McBirney is buried in the Stockbridge cemetery?" I asked.

He stopped what he was doing and looked at me for a few seconds.

"Now how the fuck do you know that?" Use of four letter words is common in ORs.

"I read it in the *Eagle* a few years ago. In Bernard Drew's Berkshire history column."

"No shit?"

"Nope. Charles McBirney. He had a summer home somewhere just north of Glendale Middle Road. You know what other famous doctor is buried in the Stockbridge cemetery?"

"William Osler?"

"No."

"Harvey Cushing?"

"No. Edward Livingston Trudeau."

"Who the hell is Edward Livingston Trudeau?"

"He was a doc in New York City in the eighteen fifties and he got tuberculosis. So he went to the Adirondacks to rest, where he had a spontaneous remission, and he credited the clean cold mountain air for it. He started the sanitarium movement for TB with rest and fresh air. He was a distant ancestor to Pierre Trudeau, the Canadian prime minister, and of Gary Trudeau, the cartoonist."

The surgeon was still staring at me across the patient.

"Very goddamn interesting, professor. If you're finished with your lecture now would you very much mind helping me take out this lady's appendix?"

He went from McBirney's Point to McBirney's incision, deftly wielded his scalpel with the #10 blade through the skin, placing retractors for me to hold as he went along, through the external and internal obliques and the transversalis. "There's the peritoneum," he said. He slit it open. Then he reached a few fingers in and fished around in the viscera until he found the large intestine. "See the taenia?" These are fibrous bands that run longitudinally along the large intestine. There are three of them.

"You find any one of these and just follow it south, hand over hand till you get to the cecum and turn it over and there's Mr. Appendix." Just like that. He put two clamps on the appendiceal base, slipped the knife between them, and sliced off the appendix. He handed the distal clamp with its red wormy appendix to the nurse who dropped it in the stainless steel kidney pan to go to the lab.

"Was it very inflamed?" I asked.

"Of course. When I take out an appendix, it's always inflamed. Very inflamed. Extremely. Almost ready to burst. Another ten minutes and it would have been a mess. Of course it's very inflamed. Did you ever hear a surgeon say, 'Nah, it was only inflamed a little bit?' Uh uh. We surgeons like a sense of drama. They're always terribly inflamed."

"I'm sorry. What was I thinking?" If I hadn't been sterile I would have thunked myself on the forehead with the heel of my hand.

He put some ligatures under the remaining clamp to cinch off the stub so quickly I could scarcely follow his hands. He removed the clamp. The nurse slapped a needle holder, pre-threaded, into his hand and he made a purse string suture around the stump, just picking up a little of the serosa with each bite as he went around the appendiceal stump. He tightened up the purse string suture and invaginated the stump and the little sack closed over the stump and the stump disappeared.

"Now it's time to get the hell out of here before all the donuts are gone," he said behind his mask.

He was throwing in 3-0 Vicryl sutures where he needed them. We backed out layer by layer, muscle by muscle. I held the skin edges together with forceps while he closed them with staples.

We were done. Sixteen minutes. "It would've been twelve if you hadn't given me a friggin' history lesson." The nurses bandaged her up, extubated her and took her to the recovery room. The surgeon went in to dictate the operative note and talk to the husband.

I casually sauntered into the coffee room, still in OR greens with the surgical cap on, the face mask dangling from my neck, shoe covers shushing on the floor as I walked.

"Look at Charlie: he thinks he's a big surgeon now, just back from his tough case in the OR, with his cute little OR cap still on," Will said.

I smiled.

"How did it go?"

"It was great. It was fun. That guy is amazing, you can barely see his hands move."

"I hear he's real good."

"You know it was a whole different tone. When I was a medical student, the OR was a pretty nasty place. You just stood there holding retractors waiting to have your head bitten off by the surgeon or the assistant or the resident. There was always such hostility. There was such a pecking order. They'd swear. They'd throw instruments. This was a ton of fun." I looked in the donut box but there was only one left. I wasn't going to touch it.

"Go ahead and eat it," said a nurse.

"Not me. The surgeon has his name on it."

I lounged around for a little while in the coffee room. Then I changed into my regular clothes, collected all my stuff and put it into my knapsack and said goodbye to the staff. I went downstairs and out of the main hospital entrance and headed to my car in the back of the parking lot. It was a beautiful day. It was nine-thirty in the morning, the sun was bright, I was squinting and I sneezed. The colors were starting to turn. Too bad I have to go home and go to bed. Maybe I'll take Maccabee for a long walk first.

Being that I was in a parking lot it was not a surprise to hear a car engine coming up behind me, but there were empty parking spaces closer than where I was parked. The sound got closer. It was very bright and I was squinting. I turned to look over my shoulder and a big dark car, I think a Lincoln Town Car, was drifting right over to me. I stopped and watched it. The car was black and it was a bit dusty and I could hear the sound of little pebbles on the pavement getting rubbed by the tires. It stopped right in front of me. The right front passenger door opened and a man got out. The upholstery inside was dark red. Maybe burgundy. He was big; he was sneering; I didn't like him and his nose was up in the air.

"Hi, Doc," he said as he opened the right rear door. I could see part of someone in the left rear seat.

I looked at the man standing outside the car. He opened his golf jacket to display a handgun on his belt. "Get in," he commanded.

"Oh, no." I said. "What's this about?"

"Get in," he said more firmly. "We wanna talk to you."

"Oh, no," I repeated. *Not this crap again.* My pulse went up, my breathing got short, all my muscles tightened. Reluctantly I unslung the one knapsack strap from my shoulder and moved toward the car door. As I began to bend to get in the car I swung my knapsack into the guy's belly, shoved him against the car door and sprinted across the parking lot towards the woods, trying to zig and zag a little to dodge any bullets coming my way. I sprinted like I had never sprinted before. At the far side of the lot, almost at the woods I judged myself to be more than accurate handgun distance away and I dared to shoot a glance over my shoulder to see what was going on. The guy I shoved was just regaining his balance and another guy was outside the car, glaring at me. No guns were visible but I kept running through the woods that were the uphill border of the hospital property. Fifty yards into the woods I stopped, panting. I looked back and I could see through the trees. The two men got back in the car and drove off.

I stayed there catching my breath. *Will they circle around and catch me when I come out of the woods? Where will they expect me to come out?* There were roads farther up in front of me. I walked deeper into the woods thinking about what I should do. The woods were pretty, and although I like being in the woods I was not at all relaxed. *Someone I know lives on the road above. Who is it? And is it on this side of the street?* I didn't have my knapsack with me anymore. Years ago I sometimes carried a gun in it. *Who is it that lives up there?* Susan the LPN on second floor evenings. We were at a Christmas party at her house once. She has a little kid, maybe she's home.

I kept walking up the hill trying to be quiet. Dry leaves crunched as I walked, branches snapped with every other step, it was breezy enough so the leaves in the trees made some white noise to cover my footsteps. The slope leveled off and the walking was easier. I kept going. The sun was bright and it was still cool. I walked for five or ten minutes. Finally, in the distance I saw the back of a house. I went toward it cautiously. I thought it was Susan's. I stopped and watched. I couldn't see if there was a Lincoln parked in front of it. There was a minivan in the driveway.

I sat and watched. I sat there for a long time. I thought about all this craziness that has been fermenting around me. I regretted whatever risk I was putting people under. Like my wife. Like maybe my mother. Years ago, in the dark days, Sal and his merry men had my parents' house trashed, to be a lesson to me about misbehaving. I didn't want anything like that to happen again.

The minivan on the driveway implied someone was home. If suddenly a man unexpectedly came through your backyard and knocked on your door and you had a little kid in the house it would be pretty scary. Unless you recognized who it is. Before they shot you.

There was movement in the house. I changed my position so I could see better in the window. I hadn't seen any cars moving past the house. I saw Susan lift her infant into a high chair. She came over with a bowl. She probably wouldn't do that if there was a big dark car full of thugs parked out front for the last hour.

I waited another twenty minutes. I made my move. I walked across the yard slowly, keeping my eyes on the road for the Lincoln. I went into the screened-in side porch and rang the doorbell.

Susan came to the door and recognized me through the window. At first she smiled and then she looked surprised.

"Oh, Charlie come in, come in, I was so worried about you." She pulled me in and closed the door and locked it and sat me down. Her daughter was in her blue Fisher Price plastic high chair playing with Cheerios. Sunlight was streaming in the kitchen windows where we sat, at the back of the house.

"I just heard on the scanner that there was an APB out on you that you disappeared from the parking lot. Are you okay? You're all scratched up." I assured her I was fine and must have gotten scratched when I sprinted through the brush.

"What happened?"

"Some guys tried to cram me into a car," I said.

"How did you get away?"

"I ran like hell. I better call the police." Sue already had the portable phone in her hand.

I called the GBPD. "Hello, this is Dr. Charlie Davids. I hear you're looking for me?"

"Oh thank God," the dispatcher said. "This is Ruthie, remember me? You treated my daughter once. Let me put you through to the sergeant."

MacPherson got on the line. "Jesus Chollie, where the hell are you? Are you all right?"

"I'm fine. What are you doing at work? I thought you always work in the evening?"

"Where are you? What the hell happened?"

"Three guys with guns tried to stuff me into a car and I ran away. I worked my way through the woods and I'm at Sue Dunn's house." I asked Sue the address and gave it to MacPherson. He said he'd be right over. I called Patty at work but she wasn't there. When she heard I was missing she shot right over to Fairview. I called the ER to tell them I was okay.

MacPherson was there in minutes. I thanked Sue and she said, "Sure, Charlie, stop by any old time."

I got into the front seat of the cruiser. I buckled myself in. I looked at all the stuff on the dashboard. Microphones and transceivers and radar apparatus.

"Wow!" I said, "can I play with all these buttons and knobs?"

"Damn it, Chollie, stop fucking around!" MacPherson shouted angrily. "We're going to the station to make a report. We've had units rolling all over the place looking for you. Staties too. We thought you were abducted."

"I almost was."

When we arrived at the police station there was another cruiser pulling up at the same time and a young patrolman got out. Another car came screeching into the lot. It was Patty. She hastily parked, jumped out and practically knocked me over. Her face was furrowed and her eyes were wet. She hugged me and buried her face against me.

"Charlie you bastard, don't do this kind of shit to me."

What could I say? "Patty, I didn't exactly want this to happen."

We went into the police station. I went to the bathroom. Then we all went into a small conference room. The table was bolted to the floor so maybe it was an interrogation room.

Patty and I, MacPherson and the patrolman sat down. They had clipboards and forms in front of them.

"Tell me what happened. Every detail."

I told them the whole story. I worked overnight. I scrubbed in on a case. I hung out in the coffee room. I went to my car. It was bright. I was squinting. I heard a car motoring slowly toward me. I turned and looked. Lincoln Town Car, dark, new, clean. Massachusetts plates, didn't get the number. Three guys: one driving, one in the back, and one in the front right who jumped out. I described the guy.

They asked questions in great detail about what the men looked like and said they would try to come up with a composite sketch and then look at mug shots. I told them the guy flashed a gun. MacPherson asked if it was a revolver or an automatic. "Automatic. He told me to get into the car. I hesitated. He told me again. I made like I was going to get in. Then I swung my knapsack into him, shoved him and ran like hell. Hid in the woods. Came out at Sue's house. Watched for a while. You know the rest. What do you know?"

"Well about ten-thirty this morning a lady brought an orange knapsack she found in the parking lot into the front office, said she was looking for the lost and found. Sophie, the secretary, opened it up and saw your name in it. She called the ER; they said you'd gone home an hour ago. Will heard about it. He went out to the parking lot and saw your car was still there and he thought it was fishy. He called the police. We ran through the hospital, couldn't find you. We called Patty. A little old lady on the third floor was looking out the window and saw the whole thing. She remembered a big car coming up to a young man in the parking lot, one man shoved the other and ran up into the woods. So that's what we know. Tell us what we don't know."

"What do you mean?"

"Tell us what we don't know. Tell us what's missing. Who were these guys?"

"I don't know."

"Who do you guess they might be?"

"I don't know."

"What's been going on with the FBI?" I looked at Patty.

"They told me not to talk about it."

"Now we're asking you to talk about it. How do you expect us to help you if you don't level with us? We're here in town to help you. To protect you. Do you see any of your FBI friends in here right now?"

Patty opened up her purse and took out the FBI agents business cards and slid them across the table to MacPherson. "They are not our friends. Please call them up and you can talk to them person to person, law enforcement professional to law enforcement professional. Are we done here? If so, I'm taking Charlie home. He worked all night and has had a tough day."

MacPherson paused for a moment. Then he said, thoughtfully, "You know, I could push you much harder on this. But we're friends. I don't think its wise for you to think you don't need our help. It may not be wise for me not to push you harder. I hope nothing happens that will make me regret this."

Patty said nothing.

MacPherson shrugged his big shoulders. "If you have nothing else to say then I guess we're done."

Patty beckoned for me to get up. I did. "Thank you, gentlemen, for your effort and your concern," I said, and then Patty and I left the police station.

Chapter 15

I was happy to get home after my Saturday day shift. It was busy at work but thankfully there weren't any codes or motor vehicle accidents or nasty stuff. I was tired. I wanted to get home and hug my sweetie, maybe the two of us could take a walk around the block with our puppy and then we could kick back and relax and have a beer or two. Patty had been away most of the day at some hotel in Springfield at a CVS corporate conference on security or something. She never liked those very much.

It was early October and it was dark and cool and the evening smelled good, like fall was in the air. As my footsteps on the wooden porch drummed a signal into the house I could hear Maccabee start to welcome me. Patty's car was in the driveway, the lights were on in the house. I was in the living room playing with Mac and rubbing behind his ears as he was jumping on my knees.

Patty came up from the back of the house barefoot in jeans and a sweater. She gave me a big long wrap-around hug and a kiss and I melted.

"Come back and let's have a cold one while I finish cleaning up. How was your day?"

"It was good. It was busy. Heard some good jokes. Nobody died or got badly hurt. Only one admission. It was good but I'm pooped. Margaret says hello. How was your conference?"

"It was very good. I learned a lot. I did some shopping. I got some things for us. Let me show you, I'll be right back." She put her Genny Cream down on the table and walked out of the kitchen.

I sat down at the kitchen table and took off my shoes and stretched. Mac came over and I picked him up and put him in my lap and he immediately began chewing on my tie. I took it off, rolled it up and put it on the middle of the table where he couldn't get at it and finish ruining it.

Patty came back into the kitchen carrying two blue plastic boxes, one on top of the other. They were the size of cigar boxes. She sat down opposite me at the table with the boxes in front of us.

"I got us a couple of guns," she said very matter-of-factly, as if she said she got us a couple of nectarines.

"You what?!" I exclaimed explosively, in annoyance and disbelief.

"I got us a couple of guns, like I said. In case you haven't really been taking it all in, we haven't exactly been living the most secure lifestyle lately. I took a handgun course today and I bought these weapons and I want to tell you what I learned."

"You took a handgun course? I thought you were going to a pharmacy course."

"I told you I had a course in Springfield today, about security. You filled in all the other blanks yourself."

"That's because your pharmacy courses are usually in Springfield on Saturdays at hotel conference centers. Don't you think that that was just a little devious and disingenuous?"

"Oh Charlie, settle down. I'm trying to do something to make our lives a little safer. One of us has to."

"That's not fair. I've been trying very hard to keep us safe and keep my mouth shut and resist my inclination to help out the Feds. And I don't see how bringing guns into the house is going to do anything but make us less safe."

"Need I remind you that you were very nearly abducted not so long ago?"

"Where did you take this course anyway?" We were still sitting at the table with the blue boxes between us and I was trying very hard not to raise my voice. I don't remember ever being this upset with her.

"At the Smith and Wesson Academy. Their factory has been in Springfield for a hundred years, or more, and a few miles away they opened up this training center. They have all kinds of courses for civilians, police, all kinds. They also have a store there, which is where I bought these. They're used, slightly, not new. They were much cheaper than the current models."

Great. She saved us money by buying used guns. I'm so pleased.

"How did you buy them? Don't you need a license to buy a firearm?"

"I've got one."

"When did you get one?"

"Shortly after you nearly got kidnapped."

"Why didn't you tell me?"

"Because I knew you wouldn't like it. But it's something I think is important and I don't need your approval."

"How did you get a license?"

195

"I went to the Great Barrington Chief of Police; he even had it expedited for me."

"For what reason?"

"Isn't it obvious? But I also told him I'm a pharmacist. Sometimes I'm the first one in the drugstore in the morning. Sometimes I'm the last one out at night. He agreed that a lady pharmacist, alone, was vulnerable and that it was sensible that I was asking him for a way to defend myself."

"You've never been threatened on the job, so far, have you?" I asked, though I guessed if it ever happened she would have long since told me about it.

"No. Hasn't happened. I hope it never does."

"Do you think about it? Worry about it? What do they teach you about it?"

"Every chain must have its own policy. But mostly it's give the guy what he wants, be it money or drugs, make it quick and easy so he gets out and doesn't hurt anybody. And if you can, hit the hidden button for the silent alarm. There's got to be some solo private pharmacies where the old guy's been robbed so many times that he keeps a gun or a baseball bat." I nodded.

"But your real reason for getting these guns wasn't for the pharmacy, it was for this stuff going on with me, wasn't it?" I asked. She nodded, reluctantly.

"Patty, I've had a gun, I've practiced with a gun, I've lived with a gun, I've had them flashed at me and pointed at me and I've been shot and I don't like them or want them. They're killing tools."

"Funny, I'm thinking of them as lifesavers. Look, Charlie, I understand, I know what you've been through. But you're being emotional. I'm trying to be pragmatic. I wish you would be too."

"Aren't you the one who gave me a long diatribe about how much you always hated guns, and about JFK and Mr. Levinson's cantaloupe head and how you have to cross the street when you see a cop with a gun-belt?"

"Yeah, that was me. But things are different now. It isn't as contradictory as it might seem to you. Faced with new threats, I'm adapting. To survive."

"Explain it then."

"Well, I was never personally threatened before. We have been now. A threat to you is a threat to me. I am personally involved in whatever happens to you, you know. Oh Charlie, it's an animal instinct. It's like the mama bear that doesn't even know she's pregnant but a minute after her cubs are born she'll fight to the death any wolf that even comes near.

"Yes, I've always been terrified of the horrible damage that can come from the end of a gun. But now we're threatened. I've never been threatened like this before in my life. And I need to have some power to protect myself. And you. I need to have some sense of control over this threat. I want to be behind that gun, and have that kind of power available to me if I need it. It gives us an option. It gives us an option we didn't have before. It gives us the option to be deadly if it comes to that. And yes, I do appreciate how very scary this is. This has not been at all easy for me, I want you to know that."

She sat there looking at me waiting for me to respond. I glared at her and finished my beer. I thought about just getting up from the table and walking upstairs.

Slowly, cautiously, tentatively Patty opened the top box. She lifted the hinged lid and turned it so I could see it. "This is the one I got for you. It is a Smith and Wesson Model 'Chief's Special.' It takes .38 Special plus-P cartridges, five of them. It's okay to have all five chambers loaded, you don't need to have an empty chamber under the hammer for safety because there's a transfer bar. It has a blued finish and a three-inch barrel. The grips are walnut and it weighs twenty-four ounces."

I just stared at the thing. It was ugly. There was a lock on the trigger. "It's unloaded, right?" I asked.

"Yes. Locked and unloaded." Then she closed up that one and opened up the other one.

This one was a little smaller, was gray in color, had a smaller barrel and smaller grips. "This is the one I got for myself. It is smaller as you can see, it also takes .38 Special plus-P bullets. It has a two-inch barrel, five chambers also, and it weighs fifteen ounces. The cylinder is titanium and the frame is an aluminum alloy. This model is called the 'Lady Smith.'"

"You gotta be kidding."

"What?"

"It's called the Lady Smith?"

"Yeah. Why, is that funny?"

"Is there a Lord Smith? Are we into the aristocracy of guns now?"

"That's just what they call this model of gun that they market toward women."

"How demure. Is the grip designed to fit more comfortably in a woman's smaller hand? Is it ergonomically designed to better conform to a woman's dainty frame? Can you get bullets that have fragranced gunpowder so the crime scene will be pleasantly perfumed? Jasmine? Sandalwood?"

"Charlie, stop it."

"Is it designed so it won't get lost in the bottom of your handbag? Does it come with different colored grips so you can accessorize your wardrobe? Is it designed so the recoil won't chip your nail polish? Can you get matching bullet earrings? Does it come with a vibrating attachment for personal gratification?"

"Charlie, stop it!!" Patty shouted. "You're being obnoxious!"

I didn't say another word. I got up and opened another beer. I flopped down at the table with body language that I hope expressed my annoyance. I gave a little whistle and Maccabee came running over. I put him in my lap again. We played. Then I took him out in the backyard. Both of us were barefoot. It was cool. We were at the point where we could trust him off his leash when we took him out at night. The grass was cool and wet with dew. We hadn't had a hard frost yet and the leaves were still on the trees, I looked up and still had a limited view of the stars. I walked over to the garden and plucked off a mint leaf and put it in my mouth to suck on. I could hear but not see Mac moving around in the bushes. Guns. Never good things to be around. There's going to be tears.

I rolled my shoulders and started walking carefully in the dark toward where I last heard Mac. My hands were in my pants pockets and I was walking slowly lest I bang my bare toes into something.

The back door opened and Patty stuck her head out. "Aren't you two guys going to come back in?"

Mac went running over to the door and I followed. I wiped my feet on the doormat. We hadn't taught the dog how to do that yet. The blue boxes were still on the table.

I sat down at the kitchen table again. I picked up the beer bottle. Patty sat down across from me. She reached across and held my hand.

"Charlie, darling, I know how much you hate violence and so do I. But we have to do whatever we can to be prepared. To have a gun and not need it is better than to need a gun and not have it."

"That sounds like a sound byte from their advertising department."

"Charlie, I mean it. I want you to respect what I'm telling you."

I said nothing.

Patty went on, "We should have one of them upstairs loaded in the bedroom and another in the living room on the sideboard hidden in a folded newspaper. Both loaded."

"Well, if they taught you anything about firearm safety today then they told you about not having loaded guns around the house. They should be stored locked and unloaded, the bullets in a different room from the gun."

"Now Charlie, what kind of sense does that make? If those thugs come back do you think they'll give us time to run around with keys from room to room to get prepared? We aren't talking about storing a deer rifle or a shotgun for duck hunting, we're talking about home security. That's what I was learning about today. I'm going to load them and put them where I said. And we can take them with us when we're out and about."

"I don't want to have loaded guns in the house."

"Why?"

"Because our nieces and nephews might find them when they come over."

"Charlie, we don't have any nieces and nephews who come over." She looked at me strangely.

"Well, when our friends come over with their kids they might find them and think that they're toys and get hurt with them."

"Charlie we don't have friends whose kids come over." She looked at me quizzically.

"Well then, maybe what if the cleaning lady comes across them?"

"Charlie, we don't have a cleaning lady." She looked at me and smiled.

"Well, what about when we invite the neighborhood over to trim the Christmas tree?"

"Charlie we don't have a Christmas tree. Why would

we? We're Jewish. You're being silly."

"Jews with guns. It's an odd concept."

"Well it shouldn't be. You know how effective the Israeli army is. Some people say that if the Jews and gentiles in Europe hadn't turned in their personal weapons, Hitler would never have been able to do what he did."

"Ah, come on. Is that another one of your Smith and Wesson and National Rifle Association propaganda stories? That an irregular number of untrained civilians with an assortment of random weapons could stand a chance against the millions of well-equipped well-trained Nazi soldiers?" I got up and picked up the blue boxes and put them in a closet so I wouldn't have to look at them sitting there between us.

We ended up in the living room and we were facing each other from opposite sides of the couch. I wasn't mad anymore. My hissy fit was over. Our legs were up on the couch and we could play footsie. Patty had Mac between her legs. He was uncharacteristically calm and quiet. He was upside down with his four legs up in the air and Patty was scratching his belly. He was in heaven.

"Okay, tell me something, because I've never understood it," I said. "Years and years ago when I took a modern history course in college they showed us World War Two movies and film clips. When they were telling us about the Holocaust they showed us some Nazi film clips. One of them was of a whole lot of emaciated naked concentration camp inmates who were standing at the edge of a big hole in the ground. There were no leaves on the trees and the Nazi guards were all bundled up in heavy winter clothing with overcoats down to their knees. The victims were just standing there, with their hands covering their privates. Men, women and children. Then the Nazis started firing at them very methodically and one by one they just fell into the hole. They just stood there. They didn't run or defend themselves or try to rush the soldiers. Not that it would've done any good. Why did they just stand there?"

"Those films were probably from Babi Yar in the Ukraine. It was a mass execution. Many hundreds, if not thousands. But you have to put yourself in these people's frame of mind. They were starved, beaten into submission. They had no clothes. They were freezing. Where could they run? If somehow they could over-power some soldiers, how much longer might they have survived? They probably already were crushed from seeing loved ones annihilated. They might have thought that if they made trouble it might have made it worse for those who'd come after them. Likely many of them were resigned and ready to die.

"You and your classmates were probably strong healthy Americans who played football and knew how to tackle people and run and you were sitting securely in a warm classroom with your American Bill of Rights, thinking, how could this happen? But these people in Europe weren't like you. Or me. They were Jews and Gypsies and homosexuals and they weren't first class citizens anywhere like we are. They were variably tol-erated where they were allowed to live. Memories of scourges and massacres and pogroms were fresh in their minds. There was also a different ethos then. Peo-ple then, in Europe, were more submissive to author-ity. It wasn't like it is here, decades later, when college students and hippies put flowers in the rifle barrels of the soldiers, when they were protesting the Vietnam War."

"Okay," I thought about it for another minute. "Nice explanation. Now, what about the Warsaw Ghetto Uprising?"

"What about it? You know the history."

"Okay. So the Nazis create a walled-off ghetto of what, a quarter-million Jews, with minimum food and supplies, and in a year or two a large number die off from disease and starvation. Then they start evacuating large numbers to be shipped to the camps and when there's maybe fifty thousand people left, somehow they get guns, smuggled in by the underground or something, and they start killing off as many Nazis as they can. So the Nazis are surprised and annoyed, and within limits the Jews do a pretty good job of it, until the Nazis bring in their big guns and get serious and incinerate the whole ghetto. Isn't that about it?"

"That's the story in a nutshell. What's your question?"

"Well, it's the flip side of my first question. At Babi Yar people didn't fight back at all; in Warsaw they fought back but what was the point? What were they thinking they could really accomplish?"

"Well, it was taught to me that it was like a David and Goliath story that didn't have such a good ending. Or the Chanukah story. But they tried. They had spirit. They gave it their best shot. It gave them hope. It gave hope to other people elsewhere who heard about it. Does it strike you as useless and ill advised?"

"What chance did they have? Did they really think they could have staved off the Nazis? Maybe they enjoyed getting their licks in. Maybe they enjoyed pestering the Nazis."

Patty said, "But there's another example of where the same desperate spirit to resist, to fight, was successful. In modern times."

"What do you mean?"

"You know, Charlie, you read *The Source*. In May of nineteen forty-eight when the British pulled out of Palestine and the five Arab nations were converg-

203

ing together to push the Jews into the Mediterranean, nobody thought the Jews could have prevailed. It was another desperate fight against overwhelming odds. That time it worked. In Warsaw it didn't."

"Okay," I pondered, "you explained it very well. As usual. I wish I took the courses you did."

"Aw c'mon, Charlie, I don't know anything you don't."

"Aw c'mon, Patty, you do too. I guess what always puzzled me is how they could be so helplessly docile at Babi Yar and so hopelessly determined in Warsaw. You explained it well. Thank you."

"You're welcome." A moment later she said, "Charlie?"

"Hmm?"

"So regarding whatever kind of threat comes our way via the FBI or via organized crime, are we going to be helplessly docile or hopelessly determined?"

Nice maneuver. She's clever. "How about hopefully determined?"

Patty nodded. "That'll do."

Chapter 16

I got to work at ten minutes to eight in the evening and there was a pall all over the whole hospital and everybody was talking about the day's tragedy. I was relieving Will Connor and even he seemed affected by what had happened. And he was a real macho guy who had the reputation for always being objective and never being emotional. Everyone was buzzing around, everyone was busy and I finally found Margaret to tell me what had gone on.

So it's fall in the Berkshires. If you want to go turkey hunting, it is in season for a few weeks. From Monday to Saturday you can go try to shoot a turkey from a half hour before dawn until noon. People, mostly men, go into the woods in complete camouflage, armed with shotguns and turkey calls. They hide in the woods and try to sound like a turkey, in order to lure a real turkey. When a turkey starts to move in toward a hidden hunter, and gets within range, they shoot at it.

Getting a turkey proves great prowess around here. Amongst the hunting crowd, it is a sign of great wood-craft to be able to conceal oneself properly, remain motionless, master the art of making the sounds of talking turkey and fooling a real one into coming to find you, and then, with all your adrenaline flowing, to be able to control your jitters and make the shot.

Well, earlier this day, a man was out hunting with his teenage son and two other adult men. To make a long sad story shorter, the father took a shot at what he thought was a turkey. When he ran over to see his trophy, he saw that he had shot and killed his own son. Heaven only knows the wails of angst that rang through those woods. The two other men came running. Heaven only knows the pathos of the scene they beheld. They told the father to stay there and they would go for help. But when they got back an hour later, the father had tried to kill himself. But he wasn't dead yet. He still had a pulse.

I didn't get every lurid detail but somehow it was determined that the father had an organ donor card in his wallet. I don't know who contacted the wife, or how the news was broken to her, or what kind of hor-rible scene must have transpired. I don't know who had to break the news to her that her son was dead by an awful mishap by his father, that the father had tried to kill himself but wasn't dead yet. *By the way, Ma'am, he wanted to be an organ donor, can we harvest his organs while his heart is still beating?*

Sparing the details, Margaret said that the ambu-lance brought the father here, Will intubated him and resuscitated him. They somehow got a cardiologist and a neurologist here to say that he was brain dead. They called the organ bank and things started to roll. Will got him on a respirator and into the OR while they waited for the transplant team to get here.

There's always a regional team on call that consists of a bunch of surgeons who are probably transplant fellows, who come with their technicians and nurses. They fly to the nearest airport in a Lear jet, using whichever corporate one is on schedule for a tax deduction that day.

The transplant team is picked up at the local airport by an ambulance and they are transported, with all their Tupperware containers and Coleman Coolers for the organs, to the local hospital. These transplant surgeons blow in, act like they own the place and take over the OR for a few hours while they do their work.

Margaret said these guys have an attitude. First of all, they are surgeons. They just finished their general surgery residency and feel like they're on top of the world. Then they get to be transplant surgeons. Then they fly through the sky in a million dollar airplane to go see some dying soul and remove his organs, who therefore finishes dying. Then they get back into their celestial vehicle and fly through the heavens to somewhere else to install these life extending organs into people who need them. How much closer to god-like can you get? Margaret said it was ghoulish and it gave her the shivers.

They got the two corneas, the two kidneys, some bone, and the heart-lung complex. Maybe the liver, Margaret wasn't sure. They didn't say much or interact much with the in-house staff, though they did accept a few cups of coffee.

Despite their attitude problem, these people do amazing things and are able to provide maybe half a dozen people with organs they have been praying for, for months if not years. If anything good can be squeezed out of a horrible tragedy to befall a family, this has to be one of the best. But it depends which side of the fence you are sitting on. Here at home in southern Berkshire County we are all grieving for this man and son and their wife and mother who suffered such an unexpected and calamitous tragedy. No doubt there will be a big human interest story in the *Berkshire Eagle* tomorrow. On the other side of the fence there are numerous members of multiple families whose loved ones are getting a new lease on life because of someone else's misfortune.

While Margaret was telling me this story, full of a tossed salad of emotions, including grief, sorrow, loss, heartbreak, admiration, pity, all I could think about was how I couldn't blame the father because I probably would have thought about doing the same thing. I thought of the story Mr. Jones told me about being there when his kid nearly got squashed by the tree, and about the poor guy who drowned in the river after jumping in to save his son and like Patty said, the guy didn't really have a choice or a chance.

We were sitting in the coffee room while Margaret was giving me this narrative. Then she got paged and took the call and needed to go upstairs. I was heading toward the doctors' room and saw Will exiting it, his coat on, no smile on his face.

"Gee, Will, a real tough one, huh?'

"Yeah, Charlie. It was a bad one. All around. Stuff happens, you know? Have a good night. I'm outta here."

The ER was empty. I drifted back to the coffee room. I sat and leafed through the newspaper.

Chapter 17

I felt like crap. I caught a miserable cold from some twerp who'd come to the ER because he thought a cold deserved an emergency visit. Who knows which person I caught it from. I decided to blame it on the person who was the most annoying.

I couldn't fall asleep when I went upstairs to take my nap. When I lay on my back the mucus gagged and choked me. When I lay on my stomach my nose would pour and when drops of secretion hit the end of my nose I would jerk awake with the unpleasant tickle on the little nose hairs that felt like an electric shock. My head hurt, my ears were stuffed, I was sweaty.

I gave up trying to fall asleep. It was hopeless. I moped my way into the bathroom and took some more Sudafed. I got in the shower and my muscle aches loosened up some. The steam cleared my head. I stayed in there a long time. When I finally felt the hot water running out I emerged, toweled off, took some Tylenol and got dressed.

I went downstairs and found Patty in the kitchen. She was holding a big bowl of cold leftover tortellini. I trudged sleepily over to her with my mouth open hoping she'd share.

"Do you feel as crummy as you look?" she asked

"Yeah. Do I look that bad?" I asked, and pointed to my open mouth, hoping for a tortellini. She tossed one in. I ate it. It was hard to breathe as I chewed.

"You look pretty uncomfortable," she said as she tossed in another piece of pasta. "Why don't you call in sick?"

"You know that isn't done," I replied, and stood there with my mouth open so I could breath and maybe catch another tortellini.

Patty stepped back the distance of a nine-inch linoleum floor tile and tossed another tortellini into my gaping mouth. I caught it.

"You know we don't do that. Not for a cold. We need to have a positive spinal tap to get off."

"You guys always say macho stuff like that: 'We have to have a hundred four degree temperature and a positive blood culture to get off.'"

"It's true. It just isn't done unless you're really incapacitated. I can still work."

She stepped back another square and tossed another piece. I caught it.

"And what is missing one shift going to do? Like I'll be all better tomorrow? Or the next day? It won't make any difference. I'll still feel crappy. What's the point of disrupting the whole schedule and everybody else's?"

She was now five squares, forty-five inches away and I almost missed one.

"I still think you should call in sick. It wouldn't be fair to the patients."

"I'll wear a mask all night and wash my hands a lot. It's not like we have a lot of back up. To call in sick usually means someone has to work a double."

She was fifty-four inches away and she missed; the tortellini hit the floor. Maccabee heard it and came right over and sucked it up. She tried it again from that distance and Mac looked at us hopefully. She missed again and Mac caught it on the rebound. She tried it again and got it right in my mouth. Good thing the pieces were too big for me to suck down my windpipe.

"When I was in training there was always someone who was trying to wimp out of night call. They had a cold. Or a sore throat. They were always looking for someone to switch shifts. Except they'd always be reluctant to make it up to you because then they might be on for two nights in a row. Payback is tough. Or they'd want to switch because they wanted to go to a concert. Within a month or two these people would be pretty unpopular. We tried real hard not to dump on each other. It was an important lesson."

"Well you aren't an intern anymore."

"Yeah, but the same ethic persists. Don't wimp out unless you have to."

She shook her head and missed again from sixty-three inches. Mac was just having a grand old time on clean up patrol. He was sitting there with his tongue hanging out drooling, watching Patty wind up for the pitch, watching the noodle fly through space and hit me in the nose or chin or cheek or eyeglasses. He was getting the hang of this and sometimes caught the little dumpling before it hit the floor.

She was stuck at sixty-three inches. Seven floor tiles. Miss, miss, miss.

"Come on, Mac's getting fat and I'm getting old waiting for you to improve your aim."

"Just one more. You know, I need to end on a positive note."

She finally got one in at seven tiles. Good. I sat down at the kitchen table and slouched and Mac put his saliva-soaked chin on my chinos. Yuck. I petted him on the head.

Patty made me some instant chicken broth since we didn't have a can of chicken soup. I could barely taste it but the warmth and the steam and the notion of it was nice.

When I finally got to the ER the place was dead. I went into the first cubicle and got a surgical mask. I struggled to get it tied on. I dumped my stuff in the doctors' room and then began looking for everybody. No surprise, I found them all in the coffee room. Will was in charge. He was sitting next to a big bowl of left-over Halloween candy.

"What happened to you? Patty smack you in the nose??"

"No. But she did hit me in the nose with a cold tor-tellini. I have a cold and I'm trying to keep my germs to myself." My nose, of course, was running and I was trying hard to not think what the inside of the mask was like. "How was your day, Will?"

In a loud and theatrical voice, Will began, "Well it was a very busy day. Very, very busy. First, I saw a kid who was running with a sharp pencil. He fell and the pencil poked him in the forearm. To get the little splin-ter of graphite out I used the eraser. Then there was a kid who was drinking a cup of hot chocolate with the spoon still in it so when he took a sip he poked himself in the eye. With the spoon. Then I saw a high school student who went to gym class with socks that weren't white, so the dye got into his pores and I had to take care of that."

Will was just warming up and the nurses and I were giggling.

"Later there was a kid whose mother told him that if

he ate one more slice of pizza he'd turn into one. So of course he had to try, and of course, he turned into one. They carried him in on a stretcher, a big round cheese pizza. Smelled good too. Had to change him back."

"How do you do that, Will?"

"What's the matter, did you miss that week in med school, Charlie? Then a mother brought in her twelve-year-old boy who she caught both drinking coffee and smoking a cigarette. So of course I had to unstunt his growth. That was a tough one. Then there was a teen-age girl who went out of the house with a wet head and she got pneumonia and I took care of her. So it was a real busy morning. And in the afternoon there was a kid who went to football practice without his jockstrap so he got a hernia."

"Of course," I added, laughing and gurgling and coughing and choking behind my mask.

Margaret piped up in a voice even more throaty than mine, "And later there was a lady who cut her thumb when she was slicing a bagel and she thought it was infected so I poured some peroxide on it and it bubbled so that proved it was infected and Will gave her antibiotics."

Will started to say something but Margaret held up her hand to cut him off and interrupted him and said, "Then there was a lady who didn't get enough sleep so she got rings under her eyes and we had to take them off."

And Will said, "And then there was a guy who ate a steak that had been frozen and thawed more than once and he came in very sick."

And Margaret said, "Oh yes, very, very sick."

And Will said, "A man came in who was sleeping on too soft a mattress and last night it ruined his posture so we had to straighten him out."

And Margaret said, "Then there was a guy who

213

worked on hard concrete floors for one day too many and he got all these varicose veins."

And Will said, "The fourth grade class clown at the grammar school was making faces and crossed his eyes and someone smacked him on the back of his head and his eyes got stuck that way and Margaret and I had to unstick them."

And Margaret said, "There was a kid blowing bubbles out of his butt because he swallowed his bubble gum and we had to get him cleaned out."

And Will said, "Then a lady came in who ate a plum she hadn't washed and she had unrinsed produce disease."

"Hey Will, I haven't heard of that one," I said.

"There's a short chapter on it in Harrison's textbook, man, you better get with it."

By this point I couldn't breathe and I ran into the bathroom still laughing and tore off the face mask. Disgusting. I rolled it up and put it in the garbage. I washed my face and my hands and tried to gargle loose some phlegm. I got another mask from the cubicle and tied it on and put a spare in my pocket. I was breathless from laughing.

I headed back to the coffee room and slumped down. It was quieter. They had finished their comedy routine and I wish they had this on tape. Just thinking about it made me grin.

It was Margaret, Helen the receptionist, Roy the respiratory therapist, Will and me. Will was just sitting there reading the paper.

"What are you still doing here?" I asked Will.

Without batting an eyelash, he said, "I'm waiting to see if I'm going to need to intubate you."

"I'm okay, I just have a cold, you won't need to intubate me, I promise."

"You want me to set up a ventilator now?" Roy asked Will.

"No, not just yet. But maybe you could do some deep suction, some chest percussion and postural drainage," Will replied.

"Sure, I can do that," Roy said, quietly getting up and heading out of the department. "I'll get my stuff. Maybe an updraft nebulizer too." He disappeared.

We sat in silence and I hoped I could doze.

A minute later Will sat up and exploded, "I can't friggin' believe this! Did you read this? Did you read the paper today? You aren't gonna believe this!"

What happened, we all asked?

"You know how there'd been a shortage of flu vaccine this fall? Well there was a GP in New Jersey who somehow got a big batch of vials of vaccine and doubled his price to give people flu shots. The attorney general was all over this guy like a bad rash for price gouging. And then it says, '... profiteering at the expense of public health is unconscionable and unacceptable...' What bullshit! Here's a poor guy just tryin' to make an extra buck like anyone else. You don't hear the AG going after the drug companies for their ridiculous prices. You don't hear the AG going after all the insurance companies who charge so much and provide less and less and pay their CEOs millions. You don't hear about the AG going after hospitals when they charge an inpatient five dollars for a Tylenol. You don't hear about the AG going after lawyers for charging eight hundred dollars to do a real estate closing in twenty minutes. You gotta be kidding me."

"Oh, come on, Will, you and I wouldn't do that," I said.

"Oh come on yourself. You and I are dinosaurs. We're warmed-over hippies. We're practically social ists. But remember, being a doctor is an occupation and a practice is a business and not everyone is as altruistic as you and maybe me and some people want to maximize profit in their business and there's no law against it and if patients don't like their price they have the choice of shopping around and going somewhere else. Hell, it's business. You know how much the airlines jack up their prices during school vacation week? Hotels and restaurants also. How fair is that?"

The intercom came on and Helen told me I had a patient in cubicle one. As I got up I said to Will, "Take it easy, Will, don't get so excited or you'll give yourself a coronary and you might be the one who gets intubated. Go home and have a beer, you'll feel better."

I got my stethoscope and went into cubicle one. I pulled back the drape and went in and introduced myself to a mother and daughter who both looked a whole lot more healthy and comfortable than I did. The girl was the patient. She was sixteen. Her hair was brown and tightly pulled back and gelled. She had on heavy eye makeup. The hoop earrings that were dangling from her lobes must have been three inches in diameter. One wrist had a dozen bangle bracelets on it and there was a boy's name written in ballpoint pen ink on the back of her hand. She was wearing a skin-tight scoop necked short-sleeved leotard top that left very little to the imagination; she was almost spilling out of it. She was wearing faded blue jeans which were tighter than skin from the knees up. It was late fall and it was cold and she was barely clothed. She smelled of cigarette smoke.

I introduced myself and apologized for the mask I was wearing but it was for their safety. No problem. They barely noticed.

I picked up the ER encounter form and there was little information on it. "How can I help you?" I asked the teenage girl. She shrugged and turned and looked over her shoulder at her mother in the corner.

She was heavy set and her makeup made her look very pale, offset by very red lipstick. She was wearing a faux leather jacket.

"She needs a note to get out of gym class for the semester," her mother said.

I didn't get it. "How come?" I asked bewildered.

"Cold sores," she said. I didn't see any cold sores.

"I don't see any cold sores."

"She had them in September," the mother replied.

"Why would cold sores keep you out of gym class?" I asked what I thought was an innocent question.

"She broke out with a cold sore in September and came here to the emergency."

"You came to the emergency department because you had cold sores?" I asked as if it didn't make sense to me.

"Yeah," she sneered, "we came because she had this big ugly half-inch sore on her lip," as if my question didn't make sense to her.

"What did they do for you, what did they tell you when you were here?"

"It was you," the girl said in an accusatory tone of voice. "Don't you remember?"

I thought for a minute. It wasn't easy. "Let me get your old records." And I excused myself. I went to Helen's desk and pulled up the patient on the computer. I ran to medical records and was back in three minutes. It is a little hospital.

I had seen her in September. I didn't remember. It wasn't worth remembering. I went back into cubicle one.

"I have the record. You had a clinically typical cold sore, no sign of bacterial infection, no significant lymph node swelling around it and I gave you Acyclovir Ointment to put on it. Then what happened?"

"It finally cleared up. But it took such a long time. Almost a week."

"Did you have any recurrences?" I asked.

"No."

"Then what does this have to do with gym class?" I asked, really not comprehending.

"I didn't want to go to gym class with a cold sore," she whined.

"Why can't you go to gym class with a cold sore?" I asked, unless they were doing intramural kissing, which might have been how she got the sore in the first place.

She looked at me and shrugged and then looked over her shoulder at her mother.

"Why would you miss a semester of gym class because you had a cold sore for a week?" I asked. I thought it was a reasonable question. I guess I was wrong.

"Well if I don't get a note from you I'm gonna get an 'F' for the semester."

"Aha. I see." *So we have a bratty kid who doesn't like gym and is manipulating me to get her out of it. So I can do the right thing and refuse and get them mad at me or I can do the wrong but easy thing and give them a note and let her succeed at being irresponsible. Let's see, what would Dr. Barker do?*

"Listen," I said, "I didn't tell you you had to stay out of gym. You made that decision yourself. You're the one who has to be responsible for it. Getting an 'F' in gym isn't the worst thing that can happen to you. I think you'll survive it. It won't keep you out of college."

"You're not going to give me a note?" she asked incredulously; she looked like she might cry. I suspect that sometimes it helped her get what she wanted.

"No, young lady, I am not." And I turned to leave the cubicle.

"Well, up yours, Mister," the little brat shot out at me. "What the fuck did we come here for?"

I turned quickly on my heel and I was incensed. Still controlled but in a low growling voice, I said, "That's easy. You came to try to get me to bail you out from your own lack of responsibility."

I left the cubicle and the curtain splayed out behind me. The stress gave me a little adrenaline rush and my skin felt sweaty and prickly and for a few seconds my nose cleared and I felt my pulse pounding in my temples. I was agitated and provoked and I walked into the doctors' room to be alone while I cooled off. Dirtballs. Wait until the hospital president hears about this one.

My next patient was a twelve-year-old girl who came in with her mother. They also both looked healthier than me. But maybe not. They were visiting from out of state. They got a call from the parents of one of her classmates back home that there had just been a case of meningococcal meningitis in one of their classmates. They were tracking down all of the classroom contacts to send them for antibiotic prophylaxis as soon as possible. Like immediately.

Meningococcus is an extremely nasty bacteria that can spread rapidly from person to person, especially young people living close together, like in classrooms, college dorms, military barracks. Sometimes people can catch it and go from healthy to dead in twenty-four hours. Or even less. It is a real infectious disease nightmare. You have to round everyone up right away and give them a dose of rifampin, a heavy-duty antibiotic used mostly these days for tuberculosis.

We didn't have any rifampin in the drug closet in

the emergency department. I called Margaret who was the nursing supervisor for the shift. She met me at the pharmacy department downstairs and with her big ring of keys she let me in. I turned on the lights and looked through the shelves. For the most part it was alphabetical. I could find the 'R's but no rifampin. Then I found a separate set of shelves full of antibiotics, all alphabetical, and I found it. I took a single 500 mg capsule, put it in a little plastic cup. Margaret locked up behind me and we went upstairs.

I gave the cute little girl the pill and a cup of water only to find that she can't swallow pills. *Oh. Now what do I do?*

I bothered Margaret again and she let me back into the department. As I poked around in the pharmacy I thought about how provincial this was. Here it is, 1987 and I'm a country doctor in a little rural hospital late at night flying by the seat of my pants. The only doctor in the whole hospital at this time of night. I found a jug of cherry-flavored dilutant and mixed the contents of the capsule into it. I left a note on the counter for the pharmacist telling what I'd done and then I went upstairs.

I gave the little girl the medicine and she it took cooperatively, down to the last drop. She and her mother were very sweet. They left the department and I wondered if this would have been a precaution or if it would have been the real thing. Did she already have the germ in her nasopharynx and she was now saved, or was this a false alarm? No way to know. If you vaccinate a million kids for polio, you don't know which ones you've saved from an awful future, but you know you'll save a lot. An abstraction.

The department was empty and it was almost eleven and I sat with Helen until shift change. We didn't have a receptionist from 11:00 PM until 7:00 AM so the one nurse in the ER did it all. There was usually a float in the house who could help out in a pinch.

I went to the doctors' OR locker room and changed into a set of greens. Then I went back to the ER doctors' room and stretched out on the sofa bed. I didn't think I would sleep. I was too wired from all the decongestants I'd taken. And too much coffee. And the Neo-Synephrine nose drops. Neo synephrine. Neo for new. Syn for synthetic. Ephrine for epinephrine. New Synthetic Epinephrine. Neosynephrine sounds better. I had a headache. It banged in my head with each heartbeat. Maybe it's a virus associated vasodilatory headache, like a migraine. Maybe I should go scarf some migraine medicine from the cabinet.

I settled down on the sofa bed. I was pretty uncomfortable but the next thing I knew I awoke with a start. I closed my eyes again and tried to recall what I had been dreaming about. It was such a nice dream; my father was there. I didn't want to lose that feeling so I decided to get up and write it all down.

I'm in an elevator accelerating rapidly. My stomach is queasy for a moment. It's a real long ride up. It's just me in the elevator. Nice wood paneling. Muzak. It's a little misty inside; cloudlike. Makes sense. Finally the elevator starts slowing down and then stops. The doors swish open and I step out into a hotel lobby. It looks very nice. I walk up to the front desk and pull my out credit card.

"Hello. My name is Charles Davids," I say to the man behind the counter. He looks up at me then glances back down at the computer.

"Yes, hello, Dr. Davids, we've been expecting you. Welcome to Heaven."

"I didn't realize you were computerized up here."

"Oh sure, we have all the modern conveniences."

Behind the counter and off to the side was a big set of gates.

"Oh, so these must be Saint Peter's Gates," I said to myself out loud.

"Or you can also call them Gabriel's Gates. You're Jewish aren't you? See my scales over there?" I looked and there they were. "Really, they're just for show."

"Pardon me, sir, are you Saint Peter?"

"No, I'm Gabriel. For Jewish people I'm usually Gabriel. But I can be Saint Peter for you if you like, watch this." He blinked and there was a little puff of mist and from it appeared a much older, baldheaded man with a pink face, white beard, long white robes with a gold braid, wings and everything.

"That's amazing," I said.

"Yeah, but you'll get used to it." He blinked again and he returned to his former self. He looked more comfortable in the corduroys and cardigan sweater.

I looked around. The place was surprisingly empty. I must have looked confused.

"Is something wrong?" the man at the desk asked.

"I thought it would be more crowded. There isn't even a line. I would've guessed there would be a lot of people checking in here every day."

"You see, we have eternity here Dr. Davids. All we have is time. It's never crowded, there's never a rush. We have a lot of entry points, too."

"Listen, sir, just a simple room will be fine for me. I don't need anything fancy. A twin bed would be fine."

"Up here it doesn't matter. You don't know this yet. You're still trying to be frugal, trying not to splurge. Doesn't matter. You can have all the comfort you want. This isn't the retirement you've been saving for.

"Also, see, it's pretty much nonsectarian up here. We're all God's angels here in heaven. Doesn't really matter what religion you came from. That was just a path to get you here. Being a righteous person is all that counts. You can go Jewish if you want to. You can go Christian if you want to. Or Hindu or Buddhist. It's multicultural up here if you want it like that."

Wow. It was a lot to take in.

"You can wear anything you want up here, too. A lot of new people wear robes for the first eon, you know, when they first get here. They like the novelty and the tradition, but then after a while they dress in something more practical."

"So I can wear anything I want? I could wear old blue jeans and a faded flannel shirt?"

"Certainly. The only thing we advise against are Birkenstocks."

"I see. Excuse, me, would you know if my father knows I'm here?"

"I'm sure he does. You know, up here, we run a very efficient operation." We shook hands and he left. I looked around. It was pretty nice. I heard something behind me and I turned around and there was my father and he looked great. He was carrying *The New York Times* crossword puzzle folded under his arm.

"Charlie, it's so good to see you. I heard you were coming. How was your exit, I hope it wasn't too unpleasant."

"No, Dad, not too bad. I don't really remember it."

"That's just as well," he said. He opened his arms and I walked into his embrace, something I'd been missing for a long time.

So Dad and I sit down and he starts to orient me about what it's like in heaven.

"It's really wonderful. It's better than the best Elder Hostel vacation I ever took. Yesterday your mother and I went to a lecture on Russian Literature."

"Mom's here?" I interrupted, surprised. "I didn't know she died."

"No, she didn't, I just imagined her up. When I miss her I just imagine her up, and I knew she'd be interested, so we went to see a lecture on Russian Literature. You'll never guess who gave the lecture."

"I give up. Who gave the lecture?"

"Fyodor Dostoeyevsky. Himself. Yesterday we went to a lecture about psychoanalysis, guess who gave it?"

"Sigmund Freud?"

"No, he was tied up, it was his daughter, Anna, who gave it. She was very good. And then she spoke a little about child psychology. You know, that was really her shtick."

"So how does it work here, Dad?"

"Well, you can do anything you want. Just imagine it up."

"You mean like you can imagine up Mom?"

"Yeah, just like that."

"But it's not very real, is it?"

"Charlie, you just aren't in the heaven mindset yet. 'Real' is a very earthly term. It'll come to you. It takes a while to get used to it. It's an adjustment."

After a while Dad said, "I have to go now."

I was brokenhearted. "Dad, why do you have to go? I just got here. I haven't seen you in such a long time. I always say Kaddish for you. Can't we have supper together?"

"Sure we can. Just imagine me up! It's the first thing you need to learn around here."

"Why can't we really have supper together," I asked again.

"Imagine me up," Dad answered again.

"So if it's all imagination, what is real here?"

"What is real here, Charlie, is that every good, kind thing that you ever did for another person all goes into your celestial bank account as an asset."

"What good does it do?"

"Well, that's how you got up here. And you know what, it doesn't even earn you interest because interest doesn't matter here, it means that you added to the positive energy of humankind since it existed during your tenure on earth. It's like Buber said, 'every good deed adds strength to the divine spark of mankind.'"

"That's all there is to do here is to imagine up any form of amusement?"

"That's one way to look at it. I admit it, it's a tough concept at first. Remember when you were a little boy and we went out at night to look at the stars and you insisted that on the far side of the stars there had to be a brick wall that was the end of the universe? Infinity is a tough concept. Human minds do not easily think that way. There are some different concepts up here that you'll get more used to over time. We've got lots of time up here. Tomorrow night I'm playing bridge with Grampa and a few others. You should come over."

"I don't know how to play bridge."

"We'll teach you."

"Doesn't it take a long time to learn how to play bridge?" I asked.

"You'll learn easily up here. All we have is time. A long time is nothing up here."

"So Dad, does religion matter up here?"

"Sure it does. But religion is just a road map to get here. We're still Jewish but up here it's not so important. Judaism is one of many paths to God's heaven. You know, there are a lot of ways to cook a meatloaf. Lots of good recipes. All good, none of them are wrong. You can have your favorites, but they're all nourishing."

"Dad, does Mom know I'm up here?"

"Oh, I suppose so. Wasn't she at your funeral?"

"When Patty dies, will she be up here with me?"

"Oh sure, presuming she continues her righteous behavior."

225

"So I'll be able to live the rest of my life with her up here when she gets here?"

He looked at me. "No, Charlie, your life is over. You'll live with her here for the rest of eternity."

"What about those cultures and religions that have a much more formal idea about heaven? This seems kinda loosy-goosy."

"Oh, they can have it any way they like it. Once in a while you'll see a Chassid walking around in a hurry and even up here they don't look happy, but that's how they like it.

"Don't forget, in the old days when people were cold and hungry and miserable and so many died young they fostered the idea of heaven to give them something to look forward to, so despite their misery they'd try to live a righteous life."

"So, Dad, who taught you about all this when you got here?"

"Moses."

"Moses? You gotta be kidding."

"No. Did you know he has a lisp? Not such a great public speaker. Who knew?"

"Moses?" I asked, still incredulous.

"Certainly. Once I even saw Abraham. I saw this old guy in robes on the other side of the street. I asked a guy near me who that is and he said, 'Oh, that's Abraham.' But Moses, he can get a little tedious after a while. He always tells the same stories over and over. He'll say, 'Did I ever tell you about the burning bush?' Frankly, I think he might be getting a little bit senile. Or, 'Did I ever tell you about the time I parted the Red Sea?' I know he was a great man, but enough already."

"Dad, have you met God?"

"No. Nobody meets God. God is unknowable, incorporeal. But every day you see his influence."

"How?"

"Well just like on earth, in life every time you look into someone's eyes you're looking into the eyes of God. It's all his work. I get tired thinking about it. Remember when you were a kid and you watched The Invisible Man on TV? The scientist who drank a concoction in the lab that made him invisible? You could only see him when he wrapped his face in gauze and put on clothes? You weren't seeing the man, you're seeing the mold around him, the shape of him. That's what it's like. But I know what you mean. I hoped to meet him too. I always wondered what I would say to Him if he sneezed.

"Oh, and Charlie, the libraries up here are fantastic. The art, the culture. You thought the Metropolitan was fantastic—you ain't seen nothing. I took your mother to see Madame Butterfly. Guess who conducted it? Puccini himself. Guess who sang the male role? Enrico Caruso. He was good, really good. He put on a lot of weight, and looked too big and old for the part, but his voice was fantastic."

"Dad?"

"Yes?"

"I miss Patty already."

"She'll be here soon."

"She's going to die soon?"

"Oh no. I hope not. But up here, an earthly human lifespan isn't such a long time. You can always imagine her up. But for her to live out the rest of her natural life down there doesn't seem like a long time up here."

"If she's eighty when she dies, how will she look when she gets here?"

"However you want her to look."

"How will I look?"

"However you wanna look. And however anyone looking at you wants you to look."

I had a scary thought. "Hey, Dad, what happens if

227

Patty remarries? I mean, I hope she will. But when she dies, which husband does she live with? Will we alternate weeks? She'll be a tired girl."

"No Charlie, you'll have her all to yourself. And so will he."

"Dad, that doesn't make sense."

"It doesn't make earth sense, but in heaven that's the way it would work. Don't worry, you'll gain the heavenly frame of mind. It takes a while. Don't try too hard. Remember when you went to college and felt you had to have it all figured out the first week? Charlie, no one really knows what heaven is, though lots of people have ideas about it. It can be whatever you want it to be."

The phone rang and startled me and it was Joan at the desk calling to tell me the ambulance was en route with a man who had a stroke and they would be here in a few minutes. It was as if powerful springs yanked me back from reverie to reality.

I washed my face and brushed my teeth and blew my nose and put on a face mask and found my stethoscope and wandered out in search of a fresh pot of coffee. It was four in the morning.

I heard the ambulance doors open and a patient was brought into the cardiac room on a stretcher. While Joan was out front getting information from the family, I started in with the patient. He wasn't conversant. He was awake and looking around but didn't answer questions, or speak, or even appear to listen to me. I put an oxygen cannula on his face. I started an IV in his arm and drew a battery of blood tests. I hooked him up for an EKG and read it and there wasn't anything acute going on. I left him hooked up to the cardiac monitor.

Strokes are so devastating. This slightly overweight baldheaded man with beard stubble on his chin and saliva on the drooping left side of his mouth might have been the most colorful guy a half-hour ago. He might have been a jolly vibrant husband and grandfather with a twinkle in his eye and a great sense of humor. But I would never know. He might be a professor or a talented artisan; he might be a bronze star recipient from heroic service in World War II; he might just be a nice good quiet man who worked hard, who provided for his family, who loved his family mightily, and I'd never get to see this, or to know him, or to converse with him.

Strokes are also confusing. It might be an embolic one and you should anticoagulate him. It could just as easily be a hemorrhagic stroke and to anticoagulate him would kill him. It could be because he had a cardiac arrhythmia, a regular old atherosclerotic stroke, or the carotid artery in his neck finally finished clogging, or he could have had an infected mural thrombus that embolized to his brain or so many other possibilities that I needed to check out and search for. Poor guy. He wouldn't want to be sitting there, drooping, with mucus on his lip, unaware of it. I cleaned him up. I had some on my own lip, I was sure, beneath my mask.

Another classification system describes three categories of strokes. First, there is the mild stroke you can recover from. Then there is the bad stroke that kills you. Worst of all is the bad stroke that doesn't kill you. This poor guy didn't have a mild one.

I did a complete physical exam and neurological exam. The neurologist would see him in the morning and decide what else needed to be done, if anticoagulation was needed, and he'd have a CT scan first thing. It is real hard to forecast how much recovery a stroke patient can have. Sometimes in the first twenty-four hours the improvement can be remarkable. The more time that goes by without improvement, the more pessimistic the outlook becomes. I hope in the future they'll have more to offer people who have suffered this catastrophe.

I spoke to the family, got some more of this guy's past medical history, and answered all their questions that I could. But I couldn't say if he'd ever bounce his grandkids on his knee again; I didn't know if he'd ever give his wife a meaningful hug again, or if he could ever tell a joke again. Such desperate questions. Time would tell. So sad.

We got him admitted; he went upstairs. I might never see him again. His attending physician would take over in the morning. He was a shell of the man he once was, a brain full of short circuits that could no longer function the way it once could.

I moped around the department with my lukewarm cup of coffee wondering if the missing part of this man's life could already be up in heaven or if it needed to all go in one package.

I ambled my way up to the third floor, went down the hallway to the north end of the corridor and stopped at the big picture window facing east. I sat down in a wheelchair and rolled myself up to the window, holding the Styrofoam coffee cup in my teeth as I used my arms to roll the chair. I put my feet up on the sill and I watched the pink tinged horizon on the dark gray sky. Some day I could be sitting just like this, in a wheelchair, parked in front of a window, with stubble on my face, drool on my chin and a brain and body that no longer worked like they used to.

The floor was quiet; I could hear the occasional snore here or there. There were soft sounds from the nursing station down the hall. The band of pink broadened on the horizon.

A chiming sound came from the desk. Someone must have pushed their bedside call button. In a moment there was the swish swish sound of a nurse's white polyester uniform and the squeak squeak of her white rubber shoes on the polished linoleum hallway floor. It came closer. It stopped.

"Oh, Dr. Davids! You startled me. I didn't expect to see you up here. What are you doing?"

I turned around. It was Harriet, the nurse I once took care of after she got pricked by a contaminated needle.

"Oh, I'm just hanging out, watching the sun come up." I answered.

She looked out the window appreciatively. "Beautiful, isn't it?"

"Yes," I said. I hoped I would continue to appreciate it for a very long time. I doubt the poor man with the stroke could anymore.

"See you later," Harriet said, and she disappeared into a patient's room.

Chapter 18

"Charlie, there are two gentlemen to see you," said Candy, the seven to three receptionist. I was in the back looking at some X-rays of a lady who probably broke her wrist. A Colle's fracture. The kind you get from falling on an outstretched hand. *I hope they aren't the FBI guys. Maybe they're just pharmaceutical representatives and they also brought me lunch. A grinder would be nice.*

"Will you see them?" she asked.

"Sure. I'm almost done. Maybe you could put them in a cubicle?"

"Sure."

A minute or two later I went into cubicle number two and introduced myself to special agents Agostinelli and Parker, from the FBI. If this had been my first time I would have been nervous, but now I was just annoyed. I shook their hands. There were two chairs on their side of the cot and I sat on a rolling stool on my side of the cot. I sat down. I acted tired. I was tired. And a little put off.

"Which office are you guys from?" I asked.

They looked at each other. I looked at them. Agostinelli was an inch or two shorter than me. He was barrel-chested, had a tan and a heavy five o'clock shadow. And it was only eleven in the morning. His hair was nicely styled and gelled. He had on an olive double-breasted suit with a foulard necktie. He wore a gold ring on his right pinkie. His partner was just as nicely dressed, in a suit and necktie with a gold collar bar behind the knot of the tie. Neither of them had a wrinkle on them. They both wore European loafers that looked like slippers. These guys dressed much better than Morse, Fremont and Goldstein. Both of them were husky.

"Springfield? Albany? Boston?" I asked.

"Springfield," they said.

"What happened to Fremont and Morse?" I asked.

"Oh, they weren't available," Parker said.

"May I see your identification?" I asked.

In unison they both reached into their coat pockets and delivered identical badge wallets. The wallets were black and shiny and the corners weren't dog-eared like my wallet. The badges were shiny and weren't burnished on the edges from wear like Fremont and Morse's. The ID cards were there, under the plastic window. The plastic window wasn't molded to the badge like Morse's and Fremont's. There wasn't any lint.

"Do you have business cards?" I asked. The other guys all had business cards.

They looked at each other. "No, we don't have business cards." Parker said. *Badges? We don't need no stinkin' badges*, I thought, recalling a line from a movie.

I took their badge wallets and set them in front of me on the cot. I took a prescription pad from my lab-coat pocket and tore off a sheet. On the back I copied down the information from their ID cards. I handed them back their wallets. "Excuse me, please, I'll be right back. I have a call to make." They looked perplexed and I got up and took my piece of paper and left them in the cubicle behind the drawn curtain.

I went to the doctors' room and sat down at the desk. I pulled Goldstein's business card out of my wallet and called the number. Now I was finally glad I'd kept it. I got through to a receptionist.

"FBI, Inspector Goldstein's office," a female voice said.

"Good morning. My name is Dr. Charles Davids. I'm a medical doctor at Fairview Hospital in Great Barrington, Massachusetts. Is Mr. Goldstein available?"

"No, I'm sorry, he is out of the office. May I take a message?"

"Yes. You see, he came out here a month or two ago to ask me some questions and he asked me to call him if I had a question. Now I do. Right now, there are two gentlemen here with me in the hospital who say they are from the FBI. I'd like to confirm if they are part of your organization or not. And if this is where they're supposed to be today. Their names are Agostinelli and Parker," and I gave her the details.

"Doctor, I'll be sure to give Inspector Goldstein your message."

"Would it be possible for you to tell me if you have any employees by those two names?"

"Doctor, they don't sound familiar to me. Let me pull up a different screen." They were more computer able than we were. "No, I don't see those names here at all."

"Thank you very much, madam, you've already been very helpful."

"Just one moment, Doctor, we are very concerned about imposters posing as government agents; that is a very serious offense. Our protocol is to alert and send out the local police ASAP to begin investigating."

"Thank you, Ma'am, please give my message to Agent Goldstein. Goodbye."

Just as I thought.

I went back out to cubicle two and it was empty.

I went out to the reception desk and asked Candy where the two men went.

"Well they left about five minutes ago. Didn't you know that? What was that about?"

I just shook my head and went in to see the next patient.

The ambulance radio squawked and whistled and shrilled. They said they were bringing in a forty-eight-year-old man who had collapsed at work and was unconscious. They said he had good pulse and high blood pressure and respirations and was hemodynamically stable. We got the cardiac room ready. Well, it was really always ready.

The ambulance backed up to the doors, its warning beeper keeping time with my pulse. The guys hopped out, opened the rear door of the vehicle and rolled out the stretcher. The legs of the stretcher ratcheted down harshly, the legs and their wheels met the ground and they wheeled the guy in.

The man on the stretcher was tall. He was thin and had thick longish wavy brown hair and a matching beard, slightly flecked with gray. Even with the oxygen mask on his face I could see he was a nice looking man. And he looked vaguely familiar. He was wearing a yellow, Oxford cloth, button-down shirt under a burgundy, v-necked sweater vest, and dark brown, wide wale corduroy trousers. Suede desert boots.

The EMTs told us he was a high school teacher in Canaan. He was proctoring a midterm exam. He was just standing around in a room with fifty or so kids while they worked. Suddenly he put his hands up to his temples, closed his eyes tight, sat down and said, "Oh God, this is the worst headache in my life," and then he keeled over. One of the kids ran out and called for an ambulance.

That story was enough to know that this poor guy was doomed.

There's a thing called a Berry Aneurysm. It is a little sack on a blood vessel that looks like a little berry. They occur on an arrangement of arteries called the Circle of Willis that surrounds the brainstem. Think of the busiest and most hectic traffic circle in Boston, with roads emanating from it like spokes on a wheel. Think of a hexagon of blood vessels with arteries exiting from each corner. The problem is that the arteries themselves have weak spots at each junction and division. Not always such good plumbing. Sometimes these weak spots slowly stretch out over time, as a result of arterial pressure, just like you blow up a balloon. Then you get a little bulge called an aneurysm. And they are weaker still. Sometimes they are congenital.

Sooner or later, as a result of the blood pressure, the aneurysm continues to stretch out a little bit more and thin and weaken until it ruptures and then blood gushes into the skull under arterial pressure. The skull is a closed space, it has a fixed volume. Blood is pumped rapidly into the skull, where the brain is supposed to live. The brain is only a little firmer than cooked caulifower and it gets squished aside by the expanding collection of blood. Important stuff in there gets squeezed and disrupted and stops working. Within minutes the volume of blood presses the brain downwards and squeezes the brainstem through the hole at the bottom of the skull through which the spinal cord exits. The brainstem is where the cardiovascular and respiratory centers are. They get crushed as they are squeezed through that opening and then it's over.

They rolled him into the cardiac room and transferred him from the stretcher to the bed. One of the nurses started an IV in the left arm and drew various vials of blood once she got in the vein. The EMT removed the oxygen mask so I could look at him. He was moving air okay, I could feel him exhale and hear the airflow in his neck and chest with the stethoscope. I put in an airway protector and then Roy, the respiratory therapist, began ventilating him with an Ambu-bag. His heart sounds were loud, fast and there wasn't a murmur. His blood pressure was 180/120. One of the nurses was cutting through his clothes with emergency medical scissors that in the ads can cut through a penny, then she put self-adhesive electrodes on his limbs and chest so we could get an EKG.

"Does this guy have a wife? Should we get a priest in here for last rights?" I asked, expecting one of the nurses milling around to transmit this to the secretary to find out.

His pupils were wide open. They were big and black with just a little rim of walnut brown around them. I shone my penlight in his eyes and they did not constrict at all.

His arms were at his sides and the hands were fisted and flexed downwards and the muscles in his arms and forearms were tight. This is an appearance called Decerebrate Posturing and was a grave sign of global brain injury. I tapped his tendons and there were no reflexes. I poked his palms and soles with a pin and there was no withdrawal reflex.

I asked the nursing supervisor to arrange to transfer this guy up to Berkshire Medical Center where they had neurologists and neurosurgeons and to get one of them on the phone for me.

His EKG showed no abnormalities other than

increased amplitude of the waves due either to his hyperdynamic state, or cardiac hypertrophy due to being an endurance athlete or having long-term high blood pressure.

The labs started drifting back and there weren't any results that were noteworthy. His arterial blood gases were close to normal.

I spoke to the neurosurgeon at BMC and presented the case as succinctly and objectively as I could. Send him up, he said. Probably nothing I can do, but send him up.

We transferred him back onto the stretcher, carefully, with all his tubes and wires and a portable cardiac monitor-defibrillator. Just as we were wheeling him into the hallway toward the ambulance door his wife ran in and threw herself across his chest, sobbing uncontrollably.

Go, go, go! I wanted to say. *Get moving!* But I didn't say it out loud because it wasn't going to make any difference and his wife was having perhaps her last moment to hold him while his heart was still beating. I just stood there, watching. *This is it, kid. The cutting edge. Life doesn't get any more dramatic than this.* You could feel the emotion in the air.

Finally she stood up and motioned for them to get going. There was a palpable wind of frenetic energy as all those people, the patient, the EMTs, the respiratory therapist, the nurse, the orderly, exited through the big double doors.

As the doors swished closed behind them we watched the big vehicle, lights blinking, roll down the hill from the hospital.

Those of us who were left in the building stood still, watching, amidst the flotsam of the tragedy. We stood amidst the cardiac bed all askew with rumpled sheets, yards and yards of EKG paper on the floor, wires and

IV tubes and lab slips all over the place. And the shreds of his sweater and shirt.

"Thank you, everybody. You all did a great job. Everybody knew their job and did it."

Poor bastard. I didn't even know his name. But at least he wasn't suffering. He wasn't feeling pain and he had no awareness. Not that it wasn't a tragic loss. It's his wife who was suffering now and will for a long time. So often it's worse for the survivor than the patient.

Someone like Will might say lightly, "Well, wasn't that an excellent example, a classic presentation of an acute severe subarachnoid bleed." Just like an ornithologist might say, "Isn't that a perfect specimen of a pileated woodpecker." Will is an excellent doctor. He is caring yet objective and detached. And he probably sleeps better than I do.

I took the ER chart and sat down in the nurses' station to start writing it up. Details, details. I was writing for ten minutes. I heard Helen speaking on the other side of the partition. "Hey, Helen, are there any old records on this guy? I keep thinking I've seen him before." She said she'd check the medical records computer and get them for me if they were there.

Just as I was finishing, Helen breezed behind me and put a file next to me on the counter. "You were right, Charlie, you saw him here two years ago," and she continued through the half door to her post at the reception desk in the ER waiting room.

I picked it up and began reading it as I walked back to the doctors' room. I had a glimmer of recognition. I could have used one of Patty's martinis, but since that might be frowned upon, I went and got another cup of coffee.

I went back to my room with a cup of stale, bitter, inky coffee and put my feet up on the corner of the desk and began reading my own notes from the time I saw this poor guy two years before.

He'd come to the ER on a quiet weeknight early evening with a headache. It had been bothering him on and off for a few days. He asked, specifically, if he might have some morphine for it. He preferred morphine because he knew it to be more natural than all of the other opioid-derived major analgesics.

Now, all doctors, especially ER doctors, are asked by patients all the time for narcotic analgesics. There are lots of patients out there who "exhibit drug-seeking behavior." A guy gets gout and the only thing that works is Tylenol #3 with codeine. The one who says he twisted his back at work and is in awful pain and is a pretty bad actor and says if only he had some Talwin he knows he'll feel better. Often these people are passing through town and rather than take in a movie, they'll try to scam drugs. We've all heard the same story many times: Some person is being treated for something painful and they accidentally knocked their bottle of pills into the toilet and could I give them a prescription for just enough to make it through the weekend.

But Mr. Burroughs was not the usual drug seeker. There was some kind of a disconnect here. As I thought about it, it came back to me as if it were a scene from a movie I'd seen last night.

We were in the cubicle together and I was asking him the nature of his headache; how long he'd had it; what part of his head it involved; whether he had a history of migraines; whether there were any other associated symptoms like light-headedness, discomfort from bright lights or neck stiffness.

He seemed disinclined to go into it with me.

"Y'know, doctor, I didn't really mean for you to get into a big process about this. I just wondered if I could get some relief."

I was a little surprised. "Well, sir, there can be a lot of reasons for a headache. Some of them are very mild and annoying and some of them can be very serious and have a lot of repercussions. Before I can give you potent medicines to deaden your pain I need to have a sense of what's going on with you. If there is something bad going on and I obscure it by doping you up you could get into big trouble."

"Well, I'll give my doctor a call. He's familiar with me and he might not need to go through all this."

"Who is your doctor?"

"Oh, he's a naturopathic practitioner in New Lebanon." New Lebanon is a small town just over the border in New York State. "I've been going to him for years."

I was looking at his vital signs on the ER chart. "You know, your blood pressure is kind of high." I took it again myself and the numbers were in the same ballpark.

"Yeah, I know, it's been like that for years. I drink special teas to keep it under control."

"But it's not under control. What tea is this? Is this from your doctor in New Lebanon?"

"It's some special herbal tea that also has ginseng in it. It has to be doing something for me." *Yeah. Right.*

"So, tell me, how many years has your blood pressure been high? It was one fifity-five over ninety. What does it usually run?"

"That's about the usual. But he feels the pulse wave in my neck with his fingers and he says the upstroke is soft so the numbers don't matter as much."

"Sir, I don't want to contradict him, but the numbers matter a great deal."

"He says that conventional doctors aren't trained in palpation of the upstroke and don't understand the nuance of it. He's a very skillful practitioner."

And you aren't as smart as I'd given you credit for.

241

"Mr. Burroughs, there are lots of reasons for high blood pressure. The simplest is called essential hypertension. There's no known reason for it other than genetics. Or, a person can have renal artery stenosis, which means the artery to the kidney is narrowed and to make a long story short the blood pressure goes up. People can have a tumor of the adrenal gland called a pheochromocytoma that can cause headaches, high blood pressure, flushing and sweats. These are all extremely important to find out about because prolonged high blood pressure can affect the blood vessels in your brain, in your heart, lead to strokes and heart attacks and kidney failure. This is real stuff, this is an eventuality, not a maybe."

"I appreciate you telling me this, but I know it's none of those."

"How can you know that? This is not within the ability of a person's five senses to perceive. We had to develop tests in order to reveal these things."

"I'm sorry doctor, I take a much more fundamental understanding about health and disease than this. I'm much more comfortable with a naturopathic approach."

"Mr. Burroughs, I have nothing against a naturopathic approach when it doesn't ignore a problem that can have serious consequences. Please let me do some tests tonight; we can do them right here. Let me examine you properly. Let's get an electrocardiogram, let's check some kidney function tests. When was your last electrocardiogram?"

"Oh, I've never had one. I've always been well."

Shit. Hasn't this clown ever heard of preventative medicine?

"Well, Mr. Burroughs, one of the best reasons for having an EKG when you are well is to have a basis of comparison for when you might not be well."

"I don't really think I want to go through any testing tonight."

"Mr. Burroughs, long-term hypertension is serious stuff. I don't think you appreciate this. This is not something you can overcome with enough tea or yogurt or tofu or chanting a mantra or walking through fields of daisies."

"Pardon me, but I think you're getting a little sarcastic."

"I guess I am and I apologize, but you aren't taking this seriously enough. Look, you came to this hospital tonight, this building where we do our best to provide modern, scientific health care. This is what enables people to live decades longer, on average, than a century ago. Please, I beg you, avail yourself of what we have to offer!"

"So, are you going to give me anything for my headache?"

"Are you going to let me evaluate you?"

"I'll have my doctor do that."

"If I can't evaluate you, I can't treat you. It would be blatant negligence to do otherwise."

"So, I guess I came here for nothing."

"No. I offered you a great deal. You chose to accept nothing. I hope you'll reconsider before something bad happens."

I was sitting there with the ER record from two years ago in my lap and a mug of awful coffee in my hand.

Helen walked in and told me Mr. Burroughs expired in transit.

When I got home after work Patty and Maccabee were in the kitchen having supper. There was a place set for me. They started eating before me because they were famished. She gave me a hug and kiss and Mac jumped all over me. When he finally calmed down I ladled myself some pasta and basil pesto sauce, opened a Genny Cream and sat down across from her.

We told each other about our day. I told her about Mr. Burroughs. I told her about the two hoods who were trying to pass themselves off as FBI agents and how they disappeared after I copied down their credentials and went to make a phone call. Patty listened attentively, her elbows on the table, slowly shaking her head as I told her about these two phonies.

"I just wonder what all these guys want from us," she said. I nodded my head in agreement.

"I want to contact Sal."

She turned, surprised, and said, "Why in heaven's name would you want to contact Sal?"

"Because there's a lot of stuff going on that we don't understand and we don't know what it is or why it's happening. I think those were mob guys who came to see me today. First it was FBI, now it's the Mob. I think it has to do with the stuff from the old days. Sal said they would leave me alone. He might be able to shed some light on it. We need all the help we can get."

"Charlie, are you crazy? Why would you go to him for help, of all people?"

"Well, we did a lot of work together. We worked pretty well together. We bonded."

"Charlie, are you friggin' crazy? This guy nearly had you killed."

"He did not. He was just trying to teach me a lesson."

"You're friggin' crazy. Any way you look at it, attempted murder is still looked upon poorly. Are you nuts?"

"Well, he said I'd be protected. It's not happening. I want to talk to him."

"Charlie, this is crazy. Just look at us. Look at what

has happened to us since the summer."

"That's what I'm saying. What peace can be found between the hammer and the anvil?"

"Who said that?"

"T.S. Eliot."

"How do you remember that? I hate it when you pull out quotes like that."

"This is nuts. Let's take a walk."

We went outside. It was dark. We walked hand in hand as we started down the block. I wondered if there were any parabolic dish listening devices aimed our way.

"Charlie, how can you want to go to that guy for help?" she asked in a soft voice but louder than a whisper.

"I told you. Maybe he can explain all this to us."

"But the guy is a sociopath."

"Aw come on. I think he's a guy who had a sordid past now doing the best he can do given the situation." Who had a temper.

"Then why didn't he let you give all those people the proper kind of care they really needed?"

"Well, without him, and me, they probably wouldn't have gotten any care at all. Don't you think that a person can turn over a new leaf? Don't you think he could have realized the error of his old ways and become a good person?"

"Charlie, I think you are letting that big heart of yours get in the way of your common sense."

"Remember Jean Valjean from *Les Misérables*? He was a nasty guy who became a good man."

"That doesn't apply. He was a good man in the beginning who only stole a loaf of bread for his sister's starving children and he was thrown in jail and had to learn to become a savage in order to survive in prison. That's not Sal's story at all. Besides, that's fiction. You

245

know that the recidivism rate is extremely high. Be real."

"Well, speaking of quotes, what's the quote you like from *The Little Prince*? 'If you want to see something really clearly, see with your heart and not with your eyes.' Did it go something like that?"

She was silent for twenty feet. "I told you I hate when you do that, Charlie. Really I'm just jealous."

"But it's a quote I learned from you. See, I listen to you. How many husbands can say that?"

"So, tell me again, what did Sal say to you?"

"When I saw him in the CCU we had a long talk. And at the end he thanked me for the service I'd given him, that he was releasing me, and that I'd be protected."

"And you believe him?"

"Why not? I haven't heard from him since."

"He might be retired. He might be dead."

"That's possible, I suppose. But what's the harm in just talking to him?"

"I think he suckered you. A good sociopath can be very charming. He played you like a fiddle to get you to do what he wanted. How about if we sleep on it for a while and see how you feel in a week?"

Chapter 19

It was ten minutes to seven on a Thursday morning and I was almost out the door to go to the minion service before going to work. I was wearing light brown corduroys, a yellow oxford cloth shirt, tie, and a sweater Patty gave me last year from L.L.Bean. I was putting on a windbreaker.

"Take your gun," Patty shouted from the kitchen as she cleaned up after breakfast. Maccabee was with her hoping for a scrap.

"I'm not taking a gun to synagogue," I responded, irritated. I glanced at the sideboard in the living room. On it was a carefully placed newspaper that was covering one of her two carefully hidden revolvers. My stomach churned to think about it. Sheesh. Years ago it was my mother shouting "Take your hat!" each time I went out the door.

As I approached the front door Maccabee charged over to see if I had a leash in my hand. I didn't, so he trotted back to the kitchen. I went out, closed the front door and the screen door. November was in the air and there were brown leaves accumulating on the front porch that I'd need to sweep up pretty soon. I hopped down the steps to the walk, hit the sidewalk and turned left heading for Ahavoth Shalom.

As I was walking in front of my next door neighbor's house a big Cadillac sedan with Connecticut plates cruised toward me and quickly pulled over to the curb right next to me. Just as quickly three men got out and looked at me. I did not recognize any of them. I nodded a quiet greeting and intended to keep walking.

"Dr. Davids, we need your help," said the oldest of the three. He had been in the front passenger seat. He was the smallest; about five feet eight, maybe a hundred seventy pounds. He had wiry dark blond hair. He had bright blue eyes but they didn't both point in the same direction. His nose was flattened and pushed to one side; he'd probably had it broken. He was dressed like he was going to have lunch at the country club.

"Do I know you?" I asked politely.

"We have a patient we need you to see," said the first guy.

"I'd be very happy to see him at the hospital," I said softly.

"No. You need to come with us."

"I'm sorry. I can't do that. I can see him at the hospital. We can keep it private, anonymous."

"No, you gotta come with us." The two younger larger men were standing on either side of him, one by the back bumper of the big car, one by the front.

"I can give him better care at the hospital than on the outside." I said. *Why am I not running? I'm pretty fast. Because my wife and dog are fifty feet away.*

"We can make this difficult for you," he said.

"If you hurt me I won't be much use to your patient."

I've been there, I've done that, I'm not doing it again. I'm not getting in that car. The two younger men leaned forward as if they were starting to move in for me.

A door suddenly slammed and in an instant Maccabee was orbiting around the four of us, doing his happy dance, hoping someone would throw a stick for him, or maybe a tennis ball or at least pat him on the head.

Patty appeared a few seconds later. She was walking toward us slowly. She was wearing my winter coat, unzipped. The coat was too big for her. Her face was white. She was walking slowly. She looked tall. Her bangs were to her eyebrows and her eyebrows were knit and lowered. Her jaw was clenched, which made her cheeks look more hollow, and she was not smiling. Her shoulders were hunched up.

She stopped walking and stood six or eight feet to my right. She looked at the older man in the middle. "I want you gentlemen to leave," she hissed, "nobody's going to kidnap my husband."

"Listen, lady, we were just talkin' to him."

"I want you gentlemen to leave," she said again louder, and her face looked as menacing as Cruella deVille's.

The men were looking at Patty's face, but their eyes kept glancing downwards and then back up to her face again. Again and again. What were they looking at?

I turned to Patty and looked at her. Her shoulders weren't hunched up any more. She still had on her Cruella deVille face. Her coat was still open. Extending from the bottom of each sleeve was an inch of gun barrel. I swallowed hard.

"Hey, lady, you shouldn't show a weapon unless you're ready to use it."

"Who says I'm not ready to use it?" she said without a millisecond delay. "No one is going to kidnap my goddamn husband. I want you to leave."

One of the junior thugs got in the car and started it up. "C'mon, boss, let's go." I could hear a siren in the distance.

The older guy moved to the car and opened the door. Still standing he turned and said, "I'll be seeing you again, Doc. You too Miss." He stooped and swung into the car awkwardly, as if his back hurt. He slammed the door and they drove away.

We watched them drive off. When they were way down the street I turned and looked at Patty. She looked at me and took a deep breath and the tension drained out of her face. The corners of her eyes and mouth turned downwards and her eyes welled with tears. I walked toward her and opened my arms. She dropped the guns in the front pockets of the coat and we hugged. "Thank you," I said, as the siren came closer and closer.

"You're welcome," she said with a quiver in her voice, and she sniffled. "I called the police and then left the phone off the hook."

As I held her she began to tremble. I looked at her and her cheeks were wet. She shuddered and sniffled and wiped her face with her hands.

Maccabee returned from wherever he'd disappeared to and was searching around my neighbor's foundation plantings looking for the right place to pee. I took him by the collar and put him in the house and then returned to where Patty was standing. The police cruiser pulled up and stopped right where, a moment ago, the bad guys had been. A young Great Barrington Police Department patrolman got out of the cruiser, put on his hat and slipped his baton into its belt holder.

"Did you people put in a call to the police?" he asked.

"Yes we did. The danger is over now," I said.

"You're Doc Davids, aren't you?"

"Yes."

"What went down?"

How much do I tell him? I better tell him what happened, but not more than he needed to know. I didn't want the whole story to unravel.

Patty spoke up. "Three men were trying to accost Charlie." She was now composed.

The policeman looked at us, confused, as another car sped down the street toward us. It was MacPherson's blue Blazer. He braked hard, pulled to the curb, the vehicle lurching. He popped out of the car, looked at us, saw us intact and his demeanor became more relaxed. It was early in the morning and his shift was in the evening. He was in civvies; blue jeans, a plaid flannel shirt. He had on his duty gunbelt and badge.

"I heard it on the scanner and I raced over," he said, looking from us to the patrolman. "What happened?"

While I was trying to think of the right way to say it Patty blurted out, "Three guys tried to kidnap Charlie."

MacPherson swallowed hard and pressed his lips together and looked at us, from one to another. He turned to the patrolman and said, "You can go, Travis, I'll take care of this."

"Okay, Sergeant." He turned to us. "Have a nice day, folks," and got in his cruiser and drove away.

"Let's go inside," he said. We sat down in the living room. Patty was next to me on the couch. MacPherson was in the wing chair. Maccabee wouldn't leave him alone. I said, "Mac, come here," in a stern voice. Mac came and MacPherson looked at me.

"Chollie, do me a favor," MacPherson said.

"What?" I asked.

"Next time you get a dog, name him something else."

I chuckled and put Mac in his crate.

"Tell me what happened. From the start."

I told him I was just on my way to synagogue like always to say prayers for my father. A new big blue-gray Cadillac drove up. Connecticut plates. No, I didn't get the number. Vinyl roof. Three guys got out and I described them. They wanted me to go with them to take care of a patient. I refused and suggested they bring the patient to me at the ER. They insisted I go with them and said it could be difficult for me if I didn't go. No, they did not issue a specific verbal threat. No, they did not display a weapon. No, I never saw these guys before. No, I had no idea why they would want me or how they might know me.

"Why did they go away?'

"Patty came out and talked to them."

"Patty came out and talked to them. What the hell did Patty say to them that got three thugs to go away?"

"I said, 'nobody is going to kidnap my husband.'" She was looking at the ceiling. She was tense. She was white. She was reliving this.

"You said, 'nobody is going to kidnap my husband' and then they just got in their car and drove away?"

"Well...."

"Well what?"

"Well, I had a gun in each hand."

"You had a gun in each hand. I see. Well. We're really getting somewhere now, aren't we? Where are these guns now?"

"They're in Charlie's coat pockets in the closet."

"Now they're in Chollie's coat pocket?" MacPherson asked.

"Well, I was wearing his coat."

"And just where did you get these guns?"

"At the Smith and Wesson store over in Springfield.

"And I presume you have a license for these guns?"

"Yes."

"I'll be wanting to see the license. And the certificate of purchase. And the guns themselves. I presume you've been trained in firearms?"

"Yes."

"Where?"

"At the Smith and Wesson Academy. I took their Basic Handgun course."

"I see. So you're an expert now."

She glared at him. "There's no need to be arrogant, Sergeant," Patty said.

"Did you point these guns at anybody?"

"No."

"You should never display a weapon unless you're ready to use it."

"That's what the bad guy said. I told him I was ready to use it."

"You really have brass balls, Patty."

"Well, dammit, MacPherson, they were gonna kidnap my husband!" Her eyes were wet again. "What would you want me to do? Wait until I took the Advanced Handgun Course?"

"May I see the guns and paperwork please?"

"Are you going to confiscate them?"

"Not if everything is in order. No, not if you have a proper permit. After all, you're the complainant here."

Patty brought my coat over and handed the coat to MacPherson. "There's one in each front pocket. Be careful, they're loaded."

MacPherson took them out one by one, unloaded them, smelled them, looked at the barrels, wrote down the model number and serial number on his clipboard.

"What kind of loads are these, Patty?"

"Winchester Silvertip."

"Silvertip? Wow, Patty, you really did your homework. You got a hundred twenty-five grain semi-jacketed hollow point plus-P," he said as he examined the cartridges.

I was disgusted with all this and was standing looking out the front window. "What the hell is a silvertip? Something to shoot a vampire in the heart?" I asked.

"It's a highly effective self-defense round, one of the best on the market. A real snotty little round. A lot of impact. A lot of knockdown power." MacPherson looked through the paperwork that Patty brought him and took notes.

"Well, you did everything right. It's a good thing Patty was holding the weapons and not you Chollie."

"How come?"

"Well if you held them they'd've had to kill you. To save face. But if a woman did it, that they could ignore because she's just a broad and a threat from her doesn't really count. It's a testosterone thing. But then they might have been wanting to take you away to kill you anyway."

"Why do you think that?" I asked quite apprehensively.

"Psychology of the criminal mind. CrimSci three-o-four. I got a bachelor's in criminal science, you know. Night school. This way the town of Great Barrington has to pay me two thousand dollars more each year to do the same work. Listen, you both will need to come to headquarters to help make some composite drawings."

"I'm going to make some coffee," Patty said, and we watched her walk down the hall to the kitchen at the back of the house. Maccabee whined as she walked past his crate.

"You really got a tiger by the tail there, that one, " MacPherson said. I nodded.

We sat in silence until Patty came back with the coffee. MacPherson put the guns back in my coat and I didn't tell him I didn't want them there, even though they probably just saved me a lot of trouble, if not my life.

We were sipping our coffee.

"So Chollie," MacPherson said, "you know I have an informer in the hospital. My wife tells me everything. You get visited a couple of times by a pair of FBI special agents. Someone accosts you in the parking lot and you run off into the woods and you're a missing person for an hour. Some jamoches posing as FBI agents come to see you in the ER. And today three guys try to hustle you away. What is a guy like me supposed to think?"

How much can I tell MacPherson? If I tell him the whole story can he keep it a secret? Is he allowed to keep it a secret? A doctor can keep a secret with a patient, so can a lawyer with a client. So can a newspaper reporter with a source. But if I told a cop about my involvement in criminal doings, even if I had been coerced, was I opening myself up to lots of trouble?

MacPherson looked at me as he drank his coffee. I hadn't answered his question and it continued to dangle in the air between us. I was quiet.

Finally he turned to Patty. "That was great what you did, Patty, what were you thinking?"

Patty was tense. She was edgy. She'd been pacing.

"I wasn't thinking anything at all. I wasn't figuring anything out. I wasn't working up a strategy if that's what you mean. I just imagined them pulling Charlie into the car by his hair and driving off with him and I'd be standing there in the street terrified, screaming my lungs out, banging my fists on my thighs wondering if I'd ever see him alive again. That's the only goddamn thing I was thinking." She turned to me. "Wouldn't you have done that for me?"

I paused. "I would. I think I would. Of course I would," I answered.

"Charlie, you know how much I love you, but sometimes you think too much." She turned and went to the bottom of the stairs and then turned back to us. "Don't you guys get it? Don't you realize?" Her voice was quivering. "I just nearly lost my husband. I just used guns to scare off three gangsters. Don't you know how scared I was? How scared I still am? They may be gone now. But they're not gone for good."

She ran up the stairs in tears, leaving MacPherson and me in the living room with our coffee.

I looked at MacPherson. "I better go upstairs." I said.

Chapter 20

I still felt strongly about getting in touch with Sal. Patty and I were both off from work. We had a light breakfast and laced up to go out for a three mile run. We took Maccabee with us. He was getting so big. We headed left on State Road, turned up Route 41, ran under the railroad overpass and continued up Christian Hill Road. It was a pretty section. There were few leaves left on the trees and here and there was a house with Halloween decorations. We turned around in the parking lot of the Willowood Nursing Home and headed back home. As we descended we passed another runner going uphill on the other side of the street. We waved and I shouted, "This way is easier." He smiled but did not laugh. I think I'm funny. Maccabee was doing great; I was holding his leash and he was pretty well-behaved running by my side. It was funny to watch him run. His ears flopping up and down.

"Aren't you glad your ears don't flop up and down when you run?" I asked Patty.

"I have other things that flop up and down when I run."

We got home, showered, and headed for Pittsfield. Mac was in the back seat. We were going to Berkshire Medical Center. We went up the back way; the scenic way. As we passed the Lee Library, I said, "Do you know that in the Lee Library they have a signed portrait of Abraham Lincoln and it's framed in wood that came from the cabin where he was born in Springfield, Illinois?"

"No, I didn't know that. How do you know that?"

"There's a little card on it that says so."

"What were you doing in the Lee Library?"

"I don't know. You know, I like libraries. I've stopped in lots of them. You've been in the one in Great Barrington with me. The one in Dalton. Have you been in the Lenox Library? It's a beauty. Don't you think it would be fun to create a book about quaint little old rural New England libraries? Like a big picture book? A coffee table book? It would be a nice retirement project."

"Yeah. If we live that long."

We pulled into the BMC parking lot and headed to the medical records department in the basement. As we walked through the corridors, an occasional nurse or other employee would recognize me from my tenure there in the past and say, "How's it going, Charlie?"

I went into the medical records office and looked for Rosemary, the supervisor, another acquaintance from the old days.

"Dr. Davids," she exclaimed happily, "what are you doing here? It's nice to see you!" she said with the sound of genuine enthusiasm in her voice. "Is this your wife?"

"Yes, Rosemary, please meet Patty." They smiled and shook hands.

"Oh, Patty, you're a lucky girl. Dr. Davids was one of my favorite residents. I could always read his handwriting."

Quickly I said, "And I'm a lucky guy," before Patty had a chance to say it.

Patty nodded and added, "Yes, I was always able to read his prescriptions without a struggle."

"Oh, are you a pharmacist?"

"Yes, down in Great Barrington."

I interjected, "Yeah, but Rosemary, you weren't so happy with me when you had to chase after me to do my discharge summaries."

Rosemary just smiled and shrugged. "So what can we do for you?"

"Well, you know I've been working down in the ER at Fairview for the last five years. A few years ago I saw a patient who I sent here with a heart attack and I wanted to look something up in his chart."

Rosemary looked at me for two seconds and said, "Sure, what's his name? Is it a male or female?"

"Male. Salvatore DeCensi. I think it was in February or early March of nineteen eighty-four." We were sitting in plastic molded chairs in front of her desk. Half the desk was occupied with a big computer that Rosemary was logging into, tilting her head up and down to look through the bottom or tops of her bifocals.

"How do you spell that? I come up with nothing in the usual spelling, D-e-c-e-n-s-i."

We tried a few other permutations of the spelling without luck.

"When did your department go digital?" I asked.

"Way before this date," she replied.

"I'm quite certain that's the correct spelling," I reiterated..

"Let me check D-i... Still nothing."

"He was in CCU for a few days. Would the EKG department or the lab have a record?"

"Well, they would, of course, but the computer is all centralized, so if he's not in here, he's not in there. Are you sure it was this hospital? Could he have been at Hillcrest Hospital?"

Hillcrest was a smaller hospital across town. "No, I'm sure he was here. I remember visiting him in the CCU here, room four."

"How on earth can you remember what room he was in four years later," Patty asked, rolling her eyes.

The three of us looked at each other. "I'm not insinuating anything, Rosemary, I know how compulsive we all are about record keeping and details, has this ever happened before? Does a person's chart ever vanish?"

"No."

"If they die, where does the chart go?"

"It stays right here."

"Oh. Make believe that there was a CIA spy who was admitted and then later needed to erase his having been here?"

"Can't happen. Someone would have to be intimately familiar with this computer program and have all the necessary passwords to do that, I'm not even sure if it can be done. Now I'm intrigued. What's this all about?"

I paused. "Well he was a colorful guy who had some unusual interests and I wanted to look him up. But I guess we came up dry. Thanks anyway. Thanks for your effort, Rosemary."

We got up to go. "I can't understand how it's possible that he was ever here and his records are gone. It can't happen. Even if his paper chart was misplaced, there'd be no way to expunge his record from the system. You must be mistaken."

"I must be. Thanks so much for trying."

"It was nice to meet you, Patty," she said and we shook hands all around.

We were walking down the main corridor on the first floor, heading to the lobby.

"What do we do now?" Patty asked.

"We go to the bank."

"The bank?"

"The bank. The safe deposit box."

"What safe deposit box?"

"The one in Allendale where I kept records of all my doings during those days."

Allendale was a neighborhood in east Pittsfield on the way to Dalton. When I lived in Dalton I used this bank.

"If you have the information in the bank, why did we bother going to the hospital?"

"I know. It doesn't make sense. It's hard to explain. It's emotional. That stuff in the safe deposit box, I hoped I'd never see it again. It's like an evil sealed tomb that I just didn't want to disturb. Like Pandora's box. I was hoping we wouldn't have to open it."

We drove to the small Allendale shopping mall. It was noteworthy for a steel ship that was upended in the middle of the parking lot, sticking up forty feet in the air, sinking into the asphalt. It was someone's idea of sculpture. The bank was a separate building across the parking lot from the mall itself. I parked at the mall. Near TJ Maxx. We both walked in, together, to the clothing store. Then we threaded our way from store to store and walked separately, to the bank, arriving there a few minutes apart. If we were being followed, I wanted them to think we were shopping, not banking.

From the time we left the hospital I was getting

increasingly uncomfortable. I had not been in this bank for three years. I'd been in the bank many dozens of times in the year before that and it was always to hide difficult information in the vault. I became sweaty and nauseous. I felt my bowels churning. Patty thought I was nuts for insisting we enter the bank separately and sneakily.

We went to the client service desk near the big vault door. I told the clerk what I needed to do. She pulled the card from the file box and looked at it. "Well, Dr. Davids, we haven't seen you for a long time."

I just smiled and nodded. I signed in on the card and handed her my vault key.

We followed her into the vault with the wall of stainless steel doors in neat ranks of varying size, each with two brass keyholes. She reached up with her master key and my key and swung open the little four-by-four-inch steel door. She pulled out the long plastic box. She handed it to me, so much like a shoe box. As I reached up for it I saw that my hands were trembling. I hoped she didn't notice. I don't think she did. She left the door open and gave me back my key.

"You can go into this little private room here. I assume you're together?" she asked, gesturing at Patty.

"Yes. Patty is my wife."

I took the long plastic box, holding it against my chest like a baby. We went into the little room, Patty first. I set the box down on the little counter. I closed the door behind me and locked it. There were two chairs. The counter top was beige formica, the walls were painted a lighter shade of beige. The room was well lit by an overhead fluorescent fixture. On the counter were a small bank calendar and a cup of pencils and some scratch pads.

Patty sat down. I was still standing, looking at the box. I was sweating and I was hyperventilating a little.

"Aren't you going to open it?"

"You open it."

She opened it.

It was stuffed with business-sized white envelopes. There was a dusty Genesee Cream Ale bottle in a plastic bag. There were pictures of Patty in it, from when we first began dating. There were Tanglewood concert tickets in there from concerts we'd been to. There was a lock of her hair in it. There was a list of phone numbers in it topped by the one belonging to my old friend Michael, the lawyer. There was a generic fill-in-the-blank last will and testament.

Patty took a rubber band off a big stack of envelopes and began going through them. She turned around to look at me with big eyes. I was still standing, behind her, too nervous to sit. "Charlie, there's tens of thousands of dollars here!" I nodded.

Slowly I reached over and picked up another stack of envelopes. I removed the rubber band. I took out the bottom one from the stack. It was marked March 1984. "This is the one we want." I opened it up. In it were many pages in my handwriting. The last page was a photocopy of Sal's Berkshire Medical Center inpatient registration sheet. I made it when I saw him in the CCU. It had his name, address, date of birth, social security number, phone number, insurance data and all that. It was spelled D-e-c-e-n-s-i. Patty, looked at me, amazed, confused.

"I wonder why he went through all the trouble to remove his records," she said.

"I don't know. When we see him we can ask him."

I took a pencil from the cup and copied Sal's address and phone number onto a slip of paper. I had taken the top piece of paper from the pad and put it on the counter, so there'd be no sheet beneath it to hold an impression. I put it in my shirt pocket.

"Come on, let's get out of here," I said, thinking about a bathroom.

"No, wait. I want to read this stuff." I nodded. I couldn't pace in that small room. Patty opened the first envelope of the narrative stack, April 1983. She began to read about the time when I first met Sal. I couldn't take it.

"Patty, I gotta get out of here."

She looked up at me, with the page in her hands. "Why don't you go get some air?"

I excused myself. I closed the door of the cubicle behind me. I told the clerk that this was going to take awhile, family papers, you know. Is there a bathroom I could use? Ten minutes later I emerged, having memorized Sal's address and phone number and flushed it down the toilet. I went outside the building. I needed some fresh air. I needed to move. I walked around the bank a few times. It was contrary to the discretion I'd intended. I wouldn't make a very good covert operative. I went back into the bank and sat down on a padded chair and read their brochures about home and auto mortgages, certificates of deposits, NOW accounts, stuff like that.

Twenty minutes later I asked the clerk if I could reenter the cubicle. "Of course," she said, surprised that I asked. I tapped softly on the door and said, "It's me." Come in, she replied. I took a deep breath, entered and closed the door behind me and locked it.

Patty was still in the same seat. She looked up at me and there were tears in her eyes. She had a thick sheaf of pages in her hands, a pile of empty envelopes and crumpled tissues on the counter.

"I've been reading them and putting them in order. Oh Charlie, I knew you had a bad time, but I never knew it was this bad," she said and there were tears on her red cheeks.

I nodded. I pulled the other chair out from the counter and sat on it sideways, my back against the wall, facing her, staring at her as she kept reading and sniffling.

We were having a late lunch at the Five Chairs Restaurant on Pittsfield-Lenox Road. We ordered beer and sandwiches and I went to the men's room.

When I sat back down the food had arrived and Patty was wolfing down her Reuben sandwich and drinking a Heineken.

"I have another idea for a book." I announced.

"What now?"

"You've seen big coffeetable picture books like *Summer Mansions of the Berkshires*?"

"Yeah?" she said and raised her glass for another gulp.

"I was thinking, *Men's Rooms of the Berkshires*."

Patty had just taken a mouthful of beer and she lurched forward and foam came out of her nose as she tried to restrain a laugh, and she grabbed her napkin and leaned forward over her plate, coughing. She finally composed herself but she continued clearing her throat for a long time. People were looking at her as if they might need to come over and give her the Heimlich maneuver.

"Charlie, how do you think this shit up?"

"Well, they have very interesting wallpaper in the bathroom here. It's a black and white pattern of these naked cherubic Reubenesque ladies all over the walls. And you know Sullivan Station in Lee? They have a cork bulletin board on the wall right above the urinal and they always have the front page of the sports section tacked up. And in Jimmy's Restaurant on West Housatonic Street they have *Far Side* cartoons above the urinal. You didn't know this, did you?"

"No, I didn't. I don't know how I could have lived without this information."

"But maybe the most interesting bathroom is the one in Joe's Diner in Lee. You know it's just along the rail-road tracks, so the back of the building is sort of built on a diagonal along the tracks. There's this tiny little trapezoidal bathroom in the back. You can hardly turn around in it. There's no radiator and it's freezing cold in the winter. And this room is just a pissing distance away from the tracks. And if you're in there when a train comes by, you think it's gonna crash right in there and you'll be nothing but a hood ornament on the loco-motive. It really tightens you right up. And there's a condom dispenser on the wall."

Patty was sitting there with her elbows on the edge of the table, her head down, tipped into her hands and she was shaking her head slightly from side to side.

"Charlie, I don't know where the hell you get these goofy ideas."

"C'mon, don't you see the potential? Some creative photography, pictures taken from interesting angles, interviews with proprietors, guests and all?" She looked at me, smiling, shaking her head.

"No, huh?"

She just kept shaking her head.

"Maybe the concept needs a little more work."

"Honestly, Charlie.

"So when are you going to call him?" Patty asked.

"Sal?"

"Yes. Sal. Who else have we been talking about call-ing?"

"Might as well call him today," I replied.

We finished our lunch. We got in the car and Mac nearly jumped in my lap. He smelled my breath and demanded to know what I'd eaten.

"I had turkey on rye with mayo and lettuce and

tomato and a side of potato salad." He seemed content with that knowledge and went back to his seat.

"Do you always tell him what you've just eaten?"

"Only when he asks." She shook her head.

We drove south on Route 7 and into old downtown Lenox. We parked on the street adjacent to Lilac Park near the old Civil War cannon and walked across the street, within view of the old Curtis Hotel and the Lenox library with its columns, massive front door and stately cupola. Two hundred years ago it was the county seat. We walked past Matthew Tannenbaum's bookstore to Keith's luncheonette on the corner of Church and Housatonic Street. I went into the phone booth and closed the doors. I had a roll of quarters in my pocket. I had lots of people to talk to for advice, not that it's done me much good.

I put a quarter in the slot and took a deep breath. I punched in the phone number for Sal. The operator came on and told me to deposit a huge amount of money. How come they can charge so much more for a call from a phone booth compared to the same call you can make at home? I fumbled with all the quarters trying to get them into the slot. The phone started to ring.

After five rings, a woman's voice answered the phone.

"Hello?" she said.

I took another deep breath and in a soft, slow, clear polite voice, I said, "Hello, My name is Dr. Charles Davids. I'm calling to ask if I might speak with Mr. Salvatore Decensi?"

"Well, he's not here right now, Doctor, can I have him call you back? What is this in regards to?"

How much do I tell her? Enough with the lies, the white lies, the subterfuge, the covering up. "Some years ago I gave some medical care to some people Mr. DeCensi knew. Some things have come up and I'd like to talk to him about it."

"I see. I remember hearing him talking about you. Quite warmly I might add. Is there a number where he could reach you?"

I'd better not have him call me at home. I'm still not positive my phone isn't tapped. I gave her my number in the ER and asked that he leave a message for me there if I'm not in. She said she would, thank you very much and goodbye.

That was easier than I expected. I thought it would be like calling Murder Incorporated, or the Mafia Hotline, and there'd be codes and passwords and interrogations just to get past the receptionist.

I exited the phone booth She sounded like a nice lady.

Patty was outside on the sidewalk next door looking in the window of Suchele's Bakery.

"How did it go?" Patty asked.

"Well. Surprisingly well. A lady answered the phone; I asked for Sal, she said she'd have him call me. I gave the hospital number. So we know he's still here, alive, well and hopefully he'll call me back. It's a step."

"I just hope it's a step in the right direction," she said under her breath.

It was three in the afternoon when we got home. I had to work that night. I brought the newspaper and the mail up to the bedroom to peruse before my nap. It became dark and gray outside and I turned on the bedside lamp even though it was daytime. I stripped to my boxers and T-shirt and got in bed to read. In a minute Patty and Mac came in. She lay down beside me on top of the covers. Mac was between us. He was getting calmer lately. Which was a good thing.

"What are you thinking?" she asked.

I sighed and put the paper down in my lap and stared out the window into the distance.

"I don't know," I answered quietly.

"Don't let this worry you. We shouldn't let it be a wet blanket on our lives. Whatever it is, whatever happens, we'll deal with it. We'll be together. Don't let it overwhelm you."

I looked at her and smiled. I'm glad she can be so confident. How can she be so goddamn confident?

"Take your nap," she said. She took the mail and the newspaper away from me, and the dog, and turned off the lamp and kissed me and left the room.

I stared at the ceiling. I got my earplugs out of the drawer and screwed them in and listened to them snap and crackle as they expanded and closed out the sounds of the world, thinking about me and Patty and our house with a baby in it someday.

Chapter 21

It was Sunday morning and I had to work so I called the ER and asked if anyone wanted a Code Eleven. That was our code for a breakfast platter from McDonald's. I took the orders and Patty came with me.

It was early November and as we opened the door to leave the house it was bright, brisk and windy. Not a leaf was left on the trees.

We came through the hospital doors at ten of eight. I was relieving Will who was on overnight. The nurses' shift had just changed at seven. Will immediately began flirting with Patty. That didn't really mean much because Will flirted with everybody. Patty only flirted with two people. Me and Will.

We were all sitting in the coffee room with our Styrofoam meal trays on our laps, talking and teasing.

Helen, the receptionist, was talking about a new car she was getting. "I'm so excited! I've been driving the same Honda for eleven years and it's got a hundred eighty thousand miles on it. I'm going to trade it in this week and I just hope it doesn't break down before then. When I give it up I'm going to say a little prayer to it to thank it for so many years of safe travel with all my kids."

I rolled my eyes.

"Why did you roll your eyes, Charlie?" someone asked.

"Did I roll my eyes?"

"Yeah, you did. How come?"

"Oh, it didn't mean anything. I was just stretching my eye muscles." Then I stretched my neck and shoulders.

"Yeah. Right. Why did you roll your eyes?" asked Will. Now he was in on it.

"Oh nothing."

"We want to know." Patty asked.

"I'd rather not say"

"Why? You started it, now we all want to know, you have to tell."

"You'll think it's corny and it might open a can of worms."

"Will you tell us already?"

"Okay. You asked for it. It's nothing special. You'll be disappointed. You don't pray to a rusty pile of junk for a hundred eighty thousand miles of safe travel, you pray to God to thank him for the privilege of traveling that distance in that piece of junk that's going to be in an anonymous scrap heap soon anyway. You give your thanks to God, not the car."

"Boy. Touch-y. You're really getting religious on us. You've gotten real religious since your father died. What are you now, Orthodox?"

"No. I'm not. I'm only mildly religious. I'm not getting more religious. You're just more aware of it. I told you I didn't want to bring this up."

"How can you really believe in God with all the crap that's going on in the world?"

"I don't know. Lots of people do. Lots of people don't. Lots of people have doubt. I have some doubt, but that doesn't change anything."

"What does that mean? How can it not change anything if you have doubt?"

Patty interrupted. "Let me explain this to you. As you know, Charlie is inarticulate unless he's talking about physiology or differential diagnosis." I shot her a glance. For an instant she turned her head toward me and gave me half a wink.

"Abraham started something in the desert thirty-five hundred years ago and it hasn't stopped since. Since then a whole lot of smart wise people sat around and observed and thought and talked about life and virtue and fairness and appreciation and people and peace and society, and whether there is or isn't a God is not relevant to the great deal of good in all this. For Charlie to say Kaddish is to continue a tradition that's thousands of years old. Every time you say Kaddish for someone they say they get a little closer to heaven. Who knows if that is true, it sounds like a fairy tale to me but I like the sentiment. But it gives him an opportunity to remember and honor his father, which is a commandment by the way, and while he's there in synagogue he's with other people who are grieving too, so who says having a grief support group is a new idea? And while there he can think about his father and mother and relatives both dead and alive and what kinds of parents they were and what kind of parent he wants to be and what kind of husband he wants to be. It gives a person a formal opportunity to meditate and think and appreciate these things and this is a valuable thing whether God exists or not."

Patty was sitting next to Will on the settee and he was still flirting with her and his arm was around her shoulders. She was leaning into him slightly while she gave this diatribe.

A nurse said, "I'm spiritual but I don't feel the need to go to church or temple."

"So don't go!" Patty said loudly, "nobody is telling you what you should do. I'm just explaining why some people do. Some people go to the gym to exercise their biceps or get sexy abs. Some people engage in spiritual exercise to keep their soul in shape. It's the same idea."

Will was playing with the fabric of Patty's violet cotton turtleneck on the top of her shoulder, gathering it up and then smoothing it out. He slid his thumb beneath Patty's bra strap. He wiggled his thumb and Patty's right breast nodded up and down.

Patty lurched in surprise and accidentally, or maybe on purpose, dumped her coffee cup in Will's lap. She jumped right up, apologizing, and grabbed a stack of paper towels and handed them to Will.

"Will, I'm so sorry, you startled me, I'm so glad the coffee wasn't hot anymore or else Charlie would have to treat you for burns. Really, I'm so sorry!"

Will was standing, wiping the coffee off his lap and off the chair. He hadn't lost his composure.

"I guess I'll go change into some OR scrubs," Will said as he left the room.

A nurse asked, "But what about those crazy zealots with the black hats in Israel?"

Patty jumped back in. "They're just doing the same thing, don't you see? They're just into it to the nth degree. They're saying that if everyone follows the laws, if everyone is righteous, then the messiah will

273

come and there'll be peace and harmony in the world and for everyone in it. And at that point, everyone who ever struggled or died or fought for freedom and peace will no longer have died in vain."

"What about eating pork?"

"Oh come on, Judaism isn't about what you eat. For us, anyway. It's about what you do! Pork is unimportant. To us. There's always people who are so into it that they love to sit around and split hairs all day and extrapolate things to ridiculous extents, and beat a subject to death. 'Thou shall do no work on the Sabbath.' That includes carrying things, like a sack of grain or bricks or bales of hay. So some pedants extended this to the ridiculous level that even if you have a runny nose you can't carry a handkerchief in your pocket on the Sabbath because that would be work. That's just nonsense to me. That's arcane minutiae. Don't cloud your view of Judaism with silly stuff like that. If they carry their interpretation of the law to that extent they think they're being more holy. Forgive me, maybe I'm being cynical."

"Why are you going on and on about this?"

"Because this started out as a 'How can you believe in God' conversation and no one wants to hear that one again. I'm trying to illustrate the point that religion has value even if God is in question. Think of it as a theoretical construct."

"So? Do you think God exists?" a nurse asked.

"That's deeply personal. And private. Does spirituality exist?"

"What's spirituality? Define it."

"Spirituality has endless definitions. Mine is when a person feels there's more to life than himself. That he thinks being a good person is its own reward, that it's good for mankind, that acts of love and trust and generosity add to the greater good of society, even if they are unrecognized. And the more people who act similarly the better off society will be."

"Do you worship the Torah?"

"No. We worship with the Torah. We worship the virtue in what God says, or what Moses wrote down, or what the wise old men wrote down, like love thy neighbor, welcome the stranger, console the sick, celebrate with bride and groom, attend the house of study. How can you argue with that? Remember the Jethro Tull song that had a lyric about a god you have to wind up on Sundays? You don't have to wind up God. You might want to wind up yourself and the spiritual part of your life. This has nothing to do with reward or being saved or redemption, or a heavenly life hereafter."

"But how can you support all this? So many people have been killed in the name of God," Will said. He was back.

"Oh, nonsense," Patty said, "People like to kill people and always have and always will and they'll use any excuse they can think of. The Civil War was the biggest bloodbath in this country's history and that wasn't about God. Stalin didn't need religion to kill fifty million Russians. Pol Pot and the Khmer Rouge didn't need religion to kill three million Cambodians."

Will sat down, but not next to Patty.

"The Crusades! Everyone bought the excuse that the Crusades were religious, but one of the underlying reasons for them was so they could gain control of the lucrative trade routes through the Middle East, get them out of Muslim hands and into Christian ones where they thought they belonged."

I turned to Patty. "Let me ask you something. Forgive me if this is a stupid question. I'm not in any way making excuses for Hitler with this question. He hated

Gypsies. He hated homosexuals. He thought they were degenerates and were undermining society. He hated Jews. Was it for the same reason? Because he thought Jews had a secret agenda and were apt business people spreading all over the world and were preparing to take it over? Did he hate what we religiously believe, how we pray, that we don't accept Christ as messiah, that we speak Hebrew; or was it that he hated the culture and society of the Jews?"

Patty thought for a moment and then said, "Certainly if you ask any scholars about Hitler and the Jews they'd say he hated them for all of those reasons. At home we have a copy of *The Rise and Fall of the Third Reich* by William Shirer who, by the way, is still alive and lives right here in Lenox. There's a chapter in there, I think, that deals with this point. But as you pose the question, Hitler's hatred was more of an ethnic one, against a group of people who were identified by their religion. He had this idea of a pure Aryan race and Aryan society that he didn't want to be blemished by having Jews, Gypsies, homosexuals, or even Russians for that matter."

In the course of half an hour we covered quite a lot of ground in the coffee room. We all finished our big greasy breakfasts with eggs and sausage patties and home fried potatoes. Lots of people came into the room and listened to Patty's discourse; the chairs were filled, people were leaning against the doorjamb, nurses, EMTs, lab techs. Everybody knew Patty, it was a small hospital and a small town, everybody liked her but I don't think anyone ever heard her give such a discourse.

One of the nurses came back and said, "Charlie, you've got a suture removal in room three." I nodded and turned to Patty. "Well, love, I better get going."

"I better get going too. Mac has probably gnawed the knob off the gear shift by now." She stood and turned and looked at Will. "You okay?"

"I think so," he replied tentatively. "Always nice to see you, Patty. I think."

I walked Patty out to the parking lot. At the car I patted Maccabee on the head and gave Patty a hug and a kiss. She was going to spend the day with some friends.

I returned to the ER and removed the stitches. I went back to the coffee room but it had emptied out so I ended up in the doctors' room reading through a pile of medical journals I'd been accumulating. It was a slow Sunday morning at Fairview. I was bored.

Finally I got a patient. I was so relieved. This nice middle-age guy had been finishing spackling the wall-board of a new room he built on his house and he cut his hand on the edge of a taping knife. It was quite long but shallow and hadn't cut anything important like big blood vessels or tendons or nerves. It looked like it was cut by something extremely sharp. When I asked him about it, he said that although taping knives start out dull like a putty knife, you are always pulling them across a wall with wet wallboard compound. It's full of tiny gypsum crystals that have a very fine abrasive quality. So it's like you are always honing the edge and eventually it can get wicked sharp. A few times he even cut his jeans with it.

Anyway, it was an easy repair and I sewed him up slowly because he was a nice guy and I had been bored and I enjoyed talking to him.

Eventually it was lunchtime and I went down to the cafeteria with Roy. The cook who didn't like me wasn't there so I didn't have to feel awkward. We ate slowly. When we got done we sat around and had another cup of coffee. Eventually we made our way back to the ER coffee room where we found Margaret with the Sunday paper.

She was sitting with one of the ER nurses, and Helen.

"Charlie, what's 'Krystallnacht'?" asked Margaret, looking up from the newspaper. "There's an article here about special services being held in commemoration of it."

"It means 'Night of Broken Glass.' It took place on a night in the fall of nineteen thirty-eight in Germany and Poland and it was a state-sanctioned night of violence directed at anyone and anything Jewish. The Nazi soldiers, the brownshirts, the Hitler youth and any other thug who felt like it were encouraged to vandalize Jewish stores, shops, homes, businesses, anything. They went into a university building and threw Jewish professors out third-story windows. It was terrible. It was the beginning of the end."

"You gotta be kidding," Helen said.

I paused. "Helen, how could anyone kid about something like that?"

The room was quiet.

"How could they do that?" Roy asked.

"They were brainwashed and they were told to."

"But didn't these people have any scruples? How could they do such things? Some of them must have gone to church when they were kids."

"Sure they did. But they were taught that those ethics only applied to people like them, not to people different than them. Think about all those good Southern Protestants who went to church on Sunday mornings and sang and prayed about a righteous life. And then during their big Sunday fried chicken lunch one guy says to the other, 'what do you wanna do this afternoon?' and the other one says, 'I dunno. What do you wanna do?' and the first one says, 'I dunno, let's go lynch a Negro.'"

"I always wondered how they could get the Nazi

soldiers to do what they did," said Margaret.

"It was easy," I said. "All they had to do was call the troops out in formation to watch a firing squad shoot one of their fellow soldiers. They told the troops that this was the just treatment for a Nazi soldier who disgraced his comrades and uniform and Fuhrer by having sympathy for the vermin it was their pledge to exterminate and for not fully embracing Nazi ideology."

The room was quiet.

"Monsters," someone said softly.

I thought about it. "No. People acting like monsters."

The room was quiet.

"Charlie," Roy asked, "did you ever experience any anti-Semitism?"

I thought about it, trying to remember. "Just once. It wasn't much really. I'd gone to the movies with my friends. I guess I was in ninth or tenth grade. I left my seat to go to the bathroom. Remember when they used to have those big porcelain urinals that went all the way down to the floor and there was always a little pink camphor cake in the bottom of it like a little hockey puck and the joystick to flush it came straight out from the wall? Well I was standing there taking a leak and some kid I never saw in my life called me an effing Jew and some other stupid names and shoved me and then he ran out. But he shoved me forward and I got poked in the Adams apple by the joystick."

"That must have hurt. What did you do?"

"Nothing really. It was just a poke. I coughed a few times, it hurt a little. I didn't even get a bruise."

"Did you go after him? Did you tell anybody?"

"No."

"Why not?"

"It was just so stupid. It didn't really mean anything.

I can't imagine that this kid had ever been harmed by a Jewish person. He was just a jerky kid who was told by a jerky parent or big brother that you could pick on Jews."

"Did Patty ever experience any anti-Semitism?" Margaret asked.

"I don't know. I never asked."

"Does she know about this incident you just told us about?"

"No. She never asked. I don't think I ever told anyone about it until you guys just now. I don't think I've thought about it in years."

"How come?"

"I don't know. We're in America. We're safe here. If you don't get picked on for being Jewish, you might get picked on for being Puerto Rican, or Polish, or Italian, or Irish, or Black. Or if you're fat or skinny or have buck teeth or freckles. What's the difference? There are bigots and nasty people all over. So I met one. So what? It was my turn."

I got called out and went to see an adolescent girl with a bad sore throat and the biggest tonsils and submandibular lymph nodes I ever saw. I've eaten meatballs smaller than those tonsils. She had a fever and felt crappy and I took a throat culture, prescribed her the usual stuff and some additional meds for her symptoms. Poor kid.

I finished at eight in the evening and gathered up my stuff and said good night to all the staff. I bundled up and went outside. As soon as I got outside a man got out of a parked car and walked over and intercepted me on the way to my car. He was nicely dressed. He had a businessman's hat and a topcoat and I could see a necktie where it was exposed by a Burberry plaid scarf draped neatly beneath the lapels of his topcoat.

He was medium height, a little shorter than me, and slender.

"Dr. Davids?" he asked.

"Yes," I answered apprehensively.

"My name is Phillip Testa. I'm an attorney and I represent a family business in Springfield and I would be grateful if you would talk to me for a little while about some matters of mutual interest."

Sure. I'll talk to you. I have two words for you. One of them is a verb and the other one is a pronoun.

I paused. What is a lawyer doing working on a Sunday night? I stopped walking toward my car and politely addressed him as he had me. "Well, sir, I can't imagine what that might be."

"Permit me to explain," he said as another man, younger and much bigger, got out of the same car. "If you would kindly join us in the warmth of my car we could talk about this confidentially."

I thought about it for a short moment. "Thank you, Mr. Testa. I'm willing to talk to you in a public place. But I won't get into that car with you."

The three of us stood there, in the dark parking lot, sloping down from the ER ambulance entrance.

"You know, Doc, I could just grab you and stuff you in the car, what do you think about that?" said Mr. Testa's simian companion.

I thought about it for a short moment. "You know, sirs, I could remove something from my coat pocket that could injure you very severely, what do you think about that?"

"Tony, there's no need to provoke that kind of an exchange," said Mr. Testa.

We stood there looking at each other.

Mr. Testa broke the silence. "Dr. Davids, what do you propose?" He was being very polite and deferential which made me instantly distrust him, as if Tony's presence wasn't reason enough for me to distrust him.

I thought about it for a moment.

"We could meet at the Friendly's or McDonald's on Route Seven just north of town."

Mr. Testa answered, but not too dismissively, "That would be too public."

"I could have the nursing supervisor unlock the medical library. That would be a nice quiet place where we could talk, and get out of this cold."

"That sounds like a good place," he said.

"Then why don't you come into the waiting area and I will make arrangements. I'll ask the nursing supervisor to open it up. I'll call my wife and let her know I'll be delayed."

Tony snorted. "You hafta ask permission?"

I turned to him. I took a step closer to him. I looked up at him. I said, "I do not have to ask permission. I choose to be considerate." *You want me to spell it for you?* I continued looking at him.

Mr. Testa said, "Tony, you need to be quiet. I will do the talking here. Very well, doctor, please proceed. We will accompany you to the waiting room and warm up."

Unctuous bastard.

We all walked in to the ER waiting area, which was empty. Helen saw me with them and asked if she could help.

"No, thank you, Helen, these gentlemen are not patients. They're here to discuss some business with me. Would you please page Margaret for me?"

"Of course. To what extension, Doctor?" I gave her the extension for the doctors' room, I excused myself from Helen and the two men and went back to my office. I sat at the desk with my elbows on the desktop and my chin in my hands, looking at the phone, waiting for it to ring. I was tense. I took my pulse. It was eighty. With my running and hiking and stuff my resting pulse was usually sixty.

The phone rang. It was Margaret. I asked her to unlock the medical library and she said she'd do it in a minute.

Then I called Patty and told her what was up. That I was going to meet two men who I presumed were emissaries from Springfield Organized Crime, in the hospital library, and so far they had been exceedingly polite. She told me to be very careful, to not divulge anything, and if she didn't hear from me in an hour she was going to call MacPherson, the Marines and the Royal Canadian Mounted Police. I told her I loved her and hung up.

I went and got Mr. Testa and his gorilla. I asked them to follow me. They were holding their topcoats, I had left my own coat in the doctors' room.

I led them from the ER waiting area into the main corridor of the first floor of the hospital. We walked down the broad high hallway, which had beige ceramic tile up to shoulder height, then the walls rose up another six or eight feet to the ceiling. There was decorative molding where the wall met the ceiling. There was much newer freshly buffed and waxed linoleum on the floor. Each door we passed was tall and wide and framed with a mahogany molding, still looking stately after having been installed almost ninety years ago. They don't build them like this anymore. These days the doors would be hollow core veneer without the raised panels, the molding would be softwood ranch and the hardware would be modern wimpy stamped steel instead of the old-fashioned solid cast.

I pushed open the big heavy modern steel fire door at the ground floor landing and held it open for my two guests. Margaret had left one of the double doors open an inch. She had turned on the lights and the small library was empty. It was a room about twenty feet by forty, with bookshelves all around.

On one wall was a small chalkboard with some scribbling about acid-base equilibrium which must have been from the recent kidney physiology lecture. In the center of the room was a large table with a dozen chairs. In one corner there was an articulated human skeleton hanging from its stainless steel stand, all the bones labeled in red and blue for the origins and insertions of their muscles.

I led my guests into the room, which they scrutinized and they put their coats down on an armchair. I closed the door until it clicked. The gorilla came over to me and gestured to me to elevate my arms as if he were going to frisk me.

"That won't be necessary," I said, as he proceeded to frisk me, "we gentlemen don't have a reason to harm each other." Tony nodded to Mr. Testa, I guess to signal that I was unarmed. As I was also in the parking lot when I bluffed about something in my pocket.

Mr. Testa and I sat across from each other at the big conference table. The gorilla sat in one of the armchairs by the door, next to the one their coats were on.

Mr. Testa began speaking first. He was sitting across from me wearing a very nice dark gray suit. He was smooth. I got the impression that he was an experienced and intelligent man and knew he might be better able to accomplish more by seeming nice and gentlemanly than by being forceful and threatening. Which I was sure he was very capable of being. As nice as he had been so far, I didn't trust him, I sensed he was perfectly able to be nasty and I was surprised by how less naïve I was than a few years ago. I used to think that nice looking and nicely mannered people were usually nice.

"Doctor Davids, thank you for meeting with me

tonight. On such short notice. I am grateful, and the gentleman I represent is grateful. I understand that several other attempts were made to contact you in a less cordial manner, which you skillfully avoided."

I said nothing. I just looked at him. He looked at me in case I might say anything. I didn't.

"My client has informed me that some years ago you had a special arrangement to provide medical services to certain people."

He hadn't asked me a question so I didn't answer. But I asked him a question. "Mr. Testa," I asked, "do you have a business card?"

"Oh. Certainly. Here you are," he said as he fished out his wallet from his suit coat, extracted a card and handed it to me."

Phillip Testa, Esq. Attorney at Law. Springfield, Massachusetts. The address and phone number were listed.

"Where did you go to Law School?" I asked.

"Western New England," he answered with some enthusiasm. "Class of nineteen sixty-nine."

"Dr. Davids, I understand that some years ago you provided medical care for some people under the auspices of my client."

He paused and waited for me to respond.

Finally I said, "I don't know who your client is. You haven't told me his name."

He swallowed and looked at me. "My client, who wishes to remain unnamed, is curious to know what you recall about those individuals to whom you provided medical care."

I didn't know how to respond. I thought about it for a minute. The gorilla in the corner looked bored. He was picking at his fingernails.

"Mr. Testa, my job is here at Fairview Hospital. I've worked in the Emergency Department for over five years. I usually work here three or four-twelve hour shifts per week, days and nights. I like my job. I did a three-year residency at Berkshire Medical Center, a branch of the University of Massachusetts Medical College. I'm board certified in internal medicine and I guess I'm board eligible in emergency medicine."

I was leaning forward toward him, my chest was against the edge of the table, my forearms and hands were on the table reaching out toward him, my hands almost at the center line, showing him in body language how earnest and forthright and willing I was to talk to him. I was trying to use all the body language and subliminal gesturing I had not learned from Goldstein. But I hadn't directly responded to his statement. And he knew it.

"Dr.Davids, do you remember seeing any ill or injured patients in Springfield in the last five years?"

"For your client?"

"Yes."

"And your client's name is?"

"It is immaterial."

I paused. *It is not immaterial.* "Mr. Testa, I closely follow the code of medical ethics of which a large part is patient confidentiality. I could and would never divulge any salient details of a person's medical problems, even if I could remember them."

"Dr. Davids, I am asking you to make an exception in this case. Do you remember any details of patients you have treated?"

I paused a second time. "Mr. Testa," I said sincerely, leaning forward, looking him in the eyes, "with all due respect, you do not have the standing to ask me to make an exception in this case. Recently the American Medical Association came out with a thick tome detailing the standards of medical ethics. I read them and I remember them and I abide by them."

"Let me phrase this differently. Dr. Davids, do you recall treating patients in Springfield who were subjects of physical violence, who suffered grievous physical injury, who were badly off such that you suspected they might die after your interaction with them?"

Why do I feel like I am on a witness stand? "The only place I practice medicine is right here. And the people you describe are sadly some of the routine patients I see here in the emergency department."

There were several hard raps at the door.

"Excuse me," I said as I got up to answer the door. The gorilla stood up too and looked nervous.

I opened the door and MacPherson took two steps into the room. In full blue uniform with duty belt and everything. "Everything all right in here?" he asked, eyeing the gorilla and Mr. Testa.

"Yes, Officer, we are just having a conversation in here. Thank you."

"Okay, Doc, anything you need, I'll be around." And he ducked out the door. It clicked shut.

"And how did that just happen to happen?" Mr. Testa asked.

"I promise you that since I met you I only made two calls. One was to the nursing supervisor and the other was to my wife."

"Okay. I believe you. It doesn't really matter. Dr. Davids, do you recall a man named Salvatore DeCensi?"

"No. I do not remember." I paused. "Mr. Testa, please let me explain something to you about myself." I was leaning way across the table trying to seem earnest. Which I was. "I take my job very seriously. When I graduated we all took the Oath of Hippocrates and that pretty well sums up all the morals and ethics I was taught and all that was bred into me about taking care of patients and all that applies to that and everything that spins off from that about confidentiality and privacy. I recall nothing that you are asking about or hinting about."

Mr. Testa had brought in a soft-sided leather business folder with handles on the top and a zipper on three sides. I had been looking at it. Early on he unzipped it and pulled out a long yellow legal pad. I didn't see a gun in the folder. He hadn't written anything on the pad. He too was leaning forward on the table, his elbow on the table and his hand against the side of his head as he tapped an expensive looking Parker ball point pen on the pad. He was thinking. Tony was sitting in the armchair looking at the books on the shelves around the room most of which had titles with words with more than two syllables and he looked confused.

"Well, Doctor Davids, I am afraid I have been unable to get the information my client asked me to get. Either you never knew it, or you forgot it, or your admirable set of ethics prevents you from disclosing it. I will report to him of your cooperativeness and willingness to meet with me at this late hour and that I assess you have no knowledge that could ever be of use or detriment to him. I might wish to contact you again in the future and ask you to sign an affidavit. I thank you on his behalf and also on mine for being so pleasant and cooperative. This will conclude our interview together tonight. Do you have any further questions?"

"No, Mr. Testa, I do not." The less I know, the better, I thought. "I thank you for your courtesy."

"And to you the same. Good night, Doctor, keep up the good work. Come, Tony, let's go."

He and Tony got up and turned to pick up their coats. I said, "Mr. Testa?" I got up out of my chair and as he turned to me I extended my hand. He looked at me and at my hand and took it and we shook and then he let go and said goodbye and the two men left.

After they left I sat at that big conference table for a while, surrounded by all the books about a discipline I loved and practiced so dearly, with the skeleton of some unknown soul whose bones and engineering I found so fascinating and wondered when all these people would just leave me the hell alone.

Maybe a minute later there were two knocks at the door and then it opened and MacPherson walked in. He smiled at me and I smiled back and he sat down across from me, just where Testa had been sitting.

"I saw them leave. I didn't see you leave. I wanted to make sure you hadn't been strangled."

"Thanks, Mac."

"What was all that about?" he asked.

"I really don't know. He asked me a bunch of questions I couldn't answer. Then he left. That was it."

"You going home now?"

"Yeah."

"I'll follow you."

I called Margaret to let her know I locked up the library and turned off the lights. I called Patty to let her know I was on my way.

As I drove home there were two other headlights in my rear view mirror and as I pulled into my driveway they passed me and MacPherson gave a little goodbye honk.

When I entered the house Patty was standing in the living room with Maccabee. She was holding a martini glass.

After she kissed me she put the martini glass in my hand and said, "Here, you probably need this." There was a little shaving of lemon peel in it.

I told her what happened.

Chapter 22

The intercom squawked, "Charlie, call for you on line three."

I ran to the doctors' room to take the call. In case it was the call I was waiting days to receive.

"Hello, this is Dr. Davids."

There was a pause, then, "Doc, it's good to hear your voice again. It really is. This is Sal. How are you Doc?"

"I'm good, Sal, very good. And how are you?"

"Oh, I'm good, I'm real good. Better than ever. Remember that little heart attack I had? It was the best thing to happen to me. I retired, lost weight, quit smoking and I'm more active than I've been in twenty years and I feel great. How are you and Patty?"

"Oh, she's real good, you know, we've been married for three years now."

"Yeah, I knew that, good for you, I'm real happy about that. How can I help you, to what do I owe the honor of your call?"

"Well, there have been some people coming around, asking me probing questions about our old days, if you know what I mean."

"What kind of people do you mean?"

"Well, some from the FBI, and also, I think, from the company you used to work for."

"Oh, that shouldn't be. It shouldn't be. You were supposed to be left alone. I promised you that. That shouldn't be. I'm glad you let me know this."

"Do you know anything about this? You know of anything going on that this might be a part of?"

"No, not at all. I think we better get together and talk this out. We should talk in person, in private. When can we meet?"

"Well I'm off at eight AM. Could we meet then?"

"Sure, that would be fine. I can meet you. Should I come to your house?"

"I'm not sure it's safe. That's why I didn't want to call you from there. I can't be sure the place isn't bugged."

"Really? Okay. How about I meet you at that Friend-ly's Restaurant on Route Seven?"

"That would be fine. What time?"

"What's ever good for you, Doc? You get out at eight?"

"Yeah. How about if we meet at eight-thirty? I'd like Patty to join us if that's okay."

"Of course. Of course she can come. I'll be happy to see her."

"Okay. Tomorrow at eight-thirty at Friendly's."

"Okay, Doc, see you then, don't worry. Good night."

"Good bye, Sal, and thanks." I hung up. *Phew. That was easy.* I hoped he could help us.

Now I needed to call Patty to arrange for her to meet us without any listener suspecting what's going on.

At around ten-thirty I called home to say goodnight to Patty and Mac. "How about meeting me for break-fast at Friendly's when I get out in the morning, before you go to work?" I was waiting for her to suggest that I

291

just come home for breakfast, but she didn't. She agreed and we said goodnight. It was a plan.

Work was work. A lady came in with a violent viral gastroenteritis. This bug had gone through her family but she got it worse than any of them. She'd been pouring out both ends all day. She was all cramps, her stomach felt like she'd done a million sit-ups from retching all day. She was so volume depleted that her blood pressure was borderline and her pulse was up and her skin turgor was poor. So dehydrated. I plugged her into to a big IV and pumped in normal saline with a little potassium in it. She got most of the liter before her labs came back. Her electrolytes were okay, her BUN (blood urea nitrogen) was up, belying her dehydration, her complete blood count was consistent with a viral infection.

I kept the IVs running almost wide open until she finally filled her bladder. That implied that her tank was finally full and she could afford to make some urine. Her pulse and blood pressure were better too. We'd given her some donnatal for the cramps, and phenergan for the nausea and she was more comfortable.

"Mrs. Ricciardi," I asked, "how would you like to spend the night with us?"

"Oh, Dr. Davids, I haven't been this comfortable all day. What a relief. I can just drift off to sleep right now."

"Well, why don't we keep you here in the department for a while? It's pretty quiet, we can put you over there in the last cubicle and turn down the lights and let you sleep and I can check on you overnight. We'll see how you do and at some point we can decide to move you upstairs, or if you feel up to it send you home."

"Okay, Doc, whatever you say."

Just after we got her settled in a guy came in by ambulance. He had crashed his truck into a tree. He wasn't going fast at all but he had no seatbelt on and he was drunk so of course he hit the windshield and had a lot of dried blood on his face and shirt. We got him in and plugged into an IV and some labs drawn and sent him for some X-rays after I examined him. As soon as he went off to X-ray the policeman came in, the one who had evaluated the accident scene. The patient was lucky, it could have been much worse.

The patient was relatively cooperative. His alcohol level was 0.2, only twice the legal limit but this guy was a chronic and had good tolerance and was probably well used to it. He said he'd been out to the bars with his buddies and had his usual eight or ten beers and was real sleepy on the way home and must have fallen asleep at the wheel. Real lucky. He checked out okay, no sign of neck or facial fracture, no chest contusion, his mental status exam and neurological exam was close to normal but for him having a blood alcohol level of 0.2.

The big job was to dig the glass out of his forehead. He was a light-complected red-haired freckled guy. We had saline soaked sponges on his forehead to loosen up the dried blood so I could get to work digging out the glass. The safety glass in car windows usually breaks into little uniform polygonal chunks but there are usually also lots of little slivers that don't go too deeply into the skin but can be hard to see and remove especially in someone with such light skin. After I gently sponged away the dried blood I soaked another sponge with some lidocaine and left it on his forehead for ten minutes hoping it would get numbed up enough so that with the anesthetic and the beer it wouldn't bother him too much when I probed with my forceps in his scratches, listening to hear when my metal tool struck glass. You could sometimes hear it better than you could see it. Even with the magnifiers strapped on my head.

I dread drunks in car accidents because they often are big dumb uncooperative cry babies but this guy was really pretty easy. After a half hour I was getting bleary eyed working on his forehead and breathing the beer on his breath. Second-hand beer.

I took a break to get a cold drink and check on Mrs. Ricciardi. She was sound asleep but had complained to the nurse that she kept waking up to pee. Which was a good thing. We adjusted her IV rate accordingly.

I heard MacPherson in the coffee room. He was sitting with the patrolman, going over details on a clipboard about the guy in the car accident.

"What are you so damn happy about?" I asked MacPherson.

"Oh, I just love getting drunks off the road."

"Well, yeah," I said.

"Chollie, how many times have you had the ambulance bring you somebody on a stretcher in full arrest and you do your thing and then you have to go out and tell somebody their loved one didn't make it? How many times have I had to knock on someone's door and tell them their loved one is dead or injured because a drunk just crashed into them? What would you give to hit that rewind button and make it not happen? Every time I lock up a drunk there's some anonymous person out there I don't have to give bad news to. Someone's loved one is alive and well because I got that drunk off the road. He didn't crash into your wife or my wife or any of my kids or anyone else's kids. You know how good that feels?"

I nodded agreement, said good night and got back to work.

I finished up with the guy's forehead and bandaged him up. His wife had arrived and if looks could kill,

this lady could wipe out a neighborhood. This man
screwed up and had it coming, and he was going to
get it. I spoke with them and informed her of all the
tests we'd done and the things we'd checked out. I went
over the "head sheet" with her. This is a list we give
to everyone who's bumped their head, warning them
to let us know if they develop worsening neurological
signs like increasing headache, lethargy, vomiting and
stuff like that. She was standing there, nodding, lips
pressed, as if she'd heard it all before. The policeman
finished up with them and then the three of them left.
The patient had to appear in court in the morning.

I figured we might as well keep Mrs. Ricciardi with
us. The nurse agreed with me. So did the nursing
supervisor. I didn't want it to look like I was cheating
the hospital out of an overnight admission. The hospital likes admissions.

Thinking of the morning's meeting with Sal kept
me wired and though the department was empty I
wasn't ready to try to sleep. I read for a while. Then
I got called to pronounce someone on the third floor.
The third floor had become, for the most part, a chronic
care nursing home floor for people who were too fragile to stay in a regular nursing home. The man who
died had been ancient. He was just about vegetative
for two years, was fed through a feeding tube, and had
flexion contractures in all his limbs from his immo-
bility. These contractures always made me think that
these poor souls had rigor mortis even before they were
dead. Well, this man was dead now and I went through
the formal routine to ascertain that. His pupils did not
react to my penlight. There were no breath sounds
or heart sounds. There were no deep tendon reflexes.
There was no response to deep pain. That was that.

It had been a long time since this poor guy had anything like a reasonable quality of life, and dying was

really the only thing left he had to do, but it was still sad. The other person in the room was asleep and the drape was drawn around the bed. I took my little Kaddish card out of my clinic book.

I went out to the desk and wrote an official note in the chart and signed it with my full name and the time. At 3:25 AM I called the attending on call to let him know; I called the official next of kin; I called the funeral director.

I thought about Patty in bed upstairs in our little house. I wondered if she was sleeping soundly and what she was dreaming about.

Mrs. Ricciardi was still doing well. She was asleep and had a sweet little smile on her face. As I took her blood pressure she woke up. "Good morning," I said.

"Good morning to you, too."

"How do you feel?"

"Oh, I feel so much better. Just weak."

I nodded as I gently palpated her belly. It was soft and she had no guarding. I listened with the stethoscope and she had slightly hyperactive gurgling bowel sounds. All good.

"Do you have any appetite?" I asked

"You know, maybe I do a little."

"Let me find you some Jell-O. If you can keep it down and still feel good, you think you want to go home?"

"Let's try it."

I got her some orange Jell-O. It had whipped cream on it; I scraped it off. She took a spoonful of it tentatively, swallowed, and then woofed down the rest of it.

"Good. If that sits well with you for an hour we'll see about getting you home. Okay?"

Nothing much happened for the rest of the shift. I stretched out on the sofa bed for an hour but didn't sleep. At six I checked Mrs. Ricciardi and she was doing fine. I called her husband and he came to pick her up.

I made a fresh pot of coffee in the Silex machine and curled up in the coffee room. The hospital was coming to life. Seven o'clock came and the changing of the guard. My night nurse came in to say goodbye and the day shift came in to say hello and in an hour another doctor would come in to replace me and I could leave the hospital and meet Patty and Sal and explore some other issues of my life.

People drifted into the coffee room. Roy and Margaret were there. MacPherson stopped in. He was doing an extra day shift and came in to pick up some information about the alcoholic I'd seen. We were sitting around drinking coffee but it wasn't waking me up.

Will walked in and as always he became the center of attention. He had his little elfin grin which led me to think he had a monologue worked up. Finally he started.

"Y'know all this shit they're always haranguing us with about the way we interact with patients and how we're supposed to be compassionate and understanding even if they are arrogant shitheads, that they might just be that way because they're sick or injured or worried and in an unfamiliar environment. And that we should explain everything to them and involve them in decision making regarding their case and all that crap? Well I've been up all night writing the Ten Commandments of Being a Good Patient. But I've only written eight or nine of them so far." He paused, waiting for us to ask him to continue.

"The first is, just because you're sick doesn't mean you can't still say please and thank you.

"Second. We're here to help you because it's our job. If you're nice we'll want to help you. If you're not nice we'll still help you but we'd rather you'd gone somewhere else.

"Three. We don't want to hear what Aunt Tillie

thinks unless she's a credentialed diagnostician and she's already examined you.

"Four. Don't interrupt me with another question while I'm still answering the last one. It's rude.

"Five. Just because you're from out of town and on vacation doesn't mean your problem is any more important than anyone else's or that we can get you fixed any faster.

"Six. I am not going to call your 'world class physician' in the city. You can have him call me if you would like.

"Seven. We can be sympathetic if you deserve it. But if you can't breathe because of emphysema and you still smoke, don't count on it. If your knees hurt and you weigh a million pounds, don't count on it."

By this time we were all laughing out loud, remembering people we've all had to put up with in the past.

"Gee, Will," Margaret croaked, "it sounds like you really don't like out-of-towners very much."

"No, not at all. I like them fine if they behave and stay out of my ER. I wouldn't treat them any different."

I couldn't resist. "Hey Will, if a local and an out-of-towner came in at the same time and they both had heart attacks, who would you take care of first?"

"The local of course. But then I would give the out-of-towner my best care. Afterward."

"What if there was a local with a broken leg and an out-of-towner with an heart attack?"

"The local is always first."

"What about a second-home owner and a local?"

"The local is always first. A local with a sick farm animal or a sick dog or cat always comes first. But I'd get to the out-of-towner. It's a matter of privilege. Locals come first."

"Speaking of animals, wasn't there a story about you

doing some surgery on a Great Dane here once?"

"Oh that was years ago. You were here, Roy, weren't you?"

Roy nodded.

"There was an EMT who'd just gotten married, bought a house, was up to his eyeballs in debt. We were sitting right here in this coffee room and he was talking about a problem with his dog. His dog had a growth which was just a fleshy little tumor on its hip. He didn't have the cash to go to the vet to have an operation, so I thought, what the hell? He brought the dog to the ambulance door, I took a look at it and thought it would be an easy little excision. I pilfered ten milligrams of valium from the cabinet, gave it to the dog and told him to bring the dog back in an hour. He came back an hour later and the dog was a little spacy. We laid him down in room three. There was nothing going on in the department. He let me numb it up. The dog was real nice, he was on his side and the owner was lying over him keeping him down and distracted. He didn't tighten up at all when I anesthetized the area. Then I soaped it up, cut it out as an ellipse, threw in a few Prolene three-o sutures. I painted some collodion on it and he was out of here. If only the president of the hospital knew what kind of stuff I used to do."

It was ten after eight; I'd lost track of the time. I had to change and go meet Patty. I excused myself and apologized for not staying to hear the rest of the commandments and ran down the hall. I changed out of my greens, washed up, got my stuff together and ran out to the car.

Chapter 23

I was on Main Street driving north, shifting mental gears between the comfort and camaraderie of the coffee room and the serious business ahead. I turned right and went over the green metal bridge. Behind me was a small park with the letters "GB" spelled out in a well-manicured privet hedge. Great Barrington. Maybe the "GB" meant something else. Maybe it was a message for me. Go Back!

I saw Patty's car at the far side of the parking lot and pulled in next to her. We got out of our cars and I went over to her. It was a bright and very cold December morning. I kissed her and whispered, "We're meeting Sal." She mumbled, "I thought so." As we walked through the parking lot I saw Sal get out of his car.

I smiled. I felt genuinely glad to see him. He looked so different. He looked like an aging oversized model for the L.L.Bean catalog. He was wearing a jaunty Irish tweed hat, a nice knee-length loden car coat with toggle buttons and corduroy slacks. He was tall and trim and there were fifty or sixty pounds less of him. He smiled broadly as he neared us.

"Doc! Patty! It is so good to see you both. I'm happy to see you, really I am," he said with true enthusiasm. He shook my hand vigorously and then Patty's more gently.

"It's nice to see you too," I heard myself saying and I heard Patty mumble something I took to be agreement.

"How have you two been?" he asked.

"Oh, we've been just fine," I said. "You look terrific. I almost didn't recognize you." His cheeks were no longer full and round and hung down in flaccid jowls. He had new dentures or caps.

"This is the new me!" he said, raising his arms out to the side. "I feel great. I'm relaxed, I took up golf, my wife and I go to Florida now and then! Did you kids eat? I'm sorry, I didn't mean to call you kids, you know what I mean, you're like kids to me. I didn't mean that, I said that just because you are such young people."

I chuckled, "That's okay, Sal, we know what you mean, we didn't take offense." I turned to Patty, "I could eat; you?"

We all went in and were seated in a booth. We hung up our coats on the coat rack. Sal was wearing a Fair Isle sweater I remembered seeing in the holiday L.L.Bean catalog.

The waitress brought us a thermos pitcher of coffee. Sal sat across from us. As he looked at the menu I looked at him. Though he was so much thinner, his width still took up almost as much of his side of the booth as Patty and I did on ours. Sal was searching to see if they had low-fat granola.

"Eggs and bacon, eggs and sausage, pancakes and eggs and bacon, omelets and bacon and homefries. Isn't there anything here for people with heart disease?" It reminded me of a line from a Tom Robbins book that referred to a diner breakfast as "hot hog heaven."

Sal finally ordered a bowl of oatmeal with fruit; I ordered just an English muffin. My skinny little wife ordered a Super Sizzler with two scrambled eggs, two bacon strips, two link sausages, wheat toast and home fries.

When the food finally arrived, the waitress handed the biggest plate to the biggest person. "No, it's for her," Sal said. He leaned forward, staring at Patty's huge platter of food. He smiled. "Are you eating for two?"

Simultaneously we looked at each other and said, "We wish..."

We made small talk as we sat there eating. Sal and I had long since finished our modest breakfasts and we watched Patty working her way through her platter. Sal looked at me quizzically. I shrugged. "She always eats like this. I think maybe she's hyperthyroid."

"Sal," I finally said, "I was reluctant to call you about this. I didn't want to disturb you, I didn't know how you were, or if you were retired or not, or if you'd be interested in talking to us."

"It's okay, Charlie. Really, I'm glad you called. This shouldn't be happening and I'm glad you called. I'm sure I can help find out what is going on. Of course I still have contacts, you know, in the company I used to work for. Once in a while, you know, I get a call from someone from the company for a little advice. I try to sound interested but I give pretty obvious advice that probably won't help them much so they call me less and less. They might be thinking I'm getting a little old and slow. When we finish eating we can go for a drive and talk it over."

Sal insisted on paying for breakfast and he left the money on the table. We walked together out to the parking lot. "Have you checked your pockets?" Sal asked.

"For what?" Patty asked.

"For any little object like a button or a coin or a pen

that you didn't know you had. Maybe in your purse?" Sal answered.

Patty smirked as if this wasn't possible.

"It doesn't hurt or cost anything to be careful," I said pleadingly.

"We can put your purse in the trunk of my car, in case there's anything in it. The road noise would cover us. Might as well put your coats in too."

I hoped no one was listening to us right now.

I got in the front seat with Sal and Patty was in the back seat. He started the engine and got the heat up high.

As we drove around I told Sal all that had gone on, about how Morse and Fremont showed up with pictures, how they asked me about prescriptions I'd written. We told him of our meeting with Goldstein. I told him about the guys who tried to nab me in the parking lot of the hospital. We told him about that strange-looking guy in the Caddie with Connecticut plates that Patty scared away. He was impressed with that. I told him about the two guys who came to the ER posing as FBI who I didn't think really were and I guessed might have been from Sal's company. I told him about the lawyer who intercepted me one night on my way out of the hospital, and about the questions he asked me in the doctors' library. I told him about our friend MacPherson, the cop, who we were trying to keep in the dark but who knew something wasn't kosher.

Sal took this all in. He was a good listener. He didn't ask the same question twice. He asked me to describe the appearances, in great detail, of all the people I told him about.

"Well," Sal finally said, "let me do some asking around. It all sounds very fishy. I haven't known anything about it. But I still have my contacts and I'll get right to work on it. None of this was supposed to happen. You were supposed to be clean out, that was the promise, and protected. It's not supposed to happen this way. I'll see what I can find out, and figure out what we should do. I'll get back to you. I'll call you at work, Charlie?"

"Gee Sal, at this stage in your life, in your retirement, I hope we aren't burdening you with anything that might get messy."

"Charlie, Charlie, you're a nice boy to think of saying that. You're a mensch. But no, don't you worry about me. I've been dancing around on either side of this line, this kinda stuff , for fifty years. Don't worry about me."

"Maybe you should have my number at work also, Sal," Patty said, and I took this as a gesture that she was thinking well of him.

"That's a good idea," Sal replied.

We were back in the Friendly's parking lot. Sal parked next to our cars. He promised we'd hear from him soon and told us how nice it was to see us and we returned the compliment. We got out and he opened the trunk and we got our things. It was cold and I was happy to get my coat on. We watched Sal drive off; we were standing side by side.

"There goes your Uncle Sal," Patty said, smiling. She gave me a hug and a kiss and she went off to work and I went home to walk Mac and go to sleep. It had been a very long day for me and it was only ten in the morning.

Chapter 24

I was running around the department all afternoon with a variety of demanding and annoying, though not terribly sick or injured, people. When I finally got them cleared out I headed to the coffee room to sit down and relax and have a soda. I found Will there. He had a deep and authoritative voice and a commanding presence. He always had an opinion and if he didn't he could make one up on the spot; always bright, always articulate, usually funny, often sarcastic. He is very committed to his opinion and very convincing; seldom wrong but never in doubt.

"What are you doing here?" I asked. He had lucked out and had the weekend off and wasn't due back until tomorrow.

"Oh, I'm just hanging out. I had some errands to do. The kids were home with friends making a racket and I needed to get out of the house."

"Great. It's too noisy for you at home with your kids so you come in here, on my shift and start making a racket that I can hear all through the department. Thanks a whole lot."

"Easy, Charlie. Claws in, you cat!" That was one of

his favorite lines. Henry Higgins said it to Eliza Doo-little in *My Fair Lady.* "So how has your day been?"

"Busy. Real busy. You know, the usual." I got a can of Sprite out of the fridge and popped it open. It foamed over the can and onto my hand. I washed it off so it wouldn't get sticky.

"There was just one lady here today who had a real heart-wrenching story." It was me and Will in the cof-fee room and Maryann, the OR nurse supervisor, who was here on break. She had been in the army and then in the reserves. She retired as a major. Like Major Hou-lihan in MASH. I tried not to call her Hotlips.

"This thirty-something-year-old-lady has had a tooth-ache for days. She went to a dentist who said she needed a tooth pulled. He couldn't do it and sent her to an oral surgeon. The surgeon doesn't take Medicaid and she didn't have the cash. So she called around and found an oral surgeon in Springfield who would do it for less, but not until next week. So her mouth is getting worse and worse, she can't sleep because of the pain, her cheek is all swollen. She'll have to take a whole day off from work to drive over to Springfield; she has to find some-one to watch her two kids since she's a single mom. I don't understand why Medicaid considers dental prob-lems to be different from medical problems and not provide for them. It doesn't make sense. It doesn't seem fair."

By this time Margaret appeared and was leaning against the door, listening.

"That's the problem with all you liberals," Major Maryann said. "You're a nice guy, Charlie, but don't you believe in discipline and personal responsibility? This woman is a crybaby. She has a failure to adapt to adult life. Stuff happens. She should deal with it. If she kept her legs together she'd have two fewer dependents and she wouldn't have to rely on the government for support. If she had the foresight or discipline to learn a skill or a trade she might do better than minimum wage. If her transmission burned out on the way to the dentist, should Medicaid pay for that too, so she won't cry about the inconvenience and expense? How much do you think she blows each month on beer or pizza or dope or scratch tickets or cigarettes? If she got arrested for driving under the influence, how fast do you think she'd be able to come up with a few thousand to retain a lawyer? She'd find it. She'd get it from her friends and relatives. And she wouldn't whine to you about needing a babysitter while she was in court. If her big-screen TV crapped out you can bet she'd get it fixed in a hurry, and it would cost a lot more than that tooth."

Margaret piped up before Will or I had a chance to say anything. In her raspy voice, she said, "You know, last month I saw a bumper sticker that I thought hit the nail right on the head. It said, 'Liberals treat their dogs like people. Conservatives treat people like dogs.'" With that she turned on her heel and disappeared, leaving Maryann speechless for about three seconds.

Maybe there was a brief embarrassed flash of pink on Maryann's cheeks, maybe I imagined it. I tried not to grin too noticeably. Margaret might be the only one around here with the stature to pull one off like that against the Major. Way to go, Margaret. We looked at Maryann and she smiled.

"God I love getting her goat like that," she said, smiling.

She excused herself and I sat with Will, but didn't finish my soda before I got called that more patients had come in.

I was beat. I was frazzled. It was a crazy day at work, twelve hours of constant patients, some sick, some sick and whining, some just whining. I hadn't eaten. I managed to get the decks cleared and had no loose strings hanging when Barker came in ten minutes late to relieve me. Typical. I was pleased that I had no patients to sign out to him. For their sake, not for his.

I grabbed my stuff and raced home in my old Subaru. It was getting a little cranky about starting lately, which then caused me to get cranky. I listened to four minutes of the news on National Public Radio and then I was home. I parked and was planning to make a beeline for the refrigerator.

I barged through the front door. Patty was standing there, waiting, with a stern look on her face.

"You! Upstairs," she commanded.

"What's the matter?" I asked, surprised and perplexed.

"I'm ovulating and I need you to pollinate me."

"I'm starving. I had a crazy day and I haven't eaten in like ten hours!"

"I don't care. Get upstairs, brush your teeth and take off your clothes," she ordered.

"You told me you ovulated a few days ago,"

"I was wrong then. Now I'm right."

"Let me eat something first," I pleaded. Mac was sitting there watching us. We were talking in unaccustomedly loud and forceful voices.

"No. Now. Move it!"

"Boy! Some people are so bossy! C'mon! What difference does it make if junior is conceived now or in fifteen minutes?"

"Every minute counts and you're burning daylight," she barked.

I grinned at her. "Some people are so pushy!" Reluctantly I went up the stairs. "Would you mind if we turn the radio on? There's a really good interview on NPR." She smacked me on the behind and I raced up the stairs.

I completed my task and almost fell asleep. My growling stomach roused me. When I got up Patty was in a peculiar position. Her head and shoulders were on a pillow on the floor, her legs were up on the edge of the bed and her torso was in a downwards diagonal. The veins on the sides of her forehead were bulging and her face was red.

"What are you doing?" I asked curiously.

"I'm trying to get those little guys in there," she said.

"They are motile. They swim. They don't depend on gravity," I explained.

"Yours need all the help they can get."

"You really know how to hurt a guy."

I took a shower and put on pajamas and went downstairs to the kitchen. I opened a beer and began searching through the refrigerator. I cracked a few eggs, chopped in some onion and cheese and made scrambled eggs and toast. After that Mac and I had cookies and milk while I finished reading the newspaper.

I cleaned up and put the dishes in the dishwasher. Mac had a new trick. He learned to pre-clean the dishes as they were stacked in the dishwasher rack. Yummm, good crumbs and egg juice and marmalade on those plates. I left the dishwasher door open for him and sat back down at the kitchen table to read.

Suddenly there was a metallic sound and then a loud crash and I thought the house was being invaded. At the sound of breaking glass I turned, startled, to see Mac struggling to make his way through the door into the dining room with the dishwasher rack attached to his collar. He banged and banged against the door frame until the rack shifted and he got through and raced to the living room, the rack swinging left and right spewing Patty's china and crystal right and left. I raced after

309

him in an effort to untangle him. By the time I reached him in the living room he'd become uncoupled from his tormentor. In just those five or ten seconds the dog had nearly destroyed the house. I couldn't stop laughing, as I walked through the house in my slippered feet crunching over shards of tableware.

"What the hell is going on down there?" Patty hollered from the top of the stairs.

"No big problem. Mac just wrecked the place."

She was halfway down the stairs and was surveying the wreckage, looking at me and Mac, all the broken stuff, and the dishwasher rack in the living room.

"See, he was licking the plates in the dishwasher. I guess his collar got stuck on one of the pegs in the rack. He panicked and pulled out and you should've seen this poor little black dog trying to get away from this nasty metal rack monster that attacked him and was holding fast to his throat. The poor guy, he's still shaking."

When we stopped laughing we got out the brooms and dustpan and started sweeping up the debris. The dishwasher rack was bent in one corner but with a pliers I straightened it and set it back in the machine. Big bad machine. Frighten our innocent little puppy dog like that.

Patty disappeared and reappeared in sneakers, jeans and a UMass sweatshirt.

"Where are you going?" I asked.

"Let's take a walk," she answered.

I looked at the clock. It was nine-thirty. I got dressed.

We turned right down the sidewalk going toward Cottage Street. It was cold. We were bundled up. Maccabee was on a leash and was having a great time. The ground was frozen and hard and there was just a little snow covering the grass. We chitchatted as we walked along, side by side, in the dark. Mac was orbiting around on the radius of his leash, sniffing every bush and tree trunk and hydrant.

We turned left on Cottage and walked uphill toward Hillside Avenue. The streetlights were fewer but with the occasional house light and the stars it was easy to see our way. As we walked a big four-door sedan cruised slowly and steadily past us like a big barge at sea. The powerful engine hummed as it drifted by.

"That's the second time that car passed us," Patty said.

We walked down Hillside, past the big brick building that was orignially built as a grammar school. For a while it served as a satellite of Berkshire Community College and it now was being used as a district court building. We continued down to State Road, then took a left and headed to back to Gilmore.

Finally we turned toward home. As we approached the other side of the courthouse, we noticed there were rows of cars parked closely together on both sides of the street, blocking the sidewalks and forcing us to walk down the middle of the road. Somebody must be having a get-together. Our shadows fell in front of us, cast by headlights coming up behind us, and I edged Patty over to the right, close to the row of parked cars. I shortened Mac's leash. I heard a car slowly drifting up behind us.

Suddenly the driver floored it and the big engine roared. I could hear and sense the big car rocketing toward us. I jumped forward half a step and with my right arm swept Patty to the side of the road into a small space between two parked cars. I swung Mac through the air in an effort to get him off the street. As I dove after him I caught a glimpse of that same big dark sedan barreling down the street, tires squeal-

311

ing and still accelerating, nearly sideswiping the row of parked cars. It all happened so fast.

I had no way of breaking my fall because my right arm was extended backwards, having hurled Patty out of the way, and my left was bound to Mac, so I crash-landed onto the trunk of a parked car. With my face.

I slid to the ground. Mac was standing over me licking my face. *Are you okay Patty?* I was disoriented and then a wave of pain washed over me and my eye and nose and cheek and mouth throbbed. I groaned and realized I was lying on my back on the street. There was a pebble under my head and it hurt. I could hear Patty's voice yelling, but it sounded like she was a block away. I looked at the bumper of the car. This was a better lit end of the street. I looked at the license plate. There were only two bolts holding it in. They looked rusty. If it was my car I would put in two more.

My mouth hurt and I reached up with my hand to feel my front teeth and one of them felt loose; I could wiggle it. There was a warm metallic taste in my mouth; blood. And then Patty was there helping me, asking me how I felt.

"I'm okay, I'm okay," I replied and I rolled over onto all fours. "Was I graceful?" I asked.

She paused before she answered. "Not particularly, no."

I was less dazed now and the pain in my face felt more sharp. I spat some blood on the road. I got a handkerchief out of my coat pocket and held it to my nose as I got up onto my feet, Patty helping me.

"Do you feel steady? Do you feel seaworthy?" she asked. I nodded. With one hand she clung to me, with the other she took Mac's leash. We trudged home, the three of us, holding each other up.

"Patty, are you sure you're okay?

"Absolutely. It's you I'm worried about."

"Patty, what was that all about?"

"My guess is that some of your friends are trying to soften you up a bit to make you more inclined to cooperate with them."

"You don't think they were trying to kill us?"

"There are easier ways to kill us. Cleaner ways. They were trying to scare us."

"I'd say they succeeded."

We got back to the house and no one was waiting there for us. Patty led me to the kitchen, turned a chair away from the table and sat me in the middle of the room under the light. I took off my coat. She looked me over; she wasn't happy.

"How do you feel?" she asked. "You look awfully pale."

"Oh, just fine, thanks, how do you feel?" I asked.

"Don't be a smartass, Charlie."

"I feel okay, I just feel like I got punched in the face. Did you get hurt? You still haven't told me."

"No, not at all, you pushed me and I just dove and rolled. Let me get some of this blood off you."

My nose was bleeding and to avoid dripping all over the place I kept my head tilted back. Blood went down the back of my throat and I swallowed it, which was dumb since blood in the stomach can make you nauseous. Patty began swabbing my face with a wet washcloth.

"You're pretty messed up here, Charlie. You're pretty swollen." My nose was swollen and it ached. I had a cut inside my lip where my tooth went into it and my right lower eyelid was sore and swollen.

"I think we ought to take you to Fairview," Patty said.

"No, I don't wanna go."

"Yes. You need to go."

"I don't want to."

313

"You have to."

"No I don't." I stamped my feet.

"Yes, you do. I'll buy you an ice cream if you go."

"An ice cream? Really? Can I get a hot fudge sundae with sprinkles and walnuts and a cherry?"

"Yes. But only if you're good."

"Okay. I'll be good. Do you think they'll give me a sticker at the hospital?"

"I don't know. I'll ask. I'm sure if you're good they would give you a sticker if they have one."

"Okay. Let's go. Can Maccabee come?"

"No. Maccabee cannot come to the hospital with us."

I whined. "Why? I want him to come with us."

We got in Patty's car and as she drove down the road, I said, "Uh oh."

"What's the matter?"

"I forgot. Barker is on."

"So?"

"You know how I feel about him. I wouldn't let him touch me. Or you. Or Maccabee."

"Well, he can certainly look you over and get X-rays if he thinks you need them."

"That's just the problem, he doesn't think." She just groaned and moved her head as if she were rolling her eyes, which I couldn't see since she was looking forward out the windshield.

We got to the ER and entered through the ambulance door. I was holding a big wad of paper towel to my nose and Patty holding my arm. We went into the waiting room and just my bad luck, MacPherson was there, looking huge in his blue uniform, leaning over the desk, flirting with his wife.

They turned to look at us, their mouths dropped and they started laughing.

"What the hell happened to you, Chollie?"

"Spousal abuse. Domestic violence. Very sad, really. Officer, please arrest this woman; she's brutal."

They took me straight back to a cubicle where the ER nurse and Patty undressed me and got me in a Johnny. After the nurse took my vital signs, Barker sauntered in with a smirk on his face.

"What happened Charlie? One of your patients jump you on the way home?" He chuckled at his own joke, which wasn't funny. None of us laughed.

I thought about my answer. "We were just out for a walk with the dog and I slipped on the ice and fell into the back of a car."

"Oh," he said. "Clumsy, aren't you?"

Jerk.

He began to look me over, moving closer to me on the stretcher. With an abrupt motion his hands were on my face, palpating my nose and eye socket brusquely. I hadn't seen him wash his hands. He shone his penlight in my eyes but not for long enough to get a good look. It takes several seconds. He asked me to squeeze his hand, as if that's a valid way to check motor function, and then asked me to touch my finger to my nose, as if that's all you need to do to complete a neurologic exam. He took a one-second-long look in each ear with the otoscope, then he looked at my retinas with the ophthalmoscope, but he wasn't really trying. Once the bright white spots disappeared from my eyes I saw Margaret at the end of the cubicle, near the foot of my bed. Her lips were pressed together and she wasn't happy. Patty was standing next to her.

I was semi-reclining on the cot holding an emesis basin on my chest as blood dripped into it from my nose. He was getting ready to squirt some NeoSynephrine up my nose when Will and MacPherson materialized in the cubicle. Boy, was I glad to see Will.

315

Will told Barker to get lost, though not in so many words.

"I was just finishing up," Barker said.

"I'm just getting started," Will said. He rolled up his sleeves and went to the sink.

"Dr. Barker," Margaret said, "I just made a fresh pot of coffee for you." And he left.

"Chollie, tell me what happened," MacPherson said.

"Nothing." I glanced at Patty. "We were just walking down the street with the dog and I slipped on the ice and banged my face into the trunk of a car."

"Right. And how fast was this car going?" MacPherson shot a glance to Will. They were in cahoots.

"It was parked."

"Where was this?"

"On Gilmore. Across from the courthouse."

"What kind of car was it?"

"I don't know."

Patty piped in. "It was an Olds Cutlass Supreme. Dark brown, I think, it was hard to tell, it was dark."

"Chollie, I went for a walk tonight too. I didn't see any ice."

"Well there was ice where we were. Just a small patch, and don't you know it, I had to step on it."

Will and MacPherson nodded at each other. One came to each side of the bed. They eased me off the bed and stood me up and pulled off my gown. They looked me over. They squeezed my upper arms, scanned me over, looked at my knuckles, looked at my belly. I knew what they were doing. They were looking to see if I'd been beat up, if anyone bruised my arms by holding them tight to restrain me, if anyone had punched me in the stomach. Looked at my shins for kick marks.

They got me back on the stretcher. It was weird to be almost naked in front of my friends. And to be lying to them. And to be a patient in my own ER. Because my wife made me come.

They turned to Patty.

She recoiled and lifted her hands toward them, palm out, "No, not me, nothing happened to me, there aren't any marks on me!"

"Patty, what happened?" MacPherson said.

"Just what Charlie told you."

"Patty, what happened?"

"I'm telling you, just what Charlie said. He slipped on the ice."

"Patty, there is no ice. And Chollie is too agile to just trip and have this happen. What happened?"

She looked at me guiltily. My nose was still dripping into the basin. By the time this interrogation gets over I might bleed to death. Patty just shook her head.

"Patty, what did the car look like?" MacPherson asked.

"What car? The car he fell into?" she asked, her voice composed, looking him straight in the eye.

In a deeper louder voice MacPherson repeated, "Patty, you already told us what the parked car looked like. What did the car look like that ran you off the road?"

"We didn't get run off the road. He slipped."

MacPherson, frustrated, took a deep long sigh and looked at the floor. He looked at each one of us in the room, holding our gaze for a few seconds apiece. Then he sighed again. His hands were on his hips. Margaret was enjoying this. It was high drama.

"Patty, I've been a cop for a long time. I've been listening to people telling me stories for a long time. Which is a polite way of saying I've been listening to people tell me lies for a long time. You think I can't tell?"

Suddenly he stood up straight and in a loud voice

he barked, "Patty, what the hell did the car look like?"

Now she was a little sheepish looking. I looked at her and gave a little nod.

"It was a recent model full size four-door Buick with dark paint and a vinyl Landau roof and the license plate was seven-eight-two-T-K-L, from Massachusetts," she blurted out, and seemed exhausted, out of breath and relieved all at the same time.

"Thank you," he said. "That wasn't so hard, was it?"

"I'm sorry, MacPherson, but we wanted to keep this low profile, I'm sorry I wasn't direct with you. I hope you aren't mad at me for being obtuse, I'm just trying to be protective."

"Mad at you? Patty, you are the sharpest and smartest and toughest woman I know. I'm not mad at you. I want to hire you. We could use you on the force. Now tell me, do you know who the driver was? Fess up."

"Honestly, I have no clue who the driver was," Patty said, convincingly.

"Will, do your thing." MacPherson said. As he left the cubicle he drew his radio from his belt and mumbled into it.

Patty started to look a little pale herself and her eyebrows arched and furrowed like they do when she gets tearful. Margaret picked up on this and took her by the arm and the two of them walked off.

Will returned with the epistaxis tray. This was the bloody nose kit. With a syringe he drew up some liquid from a vial and then squirted it into a small glass sterile cup. Then he soaked nasal pledgets in it. "Here it comes, Charlie, a perfectly legal and appropriate use of cocaine. I hope you enjoy it." Cocaine is a great drug for ear, nose and throat issues. It is a strong anesthetic as well as a vasoconstrictor. It can shrink down the smaller bleeding nasal blood vessels and bring down swelling as well. Using a nasal speculum and a bayonet forcep he packed each side with a pledget even though it was only the right side that was bleeding. It felt awkward as hell for a minute or two until it became anesthetized and then I didn't feel it at all.

Will put me through a neurological exam that was as thorough as Barker's was abbreviated. He checked all function of the twelve cranial nerves, which Barker probably couldn't list. He gently palpated all the facial bones; put my neck through a full range of motion. But halfway through his exam I barfed into the wastebasket. It had that smelly, black, coffee-ground quality of blood mixed with stomach acid. I also saw the eggs and onions and cookies a second time. As I upchucked, the pledgets went flying into the basket as well.

"I bet you did that just so you could get more cocaine," Will said as he placed another pair of pledgets.

Will said he wanted to send me for X-rays of my nose and the right lateral orbit, that is, the wall of the eye socket.

"Why bother?" I asked, "Even if it's broken it's not displaced enough to do anything about."

"Just be quiet and let me be the doctor. Don't you know the ten commandments of being a good patient?" I didn't say another word.

MacPherson found me in X-ray and told me the plates had been reported stolen in Springfield a month ago. The X-rays were okay, my nose stopped bleeding and the cocaine solution was too dilute to make anybody high anyway, though we always joked about it.

I was back in my cubicle resting with an ice pack on my face. Patty was sitting with me. I felt the blood pressure cuff tighten on my arm as someone checked it. Then I was startled by a sharp poke in my deltoid. I jumped up and there was Will, grinning, with a syringe in my arm.

"What the hell is that?" I asked.

"Demerol seventy-five, vistaril fifty."

"What's that for?

"You know what it's for. To deaden your pain and help you get some sleep."

"You know you shouldn't give narcotics to someone with a head injury!"

"Knock it off, Charlie, you had a face injury, not a head injury. You have no neurological signs or symptoms. Quit being such a stickler and let someone help you. You and I know the face was designed as a frontal crumple zone to protect the brainbox from anterior impact.

"You should listen to him, Charlie," croaked Margaret. I didn't know she was in the room.

Will discharged me and I got dressed with Patty's help. We thanked everyone and Patty walked me out. When we got outside and hit the cold air it was bracing.

"And how are you feeling, my dearest?" I asked.

"I'm feelin' near as faded as my jeans," she replied.

"Janis Joplin?"

"She sang it but Kris Kristofferson wrote it. Will and MacPherson, they're really good friends. They're really looking out for us." I nodded.

We were home in five minutes and the Demerol was kicking in. Patty steadied me as we went up the porch stairs. She deposited me on the living room couch and Mac jumped up next to me.

"Uhhh. I need a drink. Would you share a martini with me Charlie?"

"No thanks, Will just injected me with one."

I heard glass tinkling in the kitchen. I heard Patty

walk my way. She stopped at the stereo and put in a disc. She shooed Mac away and sat down on the couch. I turned and put my head in her lap. Linda Ronstadt came on the stereo, the album she did with the Nelson Riddle orchestra where she sings classic love songs.

My eyes were closed, I was warm and woozy, she was playing with my hair. When she sang along with the lyrics I could smell the martini on her breath.

"We're going to get through this, Charlie, we'll be fine," she said and she kissed my forehead. I'm glad she can be so damn confident, I thought. And then I fell asleep.

Chapter 25

It was seven PM on the second Friday of December and my shift was almost over.

Margaret and I were standing by the ambulance doors as we watched the ambulance back up closer. We'd been standing there jibber jabbering and watching a light snow come down. We hadn't had much snow yet, by mid-December, though it had been cold. There were flood lights by the ambulance entrance that illuminated the falling snow and gave it an ethereal appearance. One of the local physicians had called to say that he was sending in an extremely elderly patient from a nursing home who was to be a direct admission to the hospital, he just wanted me to make sure she was pink and breathing and didn't need to go downstairs. That's where the morgue was.

The ambulance made an electronic beeping safety noise as it backed up toward us. My shift was over in less than an hour and I was going to meet Patty at the annual hospital holiday party. It was being held in a big old mansion in town that for the past few decades was an economics institute.

"Would you ever get into an ambulance that said that on it?" Margaret asked, in her Gravel Gertie voice.

The ambulance was from Becket. On the top of the

back were the initials B.A.D. For Becket Ambulance Department.

"Yeah," I said. "I would probably think twice if I were a patient about getting into an ambulance that said 'bad' on it."

"I mean, what were they thinking? Who was in charge of sending that vehicle to the sign shop anyway? Don't you think any self-respecting sign painter would say, 'Hey, do you really want me to paint that on here?'"

The door opened and some snow blew in on the cold wintry air. We said hello to the EMTs and noted that the patient was still pink and breathing. They wheeled on past us to the elevators to go up to the patient floors.

The party started at seven and I didn't get out till eight when Barker was coming to replace me. So I'd miss an hour of cocktails; no big deal. Margaret wasn't going to it this year. That's just as well, she said, because she has a hard time with some of the administrative staff and board members. She doesn't suffer fools gladly though she puts up with me.

I brought my suit with me and I was going to wash up and change here and go directly to the party. I resisted the temptation to change ahead of time, because with my luck, I'd put on my nice clothes and at five minutes to eight someone would come in vomiting or bleeding and that would be it for me. I only have one suit. It's a dark gray glenn plaid with a very fine almost unnoticeable gold thread running every inch or two, up and down and across. I think the salesman called it a windowpane pattern. I've had it a long time. I got it when I was interviewing for medical schools. It's been on lots of interviews since. The suit could've gone without me. It had a lot of experience.

I went to the OR locker room and washed up and shaved. By the time I got out Barker had arrived. I took my freshly laundered shirt and suit out of their plastic bags and changed.

Margaret came by. "I wanted to see you all spiffed up, Charlie. You look good. Damn spiffy. You look like you could be a doctor or something." She looked me over head to toe. She stared at my shoes. "You even shined your shoes, Charlie! What did you do, rub your shoe on the back of your pants leg?"

I grinned. I thanked her, put on my beige raincoat since I didn't own a topcoat. I gave Margaret a kiss, gathered up my stuff and headed out to my car.

I put the stuff in the back seat and began scraping and brushing the snow off the windows. The air was real cold, it was dark, my breath came out in clouds and I was thinking about this evening. Patty had been excited about this big gala.

The roads did not have enough snow on them to make them slippery and the driving was fine. I had the weekend off and I thought about the things I needed to get done. I needed to take Mac for a good long walk. He's gotten so big and energetic. He's still trying to figure out what snow is. I wanted to get a bunch of firewood cut for the fireplace. Patty said the other day that she'd spoken with Sal and we were going to meet in Springfield with some of his cronies tomorrow morning, to get some things ironed out and over with, whatever that means.

The parking lot at the institute was almost full and I pulled into a spot way at the back. This was higher up on the hillside and the wind was howling. I didn't have a hat on and my ears were burning with the cold.

I went through the big wooden front door. It was good to get indoors. I was late in arriving and there was no one in the foyer or the front of the building. I stopped in the men's room to get my hair back in place. I paused a few seconds to study my face in the mirror. The bruise from my fall against the car was almost gone. I followed the sound of voices and it led me to the ballroom. There were many people there. There was a large mirrored ball, suspended from the ceiling, slowly turning, reflecting small snowflakes of light all over the room. A small orchestra was in one corner. There were dinner tables set up around the perimeter of the room. There were waitresses in white blouses and long black skirts carrying trays of hors d'oevres. My eyes adjusted from the bright light of the hall to the subdued light of the ballroom. I scanned the crowd looking for my wife.

On the far side of the room, in the corner opposite the band, there was a bar. There was a clutch of people there. A group of men in dark suits, one of them a tuxedo, were hovering around a tall woman in a slinky sleeveless dress. She was leaning against the bar, her ankles crossed, one hand on the bar, the other behind her back. She had a long lean feline look. She looked dangerous.

I continued looking around the room. I saw some people I knew, but not Patty. I glanced back at the bar. One of the men there, the one in the tuxedo, saw me and gestured to me. The woman followed his gesture and her eyes locked on mine. It was Patty. She disengaged from the men and began to walk, slowly and purposefully toward me. She looked tall, I'd not seen her in high heels before.

I'd never seen her like this. She was stunning. She had a sly smile. Her hair was pulled back in a French braid. She was wearing a beautiful velvet dress I didn't recognize. As she approached I could see the dress was dark bottle green. The neckline plunged deeply and revealed a faint shadow under her breasts. It was tight around her waist. The top tied as a halter behind her neck. It was long, almost to the floor, and there were slits on each side so the dress flowed as she took each step. She wore sparkling diamond earrings and there was a larger diamond solitaire on a fine chain around her neck. I didn't know she had them.

She stopped three feet in front of me. I was speechless. "Hello, handsome. I thought you'd never get here."

"You're such a beautiful woman! But my wife is around here somewhere."

She laughed and took a step forward and pulled me toward her. Tightly. She was wearing perfume. She looked up at me and put her lips against mine. When our lips parted some people clapped. I was embarrassed.

Patty took me by the hand and led me to the bar. I said hello to the people there, other doctors on staff and their spouses. Patty nodded at the bartender and he poured each of us a flute of champagne, as if prearranged.

I was standing close to Patty. We sipped our champagne.

"Charlie, you look like you're in shock!" she said

"I am!" I said. "You are so stunning. You look like a model in the Sunday *Times* magazine."

It had been a secret. She and Margaret had gone shopping together at Niemann Marcus at the Holyoke Mall. Their project was to find a real knock-out dress. Margaret loaned her the diamonds. Patty spent the afternoon at the hairdresser's getting her thick brown hair plaited into a French braid that started at her scalp and continued back down her head ending between her shoulder blades. She had a long neck.

She finished the last of her champagne and set the glass on the bar. "C'mon," she said, "finish your glass." She fixed her gaze on someone far behind me and nodded.

"Come with me," she said as she took my hand, "let's dance."

There was no one else on the dance floor. She looked at me and smiled as we danced a two-step.

"The music," I said, "that's 'Some Enchanted Evening' from *South Pacific*. I was just thinking of it when I came into room and saw you. I love this song."

Patty smiled and nodded. "It is," she said, "I asked them to play it."

"Thank you. You thought of everything tonight." She nodded, smiling.

This is the woman I so nearly lost. This is the woman I neglected and was inconsiderate to, not by choice, years ago during the bad times. This woman took me back in from the snow.

This is the woman who took risks to be with me, who had the courage to confront society's monsters, who wants to protect me from my troubles.

"What is the name of the perfume you're wearing? It's wonderful"

"Tea Rose."

"It does smell like a rose. And like Earl Grey tea."

She nodded as we danced. The band was picking up the tempo. "That would be Oil of Bergamot."

I would do anything for her. I would die for her.

This is the educated woman who wants to teach college students to think, to think about science, to get them grounded in science, so they can go on to do good and maybe great things for the people of the world.

This is the woman who knows me like no one else. I looked at our hands held out to my left, with my father's wedding band on my hand and her engagement ring on her right.

There were several other couples on the dance floor now and I felt less of a spectacle, though I was so entranced, it hardly mattered.

May she never doubt that she married the right man. Let me never do anything that might make her doubt that.

Will Connor suddenly appeared and asked if he could cut in. "No!" Patty barked sharply and Will walked away with his tail between his legs. Patty held me closer and we danced cheek to cheek.

As we danced I reminisced of a time, years ago. After the dark times ended I took a few months leave from work and spent a lot of time with Patty. When I got back to the ER, Margaret asked when the two of us were getting married. "I've been asking myself the same question," I replied. She said this in her normal voice, when she still had both halves of her larynx. "Do you love her?" she asked. "Yes," I answered. "Are you infatuated with her?" "Yes," I answered. "Do you respect her?" "And how," I answered. "She's a helluva woman, Charlie. She's a helluva match for you. You may never have such an opportunity. She's her own person. She loves you, she's devoted to you, she's bright, she's good, she's good for you, you may never find another woman like that as long as you live."

I didn't really need Margaret's advice to marry Patty. It was the best thing that ever happened.

I could explain to her about medicine. I could teach her the framework of logic of differential diagnosis. I could tell her jokes and make her laugh. She could sing sweet Beatles love songs to me and explain to me, in comprehensible terms, about Camus and Sartre. And explain to me about politics and Torah. And talk baby talk to a black lab puppy in a falsetto.

Chapter 26

We got back late from the party and were still all charged up. Patty slipped off her heels and put on sensible shoes and a heavy coat and we took Mac for a walk around the dark snowy neighborhood at midnight. We were walking side by side, we'd let Mac off the leash which we weren't supposed to do but there wasn't any traffic in our little residential neighborhood in the little town of Great Barrington in rural Berkshire County this late on a Friday night. Saturday morning, actually. It was crisp and cold and we could see our breath and as we walked past the occasional streetlight, Patty's teeth glistened like her diamond earrings as she spoke and smiled. Our breaths were steamy. We kept track of Mac's whereabouts by the sound of his footsteps on the snow. The snow made it easier to see his black silhouette cruising along all the front lawns, sniffing around. We had a good time at the party and we were discussing the things we heard and the conversations we'd had. Patty finally relented and did have a dance with Will and said that he was funny and light on his feet. When we got back in the house Patty told me we weren't finished partying yet.

Mac woke us up around seven and we rolled out of bed. We had breakfast in our pajamas. I made shirred eggs with feta cheese and Tabasco sauce and chopped green peppers. We drank coffee and orange juice and had English muffins. We ended up in the shower and once her skin got wet I could smell her Tea Rose perfume from the night before.

Patty said we were due to meet Sal at the Friendly's restaurant just off Exit 3 of the Massachusetts turnpike. Then the three of us would drive somewhere to meet his colleagues so we could talk over the pesky things that have been going on and get them out of the way. That would be good. It had made life uncomfortable these last few months and I looked forward to explaining it all and clearing the air between us and getting it all the hell out of the way.

I was dressed and ready and sitting downstairs in the living room playing with Mac as I unsuccessfully tried to read the newspaper. I could hear Patty moving around upstairs, her closet door opening and closing. I could hear her going back and forth from the bedroom to the bathroom.

A few times I thought about shouting upstairs to ask "What the heck is taking you so long?" but I didn't want to sound like one of those kinds of husbands.

Finally she came downstairs and she looked like Patty. Her hair was still in the French braid. She was wearing a bulky oversized Icelandic sweater with a turtleneck collar that was beige at the top and slowly became darker brown as it went to her waist. She had corduroy Levi's on and lightweight hiking boots. No make up. She smiled at me as I sat on the couch.

"Aren't you ready?" she asked. She slipped on a windbreaker parka and we were out the door. We got into my Subaru and headed to West Stockbridge to get onto the Mass Pike. As we drove I wondered what today's meeting would be like and hoped it would go well. Patty said we might be meeting Sal's former boss and a few other people. I hoped it would be a polite interview and I would be able to explain convincingly all I wanted to tell them.

When we got to Exit 3 we drove to the restaurant and rolled to the back of the parking lot where we saw Sal's dark gray Buick sedan sitting there idling. We parked next to it and as we got out Sal did too. He went to Patty, took her hand and gave it a gentle shake and then he leaned forward and gave her a fatherly kiss on the cheek. I smiled. Such a big man, towering over my wife.

"Hello, Charlie. It's good to see you. I'm happy to see you. Really I am… You guys been good?"

"Yes, we've been fine," Patty replied. "We had a great time at a big hospital Christmas party we went to last night."

"Is that why your hair is so fancy? It looks so elegant." It was funny to hear Sal speak in such a sensitive social tone after my past experiences with him.

Patty and I got in the back of his Buick and he drove slowly along Route 20 towards Springfield. He began briefing us on what to expect.

"So, we'll be meeting with the man who was more or less my boss before I retired. His name is Lou Spellacci. In the old days his nickname was, 'the Spell,' because sometimes he had spells of rage. Don't call him that. And there will probably be a couple other guys there. It's real nice Patty, that you want to come to this, you really didn't need to. They probably won't be used to having a lady at a discussion like this but they'll get used to it. I admire the way you two stick together.

"Anyway, they'll probably be a little brusque with you at first, don't let that bother you, they just have to let you know they're in control. They'll ease off in ten minutes when they see you don't have a chip on your shoulder. At first you should probably let me do most of the talking.

"Lou has been a little stressed lately because we know he's being investigated by the FBI. He thinks he might be indicted sometime in the near future. He's probably right. But that threat has been hanging over him for years anyway, it's nothing new, but lately he's more nervous about it. He's looking to find out what weak spots he might have. He knows you were involved with me and some of his injured people. You aren't one of us so he doesn't know if he can trust you.

"I'll paint a picture like you're practically one of us. I'll tell him how much good work you did for us a few years ago. He'll see that you're a sincere quiet honest kid. At some point I'll ask you to agree with me that the kinds of patients you saw with me were just like the ones you saw every day at your real job, you can't keep them straight, who you saw, where you saw them, when you saw them. You didn't know anybody's names. I'll also make it clear that you're very good at keeping secrets, not the least reason is that you made a lot of money working for us that you wouldn't want to jeopardize. Have you spent any of it yet?"

"Not a nickel."

"I didn't think so. Don't tell him that. So, I think it'll go okay. Just let me do the talking. He might try to play games with you and try to rough you up and get you off balance. Don't let him get under your skin, don't let him unnerve you. That's what he's trying to do. Just sit there, calm, polite, not too proud. Just smile, sit there confident but not cocky, don't look worried or scared, don't look weak because that'll make him want to keep poking at you. Can you do that?"

"I think so. At work there are always people trying to manipulate me and provoke me."

"This won't be the same. Because when you're at work you're still in a position of power, you're the one they're trying to get something from. You're the one who can write the prescription. They may be arrogant but you're still the one who's the doctor. But I'm sure you can handle it with Lou. I know you won't be cocky or act like you're trying to outsmart him, that you're educated and he's not."

"I wouldn't do that."

"What do you want me to say and do, Sal?" Patty asked.

Sal paused. "Not much. But your presence will be supportive. Please don't say much, we don't want it to seem like you're pleading your husband's case."

"Pleading my case?" I asked. "That makes it sound like we're going to court. Or a kangaroo court. Are they going to be sitting in judgment?"

"Oh no, Charlie, nothing like that. It was just a figure of speech."

We drove into a condominium development off Route 20 in West Springfield, just outside of Springfield proper. He parked and we got out of the car. It must have been ten degrees warmer, here in the Connecticut River Valley. But it was gray, overcast, with impenetrable clouds and I couldn't see where the sun was.

The development was almost empty. I would have been more comfortable in a busier, more populated area. Hardly any parking spaces had cars in them. Not all the buildings were finished. The ones that seemed occupied still had building debris in piles here and there, and there was no landscaping. There was less snow around here than at home.

We followed Sal up a walkway It was concrete and was still rough and hadn't been cleaned up yet. We went to Condo Unit Number 327 and Sal pushed the doorbell. In an instant the door opened and a big young man ushered us in to what was going to be a very elegant townhouse apartment. There was some furniture in it but there were still bare Romex wires coming out of the walls and ceilings, a big pail of drywall compound, ladders, sawhorses, dropcloths.

An older man came over to us and he and Sal said hello and shook hands. The young man stood aside, with his right hand in the pocket of his overcoat. He looked vaguely familiar and it made me uneasy.

"Okay, Lou, this is Dr. Charlie Davids, and his wife, Patty."

Lou only nodded brusquely.

"Okay, Sal," Lou said, "let's see it."

Sal opened his topcoat and swung it back to reveal the big semiautomatic handgun on his right hip. Lou reached over and took it out and put the gun in his own pocket. Just a formality, I thought.

Then Lou was looking at me. *Me? No, not me! I don't have a gun on me.*

I looked at Lou and answered the question that he hadn't asked. "No, I don't have one," and that sentence came out with a sound of surprise in my voice.

"Check him," Lou barked to the young man. Then Lou walked out of the room with Sal's gun and came back in a moment without it.

The young man came over to me and patted me down. Rather roughly. "He's got nothing," said the young man. I'd seen him before but I couldn't place him.

Lou directed us over to a sofa. It was covered with a

dropcloth. We took our off coats. Sal sat at the far end, Patty sat next to him in the middle with her coat neatly folded and her mittens on top. I was next to her at the other end. We were in a mostly finished living room but there was drywall dust all over the place.

We were sitting and the other two men were standing in front of us, six or eight feet away. Lou looked about ten years younger than Sal, maybe in his late fifties. He was a shorter than me, a little heavier. He had a receding hairline and the hair on his temples was gray. His face was round, he didn't quite have a double chin. His face was deeply lined and he had dark brown eyes. His eyebrows were heavy. His teeth were perfect and they were unnaturally white. He was wearing a pinstriped sport shirt under a navy blue pullover sweater that looked like cashmere. He had a big heavy gold wristwatch on his left wrist. On the right ring finger he had a bulky gold ring with initials on it.

"So Sal, glad you can make it. I finally meet your two friends we've been talking about."

"Yeah, Lou, this is Dr. Charlie Davids and his wife Patty," he said again. "She's a pharmacist."

"Nice to meet you, Mr. Spellacci," I said, and Patty nodded. He didn't step closer so we could shake hands. I kept glancing at the other big man, trying to place him.

"Charlie did us an enormous load of good work a few years ago," Sal continued, "he really went way beyond the call of duty and me and a lot of the people he helped are very grateful to him."

"I'm sure he was very well paid, that's how we show our gratefulness around here, and when it's paid, it's over." I swallowed hard as I heard the limits of his gratitude.

"They've been a little nervous lately," Sal explained. "Phil Testa had a talk with Charlie recently. A couple of months ago some guys tried to grab him on his way out of work and take him for a ride. Some wiseguys posed as if they were FBI agents to talk to him. And then three guys tried to kidnap him in front of his house."

"Who was that?" Spellacci asked. "I didn't know about that one."

I told the story of the Cadillac with Connecticut plates and described the three men. I didn't tell them what Patty had done.

"No," Spellacci said, "I don't know who those guys were. Do you, Sal?"

"No. Not a clue."

No one spoke for part of a minute. Spellacci didn't seem too concerned about our predicament.

"How are things with you, Lou?" Sal finally asked, breaking the silence.

"Oh, you know, I keep busy. A little of this, a little of that. I'm good, I feel good. I'd feel a lot better if I didn't have the attorney general's office up my ass. I don't know how they got all their information but it really pisses me off. Actually I do know. People keep telling 'em. That's the trouble with the business these days, people can't keep their mouths shut. No pride. Omerta doesn't mean nothing anymore. A man's word doesn't mean nothing anymore. It stinks. Our whole business is based on people respecting that. Know what I mean?" He took a few steps backwards and picked up a folding chair. He set it up in front of us and sat on it backwards, facing us, with his arms resting on the back of the chair.

A metal folding chair. That's where I saw that young guy before. I was on a metal folding chair. I was tied to it. He was holding a gun. My gun. I only saw him for a minute, but it was an intense minute. I'm surprised it was this hard to remember him. The big young thug was standing off to our left, hands in his coat pockets.

"Remember the old days, Sal? Remember the shit we used to get away with? Remember when Big Nose Sam and Skyball were still alive and the parties they used to have?" Sal was nodding his head, smiling.

"Remember when we were kids, well, I was a kid, you're what, ten, eleven years older than me? Remember when I was first getting started and we went and torched the cars in that guy's used car lot in Ludlow? God that was fun. And then we got so stinking drunk afterwards. Remember that?"

Sal turned slightly toward Patty and me and smiled softly and nodded guiltily.

Why the hell was he saying these things in front of us?

"Remember the time when we had that numbers operation running so smooth for what, five years or so? We never saw so much cash. Wasn't it great? Then that fuck-up from Hartford had to try to get his greedy little hands in it. We shoulda knocked him off when we had the chance. But oh no, he's from Connecticut, we couldn't do that. Bull shit. We shoulda done it. He's probably the only one I don't have to worry about squealing on me. He's got shit deeper than I do. But the feds in Connecticut aren't as gung ho playing the big man as they are here in Massachusetts. They want to hang me up to dry. Remember when we were running that protection racket in Springfield and Holyoke? God that was fun."

"Oh, Lou, you know, you don't have to worry about us. You know me, I'm from the old school, I know how the game is played, I know the rules. I've lived by them all these years. And these two kids over here, they don't know anything. We kept Charlie deep in the dark. He never knew who he treated or how they got injured or anything. He was never alone with any of them, they never told him anything. We treated him like a mushroom. We kept him in the dark and fed him horseshit."

I nodded, quietly, politely. I kept glancing back and forth between Lou and the thug.

"And Patty. She was never involved. This all happened before they were even married."

The young thug took a few steps closer to us.

"You know, it's better to be higher on the food chain than it is to be lower on the food chain," Lou went on. "I'm in a tight spot, with all these feds. They know too much. And there're too many other people who know too much. It's called risk management these days. I gotta practice risk management. Know what I mean? It's just business, you know this of course, it's just business, it's nothing personal, you and me, we had a good time for a lotta years."

Am I really hearing this? Did he say what I think he said?

As I was listening, dumbstruck by Lou Spellacci, I caught a small movement of the thug's right hand as it moved in his pocket. It was subtle. But I was sure I saw it and I knew what it meant.

Sometimes when you're listening to a patient's heart with a stethoscope you might pick up a very subtle heart sound called an S3. It comes just after S2 and it is a bad omen. No more than a soft whisper. It happens when there's been cardiac muscle damage and the patient could be on the brink of big trouble. You may not hear the S3 with every beat; it just may occur now and then, you might hear it just at the end of a big inspiration. But if you hear it, or if you only think you hear it, you better pay attention.

Lou Spellacci had said some scary things. The thug made a small movement. They were going to kill us.

Like a Poseidon missile launching from its submarine

tube I shot up from the couch using all of the muscle strength I could gather from years of distance running. I was fast but I saw it in slow motion. I had maybe six or seven feet to cover and my target was to get that guy in a bear hug and pin his arms to his sides so he couldn't get his gun out of his pocket.

Slow motion. Click…click…click… went the frames of film in the movie projector, what was it, sixteen frames per second?

In the first sixteenth of a second I thought how wrong this meeting had gone, we came here to assure him of our silence, not to be slaughtered.

Click. Then I saw the thug's face as he first recognized my ballistic movement toward him. I was fast and he was big and he'd be a hard target to miss. As I launched I saw the surprise in his eyes and in his face and I saw him fumble and it looked like the hammer of his gun got hung up in the top of his pocket.

Click. In the next frame I thought of those wretched, starving, freezing, naked Jews standing on the edge of the pit at Babi Yar and I was not going to be passive; I was fighting back for them too.

Click. I thought of those brave hopeful souls in the Warsaw Ghetto who fought back against overwhelming odds but fought back nonetheless. I am their brother, I am fighting back too.

Click. I thought about brave people like my dear wife who had the determination and compunction to buy guns and learn how to use them to protect us.

Click. I thought about Mr. Franklin in the synagogue minion group who said that people who treat each other as equals don't harm each other.

Click. As I was airborne with my arms outstretched to embrace and entrap that thug I saw a flash of panic in his eyes as he perhaps thought this might not be so easy after all.

Click. As I made contact with that thug I got my arms around his lower chest and my hands found each other and I squeezed with all my might pinning his elbows against him. His gun hadn't cleared the pocket. Maybe I should have first tried to hit him in the larynx and break it.

Click. Somewhere in the background I could hear Patty's distant voice shouting, slowly, CCChaaarrrllli-ieeeee!

Click. In the next frame I thought of that poor man who jumped into the swollen river to save his son, he had to do or die, any chance was worth it.

Click. I tried to rotate him so his right hand, his gun hand, would be on the far side from Patty.

If this worked, if I could delay things for even seconds, if it would afford Patty to have even a few more breaths of sweet air, it would all be worth it. If I died trying right here in a nasty and violent way rather than dying warmly and softly and quietly in my bed as an old man it would be okay if she gets even a little more of a chance.

I was unsure of the grip of my weak left hand. The side of my head was against his chest and my arms were steel bands and the fingernails of each hand were digging into the skin of the other as I locked this murderer's hands down.

In my peripheral vision I saw Lou Spellacci had gotten up from his chair and was digging under his sweater for a gun in his waistband.

My thug was trying to hit me but since I had control of his elbows he couldn't hit me very hard. He tried to bounce me up and down to break my grip but I held tight. I kept trying to rotate him away from Patty but he was so big.

Click. I thought about the man whose kid nearly got killed in front of him in that logging accident and the gratitude he must have felt to avoid that horror. I wasn't there yet but I was trying.

The thug was banging the gun in his pocket against my ribs but there was no force to it, they were just blunt bumps. I wasn't sure why he didn't shoot, the gun was sandwiched between the two of us and he could've hurt himself as much as me if he had.

Let that girl live. Let that girl get out of here. She's fast, why is she screaming instead of running?

Click. He was trying to pick me up so he could carry me to the doorway and bang me against it. I could sense what he was planning and resisted.

As we struggled I caught another sideways glimpse and saw that Lou Spellacci had cleared his gun from his pants and was raising it toward me in a big sweeping arc.

As I saw this I tried again to rotate my thug to get him between me and Lou Spellacci's gun. As we rotated a few degrees I saw Sal leaning forward on the couch holding Patty's mitten and pointing it at Lou's chest. There was an explosion, a deafening blast and a spear of flame as Sal shot Lou with Patty's mitten.

The thug's balance faltered with the surprise of the gunshot and I was able to turn him a little more and then I could see Patty. She was on her feet and getting closer.

I looked at her in that Eskimo sweater. It was bulky. She was lost inside it. The wool looked like it would be coarse and rough on the skin, like burlap. She didn't wear that sweater very often, which was okay with me because I never really liked it.

Patty was coming closer to me rather than farther away. I watched her come closer to me in jerky slow motion film frames.

Someone was shouting, "RRRUUUNNN!!!!!" It sounded like me.

Sal was up off the couch moving toward Lou. Lou's mouth was half open. His neck was bent back and his eyes rolled back in his head and he was halfway to the floor.

Patty kept coming closer and closer to me instead of going farther and farther away. Her brow was furrowed, she was squinting at my thug, she had on her Cruella deVille face, there was saliva in the corner of her mouth and her face was white.

Patty raised her left arm high above her head and her right hand was under her sweater as if on her heart. She bumped her left shoulder against my thug and there was a tremendous boom and my thug and I shuddered. I wasn't sure what happened. My thug finally got a shot off. I didn't feel anything, but the loud noise was disorienting. They say in the heat of combat you may not know that you've been hit. Patty moved a foot away from us and there was smoke coming from the side of her sweater. *Oh God, she's been shot! Oh God, oh God, oh God.*

I looked at her fearing the worst but she looked alright. I looked at her and she was just standing there, three feet away, looking at my thug, with a singed hole in her sweater. I still felt okay.

My thug relaxed. He was still. He was leaning on me. He stopped struggling against me. He began to slip and I wasn't strong enough to hold him up. As his elbows slipped from my grasp he got his hands out of his pockets and clung to me as he slowly eased himself down to the floor. He collapsed. Did he shoot himself while trying to shoot me? How come Patty had a bullet hole and looked fine?

I looked around. Patty was still upright and intact and I still didn't understand what happened. I looked from the thug at my feet to Patty, and back and forth again. I looked back at Patty questioningly.

Patty pointed at her sweater. "There's a gun under here."

Lou was on the floor looking very dead. Sal was holding Lou's gun looking like he was expecting more threats to come from elsewhere in the townhouse.

My thug was on the floor on his side. I got down over him on all fours and rolled him on his back. I put two fingers on the carotid artery in his neck to feel for a pulse. My ear was near his mouth listening for breathing as I watched his chest to see if it rose and fell.

"Doc, what the hell are you doing?" Sal barked, "get the hell away from him!"

"He's still got a pulse," I said, frantically.

"Get the hell away from him," he shouted.

I didn't and was getting ready to do CPR when Sal put his foot on me and roughly pushed me over and I rolled across the room.

As I regained myself and began to get up from the floor I saw three pairs of legs come racing in the front door.

"Where the fuck were you?" I heard Sal bellow in a volume like a loudspeaker.

I looked up to see Moore, Fremont and Goldstein followed by several other men I didn't know, all carrying guns.

"You weren't ever supposed to let it go this far!" Sal continued bellowing. "Weren't you listening?"

I wasn't up on my feet yet and Patty was moving in my direction to help me.

"I asked you where the fuck you were," Sal bellowed again at the men.

"We were delayed in getting here. We didn't hear the whole thing."

"You were delayed? You were delayed?" Sal said again in disbelief, still at top volume. "What the fuck delayed you? What could have been more important

343

than backing up this set-up? How could you do this?" Sal was still holding Lou Spellacci's gun but it was safely down by his side. He realized he was holding it as he was bellowing at a bunch of armed FBI agents and he surrendered it by turning and tossing it on the couch. One of the men came and picked it up.

"We can't tell you what delayed us, it's confidential," Goldstein said.

"Confidential my ass. You guys set us up. We were bait. You didn't care what happened in here as long as those two guys didn't walk out. What, did you have a shooter outside in case they did?"

Patty and I were standing side by side with our arms around each other and we were dumbfounded.

Goldstein walked briskly up to Patty. "Let me have the bug," he said, and he tried to turn her and reach up to her hair.

Patty nearly slapped him, and barked, "Keep your filthy hands off me!" She reached up and unraveled her French braid and produced a small black cylinder thinner than a lipstick tube.

As she handed it to Goldstein, Sal grabbed it, threw it on the floor and stepped on it.

"Oh," he said softly and slowly and quietly, "an electronics malfunction. How disappointing," he added in a tone of regret.

Chapter 27

We were sitting in the back seat of an unmarked police vehicle. They read us our Miranda rights. They had Sal in a different cruiser. Probably wanted to keep us separate, to see if our stories matched. Of course they would match. The only one who didn't really know what happened, or what was intended to happen, was me. It was cold. We were stunned. I tried to open the door so I could ask the cop who was leaning against the car if he would turn on the heat. He must have thought for a second that I was trying to escape and got bent out of shape. The door wouldn't open from the inside nor could I roll down the window. I told him we were cold and he said, "Oh sure," and he reached in the driver's door, started the engine and the heat.

It was still gray outside. There was an occasional flurry of snow. Through the car windows I could see Sal sitting in the back of a similar car, a few yards away. There were policemen milling around, some in uniform and some in plainclothes. The cop who put us in the car said we had to wait here until the Police Crime Scene Team came. There would be photographers, fingerprint people, ballisticians, a lawyer from the DA's office. People would come to take our story. There were policemen running yellow plastic tape waist high all around the condo unit. Just like on television.

I still didn't know what happened. Clearly something had been planned and I wasn't in on it. I knew sooner or later Patty would explain it to me. She was shivering though she was in her Eskimo sweater and the car was beginning to warm up and she was right next to me and my arm was around her. There were little bloody scratches on my hands from my own fingernails. Her hair was wavy, holding the memory of the braid and the electronic device that I didn't know about.

She was distraught. When I asked her a question, she would just nod, sniffle, but not really answer. I'd get the story eventually. I hadn't seen that much blood in a long time. You could smell it in the air, in that apartment. Metallic. Once, in our first year of med school, we had a dog lab in physiology. We had to insert arterial lines. We got blood everywhere. The ceiling, our faces, our notebooks. You could smell it. We were new at it. It bothered us. We began to laugh. We weren't proud of it. I never forgot it. But we wouldn't be laughing about what happened here today in Springfield.

I leaned forward and reached from the back seat to the dashboard and turned up the heat and the fan since Patty was still shivering. How much was cold or emotion I didn't know. I couldn't know how she felt. She had just killed a man. To save me.

Various men came into the car to talk to us and they took notes as we told them what happened. Patty had more to say than me. She explained that we'd been increasingly threatened all summer and fall. Against her better judgment we'd gone to talk to Sal about this. I'd known him from some past medical business I'd had with him. The FBI had been bugging me about what had gone on a few years ago. Sal and the FBI got together and made a plan, which would offer Sal immunity for any wrongdoings he'd ever been involved in up to this point if he'd cooperate in a set up with Lou Spellacci. Although the FBI had expressly forbade them to carry any weapons, Sal knew better and had equipped Patty with the hidden derringer she had taped under her left breast, under that bulky sweater, and the other derringer hidden innocently in the mittens she carried. *That's why she took so long to get dressed this morning. Great sweater.*

Why did Sal do this? He was retired. I never heard that he was being investigated, or that he was up for indictment. What was his motivation to be involved in this dangerous meeting?

The first time she was asked to tell that story, the agent asked where that gun was now. With a surprised look on her face she realized it was still under her sweater. Loaded, with another bullet still in it. He could have yanked her out of the car, spread-eagled her on the ground and safely disarmed her himself. Graciously, the agent permitted Patty to reach under the sweater and peel it off herself. She made some pained facial expressions as she reached under with both hands and peeled tape off her skin. I asked her to be real careful since I was sitting to her left. I'd seen what it did to that thug. She produced it from under the sweater and carefully handed it to the agent in the front seat, duct tape and all. *Please unload it.* He took it. "It's warm," he said as he held it in his hand. *Well, yeah. Where did it just come from,* I thought. *Patty, you could've blown off your breast.*

After I heard this story being told for the first time, I asked Patty why I knew nothing about it. How come she and Sal were making all these plans without me? How come he was providing Patty with weapons, especially one to tape over her heart, without telling me? Why we were walking into a situation far more dangerous than they let me know about, with armed men, good and bad, or maybe bad and worse, all over the place, and they didn't let me know? What did they expect to happen? What surprises did they try to be prepared for? How could they lead me into such a situation without letting me know, without even preparing me?

"Charlie, we talked this over long and hard, Sal and me and Goldstein. Please don't hate me for this. I'll understand if you do but please don't hate me for this. We thought it was the best way to do it. Sal has seen you in tough emotional situations. Goldstein thinks he's a good judge of people's character and behavior and abilities in a crisis. I know you so well. I remembered how upset and stressed you got when we went to the safe deposit box. We weren't expecting this meeting to go like this. This was worse than the worst case scenario we planned for. But we made it. And it's over. And we're safe. All three of us. And those two monsters are dead. And you were terrific. We didn't count on you to be so effective in there."

"What do you mean, did you think I was just going to sit there and let those guys kill us off?" *Was she being patronizing?*

"I don't know what we should have expected from you. But we thought there would be a chance that you would have had a long philosophical discussion with yourself about the appropriateness of doing something violent and by the time you came to a decision it would've been too late."

I thought about what my wife just said to me. They didn't trust me to act quickly and decisively in a crisis. Sure I like to think things through if I have the luxury, but there are lots of times at work I have to act immediately, based on a visceral instinctive decision. *I don't get it. How could they keep me in the dark? Wasn't this the girl who woke me up in the middle of the night to promise I would tell her everything that happened? And then she went scheming with a hoodlum from the mob and another hoodlum from the FBI? But it worked. We are safe.*

"So I surprised you then?"

"You did. You surprised us. You were spectacular. I didn't think a person could move so fast. You saved us. I'm proud of you. Sal's proud of you. He said to me that he didn't know you had it in you." *Now maybe they're both being patronizing.*

"So you were hiding a gun for Sal in your mitten?"

"Yes. It was another derringer like the one I had taped to my chest. We didn't think those guys would check us that thoroughly after they took Sal's gun off his belt and patted you down and found nothing. We were betting that they wouldn't bother to search me, a lady, in front of her husband. We rehearsed it. I put the mitten on my lap so Sal could grab it."

"You guys were pretty crafty," said the FBI guy. "And we told you not to bring any weapons."

"Yeah," Patty said, sarcastically. "A lot of help you were. If we did what you told us we'd be dead right now. Thanks a lot. Thank God Sal knew enough not to listen to you." The FBI guy didn't respond.

We went through the story a few more times, first with the field agent, then the special agent, then the inspector.

We had a lot of time to sit in the car between interviews. A lot of people were coming and going. There weren't any news reporters or photographers. When the men from the morgue finally came out rolling two stretchers. I looked away feeling nauseous.

Then someone from the DA's office told us they were going to let us go home but we had to appear in the DA's office first thing Monday morning to go over it all and sign affidavits, and no, we didn't need to have a lawyer with us but we could if we wanted.

We got out of the car and it was good to stretch and get some fresh air. The inspector we spoke to was still in the other car with Sal. We waited. Finally they got out and Sal came over to us.

"You guys okay?" he asked.

"Yeah. We're okay. We'll be okay."

"Let's go. I'll take you back to your car. You want to have a dinner? I know some real nice places."

I didn't ask Patty. I just said, "No thanks, Sal. I don't think we have an appetite. We just want to go home."

We got into Sal's car. I got in back with Patty, who had become quiet again.

As we drove, Sal told us, "You guys are in a state of emotional shock. It'll change; it'll get better. In a few days it'll really hit you. Don't be surprised. Just remember I told you this. You'll feel like shit for a few days and then you'll get stronger. I promise you that. Don't let it get you too down." We drove along Route 5 and then onto Route 20. We were silent. It was dark out. We were in that parking lot for hours. We hadn't had anything to eat since breakfast, nor could we eat anything now.

"Hey Charlie," Sal asked, "how do you feel when you have a patient with an infection like pneumonia, and you get him on the right antibiotic, and he gets better and his fever comes down?"

350

I paused. *What kind of question is that?* "I feel great,"
I answered.

"Do you feel badly for all those poor germs that you
are killing off?"

"No, of course not."

"Then just keep thinking of those two goons in
there as germs. You two shouldn't feel badly about their
deaths. They were bad men. They'd done bad things in
their life. The world is better off without them. Take it
from me."

It sounded familiar. I'd heard him say those words
before. We almost got killed. We didn't, but we could
have. We could so easily be dead right now. Sleep with
that one.

We got to Friendly's. Our Subaru was where we left
it. Sal parked next to it. He turned around in the front
seat to look at us and talk to us in the darkness.

"You two are great kids. I'm proud of you. I really
am. You both are a couple of mensches. Go easy on
yourselves. I'll see you on Monday at the DA's office.
Don't worry about anything. Nobody in the organization is going to bother you about this. If anything,
they'll be relieved. You should go in here and eat something before you drive home. Get some coffee."

We said goodbye and I thought of Mac at home in
his crate, him wondering where we are, him sitting
there with a full bladder.

I got Patty in the front seat and locked her in the car
and I came back quickly with two black coffees.

We sipped coffee as we drove along the Mass Pike.
We didn't say much. There was a lot to process.

"Thank you for what you did back there. Thank you
for saving me."

"You're thanking me for saving you," she said, and
I could see her shaking her head in my peripheral
vision. "How is it that you don't get this? What the hell

351

did you expect me to do? Did you really expect me to run off and save myself and let you get killed? What the hell kind of a person do you think I am? You think I could live with myself if I did that? What's my life worth without yours? You think I'd want to live without you? Why do I even have to explain this to you?" She sounded irritated and angry. She fidgeted in her seat.

"I've had enough of this coffee," she said. Suddenly she rolled down the window and threw the coffee, cup and all, out of the car. She closed the window. She looked out the side window. I could hear her teeth grinding.

"I can't believe I just did that," she said, and then she started crying.

I parked in the driveway and we went in the back door. Mac was squealing and I let him out of his crate, snapped on his leash and jogged him down the street. He stopped at every tree. I could have run for miles on nervous energy. When I got back Patty had the teapot and some English muffins on the table.

Afterwards she went upstairs. She undressed and we looked at the skin on her chest which was red where the duct tape peeled off. There was a shallow erosion and first degree burn under her breast from the muzzle flash. I gave her some Silvadene Cream to put on it. She went and took a long shower, by herself, to wash the day off her. I sat in the bedroom, motionless, with Mac at my feet.

Just as we were getting into bed the phone rang.

"Hello?"

"Hi Chollie, it's MacPherson. Goldstein told me what happened. In five minutes I want you to go downstairs without turning on any lights and let me in the back door."

"Why?"

"Just do it," he said curtly. Then he hung up.

I told Patty. I went downstairs in the dark.

I sat at the kitchen table. I heard a soft tap at the blackened back door window and let MacPherson in. He locked the door behind him.

In the faint light from the house I could see my big husky friend was dressed in black with a tactical vest on his chest and a big gun on each hip.

"I'm gonna babysit you tonight," he said.

"Sal told me that no one would bother us." Although he'd said that before too.

"And I hope Sal is right. And if he's not right, I'll be here."

"Do you really think it's necessary?"

"I hope it's not, but I'll be here anyway."

"Are you going to sit here in the dark all night?'

"Yeah."

"How are you going to stay awake? I'll make you a pot of coffee. I can put it in a thermos so it won't get bitter."

"No thanks, I brought one."

He didn't answer my question. "How will you stay awake?"

"I was a Marine, we do this stuff. By the way, I have trip wires all around the perimeter of your house. I'll take them down in the morning when I leave. You have a second bedroom upstairs?"

"Yeah," I answered, puzzled.

"I want you and Patty to sleep there tonight. Move into it without turning on any lights. Close both bedroom doors and barricade the one you're in with a chair or something."

"Do you think this is necessary?"

"You survive by hoping for the best and preparing for the worst. Speaking of which," he said while taking a small handgun from his pocket, "take this and keep it with you tonight. In the unlikely event anyone gets past me."

In the near darkness of the kitchen I was looking at the pistol in my hand though I did not remember taking it from him. I looked MacPherson in the eye.

"Thanks, Mac, for caring so much."

"That's what friends do. They take care of each other. Go to bed. Goodnight."

We shook hands and I went upstairs.

Chapter 28

I didn't sleep well. I kept waking up and instantly I would think of what had happened. And when I fell asleep I still dreamed of it so it was hard to tell if I'd been thinking or dreaming. I looked at the clock a million times. Patty was still the whole night. It was strange to be in this bedroom.

Dawn was coming. This late in the year, so close to the winter solstice, it took a long time for dawn to finish and for the sun to finally creep up. When it finally seemed lighter outside than in the bedroom I went downstairs to let the dog out. Halfway down the stairs I remembered that MacPherson was here. When I got to the kitchen there was no one there but Maccabee. The coffee pot was on and there was a note from MacPherson that he'd let Mac out and fed him and the coffee was fresh. He said he'd talk to us later, he was going home to sleep. Hard to find friends like that. I hadn't heard either of the Macs all night. Maybe I had been asleep. I let Mac out of his crate. We were going to need to get him a bigger one, he'd grown so much. He was now eight months old and sixty-one pounds and his back was above my knee, he was all legs and a wiry, lean puppy body. By the size of his paws he still had some growing to do. MacPherson must have fed him a big portion because he was unusually lethargic. Must have a full belly.

I brought two cups of coffee up the stairs and Mac followed me. He lay down in the corner in the bedroom and I put one cup on Patty's nightstand and put a paperback on top of it to keep it warm. I climbed into my side of the bed carefully so I wouldn't rock the bed and disturb her. It was odd to be in this small spare bedroom. I sipped and watched the world slowly brighten out the window.

"Mmmm, I smell coffee," Patty said sleepily with closed eyes, and rolled over and was still.

I finished my cup. I looked at Patty to my left, lying there on her left side, facing away from me. She was in a fetal position. Funny how such a slender girl could make such a big lump under the covers.

Slowly she came awake and moved and stretched and emerged and kissed me. She sat up and stuffed her pillow behind her and picked up her coffee. She took a sip and made a yummy noise. "Mmmmm. Strong."

"MacPherson made it."

"Oh. I forgot he was here."

"So did I. I never heard him."

"Is here still here?"

"No. He left a note. He took care of Mac and fed him and let him out and made coffee."

"I wouldn't have thought in this small house you could do all that and not be heard."

"I didn't either," I replied

"How'd you sleep?"

"Poorly. You?"

"Poorly."

"Any thoughts?" I asked.

"About yesterday?"

"Yeah."

"No. Nothing more. Yet. Still processing. You?"

"Yeah. Nothing yet."

"Tough stuff. I'm not sorry I did that to him. I'm sorry I had to."

"I've been amazed at how cool and confident you've been all these months," I said.

She made a little shaking motion of her head and looked up at the ceiling.

"What?" I asked.

"I wasn't confident. I was faking it. Just like you tell me you fake it at the hospital when you're worried. It was all just bullshit."

We sat in silence and stared at the bare branches out the window moving in the breeze. From our vantage point we could only see trees and the roof of the house next door. And a telephone pole.

"What do you want to do today?"

"Not much. Vegetate. You?"

"Sounds good to me. We can have a nice breakfast. We can take Mac for a walk and pick up the Sunday papers."

I made shirred eggs again. I made Medaglia D'Oro espresso coffe in a little aluminum espresso pot Patty picked up at a tag sale. I toasted English muffins kind of dark. We ate in the dining room and we had the classical music station on the radio. We didn't talk much. We were both ruminating.

Patty was standing looking out the kitchen window while we cleaned up.

"Know how you can tell when it's cold out from when it's damn cold out?"

I turned from the sink and looked at her. I paused. "How?"

"See the azalea bush next door?"

"Yeah?"

357

"When it's mild out all the leaves are normal. When it's cold out they start to curl up. When it's damn cold the leaves curl into tight little tubes and you can see through the bush. See?"

I looked at the bush. It was true. It didn't look like there were any leaves on it, just toothpicks.

While I was cleaning up Patty brushed Mac.

"The vet told me I should start brushing his teeth too."

"Do you think he'd let you?"

"Yeah, I do. Mac would let me floss his teeth."

We bundled up and put Mac on a leash and headed out down Gilmore. It was frosty cold. In the low teens. I offered to go by myself but Patty wanted to come. Maybe she's not ready to be alone. I suggested we go back and take the car to get the papers; she called me a wimp. We walked down to Cottage, turned right, then turned left on East Street and walked many blocks down to Bridge Street. It was so cold and so still that the smoke from chimneys went straight up like solid white cylinders. Mac was having a great time sniffing everywhere and leaving his mark. As we crossed the bridge over the Housatonic River we stopped and looked upstream and down. It was low and mostly frozen. There was a trickle of an open channel meandering down the center, and it was steaming. A thick layer of mist hung over the channel like cotton batting. The trees and brush along the river were white as if powdered with confectioner's sugar.

On the corner of Main Street and Bridge is a big old three-story, office building and in the back of the first floor is a newsstand that's been there for generations. We picked up the *Berkshire Eagle*, the *Springfield Journal* and *The New York Times*. We chatted with the proprietor who was a much loved local personality.

On our trip back home the wind picked up. Every time there was a gust it made me swallow and feel like the breath got sucked out of me. We walked fast. The cold didn't bother Mac at all. Like most Labs, his tail wagged constantly and with great energy. "If that tail were made in Detroit, we'd've had to replace it by now," Patty said.

When we got home we were chilled. We plopped down in the living room and dug in to the papers. I took the classified ads and used them to get a fire started in the fireplace. I ran out to the garage to bring in an armload of wood. In twenty minutes we were toasty warm and content. Almost content.

I was supposed to work tomorrow. We were supposed to be in Springfield tomorrow. I'd better call and try to get someone to cover for me. I better call the director first and let him know what happened, before he hears it from someone else, through the grapevine, distorted.

I called and told him the whole story. He was flabbergasted and he was usually a man of few words. He appreciated hearing it from me first. He told me he'd take my shift himself, not to bother calling Will or the others.

We sat on the couch and worked our way through the sections of the newspapers. Periodically I got up to throw more logs on the fire. After we'd been reading for an hour or so I saw Patty sitting there, gazing into the fire, papers in her lap, her feet on the coffee table. Her finger was pressed on her lip, which was usually a signal of deep thought. I watched her.

After a while she returned to this planet and looked at me.

"You know what? I've been thinking. I didn't see anything in the paper about what happened in Springfield yesterday. Did you? I was thinking, if yesterday had gone badly for us, what kind of spin would those bastards have put on the story they gave to the press? It would probably be something like, 'Dr. Charles Davids and his wife, Patricia Caine Davids, were killed along with three mobsters in a shootout with the FBI in a luxury townhouse development outside of Springfield. Dr. Davids was known to have had ties to organized crime for at least four years.' They tried to set us up as bait to get killed and then they'd victimize us again once we were dead, make it look like we were dirty and we got what we had coming to us."

I kept looking at her. I swallowed hard.

"Well?" she asked.

"I guess I just find it hard to believe that they could have set us up like that."

"Do you doubt it?"

"It just seems so underhanded. I can't believe that they would just let us get killed in there."

"I can't believe that you're still so naïve and willing to think that maybe it wasn't intentional," she replied.

I didn't know how to answer, so I didn't.

By one o'clock in the afternoon I was bleary eyed and had read more than I was interested in. I glanced over at Patty and she was asleep on her end of the couch, her head on the arm and her feet against my thigh. A piece of wood in the fireplace made a loud pop and it startled us.

"Let's go for a walk in the woods," she said.

I packed some lunch in my knapsack. The three of us got in my Subaru and drove north on Route 7 to the Fountain Pond State Forest, right up the hill from the Jenifer House Shops, just down the hill from Monument Mountain. There is a four-acre pond right on the road that I always look at as I drive by. There are wood duck boxes set in the shallows. It's always very weedy in the summer. The fish must think they're swimming in a salad. There is a small parking area right off the road and a trail that goes way far back in there, up Blue Mountain. Not much of a mountain but a nice walk.

Mac was squealing with joy knowing we were going for a long walk. It was not quite as cold now. We kept him on the leash for the first couple hundred yards, which were through a copse of hemlocks so it was shady and colder. When we got to the far side of these evergreens we were in the sun again and it was warmer. I let him off his leash and he ran around joyously like a free man. Dog. Off this way and then the other. Never more than fifty or seventy-five yards away, then he'd come dashing back to check on us and get a pat on the head. Then he'd be off and come back with a stick and ask us to throw it for him. He'd never carry it in the middle but on one end, lopsided. He'd run down the trail full tilt, with a stick in his mouth with four inches of the stick beyond the left side of his mouth and three feet beyond the right side. Then he'd inevitably bang the long side into a tree trunk, it'd knock his molars and whip his head around. He'd look dazed for a second and keep right on his way. No brain, no pain. Throw it for me, Dad, throw it for me! Please! Please? C'mon Dad! Then I'd throw it for him and it would go on all over again. So easy to make him happy.

There were only a few inches of snow. It was old snow. In most places it was crusty, and crunched as we walked. In the sunnier south-facing areas the sun warmed the snow and it was quieter. We both learned to keep an eye on Mac. One time he ran past Patty and smacked her in the leg with the stick he was carrying.

There were deer tracks. Here and there were little rodent tracks that would emerge near the base of a tree, meander around for five or six feet and then circle back to the little hole. There were lots of pine needles and hemlock needles on the snow. They must always be falling. We came to a line of big Y-shaped footprints in the snow, in a perfect line. Patty surmised they must be turkey tracks, the Berkshires have lots of them.

We followed two sets of deer tracks along the trail, which led down into a little hollow. At the bottom was a wet spot, a seepage that melted the snow. It was only two feet wide. Mac deftly jumped across. The deer hadn't. We'd been following clean white deer tracks in the snow but on the other side of the seep the deer tracks were muddy. They mustn't care about getting their feet cold or wet or muddy. What would their mothers say? Ten feet later their tracks were clean and white again in the snow.

As we climbed the rise out of the hollow we came to a stone wall facing south. The snow on it had melted, and it dried in the sun. I swung off my knapsack and we sat down and settled in. We sat on the wall and the stones were cold on my bottom. Mac came over and I petted him. As he sat in the bright winter sun, his black fur was warm to my hand. He was panting and his eyes were smiling.

We were sitting under some open hardwoods. There were Red Oaks with a ski slope pattern on their bark. There were Beech trees still with a few remaining tea brown leathery leaves, like in an Ansel Adams photo. There were white birch trees, and yellow birch with curly coiled ribbons of bark. There were tall white pines, their lofty branches floating as if lighter than air.

My sweaty back became cold once I took the knapsack off. I opened it and laid out the food. We shared from a thermos of strong sweet Earl Grey tea. There was a small hard kosher salami. Cheddar cheese. Half a loaf of Italian bread. We had some apples that I peeled and sliced with a Swiss Army knife. I had a small container of coarse Pomerry mustard. Patty was hungry.

It was beautiful. It was peaceful. I felt safe. I always felt safe in the woods.

From our perch we could look south and see the mountain in the distance that I think was the east end of the same mountain that the Butternut ski resort is on. In the distance the hillsides looked slightly violet.

"When I was in college I took an earth science course. It was fascinating," Patty said, "one of the books we had to read was called *The Changing Face of New England*. It was about geology and how the land and mountains changed with the ice ages and all that. It was written by a lady and in the prologue was something I really like, it really struck a chord with me and I've never forgotten it. This lady, the author, is from the Midwest and when she was a little girl in grammar school they had packages of construction paper. She knew what all the colors were except one. Every color but one meant something to her. Orange pumpkins and green grass and red apples and yellow corn. But there was one color that didn't fit into her experience. It was a soft gray-violet color that was not something she could ever remember having seen anywhere else. Then as a young adult she came to New England. When she saw distant hills in the winter time she could place that color. It was the color of the coalescing terminal twigs and buds and bark on the trees in the distance."

"I remember that color of construction paper. I just thought it was a drab gray. It meant nothing to me."

I looked at the colors spread out before me. The salami was dark reddish brown with lighter flecks of suet and garlic. The orange-gold color of the cheddar cheese and the bright red Swiss Army knife. The granular gray of the rocks we were sitting on with green lichen. The red apple peelings that I dropped on the white snow. The brown crust of the bread, more golden in color than the beech leaves.

Patty's pink cheeks and vermillion lips. Her dark brown eyes and dark brown hair. Her turquoise knit hat. She saved my life yesterday. She killed a man.

The sun had melted the snow and ice on the south side of some of the darker-trunked trees and now as the sun was getting lower and colder, the water froze and gave the trunks a glassy finish.

"We'd better get going," Patty said. "It's two forty-five. I think it'll be dark by four-thirty." We packed up and headed back the way we came.

Mac was still running back and forth bringing me sticks to throw. The sun was going down fast. It was colder. The snow was crunchy now everywhere. The little seep in the hollow had frozen over with a film of black ice.

Patty was walking in front of me and Mac was in orbit. Patty looked up and stopped and pointed. "Look," she said, "you can see the moon."

I looked up and in the very blue sky was the moon. Just a little bigger than half full. "I can never remember if it gets full from left to right or from right to left," I said.

Patty turned and smiled and as she spoke her breath was foggy. "That's easy; it's like Hebrew. It goes from right to left."

"Okay, that makes that easy. What about waxing and waning. I can't keep those straight either."

"That's easy, too. The waning of the British Empire. The diminishing of the empire."

"But a wax candle gets smaller as it burns. Waxing means getting bigger, then?"

"Yeah. Waxing bigger, waning smaller. A big ball of wax."

I thought about that a few times as we walked along, hoping I would remember it and never have to relearn it.

We kept walking along. We'd get out just before dark. It's good we got moving when we did.

When we were maybe ten minutes from the road I heard footsteps coming toward us, and Mac lit out racing ahead to find someone new to play with. I tried calling him but he ignored me. Patty and I looked at each other and shrugged. Who would be coming into the woods at this time of day?

As we continued around a bend in the trail we could vaguely see the outline of a person walking toward us, trudging determinedly with his head down, arms swinging, and a big black dog bouncing around him trying to get him to play. Our view of him was fragmented. With the tree trunks it was like looking through the slats of a picket fence.

We lost sight of him for a minute and then we came face to face with him at a bend in the trail. We all stopped abruptly twenty feet apart and I was just about to apologize for my overly enthusiastic dog.

He was looking at us. He was not dressed for the woods. He was in city clothes with a shearling coat and loafers. No hat. But there was a gun in his hand. A big black one. Pointing at us.

Oh shit. My heart was in my mouth. *I thought we were done with this stuff.*

Mac kept bouncing up and down a few feet in front of him, hoping the guy would throw the gun for him so he could bring it back. What fun.

I looked at the man. I recognized him in a second. He was the one who tried to kidnap me in front of the house. He's the guy that Patty chased away with her guns. He's the guy with the scraggly dark blond-brown hair, the broken nose, the blue eyes, one of which was

365

always pointing somewhere else. The guy with the big Cadillac with Connecticut plates.

"What do you want?" I asked. Patty backed up and was beside me. *Should we run?* I thought. *It'll be hard to run fast in the snow.*

"What do you think? I want some information. Then I'm gonna kill you. Both of you." Mac jumped up again, right next to him, enthused, and he backed up a step. "All three of you."

"Why?" I asked. His nose was red and dripping in the cold and I could see pockmarks on his face.

"Because you killed my son."

"I didn't kill anybody. Who is your son?"

"They brought him to you to save three years ago. He had a head injury. Your job was to save him. He died. You failed. You killed him."

"I see a lot of people with head injuries. I didn't kill anybody. I might not have been able to save him."

"Same difference." he said.

"Tell me about him. When was it?" I asked him, staring at the big gun.

Mac continued to jump around him. Between jumps he was sitting on his haunches like a good boy, as if, if he sat politely he might get rewarded. But he could only sit for maybe three seconds before jumping again. When he jumped he was practically eye level with the guy.

"Three years ago. In Holyoke. Sal brought you to him. In the back of some liquor store. But you didn't help him. He disappeared. He died. They just found him and dug him up a few months ago."

"I remember now. I remember. I pleaded with Sal to let me take him to an emergency room so he could have a CT scan and a neurosurgeon. Couldn't be done, they told me. I pleaded with him. They said no. I made a fuss and kept pushing Sal until finally he pulled a gun on me and told me to shut up. I have all this written down. I can show you. I kept notes. I wanted to help him."

Patty piped in, "It's true. I've seen the notes. I've read them."

"Not good enough, Doc. You're as good as dead. What's the matter with this fuckin' dog?" he asked as Mac continued to pester him to play.

"You I'm gonna kill first, Doc, so your wife can watch. Then I'm gonna kill her much slower." He turned to Patty. "I told you you'd be seein' me again. You're gonna die much more slow. Nobody ever pulls a gun on me and gets away with it." He was shouting. Flecks of saliva were spraying from his mouth in the mist as he shouted in the cold air. He said it again. "Nobody ever pulls a gun on Anthony Spumoni and lives to tell about it. You fuckin' bitch. No broad ever's done a thing like that to Anthony Spumoni, you're gonna pay for that big time and real soon, you scrawny bitch." He was agitated and was waving the gun around, which made Mac think he was getting ready to throw it. Mac jumped near him in excitement. Spumoni must have thought he was going for the gun and jumped back.

"What the fuck is the matter with this goddamn dog?" he said again and turned sideways toward Mac who was bouncing up and down as Spumoni extended the gun towards him. Mac thought he was going to throw it.

He's going to shoot the bouncing dog.

Without conscious deliberation I pulled my mitten out of my parka pocket, raised it up to eye level and shot Anthony. I shot him in the chest. I shot the bastard in the chest twice. He just collapsed in an awkward pile. As he fell he dropped his gun in the snow. The noise was deafening. Mac was startled and ran off. He threw a rooster tail of snow as he ran. The gunshots filled the woods and echoed off the gray-violet hillsides and back to us again. He was dead in the snow before the echoes of the shots that killed him were finally silent.

I stood there looking at what I had done. I was still holding the mitten up. I was looking at Anthony Spumoni. He didn't move. He didn't say a word. He was lying there, sort of on his back, his knees folded up under him. His eyes were half closed and his mouth was half open. I didn't see any blood. I didn't see his chest rise and fall. The golden light of the late afternoon sun highlighted his dark blond hair and his Florida tan. He didn't utter another threat. Not another insult. Not another vulgarity. I liked him better this way.

Patty came up and held me from behind.

"Put the gun down," she urged quietly. I put it in my pocket. I wondered if there was anyone else with Tony, coming up from behind. Probably not.

"Don't check him," Patty said insistently, "don't touch him. Don't give him CPR."

I just stood there, looking at him. "I wouldn't want to," I said, quietly.

Mac came back sheepishly. When she saw him Patty bent over and clapped her hands and he came right to her and she put him on the leash.

"What should we do?" Patty asked. "Should one of us stay here and the other go for the police?"

"No," I said. "We stay together. We'll walk out together."

We began walking. Slowly. I was dazed. I was trying to think but I wasn't thinking. I was just walking.

"Damn," I said.

"What?" Patty said, in front of me.

"You and me. We're going through a lot of mittens lately."

"Yeah, you're right."

I don't think a can of Mace would have worked well in that situation.

We kept walking. After a while I heard Patty mumble something.

"What did you say?" I asked.

"Oh, I was just talking to myself. I said 'I'm not scrawny.'"

After a few minutes we heard more footsteps, coming toward us. Fast. The person was running fast and you could tell from the sound he was covering a lot of ground. *Oh no.*

We hid behind a big hemlock and it was hard for Patty to keep Mac behind the trunk of the tree. I had my hand on the gun inside the mitten, at my side.

The sounds came closer and I realized it was MacPherson. He was in uniform running toward us with a shotgun.

With a huge sigh of relief I put the mitten in my pocket and stepped into the trail with Patty.

MacPherson came up and stopped right in front of us. If his hands weren't full I think he would've hugged us.

"Did what I think happened just happen?" he asked earnestly while huffing and puffing billows of fog from his mouth.

"Yes," I said.

"Are they dead?" he asked.

"Yes," I said. "Just one guy."

"You two are alright?"

"We're fine," Patty said.

"I saw your car there at the pull-off a couple of hours ago. When I went out on patrol again I saw another car next to yours. A Cadillac. Not your usual hiker's vehicle. It had Connecticut plates. I pulled in and as I was getting out of the cruiser I heard the two shots. I feared the worst. I thought you two were goners. I radioed it in just before I raced down the trail."

We stood together looking at each other.

"By rights, by procedure, I should cuff you and take you to my unit. I don't have to do that, do I?" It was a rhetorical question and I didn't answer. "How far back there is the guy?"

"About five minutes. Maybe more. Not more than ten." Patty answered.

"C'mon. We'll go back to the parking area."

Slowly we walked out through the crunchy snow in the darkening gray dusk of this late December afternoon. It had gotten very cold again.

We got back to the parking lot. There were three cars. Mine, Spumoni's, and MacPherson's cruiser. I put Maccabee, the wonder dog, in our car.

"By procedure I need to put you in the back of my cruiser. I have to read you your Miranda rights. It was self-defense, wasn't it?"

"Mac, do what you have to do. Don't risk getting into trouble by not following procedure. We understand. Do what you're supposed to do," Patty said.

"Well, I'm supposed to cuff you and put you in the back."

"Then do it," Patty ordered.

I gave MacPherson my wrist and he held my hand and as he was attaching the handcuff, he said, "Charlie, you're shaking."

I was cold, I was emotional. I couldn't believe what had happened. Again.

He didn't bother with the cuffs. He put us in the back seat of his cruiser, behind the cage, with the doors you can't open from the inside. He started the motor and adjusted the heat to high. He picked up the microphone and said something in a numbered code at Fountain Pond. The voice on the radio said there was a unit en route. MacPherson stood outside the car waiting. Patty and I sat in the dark in the back seat, my arm around her shoulders. She was quietly crying. I was choked up too, but we weren't both allowed to cry at the same time.

Another cruiser pulled up. It was too dark for me to see faces. MacPherson went over and spoke with the driver for a few minutes. Then the other cruiser drove off.

MacPherson came back to the car. "I told him what happened. He's going to go back to the station and call the chief and mobilize the CPAC unit."

"What's the CPAC unit?" Patty asked.

"Crime Prevention and Control," MacPherson answered.

"Prevention and control, huh? A little late, huh?"

"It'll probably take an hour for everyone to get here that needs to. Being dark they'll need to bring in lights and generators for the analysts, the photographers, ballisticians, investigators, the assistant district attorney on call, and everyone else. Lots of people will come and ask you the same questions over and over again. They might separate you. This will probably take a couple of hours. We can probably finish most of it back at headquarters." I nodded knowingly, having been through all this yesterday.

"MacPherson?" I asked.

"Yeah Chollie?"

"Would you like me to give you the weapon?"

His eyes got big for a second. "You have a weapon on you?"

"Yeah."

"Yeah. You should give it to me now." I handed him the heavy mitten.

We went through the same routine again as yesterday except there were different faces and it was dark and colder. After a while they did take us back to the police station. And who did we meet there but Goldstein and Fremont. I cynically thought they were there to look over the situation and see how they could manipulate the story so they could get some credit for it. They put Patty and me in different rooms and we were interviewed by the chief, by Goldstein and by the county assistant district attorney. It was so repetitious. After I finished telling the same story for the nth time, Goldstein got up and left the room. The ADA was organizing his paperwork in his attaché case.

He seemed like a nice man. Late forties, maybe, thin with brown hair, a dress shirt with a button-down collar and a striped tie, the knot loose and the top button open. He was easy to talk to. He was nice. He had a pleasant and gentle manner.

I sat there in the small conference room watching him pack up his materials. Should I tell him the background of how I came to be involved, against my will, with these people from Springfield? I have now been involved in the killing of three people in the last two days. Maybe he'd want to know what went on before. Should I tell him about all the clandestine medical care I was forced to provide in all those nefarious situations? Should I tell him about the diary I kept while all that was going on?

If I told him all that, I'd have to tell him about Sal. I still didn't know if Sal was a good guy or a bad guy. I knew I liked him. Despite what he put me through. I knew he saved our lives yesterday. And even though he supposedly had some kind of immunity because of what he helped set up yesterday, I saw no point in providing information I hadn't been asked for. I kept quiet. He left the room.

I spent a lot of time alone between the interviews. When finally they put Patty and me get together again, the assistant DA told us we needed to be in Pittsfield at nine the next morning to meet in the District Attorney's office.

"We can't," I said

"Why not?" Fremont asked, nastily.

"We have to be at the Springfield District Attorney's office at nine tomorrow morning."

The officials all looked at each other. "We'll work something out. We'll let you know. Why don't you call us tomorrow morning when you finish in Springfield," said the assistant district attorney, handing me his business card.

I took it and they let us go home. It was after ten o'clock.

We went out to the parking lot. Earlier MacPherson had driven our car over. Maccabeee was curled up in the back seat. It was cold. He'd been in there a long time. Patty got in. "Wait a minute," I said and I snapped on Mac's leash. I walked him over to Morse and Fremont's car so he could pee on their tires.

"Were you expecting this to happen?" Patty asked as we drove home.

"No. I didn't know what to expect. After yesterday I thought, 'now what else can go wrong?'"

"I think this stuff is all over now," Patty said. "I didn't intuit it last night but I do now." I looked at her in profile in the passenger seat of the car, in semi-darkness.

"I hope you're right. What do you base this on? Just a feeling?"

"Just a feeling."

When we walked in the house the phone was ringing. It was Sal.

"I heard what happened and I couldn't believe it. I was so surprised. I'm so glad you two kids are all right. You two must feel emotionally brutalized by now."

That was a mobster talking.

373

"Thanks, Sal, we'll be alright," I said, not knowing what else to say.

"The guy who told me about it said that Spumoni was a real whack job. He was in the Connecticut branch and he'd been getting weirder and weirder, was becoming a real problem. Nobody there is gonna be bothered by this. In fact, they're probably relieved that this guy is off their hands, they're not gonna come after you for this."

I hope he's right. Of course he's said this kind of thing before.

I thanked him for calling and he gave his regards to Patty and we hung up.

The phone rang. It was MacPherson. "Let me in your back door in five minutes. Don't turn on any lights."

Same routine. I walked carefully in the dark to the kitchen and sat by the back door. In a moment MacPherson tapped softly and I let him. He was dressed like the night before, and heavily armed.

"Well, here we are again," I said. "Thanks for coming. Do you think this is still necessary?"

"I hope not, but I'm here to be sure."

"Patty thinks we're done with this stuff now."

"I'm almost sure she's right."

"Don't you ever get tired?"

"I feel great. I slept all day after I left here this morning. Went to work at three. You know the rest. After I took you to the station I signed off and went home for a nap. I had them call me when they released you and here I am."

"You see, Chollie, I'm just like you. I love taking care of people. I love civilians. You love patients. Some FBI guys just wanna make great cases, make great arrests, get promoted. Civilians are just in the way. You've told me about some university medical professors who love diseases and the patients who have them are just an annoyance. Go to sleep Charlie. Sleep well. You'll be safe. Kiss Patty for me. She is a tiger."

I was standing right in front of him, we were whispering.

I pointed at the shotgun. "Is that your Claymore?" I asked.

He laughed. "Yes, Chollie, this is my Claymore."

"Is it sharp?"

"Yes, Chollie. It's real sharp," he said, grinning. Ever vigilant.

"Thank you, Mac." Maccabee heard his name and his tail began thumping on the floor of his crate.

I thanked him again and shook his hand and he settled himself on a chair in the front of the kitchen midway between the front and the back doors, in the dark.

I got into bed and put my arm around Patty. The minutes went by. I couldn't fall asleep. I killed somebody today. It didn't bother me much. Yet. I was sure that in a day or two or three it would hit me hard but right now I felt okay. Like what Patty had said. I'm not sorry I killed him. I am sorry it had to happen. What a day. What a weekend. If I ever had grandchildren to tell this story to they probably wouldn't believe it. Patty was still. I hoped she was asleep.

I thought about all the good decent caring people I had the privilege to know. Of course, Patty. And MacPherson. And Will, and Margaret and all the nurses and staff at the hospital and the old men in synagogue. And maybe even Sal fit in that group too.

An hour later I was still awake watching the red numbers change on the clock. I felt her stir a tiny bit. Then her breathing got faster and irregular and I wondered if she was crying. Can you cry in your sleep?

Was she crying from stress? Was she crying from the violence we witnessed, that we took part in? Was she crying from the tragedy, of the taking of life, from the mortal threat we'd been in? Were they tears of joy that we were alive and together and it was over? If she were awake and I asked her, she might say, "All of those things. All of those reasons. It doesn't matter which one the most."